CASE WHITE

THOMAS SULLIVAN

He smells the cabbage broth from the street. Pungent today. And does he smell a bit of beef? But where is the bread? He saw it rising in the pan before he left.

He unlocks the shop door, steps inside and relocks it. A silver watch lies on top of the green felt on his bench. Katya has let in a customer. He picks up the watch and gently tests the stem. Watches talk to him this way. The sighing of time. *Broken gear tooth,* this one says, *I'm slipping.* Laying it down, he passes to the stairway. The top of the landing is steamy.

"Such a waste of broth," he sighs, entering the kitchen. "We have the best tasting walls in Vienna."

But she is in the living room and doesn't hear.

"Katya?" he calls. And then he notices the flies through the steam. Thick above the pot. It *is* beef. The lid quivers, promising surprises. He forgives Katya the omission of bread and tiptoes to the stove for a peek. "Shoo, shoo, shoo," he tells the flies, who merely make short loops and resettle with those crawling on the new cupboard above.

And then he is gasping for air and smarting with tears as the pot lid clatters to the floor. Because it is not beef he smells after all. And Katya is not in the living room. She is right here beside him. Beside him and *above* him where the flies are crawling frenziedly along the seams of the new cupboard. And as his great soul quakes and time inside it stops, as surely as it has stopped in the silver watch atop his workbench downstairs, the broth boils over with cabbage and hair and something else somewhere within that must be—must have been—the two unremarkable gray eyes of…

Of all the sources that were invaluable in the writing of this book, I wish in particular to recognize Janet Berliner-Gluckman for her astute awareness of an era she knew much too well and to Jim Hornfischer.

Copyright © 2012 by Thomas Sullivan
Cover by Dave Dodd
Design by Aaron Rosenberg
ISBN 978-1-941408-83-4 — ISBN 978-1-941408-84-1 (pbk.)
All rights reserved. No part of this book may be used or reproduced in any manner whatsoever without written permission except in the case of brief quotations embodied in critical articles and reviews.
For information address Crossroad Press at 141 Brayden Dr., Hertford, NC 27944
www.crossroadpress.com

First edition

FOREWORD TO AUTHOR'S EXPANDED EDITION

There is no funeral for history, no expiration date, no burial. On the contrary, history is constantly being disinterred. No surprise then that the history of a nation that went insane for 12 years in the 20th century, traded its Judeo-Christian beliefs for Nordic mysticism, and by some estimates caused over 80 million deaths, is still screaming with fresh revelations. And so too this novel must expand.

If it were simply fiction, it would rest on its laurels. But *Case White* is built on painstaking research and, I hope, some inspired insights that for the first time weave together the colossal underpinnings between what has actually become two histories. First, there is the straightforward recounting of events that is called mainstream history. Secondly, there is the bizarre mythology that, while acknowledged by scholars, has simply accumulated like a pile of grotesque and eccentric anecdotes that seem unrelated. Make no mistake. They are related.

The anti-intellectual Reich of Nazi Germany turned its back on humanity. It had to from the moment it damned and began murdering human beings under the specious notion of "race shame." What kind of man says, "When I hear the word 'culture' I draw my revolver"? Or, when asked to choose between two opposing cosmologies, one that we live in a universe of fire and ice and the other that we live on the inside of a hollow sphere, says, "Our perception of the universe need not be coherent. They may both be right!"? The first quote is from Reichsmarschall Hermann Göring; the second was spoken by Adolf Hitler.

Yes, German scientists understood Newtonian physics and the Cartesian world, but the aberrant goals of an amoral Reich required something quite divorced from the human family. *Case White* pulls it together in a thesis fed by fresh perspectives, meticulous research, and the lives of everyday people. Welcome to these pages and the build of living history to a pulse pounding resolution that I hope will both entertain and inform you in these disturbingly similar times where intolerance and terror infect our world…

                                                Thomas Sullivan
                                                August 1, 2016

THE WAND AND THE SORCERER

Enter the Treasure Room of the Hofburg museum in Vienna any day of the week, 9 to 5, and in a leather case lined with red velvet you will find a spear. Its history is mystical, the powers attributed to it magical. The legend goes like this:

Begin with Jesus Christ dead on the cross. His enemies in the Jewish hierarchy look on but are not happy. The radical Christ has neither renounced his sins nor begged for mercy. The upstart has even called upon the Almighty and forgiven the repentant one of the two thieves flanking him. If this is dying, he will never be dead. You can kill a mortal but not a martyr.

So Annas of the Jewish supreme judicial council known as the Sanhedrin and Caiaphas, the High Priest, want to mutilate his body to show that he is not the Anointed One, because Isaiah has prophesied of the Messiah that *A bone of Him shall not be broken.* Dusk is coming. No executions on the Sabbath. If Christ were still alive, he would have to be killed by sundown. The common method is to break the legs. Thus, the Sanhedrin petition Pontius Pilate for authority to finish the job, pretending Christ is still alive. Pilate shrugs and a party from the Temple Guard goes out.

To make it official, they carry the Spear of Herod Antipas. This is no ordinary spear. It was forged by the Prophet Phineas in ancient times. Since then it has been raised by Joshua at the fall of the walls of Jericho and hurled in a jealous rage by King Saul at young David.

When the Roman soldiers at Golgotha see the Temple Guard arrive with the Spear, they let the leg-crushing begin. Gestas and Dismas, flanking Christ, are first. The legionnaires stand about casually, but nearby, their leader watches in disgust from astride his horse.

Meet centurion Gaius Cassius, senator, philosopher, co-killer of Julius Caesar and now oddly juxtaposed to save Christ in the same manner with which he murdered the Emperor of Rome.

Officially, he is representative of Pro-Consul, Pilate. Cataracts have reduced him to what he regards as no more than a reporter of local religious activity. He has been watching with growing personal recognition at the way the Nazarene died, because he too feels unjustly terminated. A complex man in complicated times, he has escaped a hundred deaths only to live in virtual exile and extinction.

So the lesson in humble courage this day at Golgotha is not wasted on a half-blind centurion who yearns for battle duty. It is enough that the Nazarene has been crucified. Death is sufficient indignity. Out of Cassius' pent-up frustrations a compulsive outrage flares. There will be no need to mutilate this Christ. He will prove the man is dead.

Now the Spear.

Wheeling suddenly on his horse, he charges recklessly toward the high cross. The remaining Temple Guard is scattered. It will be said that it was Christ's blood that restored his vision, but whatever enables the centurion's aim, he raises his lance at the last moment and thrusts home precisely between the fourth and fifth ribs. Out of the body pours blood and water. Astonished, soldiers and Temple Guard stare, fulfilling the prophecy of Ezekiel: *They shall look upon Him whom they have pierced.*

For a few seconds the centurion has held the destiny of mankind in his hands and impelled it toward Christianity. His sight permanently restored, he becomes a convert. Known now as Longinus the Spearman, the tapered shaft becomes the Spear of Longinus. And the legend takes shape: *Whoever possesses and understands the Spear of Longinus may turn the world toward good or evil.*

Apocryphal? Perhaps. More to the point is that many men of destiny believed it was true, and the power of belief is sometimes enough to fulfill destiny.

Justinian believed.

Constantine the Great believed.

Charlemagne believed.

So did Otto the Great, Heinrich the Fowler, Mauritius, Theodosius, Alaric the Bold, Aetius, Theodoric, Martel, the Carolingians, the Hohenstauffens, to name a few. Conquerors and kings. Forty all told. All believers. And the one who wants to possess it in 1908. He believes and desires conquest, too. His name is Adolf Hitler.

THE MANDATES

1

Trust me and I will tell you history. Mostly history. Allow me just a few inventions. A Jew and a German not quite a Nazi: Mika Lott and Josef Krantz. Give me their eyes and I will give you back their souls. Composites of reality. Imagine, then, the details, the connective tissue, that binds them to the history. Bizarre history. Insane future. History that dismays and inspires. Stark, hideous, rays-of-hope, obscene, redemptive, alpha-and-omega history. But first, Mika Lott.

He runs. A small boy in the wheat fields of a place called the Pale of Settlement in southwest Russia. He runs because his father is running and because black smoke is billowing over the brow of the hill above their house. The year is 1891 and he is eight years old. He knows nothing of the Czar's Procurator of the Holy Synod, Pobedonostsev, who has decreed that one-third of Russia's Jews should be killed. But he sees his father stop in the sudden orange glow and hears his agonized cry that seems to rise through twisted fingers shaking at heaven.

A surge in the wind brings fainter screams to the boy's ears just as he catches up, and his heart vaults with the nimbleness of a child's passion. The screams are his mother's. He gets only one step down the hill toward the inferno before his father sweeps him up.

All around their house soldiers with poised rifles canter on terrified horses. Presently his brothers emerge: Saul coughing and stumbling; Lev, his new jacket from Kiev aflame; Ira, right arm raised as if to hurl an object which might be a brick from the fireplace or their mother's letter box. The rifles puff and seem to blow all three of them down before the sound comes.

The boy writhes in the old man's iron grip. Why doesn't his father do something?

Wheeling their wide-eyed horses, the soldiers ride off to the east. His father, numb and dazed, releases him. The boy sprints down the hill to shake the corpses one by one. Then he sidles around the house, crying "Mama...Mama" in a piercing voice. The heat from the still flickering fire blisters his cheeks and keeps him from seeing the mounted soldier until he is at the rear of the house where the chimney still stands. Even then, he only senses him at first, like an opaqueness in the heat-warped air. Slowly the boy turns.

The horseman regards him critically as he raises his rifle and calmly aims between the handsome boy's eyes. This is no Cossack but a Prussian, and he has killed Jews before. Killing a cornered enemy is almost ritually methodical. His finger tightens on the trigger, the hammer rears back and...catches.

The soldier is annoyed. He has fired hundreds of times and always the well-oiled mechanism functioned flawlessly. "Worthless cur!" he roars at the child, thumbing the hammer in vain. Distracted by the boy's unflinching manner, he spurs his mount away in pursuit of comrades.

When the flames are out and the charred foundations cooled, the boy's father staggers into the ruins to silently sifts the ashes with a stick and then his bare fingers until he finds a locket and a ring and a few hideous lumps. These he paws into a box he buries in the field along with the three bodies. The child watches from the hill, and, when it is over, his father clambers wearily up the slope, kneels, and sobs on the boy's knees.

Bring the boy—now a man of twenty-five—to Vienna, 1908. Give him a trade like watchmaking that he learns from his only surviving relative (Uncle Mikhail) in Odessa. Make him stout now, but not soft, with sad eyes that nevertheless dance whenever he thinks of the future. He is always thinking of the future. Let his German be refined and expanded by another Russian émigré—Katerina Popov—whom he marries six months after arriving in the capitol. She makes him think of the future even more.

But still there is the other thing he cannot put away. The horror from that day in the Pale of Settlement. That has come with him too, breathing flickers of memory like small flames popping out of ashes and forbidding him entry into a future with Katerina. "What a poppa you will make, Mika!" she tells him in her eagerness to get on with life. "Put the past aside before it gobbles up the present." He deals with it by joining something called the Temple Guard.

No longer the empowered and assertive Levites of old, this is a poorly organized Jewish underground that stretches raggedly across Europe. It gathers information against outspoken hate-mongers and publishes its own propaganda in response to a flood of defamation as inexplicable as the Prussian soldier staring down the barrel of a rifle at Mika from a day that is still frozen like a bit of ice in his memory. Except for its cells in Rome and Munich and Basel, it is badly funded and generally avoided by Jews. In Vienna there are only five members. The newest one is Mika Lott.

Another of the five is Avidan—Avi. Mika is drawn to him because the shy young man is witty and because they are both fascinated by mechanical toys and delicate mechanisms and share a taste for lemon ices.

"You remind me of my brother Lev," Mika tells him. "Never a hat...as if sunshine is inevitable."

"You remind me of my sainted Aunt Tzivia, Mika. Always buttoned to the nines...like pneumonia is looking for an opening."

Along the Danube canal in the Old Quarter of the city there breeds a special kind of human vermin that is the source of the pestilence Mika saw as a boy in Russia. He is with Avi the day he first encounters it on the wall of a warehouse. A primitive depiction of a bearded Jew wearing a yarmelke and having sex with a dog is sketched on the bricks.

"Cave paintings," says Avi.

"So well-endowed. I thought we were supposed to lack testicles."

Avi sites over his outstretched thumb as if admiring a great work of art. "You still have some catching up to do, Mika. When you've lived here long enough, you won't be shocked by this."

"Who says I'm shocked?"

But he is, and he picks up a flake of ancient brick and scratches at the pornography.

"Hey!" someone shouts from across the street. "Leave it alone." Blazing blue eyes in a smooth, self-righteous face glide toward them. "Get out of here. Jews are banned from the Old Quarter."

"Really?" Mika resumes scratching at the graffiti.

"I said leave it!"

Avi insinuates his thin frame to stop the burly accoster. And suddenly there are others—three, four—steamy breaths reeking of coffee and alcohol. A window goes up.

"Art haters," someone calls.

"Make them read the *Volksblatt* aloud," from another, countered by, "What makes you think they can read?"

The *Volksblatt* is a rabid newspaper that regularly lathers up its readers over the "Jewification of universities." The street thugs have a copy. Two men grab Mika while the paper is held in his face by a third.

Mika struggles, face reddening. He tries to come up with something clever to say, but all he can think of is that they are stretching the bulky sweater Katya knit him off his shoulder.

"Get Ehrlich's dog," is suggested. "See if he objects to being fucked by a Jew."

Lunging forward with a mighty push, Avi frees Mika. They back away together, and as they turn to run, a bucket of whitewash is hurled in their faces. The rest is derision and laughter.

Mika goes to Avi's apartment to clean up, so as not to upset Katya any more than necessary. "I had an accident while Avi was painting his kitchen," he will tell her later.

"You should have just read it aloud," Avi says to him. "What difference would it have made?"

"The *Volksblatt*? I'd die first." In fact, he had been trying to make up his mind whether to give in. "You don't really believe that would have ended it, do you?"

"We have to pick our battles carefully, Mika."

"You give that type their way, you embolden them."

Avi looks away. "Believe me, there's far worse than the *Volksblatt*."

Mika knows this. Take Guido von List's pamphlet with its crazy vision of a Reich led by Gauleiters and a mystic Führer and its hysterical rants against Jewish perverts preying carnally on the flower of Aryan virginity. Two symbols are important to von List's Reich: the swastika and the double rune of twin lightning bolts made to look like a stick version of the letters SS.

Another publication, *Ostara*, also uses the swastika. This one is written by Lanz von Liebenfels, a former monk who is establishing something called the New Temple which worships Teutonic ancestors at Castle Werfenstein in Upper Austria. One day Mika finds a yellow copy of the pamphlet lying at the foot of a bridge over the canal and for a quarter hour stands on that span utterly riveted by its xenophobic doctrine. Unable to throw it away, he continues home still reading to Katerina in whom he confides everything about the politics of the day.

They make a benign, indoor couple, ruddy-faced around a hearth. Only their hands speak of youth and nimble skills. White hands. Capable of small miracles, caresses and steady tasks.

She listens patiently as he runs his finger over the words, reading aloud of pre-Atlantean origins on an island in the extreme north called Hyperborea and of its capitol, Thule, and of the seven original races of mankind and particularly the Aryan race of near demigods—supermen—who exist in a kind of primordial ether, who survive and mutate through changes in the earth's atmosphere along with remnants of the other six races.

"Why are you interested in this?" she wants to know, dumping out a box of colored buttons on the floor to sift for mates.

The question and the sifting conjure up the memory of his father sifting ashes that day when he was eight. He faced a Russian soldier in a Prussian style uniform then and something came between them, canceling certain death, creating a debt. He has never talked about this. Never really understood it. But now he says: "The day they killed my family, I knew I'd face them again. In some form."

"The Russians?"

"The hate. The evil."

Her half smile puckers into a sensuous pout as she dives back into the box of buttons. "Any man crazy enough to join the Temple Guard is looking for hate and evil, if you ask me. But the man I love can't get enough of it in Vienna. He has to hunt up magical civilizations from another time."

Mika returns a sheepish species of her pout, but inside he is thinking that that is it. The hate is almost too irrational to be simply human.

"The man I love has been appointed to fight windmills," his wife concludes with too much glint in her eyes. "Let the Brodesteins sell vegetables, let the Hadshiners bake bread, my Mika wants to lock horns with the Devil!"

Close by, in a room on the Felberstrasse 22, behind door 16, a somewhat younger man is also fascinated by what he reads in the same issue of *Ostara*. He too senses some imposed purpose on his life.

Living alone among beggars and thieves, the young man is scarcely motivated to earn food or rent. His communication with the world at large consists chiefly of solitary outbursts at odd moments in odd places—erupting into an overheard conversation on a streetcar, exploding into a tirade against a political speaker in the park.

He has washed-out blue eyes that nevertheless pour cold fire on spellbound audiences. Already he spits and froths when he speaks, cleaving the air with rigid hands. His voice grows hoarse as he lines out the past in a robotic ballet of will and urgency. When one of these seizures lets go, he sags back into the runt of a man you took him for. Even he seems surprised.

He believes in reincarnation and in certain talismans from the past. The talismans have been perverted by Christianity, which he secretly despises for its doctrines of pacifism and forgiveness. That said, he is quick to rant against "Christ-killing Jews."

One such talisman lies in the Schatzkammer, the Hapsburg Treasure House of the Hofburg Museum, in this very city. There in the central gangway stands a dais and, on the dais, a leather case lined with red velvet and, upon the red velvet, the remnants of a spear which, nineteen centuries ago, Longinus the centurion plunged into the flesh of God incarnate, Jesus Christ. Black iron. Golden crosses. Flared wings in the base.

The young man was unaware of its existence until the day he sat outside the Hofburg sketching plans to renovate the brick with stonework.

He often does things like that. He doesn't know why, except that he has a talent for drawing and he likes to draft historical monuments and buildings as if it is given to him to lay out an empire.

But on this particular day he was at his lowest ebb. It was cold and damp and there was an ominous rattle in his lungs. He was hungry and almost without a krönen. All around him promiscuous swarms of foreigners defiled the Hofburg. His sketches seemed a waste. Suddenly the sky darkened. A cold rain began to pelt him. God was against him too it seemed. But what need did he have for a god of forgiveness and self-denial?

He sat in the rain until it soaked through his coat and his sketchbooks became sodden. The choice then was to go back to his wretched room or follow the tourists into the Treasure House. Tearing his sketchbooks in half, he entered the Schatzkammer.

At first he ignored the imperial regalia all around him, but then he half heard a tour guide say to his shuffling followers, "…in the hands of claimants who understood its power, it is said to have changed the destiny of the world for good or evil."

The young derelict waited impatiently until at last the rabble of foreign tourists moved on. And then he saw it. The Spear. His heart churned icily as he moved closer. Why should a Christian artifact absorb him? The guide said it was ancient even at the crucifixion. But somehow he knew that when he saw it. And why good or evil? He knew that, too—that it was, after all, the weapon that tore the flesh of God incarnate.

Years from now he will write in his book, *Mein Kampf,* that he saw a magical presence all around it, that he was transported through it to a unified vantage point of past and future, that he felt he had held the Spear himself in another century. It was a moment of destiny, and he believes in moments of destiny.

At closing time of that fateful day, the young Hitler was still standing before the Spear of Longinus.

Mika Lott and Adolf Hitler. A Jew and a xenophobe, each with a mandate. The separation between them will always be that orchestral darkness between a stage and an audience. Mika sees Hitler; Hitler sees Mika. Two minor figures in the plain tapestry of Vienna's streets in the year 1908. The day they meet is rather ordinary.

Mika especially is insignificant this day. A watchmaker. An undynamic man caught up in the quiet order of wheels within wheels, the precise sighing of time contained in perfect polished circles of silver or gold. But it is that very reverie of ordinal time and the fear of its disruption that also makes Mika unique. Because it allows him, on this gray oatmeal day in Vienna, to briefly glimpse what is coming.

It begins with him and Katerina preparing to go out.

How much longer, Katya?" he hollers through the panels of the water closet door.

"Waiting is good for the soul!" she shouts back. "Fix a watch or something. And why don't you put on some of that cologne I can't resist!"

He looks into the cracked bureau mirror and discovers his postponed adolescent vanity. If he had begun to train his hair back then, it wouldn't flare wildly from his temples now. If he had slept nights instead of reading hour after hour, his eyes would not resemble watery cocoa in tarnished cups. Too late. He is a mountain goat at twenty-five, hair arcing back like ram's horns.

He splashes on essence of something-or-other out of a bottle Uncle Mikhail gave him for a wedding present and struggles into his coat. But when Katya pads out wrapped only in a towel, her statuesque shoulders pink and steaming, he seizes her by the waist in a way that pulls the towel off her breasts.

"I thought you wanted to go to Demel's Cafe," she says, her unremarkable gray eyes remaining steady.

"I thought you said you couldn't resist my cologne."

She says nothing—willing to make love but not wanting to—and in that radiant deception he reads the unselfishness of her love.

"You have large breasts," he notes slowly and distinctly.

"I have large everything."

He strains to make his thumbs meet at her navel, but his fingers barely curl around her sides. "I like full women," he says.

"I'll be fuller after we eat dinner."

"Such a temptress. Get dressed. I'll wine and dine you first."

They are a good match, and when he thinks about how he almost didn't propose at all, he believes in God. He had merely gone to her house on a Tuesday instead of a Sunday. Her mother, Vera Popov, took it as a sign of serious intentions and dragged her husband, Ilya, out of the water closet with a good deal of whispering and pushing. The old man marched into the living room, believing the subject was already broached, and when Mika stood there dumbstruck, he demanded to know whether he had something to ask him or not. Rather than risk permanent alienation, Mika mouthed the proper thing right then and there.

God is good.

Katya finishes dressing and they take a streetcar to Demel's Café. Thinking it will please her, he talks of building the cupboards she wants, but she has other things on her mind.

"You could handle six sons and daughters, Mika. So patient."

"I'm not patient," he says, unfurling his napkin. "Just methodical."

"What do you want first?"

"I think I'll have a glass of wine."

"I mean a boy or girl, as if you didn't know. Most fathers want a girl first."

"Are there any other choices?"

"Choices?"

"I mean, are we really ready, Katya?"

She strokes her broad brow in a way that signifies hurt feelings. He changes the subject.

"See that clock? Broken." He can't stand broken clocks. They interfere with his pulse somehow. But she won't look, and he sighs, "Ah, Katya..." *Ah, Katyas* are capitulations. "Of course, I dream of a family."

And immediately, as if they haven't quarreled at all, she beams, "There *is* another choice. One of each. We'll have twins."

They look exactly like what they are: two slightly over-dressed people trying to make a dinner date out of a meal in a café. In the middle of the room three corpulent merchants are holding forth on Austrian independence. By the window sits a sallow man in gray check trousers, slurping soup. A couple of workers smoke and drink unobtrusively. Least remarkable is the tattered fellow who is just coming in.

Hitler has left his miserable room within the quarter hour and walked to Demel's. Now he takes a seat at a small corner table and orders tea. He wants a piece of pastry, but he only has enough money for the tea. Disdainfully he notes the rabble of Jews and merchants. Glowering at the wall, he lets out his breath in a kind of hiss to drown out the blasphemies about Austrian independence. He himself was born on Braunau-on-the-Inn in what was called

Austria; but he knows he is German. The irony is appalling. Jews and traitors allowed to sit in a public café filling their faces while he, a loyalist to the true empire, sips tea and listens to his stomach growl!

He thinks of the Spear lying in the Schatzkammer in order to calm himself. Excite himself. Always the Spear. It is the wand of a sorcerer waiting to be claimed, the scepter of a nascent king. Sovereigns of light and darkness are warring inside him—

"Toast to Emperor Franz Josef," one of the merchants shouts, and as if he has been kicked, Adolf Hitler suddenly scrapes to his feet.

Trembling, he looks around. "A toast?" he repeats nervously. "A toast to what? That pretender? Franz Josef—the gangrene in the body of true Germany, that maggot feeding off the infested wounds of betrayal?"

Something inside is shaking him, and now it begins exploding like lava through rock. He raves, he spits, his eyes grow glassy and wide as he calls them all traitors on the page of living history lying open and unfinished before them. On and on he goes—exhorting, condemning, threatening. "Austria—the prodigal child estranging itself from the Fatherland?" he sneers. "This little fiefdom will be washed off the map by the storm of pure blood that is coming, and all collaborators will drown!" His power of conviction is immense. But just when it seems the tirade will burst the throbbing veins in his temples, his lips tremble and his face goes white. Sagging back into his chair, he is suddenly limp as a glove.

Mika stares in amazement. Surely this man is on a par with List or Liebenfels as an influence in Vienna. His icy blue-gray eyes were hypnotic only a moment ago. The articulate blend of nationalism and anti-Semitism raging from the stranger's breast is insidious. Why hasn't he run across him before?

The scourged merchants mutter and glance at one another dumbfounded. Two nervous waitresses and a waiter stand hugging their trays at the sideboard. Suddenly the little firebrand is on his feet again, but this time he is out the door. Mika half rises.

"Where are you going?" whispers Katya.

He sits back down but cranes to follow through the window. "Who is he, Mika?"

"I don't know."

"What an awful man. He sounds like the one who wrote that terrible pamphlet you brought home."

Exactly.

The manager of Demel's flutters around the merchants, going table to table apologizing. But to their table, nothing. The snub is pointed.

Katya blushes duskily. Mika thumps his spoon. Two civilized people come to a civilized restaurant and encounter this sort of thing.

"I don't think I can wait any longer," Mika says solemnly.

Katya's broad brow develops a tiny wrinkle and her lips part in a question.

"…to have twins," he amplifies, forcing a smile. "Let's go home."

Tears come suddenly to her eyes, and he realizes how fragile she is inside. He helps her on with her coat, pays the bill, leads her out.

If ever there is a night when she is beautiful, it is this night. And Mika, for once, gets all the protocols right. Taking her by the arm, strolling home along the promenade, observing the almost full moon, stopping to buy a hothouse rose—he even feels like her hero. And the love-making, that too is beautiful. The climax coming like the exhilaration of a playground swing, rising, rising, until it catches on its brief, timeless hook.

"You wanted to follow him," she says when a few minutes have passed and she is stroking her warrior's head upon her breast.

"Who?"

"That man in Demel's. You wanted to follow him instead of this."

"Maybe I wanted both."

"I feel your love now because I'm touching you…because you were just inside me. But I felt your urge to follow that man from across the table."

He cups his hand around her breast, kisses the nipple.

"He's the hate and evil we talked about, isn't he, Mika? That's what you were thinking."

"We don't have to talk about this now. It's not important."

"Yes, it is. If it's that strong, it's important. You should have followed him. I thought this Temple Guard business was just a game. I thought my Mika was meant to fix watches and play with his children. But I was wrong."

He rolls away. "You've let him upset you. He said some nasty things."

"No. It's not him. It's you. When I saw that spark in your eyes, it reminded me of Sasha."

"I remind you of your father's dog?"

"She used to guard me, but if she smelled the woods she ran off and you could call till your voice cracked and it wouldn't bring her back. 'Obeying the blood,' Papa called it."

"You're comparing me to a creature of instincts," Mika says derisively. "I'm a man and I choose my path."

"You should've followed him, Mika. Maybe in a single man you can deal with this hate and evil. You should've followed him."

And this time he doesn't answer.

2

Obeying the blood! It isn't in the blood. It's in the past where a soldier rode in wearing a Prussian style uniform, pointing a rifle at his head. The thing jammed and little Mika knew then that something beyond his control was beginning. Some immense gear, like one of Uncle Mikhail's watch movements, began to turn. He knew that he would see this soldier again in the future—when the gear meshed with other gears—and now grown-up Mika has seen the soldier this very night in Demel's Cafe. A different face, a different body, no uniform; nevertheless the same.

He has not wanted to believe it. Not the return of his horseman. Not a single focused entity for all the irrational hate that shocked him as a boy. But now, like one of the four riders of the apocalypse, he has seen him—heard him. Vaguely he realizes that everything he has done in the underground was to prevent the potential of such a leader. And yet, and yet there is another path still open to him, isn't there? One he has begun with the woman he loves, who paints visions of the family he lost. Home in the warmth of their apartment, he indulges a little denial.

"There are always extremists," he says to her. "It would be extraordinary for them to take power, don't you think?"

"I don't know, my love. I'm just a simple person. Politics bore me. But I think you're guarding against that extraordinary possibility. You and the others in your Temple Guard. You keep track of these extremists. And if it turns out to be unimportant, you will have served your purpose just as surely as if you have to call out the earliest warning."

An extraordinary answer for his apolitical wife. Exactly what he didn't want to hear, as if the words were put in her mouth by an unrelenting Providence.

Mika goes back to Demel's and inquires of the surly manager.

"Excuse me, Herr Demel, but that man last night who was upset…do you know who he was?"

"What man? No one was upset. Are you trying to cause trouble for me?"

Mika haunts the place for a week at dinnertime and even roams the neighborhood. He scans the crowds at every political rally he can find, but the icy, blue-gray eyes do not appear. Whoever the demagogue is, he must be new to Vienna.

And then in the Hof library one evening he feels the same peculiar foreboding: that the soldier is near, that the rifle is pointed at his head. Icy, blue-gray eyes sweep past him as the man from Demel's returns a newspaper to a rack and strides swiftly through the foyer.

Mika has learned a little about surveillance since coming to Vienna, and he knows that he shouldn't follow—that the streets are too empty this night. But his prey seems intent on a destination. There is something martial about the plain little man—choppy gestures, purposeful strides. Pursuit terminates in the Fifteenth District when Mika turns a final corner and there is no one in sight.

Instinctively he shrinks back. His quarry might have recognized the situation, might in fact be lying in wait. And then a light fills a window in the facade of a building just up the street, and a silhouette comes briefly to the shade. Mika strolls to the entrance.

Felberstrasse 22.

He enters the building and his senses are immediately assailed with the smells of urine and mold. Piano music floats down the staircase; someone practicing Chopin. Untangling the geometry to match the apartment with the light, he slowly mounts the creaking stairs. A dead hush seems to descend upon the whole building when he sees the door—even the piano is abruptly silenced. And that is when his courage fails.

Apartment 16.

The card in his file now has an address.

"It was palpable, Katya," he tells her. "I stood there on the landing and it was as if his eyes were burning into me right through the walls of his apartment."

"You think he knows then?"

"Oh, yes. A man like that... No. I mean, he doesn't know me personally."

"Don't try to hide the truth from me, Mika."

"A man like that stands for something wholly incompatible with the rest of the world, Katya. He sees everyone as an enemy... every belief not his own is a threat. I'm not an irrational man—you know this, Katya—but..." He looks around in genuine discomfort, clasping and unclasping his watchmaker's fingers. "But you heard him talking as if outside forces are part of his vision. He believes in magic—this man—in destiny."

"What are you talking about?"

But he cannot say it. That in his own way he may be driven by something just as irrational as the demonic passion that drives the rabid pedagogue. How else to explain the instant recognition that floods his brain with white light, the old awakening that twists long frozen screws rusted into his heart?

Early the next morning he goes to the Police Administration Bureau where, for a little bribe, the clerk culls through residency records to give him a name and citizen classification: Adolf Hitler, art student.

Mika waits across the street from the Felberstrasse apartment on three successive mornings trying to pick out a routine. Hitler likes to leave early. He seems to have no classes, no job and no regular destinations. Mika follows him to the Neustadt factory district and hears another inflammatory speech. A second pursuit leads to a certain shop where pornographic and racist pamphlets are sold, and another where occult literature and drugs are available. Occasionally Hitler paints on the Ring outside the Hofburg and tries to sell his work. And always—*always*—the young radical returns to stand inside the Treasure House before the Spear of Longinus.

"Hitler has aspirations," Mika tells Katya.

"Of course he does. That's why you're following him."

"But this is more than that. I know how his mind works, Katya. This spear, I've been researching it. Even Napoleon tried to claim it!"

"Just be careful, my love. Madmen have no scruples."

"He doesn't even know I'm there."

A little white lie. Because the young Hitler *must* know. How could he *not* know? Mika is no suave Metternich spy, no Prussian agent or

Ochrana saboteur. Just a simple watchmaker following awkwardly through the streets of Vienna, often where Jews are not welcome. How else can you contain the sparks that feed the flames of anti-Semitism? People have noticed. The question—if there is a question—is whether or not Hitler is still the lone wolf he appears to be.

It is Mika's friend, Avidan, who comes up with the bad news. Avidan who braves two nights in one of the rathole cafés in the Old Quarter dressed as a tradesman and wearing a crucifix so that he can mingle with the sodden malcontents who love to rail against the rich, the Jews and the Republic.

"Hitler has his following, Mika."

"You heard them mention his name twice, you say?"

"And they quote his phrases! That bit about the old cockades and the dust of history and good German blood. Does that sound like what you hear on every hod carrier's lips?"

No. It sounds exactly like what the Temple Guard in Vienna is trying to isolate.

One cell. Five members. Barely organized, barely in touch with their larger counterparts in Munich and Rome. But if this hate thing rears its ugly head in organized ways, they can and will expose it. There are people of conscience in Vienna who will not permit such hate to infect their local government, if only they recognize the threat soon enough.

So Mika follows Hitler, and sometimes Avi watches the apartment on Felberstrasse. And thus there comes a morning near the gate to the Old Quarter—the Schweizer Tor—when Hitler turns and fixes Mika with a look of calm arrogance. Too late to duck. A pair of hands from behind send him sprawling to the pavement at Hitler's feet. There follows a crushing kick to the base of the spine and another to the groin.

Conscious but too knotted to move, he breathes in sips, like a goldfish. What little air passes through his nose smells vaguely like oranges. He hears the sympathetic murmur of a crowd above the buzz of flies already settling in his vomit.

"My God…in broad daylight. The bullies just let him have it as bold as you please and ran off."

The speaker leans over him, a balding man with trim mustache, wearing an apron.

Mika blinks away tears, tries to lift his head. The good Samaritan cradles his neck and shoulders. Half a dozen hands bring him to his feet, feeling as though everything between his chest and his legs has been removed. He wobbles along in someone's grasp, murmuring directions as he is taken home.

"Well, now you've found your enemies and they've found you," Katerina says fatalistically as he lies on the sofa with a hot cloth on the back of his neck.

"They don't know where I live, Katya."

She strokes his brow and rocks upon the footstool. "We have that to look forward to, I suppose."

"They're cowards."

"Even cowards can kill." She sniffs in a way that says she has been crying. "I've changed my mind about this policing thing, Mika. Let them talk. Let them write. Let them print their filthy cartoons. It will be good for them to get it out of their systems. It won't harm us."

"If I hadn't been careless…"

"Give up this child's game of spying. What are you going to do with this information anyway?"

"Expose them," he says with a little strength in his voice. "Even if I never get near Hitler again, I can do that."

"Expose them to whom? Everyone knows they hate us. It's a political asset."

"But not the things that go with it, the occultism, the pornography, the drugs. People don't know about those. It will discredit them. People will stop listening to them. At the very least, they'll be blocked from political office."

"And I suppose you'll lead this crusade," she says in a way that demands contradiction.

Of which there is none.

Lying in bed at night watching Katya's eyelids tremble with dreams, her soft lips reposed in what can only be called innocence, he vows to himself that he will be more careful. But it is not following Hitler through the streets of Vienna that seals Mika's fate. No, it is the thing he blurted out to Katya. *Expose them*, he said. It was the first time he put it into words to anyone. In reality, the thought of exposing those underpinnings has always seemed to him more an expression of moral outrage than a viable strategy. Who cares what Vienna's racist rabble do in their rat holes? Only, now the racist rabble is making headway into mainstream Vienna. So maybe it does matter.

Almost timidly the next morning he tips a reporter about Guido von List's satanism. Von List heads a blood lodge whose mock rituals substitute the swastika for the cross. The journalist is interested.

"I thought he'd laugh at me for being a tattletale," Mica tells Avi. "I thought he'd tell me to sober up and quit playing phone pranks, but he actually seemed interested."

Not long afterward, an evening edition of the Vienna Chronicle details the sexual perversion and medieval black magic witnessed by an infiltrating reporter. The uproar among Vienna's majority Roman Catholics forces Guido von List to leave town. Satanism has been struck a blow.

But it isn't outraged Christianity to whom it will turn for revenge. Mika Lott, the troublesome Jew whose skinned palms have not yet healed, will soon receive another hard push, and this time, he will fall for decades.

3

The bookstore of Ernst Reicher floats amid occult flotsam. His shop is small and cluttered and seems to recoil from the light. Four of ten who enter buy books, two of ten pawn or sell them, three ask advice on ritual magic, one buys drugs.

The drugs, mescaline mostly, are kept in an odd assortment of glass phials behind books in the office. The mescaline comes as peyote root from Mexico. Reicher's father once ran an apothecary business there and studied ancient Aztec magic. In lieu of a family portrait, the oldest chart on the walls of the office is an Aztec calendar. The rest is astrological, alchemical or anti-Semitic.

There are also some postcard-size watercolors he has bought from a certain young painter who has been refused admittance into the Vienna Academy of Fine Arts. He bought them because the young man promises to be an adept at ritual magic some day, and because he is an inspired vilifier of Jewry, and because he is starving.

So, when there are no watercolors, Reicher gives Hitler a few hellers for his books. The books are there now on the back shelf, not to be sold. Who would buy them anyway, with all the scribbling in the margins? There are cleaner copies available. Hitler's books are standard stuff—Nietzsche, Schopenhauer, a tattered green copy of Eschenbach's *Parzival*, among them. These are safe until the young firebrand can buy them back.

Reicher is bald, fat, hunched, a puffy fish amid shoals of books. He turns slowly and only when absolutely necessary. He holds whole conversations peripherally, or even with his back to an interlocutor, relying on a keen ear for nuance and those intuitive senses he believes he has developed. Thus, when Mika Lott enters early one rainy Friday, Reicher remains bent over the broken shelf along one wall.

Mika strolls quickly past. He knows Reicher. They are old enemies, in fact, and he has been watching through the window until just the right moment to enter.

Reicher was at Guido von List's the night the lodge was exposed. Since then Mika has not been able to keep close tabs on Hitler, because the little rabble-rouser has moved. But he knows he sometimes pawns books at Reicher's, and so he has come here three times to check the back shelf where they always sit, hoping to find a new address inside a cover and to see what kind of stuff Hitler reads. Each time he came, the shop had customers, however; and Reicher's customers are a danger to him.

Today (praise God) Reicher is alone and on his knees repairing a shelf.

A roll of thunder ushers Mika in. He stands for a moment in the mustiness of old books and the smell of varnish brought out by the rain. There are three aisles that separate the shelves, each faintly lit by a yellow incandescent bulb. Ambling along the far row to make his footsteps sound casual, he works his way to the back. There his straight, undeclared lips bud and his smooth brow tightens as he seizes the lone pile of books on the third shelf.

Besides Nietzsche and Schopenhauer, there is a copy of *The Foundation of the Nineteenth Century,* Houston Stewart Chamberlain's diatribe against the Jews in which he claims Christ is Aryan. No surprise that Hitler's heroes include Nietzsche, Schopenhauer, Wagner. Never mind that the first says evil is good and good is evil, the second denies they even exist, and the third claims Jesus is Aryan and talks about "a final solution" to save the Fatherland from Jewish influence. But the prize that totally engrosses Mika is a small volume whose margins are heavily scrawled with bold notes. He has thumbed through the first third of it when a ponderous opacity looms close enough to block the yellow light.

"You!" Reicher expostulates.

Mika is cool. Mika-the-watcher watches. "How much?" he asks, waggling *Parzival* in the bookseller's face.

"I swore I'd kill you, Jew bastard."

"Of course, but first let me pay—"

Reicher swings so wildly that he is carried to the floor, from which he rises, wheezing, to his knuckles.

"How much for *Parzival*?" Mika says. "One heller?"

"Get out, Jew bastard!" The lump of flesh bellies over trying to reach him.

"Such a hard bargainer. Two hellers."

"Give me that book!"

Mika drops three coins to the floor as Reicher struggles to his knees. He has the green *Parzival* with the notes. Tucking it into his coat, he strides out, unmindful of Reicher's pursuing roar or the bronze coins dancing past him in the rain.

The watches and clocks always seem to chatter when he arrives home, as if to search out the rhythm of his thoughts. *What have we here? Books, Mika?* And Katya now, too, suddenly appears at the dark end of the shop.

"What is it, Mika? More books?"

"Obscene books."

She arches an eyebrow and a ponderous Swiss stemwinder "tsk-tsks" its disapproval above the bench lamp. "You don't look very lustful."

"Not that kind of obscene."

"Oh. More of those sick people." She moves into the light, her eyes glassy but intent. "Come upstairs and read. I don't care how sick it is, I want you to share everything with me. What kind of wife will I be if you can't share everything with me, darling?"

He climbs the stairs behind her, but it is another quarter hour spent reading silently in the fuchsia depths of the ottoman before he raises his shaggy head and loses his reticence.

"*Kein ayin horoh*, Katya," he says then (May no evil befall). "I'm overwhelmed. This man has oceans of venom in him. Change his ragged clothes, cut his hair, clean him up, put him on a platform—"

The rain drumming on the windows between gusts of wind has the relentless quality of marching troops and goading applause.

"Is that *his* handwriting in the margins?" she asks, divining the nature of the notes in the tattered green book. "Hitler's—is that his book?"

"Like a trial lawyer he builds his case. If there's even a grain of truth in it, the world is going to grow very dark."

"Truth in what he says about us? How can you say such a thing?"

"Not in what he says about Jews." He thumps the green book. "This...this *Parzival* and reincarnation. The allegorical story of the knight Parzival's search for good in a world of evil is part of the Holy Grail tradition."

"Who would have guessed our little friend is an opera buff?"

"Yes. Evidently it's Wagner's opera *Parsifal* that Hitler admires, because his notes are all about how Wagner improved the material from the original *Parzival*."

"Improved? Meaning he thinks it fits his own view of things?"

"Oh, yes, but it's more than that," Mika warms. "Hitler thinks he comes out of a whole line of reincarnations that begins with a real life sorcerer who was born almost exactly a thousand years before him!"

"And who is that?"

"In the opera? Klingsor."

"And Hitler thinks he's Klingsor?"

"No! Yes! Klingsor. But only because Klingsor is the evil magician in *Parsifal* who represents Landulf the second de Capua in real life!"

"You don't have to shout, Mika."

"I'm not shouting."

"And this Landulf de Capua was a beast, you say?"

"He was castrated for raping the wife of a nobleman. In Wagner, Klingsor is 'clipped between the legs.'"

It is all rather murky and meaningless to her, though she is moved by Mika's intensity. "And Hitler?"

"What about Hitler?"

"Is he castrated or clipped between the legs?"

"How would I know? What difference does it make?"

"Why are you yelling at me, Mika?"

"I'm not—" He drops his voice. "I'm not yelling at you, Katya. I just don't see what difference it makes. This Landulf of Capua conducted a reign of horrific sexual perversion and Arabian star magic, from his castle at Kalot Enbolot, that involved thousands of victims. Klingsor wields the Spear of Longinus in Wagner's opera in such a way as to make others suffer for his emasculation."

"Well then, if Hitler is his reincarnation, why isn't he emasculated?"

"Katya." Patience manifest. "The point is that Hitler believes that this figure from the ninth century is the Antichrist, that he understood and used the Grail and the Spear for a power alliance with evil, and that he has survived to a new millennium through several reincarnations, the last of which is Hitler himself. He thinks he's the German messiah, Katya!"

"Well, why didn't you say that in the first place?"

A German messiah, or rather a whole gang of them, has been expected by pan-Germanic mystics for at least half a century.

"'The superstitious knights who followed the Jew Jesus betrayed their Aryan blood,'" Mika reads from Hitler's notes. "'What has the Grail path to do with Jewish carpenters? Meekness is weakness. Forgiveness and self-denial fly in the face of evolution. They are defeats of will and an attempt to dilute the powers of Aryan blood!' He spits on forgiveness and humility, Katya. *Will* is his Grail. Ruthless will."

"And this Spear—that's the one you told me is in the Hapsburg Treasure House right now?"

"Yes."

"My, how they bend everything!"

"True. They say Nietzsche and Wagner came to Vienna just to see the Spear of Longinus and wound up arguing over it. Wagner believed it was a Christian symbol—Aryan Christ, of course. Nietzsche hated Christ, Aryan or Jew. Hated Wagner too, after Vienna. Wagner hated Nietzsche in return and loved Christ. And from Hitler's notes, it's clear that he loves Nietzsche and Wagner but hates Christ! Can algebra survive such equations? Can philosophy?"

She has never seen him so worked up. But she has not forgotten the night at Demel's and the hissing, spitting weasel who astonished everyone. Hitler has become for her a kind of pathological orator, a diseased gnome fueled by drugs. This mystical historian her husband is describing, who analyzes links between dramatic allegories and real figures ten centuries removed, bears no resemblance.

"You have no idea how intricate this is," Mika says. "Hitler's version of the present is rooted so deeply in history that I have to consider the possibility that some of it is rational. The power of his hate is absolutely inhuman. The man harbors leviathans. *Kein ayin horoh.*"

Katya heaves a great sigh and stands up. "Leviathans, my

husband says. Which reminds me, we have fish for dinner." She moves to the stove. "Take my word, we're better off today than ever before. You don't know how lucky you are, Mika. Even the watch trade grows. How, I'll never know. They pile up on your workbench downstairs and you don't get to them for days. When I came to this apartment all you had was bread, potatoes and tea. You wore the same green sweater day after day. Now someone loves you, washes and sews for you, cooks for you and warms your bed. It's beyond me why you go looking for trouble. Wait till this Hitler is 'clipped between the legs,' then worry about magicians coming out of the past!"

Two days later, another Temple Guard member, Uri Spee, talks to Gustl Kubizek, a former roommate of Hitler's in the Mariahilf suburbs. Kubizek tells him that Hitler has messianic visions, but that he hasn't always been like that. That the first time he heard it was on a hill above Linz. That they were looking down at the town at night and Hitler suddenly started spouting grandiose prophecies about himself receiving mandates from the German people. The words just broke from him like a flood, says Kubizek. They were both astonished.

Both?

And one more thing, observed by Kubizek when his roommate bathed. *Hitler has only one testicle.*

4

And then Wagner's operatic *Parsifal* comes to town. Mika's whole soul roars counterpoint. Of course Hitler will be there. How could he not? The character of Klingsor will inflame him. Landulf II, the real life thousand-year old sorcerer upon whom Klingsor is based, will awaken as Adolf Hitler in the new millennium.

Despite his vow to stay out of trouble on the streets, Mika decides he must confirm this for himself. On the cold, blustery opening night he stands by the fountain outside the State Opera House waiting for the last act to end. Carriages line the street. Cicerone coachmen in melon hats smoke and chat while their steaming horses stamp their hooves. A final declarative from the orchestra pit reaches the cobbled avenue, followed by a fine rain of applause. Slowly the gloss of Vienna's aristocracy spills through the four columns at the entrance. Carriage wheels glisten damp. Spokes blur the exodus spreading now in two directions.

Mika moves into the street, side-stepping a veering team.

There. Outstriding the couples. No mistaking the ragged hair. Mika follows, and this time there isn't any Hof library or Weltliche Schatzkammer to get lost in. A flophouse in Meldemannstrasse. That's where he now lives. A flophouse!

Mika waits fully five minutes after Hitler disappears inside before seeking out the manager, a certain Herr Kanya, whose apartment is in the basement.

"I'd like a word with you about one of your lodgers," he says at the door when it is opened to reveal the pouty face of a man with a patched eye and a cigarette dangling from his lip.

Kanya blinks him into focus in the dim yellow light. "Go away before you get beat up."

Mika produces a modest bribe, held in the air like a lit match.

The door hesitates. "Hitler," he says, pointing up.

"What about him?"

"What's he like?"

"Different," says Kanya, plucking at the money but missing. "A student, I think."

"He attends classes?"

Shrug. "He paints. Reads."

"How else is he different?"

"He has"—shrug—"ideas."

"Plans?"

"Ideas, I said. A real thinker, that one. He could straighten out a lot of our politicians, no question." Kanya's disdain flickers and the cigarette burns brighter.

"What kind of ideas?"

Flicker. Shrug. "He hates Jews for one thing."

"And his friends? Visitors?"

"None." Kanya reaches unsuccessfully again for the money.

"None?"

"No one understands him. And he won't keep himself clean. Last week we had to strip him by force and send his clothes out to be fumigated."

Kanya steps forward and this time snatches the money.

"Tell me more of Hitler's ideas," says Mika.

"I've told you the one idea we all understood," Kanya sneers. "Now get out of here. I don't want anyone murdered in my hostelry."

So, the little beggar has lice. That alone is worth the bribe. A million koronas worth of laughs. Only Mika isn't laughing. Lice are just another deceit. Lice will train the lice-ee not to care a louse about what anyone thinks. Lice are just another way of underestimating him. Some day the lice will abandon ship and there will be Landulf II waving the Spear of Longinus. No. Not to laugh at Hitler.

Assume that Herr Kanya will blab to him, as well. *Some Jew-bastard has been asking about you, Adolf. I sent him away.* Hitler will ask what the Jew-bastard looks like, will compare him to Reicher's Jew-bastard, will realize who it is.

It won't hurt to stay away for a few days to avoid the cretins who might lie in wait for him, Mika decides. Time to remember that it is the twentieth century and that he is still a young man capable of hope and ambition and living in the here and now with the woman he loves dearly. And besides, he feels guilty for breaking his vow to be more cautious and exposing himself to more retribution from the radicals. He goes home to Katya and for a few days becomes the domesticated husband/lover she yearns for.

"Jesus was the last Jewish carpenter," he says after completing the cupboard she wants over the stove. "If he wasn't the Messiah, maybe he died so that none of us would ever have to do carpentry again."

"Such a fine, spacious cupboard—has anyone ever built a better one?" she lies enthusiastically.

"What cupboard? This is the room you wanted."

He looks up to find her brimming with tears. She loves him and she is happy and grateful. Beneath her squarishness, her tightly drawn coarse hair, her unremarkable gray eyes and thin lips, she is nonetheless beautiful. Quite beautiful.

But Meldemannstrasse is a magnet. A glance at the notes in *Parzival* is enough to send Mika there. And besides, nothing happened to him the night he followed Hitler from the opera. He is getting good at this surveillance stuff! A regular Scarlet Pimpernel. No danger, if he keeps his distance.

This Hitler is no dreamer, no closet scholar. His notes speak from the margins of pages in the same hoarse bursts he has used in the Kohlmarkt—a kind of demonic croaking, the unfurling snap of a flame that first ate into Mika's brain as a boy standing before a smoldering homestead in the Pale of Settlement.

Hitler has a grasp on the occult threads of German nationalism. He makes reference to yoga, alchemy, astrology, mysticism, mythology, religion. And history! The man has lived forever. The blueprints to power are filed in his head. Moreover, he has eloquent hate. Of all the anti-Semites Mika sees in Vienna, Hitler is most capable of commanding an audience.

That is why the little agitator must remain a tattered oddball among dregs. And why Mika is disturbed when he disappears from Meldemannstrasse. And why he is thunderstruck to see him back several days later. Because the wretched caterpillar returns on black velvet wings. Behold the metamorphosis!

Item: new boots. Black. Seven-league.

Item: dark suit. Crisp, authoritarian.

Item: white shirt. Self-righteous.

Item: haircut. Military.

Item: beard. Gone. Reduced to a smear above a sneer. The caterpillar is now the mustache above the lip. (And why does that mustache bother him? Something...something he read long ago in a book.)

Hitler is taller now by ten feet. Just standing there he is louder, his hate more reputable. They will hear him now, Mika fears. Respectable people. People with keys and connections. Hitler will stir their nationalism and gain their sympathies with his blame-laying. The pulse of the old German Empire beats like a bass drum here in Austria and elsewhere. Who knows where the call to pure blood may go? In *Parzival*'s tattered margins Mika was shocked to read in Hitler's handwriting:

"...pollution must be cleansed as blood was once cleansed, by letting it flow until it is fresh and pure."

Whose blood? There can be no doubt about the literal part of that. Hitler blames the Jews for what he sees as the dilution of an empire. If ever a Jew has died by hate in the history of the world, this man has ample supply to cause it to happen again. En masse.

So what should I do, agonizes Mika the Scarlet Pimpernel. What if I kill him? He preaches genocide. It would be self-defense. I might be saving women and children. It would be a very moral thing to do. But what if he's never more than a talker? What if no one listens? They listened in the Pale of Settlement. The real question is how would I do it? Mika the marksman? The garrotter? The slasher? Too physical. Poison is his medium. Mika the Medici.

Who is he kidding?

Mika Lott kill someone? It isn't in him. He can't even hunt. Can't even fish. God will have to order him. Then a nudge in the ribs. Only, God doesn't nudge ribs anymore. He lets things happen. The Pale of Settlement, Kiev, Korovo, the 1905 pogroms. Still, there might be a way. If Mika can write a letter. Munich is efficient and highly organized now. So are Berlin, Paris, Rome. It will be nothing for them to send a professional.

He awakens in the morning beside Katerina, assaying the expression on her sleeping face. For the sake of innocent faces he will have Hitler murdered, he decides. But at night, working silently into her flesh, and afterward thinking of life starting inside her, he wavers. Pobedonostsevs might deliver such edicts and murder abstractly. Hitlers might. But can Mika Lotts?

It is incredible that he even considered it. Interrupt a life! And all because of an embittered derelict's philosophies. A sick derelict. Katya was right. No one will listen to Hitler.

And suddenly he remembers the book he read as a young man in Kiev that Hitler's mustache has somehow called to mind. A book of disturbing prophecies, pinpoint predictions, which could not possibly come true. Except…

Pushing his watches aside, he hastens to the Hof library and there locates *Tri Razgovora* (*Three Conversations*), by Solovyov, the famous Russian philosopher, published by the Imperial Printing House at Tsarkoye Selo, 1900. In the back is a supplement—*The History of Anti-Christ*—Solovyov's apocalyptic vision. This he brings home and solemnly begins to study.

"Why are you fussing so?" Katya demands as he moves from chair to chair to ottoman and, finally, to the window, puffing his cheeks, shaking his head. "Another Hitler book?"

"No, but it seems to be about him."

"A biography? How can that be?"

"Not a biography. It's a book of…prophecies. I don't know what else to call them."

She pokes a fork into a steaming pot on the stove, her broad forehead flexing without wrinkling, like the skin of a child too young to have indelible expressions. "Does he predict whether babies will be boys or girls?"

"Mmmh. You shouldn't get your hopes up, you don't know yet, Katya."

"Oh, don't I?"

It is the clue she has been waiting to deliver. Triumphal information. But he isn't listening. His lips are moving as he reads. "He says there are horrible things ahead," he relates.

"It's an old book. There are good things ahead. Next spring."

"He talks about an antichrist. An everyday-looking antichrist. He says he'll be young and forceful, with a magic voice that seduces—"

"A swain. They're everywhere. How I had to fight them off before my Mika came along."

"He says the Antichrist will lull leaders into a terrifying moral apathy, that he'll stir the masses into reducing Jews to ashes. He says our skins will be turned into household articles. He says…I'm sorry, Katya. I'll read to myself."

Hardly the atmosphere for joyous tidings, she decides. She will withhold her news until he has his head out of this dreary business. Hopefully that will come before she looks like two Katerinas.

"When is all this supposed to happen?" she asks.

"The Antichrist will make himself known after a short spell of blindness. He'll begin his thirty-third year in 1921."

She laughs a single syllable. "Good. He'll stand out. Should be easy enough to identify."

"Except he won't come as the Antichrist." Mika slides his hands under the book covers, curling his fingers over the tops. "Maybe he'll come as the long-awaited German messiah. Maybe he's here now in Vienna."

"Hitler? Your Wagner aficionado in his tattered pant cuffs?"

"Why not? Solovyov says he will be so common-looking as to be underestimated." Glancing down the page, he reads in Russian: "'…he may even have a funny mustache.'"

"Your Hitler had a tuft on his chin, as I recall."

"Not anymore. Now he has a funny mustache. That's remarkable, don't you think?"

"What's remarkable about the way a man shaves?"

"I meant the prediction."

"And I meant to be sarcastic. Of course it's *not* remarkable. It's ridiculous. So, this imaginary Antichrist is a young demagogue with a hairy lip. Probably half the heretics in Vienna fit that description. If you want to take a weight off your mind, find out how old your Hitler is. That's where Solovyov made his mistake. He shouldn't have been so specific about the age. 1921 will come, and then who will read Solovyov?"

She is right again. Hitler is twenty-seven or eight if a day. That will make him thirty-six or so when 1921 arrives.

His Katya is very level-headed. Such a good marriage he has made. A very decent woman with a fine mind, who reads voraciously.

A healthy woman. A loving woman. Maybe a trifle stubborn, but perfection is boring. And when she is right, she is right, right, right. He (first to admit it) is wrong this time.

His error is in believing in the magic. Once in your soul, it rolls around like a drop of mercury you can't corner. You think it isn't affecting your logic, but it is. It's hard to know the magic, to understand it and still be noncommittal. Take the Spear, for instance. Did the Spear bring power to its possessors, or did those possessors seek it out because they were power hungry? He knows the stories, portents galore, coincidences to stymie the rational. But he has told himself all along not to make up his mind and instead just to see what others believe and to realize what a potent stimulus the Spear can be to certain personalities. It is an error, therefore, to think that Solovyov might be a prophet. The real question is, are the Viennese hate-mongers aware of the work? If they are, then that might explain the mustache. Hitler read Solovyov before he grew it.

Mika puts the mystery aside.

And then one day he is passing the Vienna Academy of Fine Arts, and it occurs to him that, if Hitler came to Vienna calling himself an art student, he very likely had hopes of attending the famed academy. And if he actually applied, then there is a record, an application...*a birth date.*

"My name is Adolf Hitler," he says to the young clerk inside. "I wish to amend my application."

The clerk glances twice. "You applied here?"

"Yes."

"Recently?"

Mika balks.

The clerk adds, "Fill out a new one, please."

"Actually I want to remove the old one."

This stops the bureaucratic flow cold. The clerk cocks his head in such a way that his glasses glitter opaquely. He has a tight, resigned expression that suddenly loosens in expectation of novelty. "Why?"

"Because it contains certain errors and blasphemies that must be corrected. This is no laughing matter. I am very upset...very upset. If necessary I will use legal means to see that my honor is restored."

"Your application contains blasphemies?"

"I have reason to believe so."

"But you filled it out."

"No. It was submitted for me."

"By whom?"

"That is no concern of yours. If you'll simply pull the application, I'll make the corrections and insertions."

"How long ago did you file?"

"A long time ago. I think."

"You don't know?"

"I told you it was done without my knowledge."

"Surely you realize it's been processed by now. Who will ever look at it again?"

"It's a matter of honor," Mika pleads earnestly. "For the record, don't you see?"

"I'll look into it." Dryly. "Hitler, you said?"

"Adolf Hitler."

The clerk dissolves among filing cabinets and returns minutes later with a yellow document. "I must ask you for your identification, Herr Hitler," he says coldly.

Mika shrugs. "This is absurd. I just want to see it."

"You have no identification?"

"Sir. *You* have my identification. Anything I show you will simply conflict with the blasphemies there—"

"I see no blasphemies. Just a straightforward application. Quite innocent, I assure you."

"Then if you won't let me see for myself, at least read me the information."

The clerk sucks his cheek.

"My birth date!" Mika blurts. "Read me that. For God's sake, you can tell me that!"

"Why don't *you* tell me your birth date, and I'll tell you if it needs to be changed."

Mika licks his lips. It is only necessary to eliminate one year. If it isn't that year, all is well. But if it is that year…

"1889," he says.

"It doesn't need to be changed."

"It says 1889?"

"It doesn't need to be changed."

Yes, Mika, Hitler will turn thirty-two in 1921 and thereafter begin his thirty-third year. Shattering, eh? That Solovyov—what did he say? *The Antichrist will become known after a short spell of blindness. He will assume his vocation in 1921.* Are you going to wait till then to find out, Mika? Or are you going to kill him now? Where is the outrage you felt when your father cried in your lap? Has the smoke from your mother's pyre all blown away?

It was plain from his change in appearance that Hitler has come into some money. Money might also mean a change of lodging.

Concerned he will lose Hitler's trail again, Mika appears every morning at Meldemannstrasse. But on the fourth successive day he waits in vain. Hitler is not there. Even before he musters the courage to enter and knock on Herr Kanya's door, he knows what has happened.

"Hitler left for good last night," the manager tells him. "Go away. I don't need your kind of trouble here."

From the stairway, where a snake of a man leans against the wall, comes a casual question. "Want to know where Hitler went?"

"Crawl back into your bottle, Lingenfelter," says Kanya. "You don't know where Hitler went."

"I know, Kanya."

"Where?" from Mika.

The snake emerges into the light—chinless, scruffy, searing eyes. Kanya grunts in disgust and slams his door.

"You're the Jew," says Lingenfelter.

"I'm a Jew."

"He went to a village up the Danube," says the snake. "I can show you. There's a peasant there who sells herbs. *Herbs*, know what I mean?"

"Drugs."

The snake's tongue darts over his lips. "It'll cost you an extra steamer ticket if I take you. And a little bit of cactus flower for me when we get there."

"Hitler uses mescaline? Why does he leave Vienna for that? Why don't I just wait for him to come back?"

"He isn't coming back. He's on his way somewhere. Said he'd stop at Wachau. Safer…cheaper there. Lodz, the herbalist, will know where he's gone."

"Your name is Lingenfelter?"

Formal nod. "Well?"

The blue Danube is green today. Mika's favorite color is green. He stands in the bow of the little steamer bound for Wachau in a green sweater, feeling quite right about what he is doing. Next to him is Lingenfelter.

Lingenfelter is colorless. "What do you want Hitler for?" he asks above the sound of the engines.

"My business."

"You going to kill him?"

Mika scrutinizes the searing eyes. Lingenfelter's question seems more than tactless. Maybe he intends to kill Mika on this trip. Maybe he is trying to assess how much of a fight he might put up.

"Certainly I'm going to kill him," Mika replies. "Don't you recognize a trained assassin when you see one?"

"How will you do it?"

"See these hands? I'm a strangler. Use to kick them to death, but I sprained my ankle."

Lingenfelter laughs inaudibly, not really sure what to make of the man. "I've heard Hitler speak outside the factories in Vienna Neustadt. He belongs on stage. My father was an actor and so I know these things. A regular actor and damned convincing, too."

"But still an actor."

"I said so, didn't I?"

"Acting is pretending things are true that aren't."

"Yes, yes, why should you like Hitler?" Lingenfelter nods. "He hates you, you hate him. That's simple enough."

"Simple enough."

Cleaved, they lean one to starboard, one to port over the bow rails, and the water that flows past is liquor to Lingenfelter, Katya's cabbage broth to Mika.

At Wachau they disembark. The herbalist has a cottage, says Lingenfelter, and he shows the way along the outskirts to a structure that is almost organic in its aromas, its collection of leafy pots and bottles and vines and even in its griminess. By contrast Lodz turns out to be a withered gourd of a man, something dried, gnarled and decaying. In a thin, soprano voice he conducts a third person examination of them as if dictating observations to an old, smoky cat at his feet.

"Lingenfelter looks well, a consequence of the hickory bark dram he got from Hans Lodz," he coos theatrically.

"I coughed up the hickory, but the base was delicious, Hans."

Lodz picks up the cat as he continues. "And with him is another refugee from modern medicine. Suffering from melancholia, perhaps. He has very likely been doused with belladonna and so needs a purgative, followed by Hans' mint potation to sweeten the humors. But we'll ask him what he wants."

"Information," says Mika abruptly, "about Hitler."

The peasant's eyes flick to Lingenfelter. "What about Hitler?"

"Where is he?"

"Gone to Munich to seek his destiny."

"Destiny?"

"I helped him discover it."

"Through drugs?"

Lodz releases the cat. "He was very much disposed to what happened. A disorganized personality, half starved. Drugs had a powerful effect on him."

"No doubt they strengthened his delusions. And you catered to his petty wish for power."

Lodz nonchalantly whisks cat hair from his sleeves. "I recognized you soon after you entered—"

"Lie."

"…the Jew who would like to stop Hitler. But Hitler can't be stopped—"

"Lie."

"…and so I don't mind telling you these things."

"Lie."

"You must believe that or you wouldn't be here." And to the silence he adds, "Not many believe it, eh, Lingenfelter? But that's to Hitler's advantage. It's the world that's drugged, eh, Lingenfelter?"

Lingenfelter, whose head has been swiveling back and forth between them, grins uncertainly and finally settles on Mika. "Well, do I get my cactus flower?"

5

Leaving Lingenfelter behind, Mika boards the little steamer for the short trip back to Vienna.

He is depressed. Going to Munich is out of the question. He has his own life. Munich has its own Temple Guard. He will write them a letter; try to explain. But he will not move to Munich to follow Hitler.

And Lodz is wrong about Hitler being unstoppable. What an absurd thing to say. Admittedly Hitler is a demagogue in the making, but unstoppable? Someone will stop him. And if not the man, then the cause. Because if you can't cut off the head, you cut off the arms. The arms and the legs and the hands and the fingers. That is Mika's role. To sever fingers. And to keep track of the body as a whole. He must understand the black heart, mind and soul of this evil so that he can deal with its extremities.

He leans over the rail in order to regard the gluey bow waves and again is reminded of Katya's cabbage broth. Why should he be the one to stop Hitler? Making a home is more important to him. Cabbage broth is more important. Katya boils it every Friday. Today is Friday. Shabbat at sundown. Of all the things that have passed through his life, cabbage broth is still with him, but Hitler he can live without.

It was different before he was married. His family was dead. He was the punctuation at the end of a sentence that had been erased. But now he is the capital letter of a new sentence. And dinner will be ready. And Katya will be talking about babies. And Mika Lott isn't an Ochrana agent (the Tsar's secret police) but a letter writer.

He will *write* Munich.

He smells the cabbage broth from the street. Pungent today. And does he smell a bit of beef? But where is the bread? He saw it rising in the pan before he left.

He unlocks the shop door, steps inside and relocks it. A silver watch lies on top of the green felt on his bench. Katya has let in a customer. He picks up the watch and gently tests the stem. Watches talk to him this way. The sighing of time. *Broken gear tooth*, this one says, *I'm slipping*. Laying it down, he passes to the stairway. The top of the landing is steamy.

"Such a waste of broth," he sighs, entering the kitchen. "We have the best tasting walls in Vienna."

But she is in the living room and doesn't hear.

"Katya?" he calls. And then he notices the flies through the steam. Thick above the pot. It *is* beef. The lid quivers, promising surprises. He forgives Katya the omission of bread and tiptoes to the stove for a peek. "Shoo, shoo, shoo," he tells the flies, who merely make short loops and resettle with those crawling on the new cupboard above.

And then he is gasping for air and smarting with tears as the pot lid clatters to the floor. Because it is not beef he smells after all. And Katya is not in the living room. She is right here beside him. Beside him and *above* him where the flies are crawling frenziedly along the seams of the new cupboard. And as his great soul quakes and time inside it stops, as surely as it has stopped in the silver watch atop his workbench downstairs, the broth boils over with cabbage and hair and something else somewhere within that must be—must have been—the two unremarkable gray eyes of…

THE MORAINE

1
FALL, 1921

Deep within the earth a groaning begins just as the crescent moon passes over the Polish Corridor. There are always groanings in the earth, but this one is different. This one begins beneath a hundred million tons of boiling sea water heated by magma seeping through fissured rock and bubbling sediment. From there it arrows inward, kilometer upon kilometer, until it is beneath a hundred billion tons of coastline. Taut as a violin string it resonates, crumbling and pulverizing the points of least resistance. Pockets of gas explode, squeezing into hairline cracks and expanding them, adding a tangled chorus of thin screams. Vast veins of feldspar become carbonated as pustules of trapped water vapor burst inside. Great shards of granite begin to snap.

The uncanny wail of the earth transmits itself to the Baltic, awakening sleeping denizens on the bottom. An underwater reign of sand and silt begins to churn as they stir. Smaller fish dart everywhere and schools of sprats fly like windblown leaves in the blackness. Pores in the skin of the earth secrete insects, worms, snakes. Burrowing animals leave their dens. Countless birds, sensing magnetic aberrations, flutter and flinch.

And when at last footings shatter, a foundation plate of the earth slips with an uncanny grating. Monoliths grope and wrestle in the hellish medium of disintegrating rock. Voids open and close. That which is permanent twists like hot taffy. From the Baltic to the village of Niski Kosciol the earth quakes.

Above the larchwood church on the village square, the bell in the tower begins to hum. Then the church and rectory shiver, hymnals fall to the floor and the bell tolls wildly in its tower. Deep in colorless dreams, Father Ledochowski is bumped out of bed on the first jolt.

The old priest braces himself on the floor, heedless of the spider that runs over his hand. Crawling unsteadily to the nightstand, he fumbles for his glasses. When the trembling stops, he spreads the wire rims and inserts his face behind the lenses.

Then he gropes through the nightstand drawer for a votive candle and the matches next to his cigarettes. The thin flame pops and cowers in the dust-filled air as he rises to his feet. Holding the candle high, he pivots slowly in a complete circle.

Not much damage. Not much *to* damage. Two small portraits of Christ and Mary have fallen to the floor, the stove door is open and a few sticks of wood have rolled away from the pile. He smells kerosene; a lamp in the cupboard must have broken.

Distant voices reach him now. And a moment later the bell in the tower begins to hum again. A woman screams. Father Ledochowski braces himself against the table. Pots and pans rattle, plates dance; and then a tug. The earth breathes free of the aftershock.

A quake! In this region? Dear God, what he hasn't lived through!

Outside, more voices join the din. He had better go door-to-door this night. But clambering stiffly into trousers, shirt and shoes, he remembers.

The moraine.

His first duty. The moraine. Even before his flock. Because if something has disturbed it...if it has somehow opened—

Securing the twine he uses to tie up his cuffs when he bicycles, he hastens out onto the plaza where he wheels an old wood-rimmed, two-wheeler to the main road, mounts and bumps slowly off over the bricks. A few parishioners call to him, asking if he is all right, to which he makes the sign of the cross. They wave him on, believing he is checking the rest of the village.

There are no collapsed houses as far as he can see, no injuries. Stopping at the first crossroads, he glances to make sure he is alone, then turns and pedals briskly into the darkness. He feels intense relief at even this simple escape, because whatever the devastation to the village, he *must* go to the moraine.

The road—little more than a cart trail in actuality—drops in the partial moonlight, making the ruts barely discernible. They might find him with a broken neck in some newly opened fissure, he realizes. Then what? Surely some Kaszubian fisherman will happen on the moraine before long. Gripping the handlebars tightly, he strains upright to pedal faster.

But what will I do if it has been breached?

What can he do? The lame answer is frustratingly obvious: search. Search until he finds what is hidden there or until he is sure it can't be found. Search a mountain of sediment layer by layer.

For nearly an hour the rusted bicycle frame shudders over the narrow road until at last he hears the coastline. Thud after thud heralds the Baltic and still he cannot see it. The smell of brine is potent, and then the abrupt swelling of the glacial moraine itself appears, a colossus of sediments rising like some scaly saurian atop a cliff that plummets back into the sea from which huge waves relentlessly mount their assault.

Once, and once only, over the years, he has violated the Vatican edict not to go to the summit. And for that he was officially censured. Whether it was fear that the local inhabitants might see him and overcome their superstitions, or perhaps that the evil feared by the Vatican is in some way palpable, he never really understood. The difference is important now because he is about to violate that edict again.

Dropping the bike at the base of the moraine, he ranges west, studying each shadow and silhouette for signs of a breach. The west edge looks intact. And the eastern end. Impregnable. It is impossible to wade out to survey the sea face, but a rock jetty that could afford him a view extends into the Baltic and this he gauges with trepidation.

He has a morbid fear of deep water. As a child he was rescued from a boating accident in which a younger sister drowned, leaving him wracked with guilt. He had grabbed the extended oar—grabbed it reflexively—when he might have grabbed little Rasina. His life seemed borrowed after that; not really his. Perhaps that is why he committed to seminary.

Is this my test, Satan?

The jumbled cubes of stone and seething foam beckon him with the hiss of a twisting black serpent. Waves crash into the jetty, leaving smooth surfaces slick with spume. Summoning both faith and will, Father Ledochowski takes a cautious step onto the first granite block.

Some of the stones are cracked and unstable; all of them are wet. The footing is treacherous. Working his way from one uneven plane to the next and trying to ignore the oncoming waves, the priest moves faster and faster. But when the first big breaker catches the corner of his eye, every sinew in his body tenses.

It explodes with a crack beneath his feet, blowing through channels like a school of whales. The reverberation drops him to his hands and knees. He closes his eyes and raises his face to the wind, paralyzed with terror while three succeeding waves soak him to the skin. And then he paws the lenses of his glasses to run the water together and staggers up into a half crouch. His calves tremble. He moves apelike, catching himself at each step with knuckles or splayed fingers. One stone block, another. At the end of the jetty the pounding sea sends vibrations through his sodden shoes, demanding his attention and daring him to look away. Slowly, like a man lifting a great weight, the priest forces himself to full height. Inching around until his back is to the Baltic, he scans the palisades.

High and dry, bone-white in the moonlight, the phantasmal crest of the moraine looks unchanged. Relief floods over him.

He is about to start back when the insidious rush of a new wave compels his gaze. This one is huge. This one is not going to meet the jetty head on. It is going to go over it. As the nerve-fracturing assault fires through and over the man-made peninsula, he probes for purchase in the crevices. But a mattress of water lifts him off the stones, and for a moment he thinks he will be carried out to sea. The borrowed life he has lived will end in a poetic drowning afterall, flashes across his mind. And then it subsides with gurgles and sighs, leaving him gasping and trembling upon the granite. Badly shaken but driven by the need to fulfill the mission, he gains his feet and scrambles ashore.

It is fully five minutes before he recovers enough to gaze at the summit where he must now go. His fear that the moraine had sheared off into the sea is put to rest, but an earthquake might easily have opened deep fissures from the top.

Still breathless, shivering from the cold, he returns to the lee side to begin the ascent. He has forgotten the severity of that incline. The slips and falls make him feel like bread dough against a granite rolling pin. And at the promontory he is struck by a steady seaward wind.

He knows nothing of air currents, but it seems remarkable to him that the breeze he felt in his face while traversing the jetty can have turned so sharply at the summit. The truncated pinnacle itself, strewn with ancient dolmens, looks exactly as he remembers it, thank God. No erosions, no chasms. He dares hope the quake's epicenter was far off. Circling the broad plateau, he reaches the seaside edge and utters a simple prayer: "Father in heaven, let there be no openings. Seal off the abominations in this place."

A violent gust forces him a step or two closer to the precipice. What a view! The roiling sea charging ashore line by line. And a horizon tinged an unearthly phosphorescent green but flickering white. And what is that odd void of darkness moving forward against the faint illumination? Very odd. He squints for perhaps a minute before detecting its peculiar vertical motion, like a skin being pulled off the Baltic. And then the meaning of it bursts upon him with terrifying clarity.

Tidal wave!

His first impulse is to turn and run. But it is already too late to pick his way to the bottom of the moraine. Precious seconds expire in deadly fascination with the tsunami's tumultuous power and speed. Conspiratorially, the seaward wind drives him another step closer to the edge. He is riveted on the incredible wall of water, and though the wind is blowing in the wrong direction, he thinks he can smell the thing, the wave—its dankness, its bottom-of-the-world decay.

One kilometer...half a kilometer...two hundred meters—and yes, it *is* taller than the moraine, he thinks. In the last three seconds he pitches forward onto his face, fingers clawing over the very brink of the abyss.

The sound when it hits is deafening. A sound that resonates bones and seems to go on forever. But the tomb of water he expects to close over him never comes. The impact shakes the granite cliff to its bedrock, shattering the wave high in the air to fall in a protracted, pelting rain over him. The moraine has survived millennia and it is neither smaller nor weaker than this newly born wave afterall.

When the torrent subsides, the old priest clambers slowly to his feet. In the gray of an emerging dawn he sees that the beach is gone. Farther inland, a flotilla of trees and undergrowth whirl in freshly created lakes. Only the area directly behind the moraine, where the wave was blocked off, escaped inundation.

Father Ledochowski descends.

His bicycle, left on the slight elevation at the base of the moraine, has missed the flooding and most of the rain. Yanking it out of the mud, he leads it along a slow journey from island to island. Some distance inland, he mounts and starts to pedal back to Niski Kosciol.

Sixty years old and he has survived an earthquake and a tidal wave all in one night. God must still have a use for him.

2

Scarcely have the tremors died in the Polish sea when far to the southwest members of the Thule Gesellschaft stir from their lairs. It is not the churning of buried things that drives them through the glistening black streets of Berlin, of course. It is belief in an ancient presence that tonight will meet them at Mehring Damm 26. They call themselves the Society (Gesellschaft) of the Thule after the legendary island of Thule, a vast civilization of demigods from whom they believe all Aryans descend. This happened in the last world order, they will tell you, before the great cataclysm, before the degeneration of the species. And so they come to Mehring Damm 26. Three stories. Stone columns. Iron fence.

There is the society's founder, Baron Sebottendorf (real name Rudolf Glauer, born in Dresden), all the way from Munich. And Alfred Rosenberg, future Reichsleiter, who has smuggled *The Protocols of the Wise Men of Zion* (a forged document that indicts "the Jewish conspiracy") out of Russia, thus winning amnesty for his Jewish name.

And another is Dietrich Eckardt, a hard-drinking morphine addict whose violent withdrawals have gotten him in and out of hospitals and asylums where he uses inmates to stage dramas about the Spear of Longinus and the Holy Grail. The aberrations are well cast. He has also translated *Peer Gynt* and edited *Auf Gut Deutsch* in Munich. He has also co-founded National Socialism. And finally he discovered an exciting proselyte, introduced to him in the Brennessel wine cellar by two friends named Feder and Röehm. The proselyte's name is Adolf Hitler.

Enter Josef Krantz, tramping down Spandauer to Bismarckstrasse, his gaze leaping from parapet to gargoyle to cornice like some

Quasimodo of Berlin. He is an honors student in architecture (and archaeology) at the Institute of Technology in Berlin-Charlottenburg. Visual textures excite him. He has a passion for subtle shadows and restful hollows. Before she died on his 10th birthday, his mother used to read him stories about strange people in exotic lands. He could never get enough details about the settings, and when he pressed her, she would turn to his father and say, "Walter, Josef wants a palace," and his father would paint a word picture to fire his imagination. Often it wasn't a palace but a pyramid or a temple or a castle.

The columns reared in the young boy's imagination soared endlessly into the clouds and supported whole cities of alabaster, gold and marble. But with his mother gone, his father could no longer build these foundations for him. Whenever he tried, his eyes would fill with tears and the cities would dissolve. Josef spent his adolescence in the ruins of his childhood.

Then came the Institute and the resurrection of his passions. The study of architecture and archaeology awakened his needs for human warmth as well. A series of awkward relationships followed, the last of which ended when the object of his affections assured him he was too afraid of commitment, too guarded, too undemonstrative to ever find a wife. That was when he met Lutka.

Lutka the actress. Human warmth—my God, it is several hundred degrees hotter than that! In three days they will leave by night coach to seek her father's permission to marry. Her father lives in a Polish village named Niski Kosciol.

But tonight Krantz is en route to Mehring Damm 26 because one of his archaeology professors has said he should hear what these people have to say. The professor is a racist and a scholar of esoteric groups. He talks of Atlantis and the legends of Midgard and Niflheim. He quotes Madame Blavatski's *Secret Doctrine*, and he says that the Thule Gesellschaft is merely the final distillation of a dozen other lodges: Theosophists, Astrum Argentinum, Germanenorden, Rosicrucians, Freemasons, Golden Dawn, Ordo Templi Orientis... Krantz was shocked to learn that the poet W. B. Yeats and Mathers were once lodge members, as was Aleister Crowley, who rekindled the sexual magic of the Landulf of Capua—Klingsor. He wonders where his professor's mysticism stops and his archaeology begins.

An uncertain breed of dog roars wolfishly through the bars of the iron fence as Krantz arrives. He waves the pass his professor has given him and the dog is checked by a handler. In the foyer he is searched. They seem more interested in what he looks like than in what he says. He is a real Aryan Adonis, blood and marble, and he moves to the large, carpeted inner room aware that he has just passed some kind of racial screening.

The low ceiling is coffered, the interior wall bolstered with bas-relief columns. About thirty people occupy a ballroom arrangement of divans and settees. Jasmine mingles faintly with the smoke, and a Victrola plays almost inaudibly in the background. Krantz is issued a drink and a lot of indifference.

The crowd on his left is talking about someone named Kurt Eisner—a Jew who led the Social Democrats and was shot down in the street—and of how his supporters forced passers-by to salute a wall poster of him over a gun barrel until a man named Eckardt had the urine of bitches in heat thrown at it, attracting every stray in the district. They don't say it, but Eisner's assassination and Eckardt seem directly linked.

"Well, here's someone I don't know," declares a graying woman, advancing upon Krantz with an ingratiating smile. Her cigarette in its holder is rather like a bowsprit, and trailing in her wake, saunters a sleekly bald man with muscular jowls. "See, Eben, we do have appeal to young, rational types. This one is a lawyer or a doctor just beginning his practice. Oh, I do hope he knows something about gallstones!"

"Gravestones, I'm afraid," says Krantz. "I'm a student of archaeology and architecture."

"How interesting. Well, you may call me Clarissa. But—oh, dear—I'm afraid I have to let you go already. That's Herr Rosenberg clapping for attention. You must sit with the novices."

She flutters fingers toward the other side of the room, and before Krantz can find his seat on a small couch, the man named Rosenberg reaches the center of the room and, turning slowly, launches into an introduction of the night's speaker:

"…his travels have taken him through the Islamic world. He has traced Arabic history from North Africa through the invasions of southern Europe where he uncovered new historical facts about such magic centers as Kalot Enbolot, site of the ancient mystery temple where the Landulf of Capua reigned supreme among ninth century sorcerers. Through his own climb to fifth degree adept, he discovered a previous incarnation of himself as Bernard of Barcelona, a ninth century European who was part of the collusion with Islam. Ladies and gentlemen, I give you Dietrich Eckardt!"

Tall, balding, burly Eckardt strikes a paternal pose with outstretched hands and immediately appeals to "the rivers of good German blood" in the room. They are the historical process, he tells them, the reincarnations who will return again and again to restore their ancestral purity.

"My ancestors were pirates," Krantz murmurs too loudly and directed at the stylish woman in a peach gown next to him. Her spontaneous smile fades as Eckardt's eyes sweep them. Already Krantz has misjudged the night's tone—not unusual for him—and worse, he has decided not to care. Even the bored Clarissa regards him with a stony expression from across the room when he smiles and flutters his fingers at her.

"...the Thule Gesellschaft witnesses the past through contact with the outer world," Eckardt is proclaiming, "and in written documents and talismans of power touched by outside forces—the Spear, the Grail.... From these we know of Thule, a vast island in the extreme north which vanished. And of its civilization whose members shared a time consciousness with celestial hierarchies and began the Akashic record. Their faculties transcended reason and the colloquial laws of the earth. They took energy from the sun and the sea and transmuted matter with their minds. But this power caused wars and created mutations. Many mythologies tell about it. The Edda records the struggles of 'Norse giants' with monsters. And even Genesis, chapter six, verse four: 'There were giants in the earth in those days; and also after that, when the sons of God came in unto the daughters of men, and they bore children to them, the same became mighty men which were of old, men of renown.' So the races degenerated into seven sub-races, and only the elite were prepared to retain contact with the unseen powers. These are your ancestors."

The room remains reverent, except for Josef Krantz, sucking his cheek, who sits one arm flung along the brow of the couch. Dear

God, he has heard more convincing pitches at a freakshow, and yet, he seems to be the only one not taking it seriously.

And then, to his surprise, Eckardt's eyes come to rest on him. "Am I boring you?"

There is a moment of shocked stillness at this break in decorum. But the speaker is known for theater. A few now crane for a look at his new sacrificial lamb.

"Which...which sub-races?" Krantz mutters, a little embarrassed—but only a little.

"Rmoahals, Toltecs, Tauranians, Aryans, Akkadians, Tlavatli and Mongols," Eckardt recites slowly, eyes remaining fixed on Krantz as if taking aim with a lethal weapon. "Some of these have deteriorated and evolved more than once. The theories of Darwin are essentially correct but limited to brief moments in the time-space continuum. The process of natural selection may be controlled by conscious memory. Those who come back again and again *will* the changes. But they must find each other first and resist the polluting of the race. They must renounce the Christian values of surrender, pacifism, tolerance, forgiveness and self-denial. These capitulations of the masses make them unworthy to become rulers. All religions which conquer in the name of such vices do so to perpetuate their own weakness and suppress superior elements. In order to defeat their numbers we ally ourselves with those powers who esteem force and will!"

There is a spectator's pause while the room's attention solidifies pointedly on Krantz. Eckardt is going to play it to the hilt, and clearly he is to be the foil.

"I must have missed a few tidbits in Archaeology 101," he ventures lightheartedly, now hoping to make peace, but no one rescues him with a laugh.

"Only advanced study would reveal what I am revealing here tonight—"

"I *am* an advanced student," Krantz undercuts him. He just can't seem to stop uttering blasphemies. "Archaeology. I do independent study under the head of the department."

"Ah! I see. A university brat. I thought so. You've been indoctrinated with traditional thinking. Unfortunately the truth about the past doesn't always present its formal credentials to doubters. Conservative archaeology needs warm bread crusts in order to believe in this morning's breakfast."

"And what evidence does liberal archaeology offer?"

Eckardt slips his hand into his right pocket, withdrawing something black and polished as he strides slowly to the small couch where Krantz sits. This is his so-called "Mecca stone," a fragment whose origins he has never revealed to anyone and to which he will one day die praying. "Touch it," he says.

Trying to remain cavalier, Krantz drops two fingers on the polished surface. Instantly the muscles in his hand contract as if triggered by electrodes. A barrage of images bursts across his mind.

Abruptly Eckardt pulls back and the stone falls to the floor. Judging by his expression, he is as surprised as the young man. "Who are you?" he murmurs.

"I told you…a student."

"The elite left us weapons in the earth. You've come to scandalize us."

And before Krantz can figure that one out, two thugs—one burly, one skeletal—have him by the elbows and he is being dragged unceremoniously across the carpet. A door opens and he is deposited on his feet in another room just long enough to take a punch below the belt. The fuzzy domed hulk withdraws an arm from the crater in his belly, and then the nausea comes like a second of intense hunger, followed by a stone in the gut. The skinny half of the duo steps across the threshold and closes the door.

"Which are you, a spy or a reporter?"

The answer doesn't seem to matter, because the massive man's fist blurs in again, snapping Krantz's head back, numbing his lips and jangling his teeth. He entertains a brief philosophical flash that this is all wrong and disproportionately cruel. Within the past hour he was standing in the street, free and full of optimism; and just moments ago he touched a stone, triggering images of a granite cliff and an undersea cavern. Now he lies on a carpet damp with his own juices.

Before the room stops spinning, he hears the door open again and the two thugs are gone.

He is in a study, he sees, blinking away blurred vision: books on shelves, desk, red leather couch, matching chair, a pair of dull paintings, half a dozen photos in frames. The light is coming from a desk lamp with a milk glass shade hand-painted in roses. Not a room to get beat-up in. There are no windows, no phone, and just the one door.

It is not over, he realizes; otherwise they would have tossed him out on the street. The two blows were just preliminary. Running his tongue over his teeth he tastes blood. So many disappearances in Berlin these days—this could end very badly.

He crawls stiffly to the keyhole, but his timing couldn't be worse. Because the door suddenly opens inward, and he takes it on the temple, which jangles the outposts and starts the pain looking for an exit again. From the floor he blinks stringy hair and a sympathetic grin into focus.

"My name is Helmut Dürer," the newcomer says with insidious politeness. "I believe in being rational."

Krantz tries to rear up, makes it to his elbows. "Nothing...in this place...is rational."

Dürer flings out a rubbery arm which snaps back to scratch his nose. "And you are Josef Krantz. You see? Rational. The next logical revelation should be why are you here?"

"Professor Stoph gave me his pass. He said I should hear your pitch."

"Alas."

"Alas? Why do I have a feeling that you've stopped being rational?"

"Ah, Josef, it may be that you were only very foolish. Very foolish. You see, they think you're a reporter come to discredit Eckardt."

"He doesn't need discrediting."

Dürer's grin rises to his eyes without giving up on sympathy. "I like you, Josef. But, you see, this kind of thing happens. Reporters looking for something sensational, infiltrating, creating a stir."

"You can't seriously believe I'm a reporter."

Dürer drops to his knees beside him and nods to the closed door. "*They* believe it."

"Then you can tell them. Can't you? Look, I'm just a student. *Please.*"

"They sent me in here to hypnotize you. If you're willing. Are you willing?"

"Hypnosis? Another parlor trick?"

"My, my, you certainly are cynical, my young friend. It's difficult for me to believe a university student doesn't recognize hypnosis as a medical fact."

"If I do, will that get me out of here?"

"It might."

"Do it, then."

"You have to want to be hypnotized, Josef. You have to let me. It doesn't work if you don't let me."

"I've never wanted anything so badly in my life."

Dürer studies him for a full ten seconds before the rubbery grin ripples back in place.

"Relax, then, Josef."

They are on their knees, face to face. Dürer's stage voice is resonant yet low, undulating gently.

"…think pleasant thoughts. Imagine leaves rustling on a soft bed of grass, imagine breezes sighing…deeper and deeper, relax. Relax. Let your body melt."

Krantz sits back on his calves, closes his eyes.

"…limp like a rag doll. Let yourself go. One, two, three…deeper. Hear the waves crash? One, two, three…deeper…each third wave taking you deeper, more relaxed, more limp. Asleep now. Asleep but you hear my voice. You know what's going on…but you're asleep."

Despite the stress of the past thirty minutes, trauma and dislocation have loosened Krantz's grip on reality. Not long after he begins, Helmut Dürer lifts Josef Krantz's hand and lets it fall.

"Now we begin," he says.

Exactly twenty-three minutes later, Dürer brings him back. It is perhaps the most important twenty-three minutes in Krantz's life. He will be years sorting it out. But in the moment, he merely blinks, remembering nothing. "Well?" he asks. "Am I free?"

"You didn't tell me who sent you."

"You bastard." He leans into Dürer's face, enduring the reek of sauerbraten. "I've got friends, you know. They're probably calling the police right now."

Dürer grins lazily. "How would you like to talk to Police President Pohner, or Assistant Chief William Frick, or Bavarian Minister of

Justice Franz Gürtner?" He nods again to the door, beyond which the novices have left and the Thule Gesellschaft has gotten down to the night's serious business. "But frankly you'd do better to confess something."

"I'm a Berliner. Lots of people know me. I'll be missed."

"Pohner says he has nearly three hundred political assassinations and disappearances on his books since the war."

"Scare talk, right?" Krantz says, nodding. "I understand. Scare the pants off me so I'll keep quiet. Well, I will keep quiet, you can count on it. Not a word. I swear. Believe me, I don't know a thing about politics. I didn't even know Charlemagne was dead until last week. Architecture and archaeology. That's what I care about. All I know, really. Buildings and ruins don't change that fast. I mean a head of state, he can go just like that. But buildings and ruins, they just don't turn over that way. Gives a fellow a chance to stay on top of things. So tell your friends. Tell them it worked. I'm speechless with terror. Okay? Tell them."

"Alas," Dürer repeats for the last time, the baggy grin collapsing as he rises. "But I like your sense of humor."

Backing slowly away, he opens the door, turns and closes it behind him.

And there is doomed Krantz alone with the last lingering whiff of sauerbraten, which smells very much like sulfur.

Escape.

It comes down to that.

The door, he ascertains with a gentle twist of the handle, is unlocked. What stands between him and free Berlin is a room full of lunatics, two pagan doormen, and in the yard a guard dog evolved only slightly from a wolf. It just might be that the world is still Cartesian, that even in an occult lodge all is not madness, and that the object of his ordeal is mere terror and not extinction. Nevertheless, he knows he has to cross that room, exit that door, and pass through that gate. At best they will let him. At worst…

The view through the keyhole is badly framed. That or a number of people have left. There is Eckardt with a woman dressed as a peasant by his side and only a handful of others. Presently Rosenberg says something to the peasant in Russian. "Da," she answers and pulls her blouse up over her head. Two men transport a table into the center of the room. The peasant, breasts flopping, removes her shoes, skirt, underwear. Unaided, she clambers onto the table to lie on her back. Then the lights are extinguished, and Krantz cups his hands around his eye to eliminate the illumination of the lamp behind him.

In the darkness beyond the door Eckardt calls for silence. Candles are lit. The flames seem to dagger unnaturally high, creating an ether with blots of ashen light adhering to faces, hands, the naked form of the woman. Faces slide in and out of darkness. Moons. Orbiting now. Phasing and orbiting in a slow march around the catafalque.

The surrogate begins to groan. Her knees come up as if she is in childbirth or about to have sex. Words slither and collide in gleeful chaos, rising. Like the candle flames. There seem to be no walls, no ceiling to bounce them back. The void gulps them instantly. Senseless words. Non-human voices now.

Only gradually and without contemplation does Krantz record a singular fact occurring on his side of the door. The lamp has been extinguished behind him. Unimportant. A power failure. God has called lightning down on Mehring Damm 26.

Much more fascinating is the insanity beyond. He, the small boy, the child of a rational world, is peeping beneath the roots of a tree into a midnight microcosm. *Absolutely insane,* he marvels. *Utterly and absolutely insane.*

And then comes the shriek. Blood-curdling. Not a note of glee in this one. An I'm-being-torn-up-inside shriek. The nude figure on the table writhes. All the whispering stops. A chill drives across the inky ocean straight into the keyhole, causing Krantz's eye to water. And while he reasons that the windows have been opened, the chill deposits a terrible odor beneath the seam of the door. Loam and suppurating flesh. Earthy cerements, gummy cadavers. All the séances have them. And if it weren't for the obvious terror beyond the door, he would laugh.

But there is terror.

The candle flames flee in every direction away from the table between them. The Baron is quailing and edging out of the circle. Eckardt tells him to shut-up. Slaps him. The others, some with handkerchiefs to their faces, seem equally unsure.

"We've unleashed it," is croaked.

"Give it room!" another.

The peasant woman respires in faucal gasps and arches like some death-locked, hissing serpent. Suddenly, impossibly, her head and shoulders rise fractionally off the table. Her breathing becomes sibilant. A voice wells forth. Masculine. Clarion. But not Russian. Not German. Not anything recognizable. And then another voice comes out of her, terrifyingly loud. And a third. Babbling. Beyond human speed.

The tenants of the room stand like pillars of salt. In the candle glow—now blue—the peasant's breathing plumes frosty white. It is Rosenberg who calls: "Speak to us of the Messiah!"

Instantly the blue subsides, the chill ebbs. The candle flames right themselves and turn crimson. The air becomes stifling, unbearable.

Half-demented, the Baron begins whimpering on behalf of all of them as a thin vapor seeps obscenely from the woman's vagina. Coiling upward, it collects in a viridescent shroud. All eyes are drawn to the cloud and the disturbing resemblance now emerging. The Baron's voice squeezes into a whimper as the thing gels: hollows, brow ridge, gaping orifices. Like a yawn, the orifices broaden and a face awakes from sleep.

Evil enough. They have surpassed obscenity. They want no more. No longer are they like wicked little boys and girls defecating on the floor, uttering vile blasphemies, defiling human dignity. This is black and foul and grave-sprung. Let *in* by them. And they fear the crashing of the barrier, for they are, after all, of the living.

And Krantz knows. Kneeling on the other side of the door, he knows. He feels it through the keyhole. A crawly, shattering, deranging thing; a smell as much as anything else. Something panic-driven that one remembers from evolution. He doesn't even realize that his lips are moving, that he is telling himself he has heard of it before, ectoplasmic faces, voices, colored flames, odors, drafts. Tricks of the trade. Not to mention, he has just been hypnotized. Séances are booming. Any number of students will tell you they have been to one, or that so-and-so is a medium.

Nothing new to the Thule either. Probably a weekly event. They like to get together and defy God, and bare their souls to Lucifer, and invite in whatever atavistic forces lie shed on the path between beast and man. So why the feeling?

Why are they so shaken this night?

Whatever the reason, he must escape now. The enemy is wholly absorbed and the door is unlocked. Go now. Ignore the new voice that erupts from the other room. German. Masculine. Ignore the thrill of horror by those who recognize it and call it by name—some recently dead compatriot killed by the communists.

Krantz places his hand on the doorknob just as a gasp goes up outside. The voice has announced that the messiah will be the next claimant of the Spear of Longinus (whatever that is). A countering voice, female, is warning that Germany will come to ashes in his reign.

Don't look, Krantz. Arguments beyond the grave are not for you. The doorknob. That's real. Cold ceramic. Turn it. Wipe the sweat off your hand and turn it. Ignore the voice, turn…turn.… The latch is free. Let the plane that separates you swing inward. Make your hellish plunge through the ether. Startle the pagan doormen, if they are still there.

The door stands open now. And the shock that rushes over him is total.

Because the room is empty.

No table, no initiates, no sprawling, naked medium, no candles, no stifling air, no odor of rot. The scent is jasmine and the room is lit and arranged as before.

Walk, Josef. Blink and wonder whether any of it was real or just some trick of suggestion. The keyhole is a cinema. Kellerman's *Tunnel* is showing next. Not funny. Not funny at all.

Fearing yet another veil being torn aside, he pivots and crosses the room, striding faster, pivots again at the front door, and out that door faster still, and through that gate from Mehring Damm, running, running, running.…

3

When Lutka Gerlak was three years old God made her an angel in Niski Kosciol. This was confirmed by Father Ledochowski who needed a tiny seraph for the village mystery play that year. After the play was over, they took away her paper wings, but no one told little Lutka she was no longer an angel. She continued to make "angel prints" in the snow by sweeping her arms up and down, and raced through summer meadows, soaring in her child's mind to the same heights Josef Krantz's boyhood columns soared. She was five before she realized it was only a role, and the knowledge sent her crashing to earth.

In a sense her youth—like Josef's—was spent in the ruins of a childhood fantasy. She longed for the freedom to be someone else, to choose an identity and make it real. At fifteen she was thin and boyish, with large, lime, limpid eyes and skin as pale as fog; but when she looked in the mirror she saw Cleopatra and Helen of Troy.

Her father frowned on her ambitions, and, though she longed desperately for his approval, every step she made in the direction of the stage drove him two steps off-stage—off their stage. By the time she had done Reduta Theater in Cracow and five productions at the Teatr Polski in Warsaw, they were in full flight from each other. It didn't matter that it was Shakespeare or Molière, an actress was an actress, and Papa disowned her when she left Niski Kosciol for the German stage.

So now she is here in the Weimar Republic, having disenfranchised her family, resisted moral peril, and learned theater, life and language without help. She has fought off grasping men, near poverty, lousy roles, isolation and loneliness. In a way that Freud would have loved, she has kept faith with her father.

Until Josef Krantz.

The young man is rabid and quite convincing when you give him half a chance. She has given him half a chance, and he has convinced her to do this crazy thing—to take her home to Papa and ask permission to marry. Maybe she is just homesick. Maybe that is why this crazy thing seems right.

So. Lutka & Josef. On a night Pullman between Berlin and Niski Kosciol.
Neither is seeing things clearly.
The man who is following Krantz for instance. He has been following him for three days, and when Krantz boards the train for the Corridor area of Poland, the man is confused. His instructions are simply to see that Krantz doesn't go to the newspapers or some other authority after the meeting of the Thule, but the Thule has a great interest in that area of Poland, and here is Krantz suddenly going there.

It seems doubly ironic considering what Helmut Dürer learned when he had Krantz under hypnosis—the fact that the young man is an architectural student with a prior background in archaeology, that he has actually spent some months in Poland at an archaeological dig near Gdansk. Such a person might become useful to the Thule when the coming Reich incorporates Poland. But here is this Josef Krantz returning there already. It might be significant. The man from Thule boards the train.

If Krantz noticed him, he would have recognized the fat half of the duo who worked him over at the séance. He might even have noticed a second man following the first. This one is a member of the Temple Guard assigned to keep track of the Thule, and he too boards the train.

It is Mika Lott, and his home base is now Munich where until recently he has been an obscure intelligence gatherer. He understands the importance of myths and mysticism, but after thirteen years he has grown tired of going through trash barrels to see who reads what, and he welcomes the chance to trail a figure as important as Dietrich Eckardt to Berlin. Now the trail has broadened and his assignment has changed, thanks to his pleas over the phone to Munich.

He has yet to divine the importance of the young lovers to the fat man, but he has learned Krantz's name. On the surface they seem like a very ordinary couple. Which is exactly what they would be if circumstances allowed.

Through design all four have taken berths in the same car. The Thulist is near the rear, Mika across the aisle about mid-way, Josef and Lutka are toward the front on the same side as the fat man. None of the berths are made up.

The fat man has been aware of Mika since before he bought his train ticket. *Amateur*, he deems, a member of the Jewish underground. The war has gotten the fat man used to killing, and two assassinations since have taught him a little subtlety. His first murder was a woman with the instincts of a cow. He simply stabbed her once and waited for her to die. But she looked at him as though nothing had happened, and then she bellowed for help throughout a dozen more slashes until he finally found her throat. The next time he used a pistol and killed his victim outright; though others heard the shot and he barely got away. Now he carries both pistol and knife, and he is carefully making up his mind which to use on the Jew.

Across the aisle, Krantz yawns and casually suggests to Lutka that they go to bed.

"What is this sleeping sickness that's come over you, Josef? First you insist on a night coach, now you're ready to die at a quarter to nine."

"It's the clackety-clack." He gestures vaguely to indicate the noise of the train.

"What part of you is it affecting?"

"How embarrassing."

"I thought so."

"What I meant by embarrassing was…was my fantasy."

"I know I shouldn't ask."

"It's childish really."

"Do you have to tell me?"

"All right, I'll tell you, since you insist. I'd like to sleep with you—not *with* you, of course. On top of you, I mean. The upper berth, I mean."

"Relax, toad, your third wish will come true."

Ordinary lovers. Sparring.

One by one the berths are made up. The car becomes compartmentalized. Some time after ten Krantz begins to drift off. He sleeps badly. It is the mingling of the clackety-clack with his dreams, like a voice from the real world. That is the way it was at Mehring Damm 26. Dreams and reality. Helmut's voice going clackety-clack, hypnotizing him, suppressing something he wasn't supposed to see. Only now he is starting to see it.

It started when he turned the latch on the inner door and got the shock of his life, because the outer room was empty—*or was it?* It couldn't have been. The things he was watching and feeling were real; *they could not have disappeared*. Either that, or the empty room was real, and the rest of it was imaginary. Maybe Helmut used some sort of post-hypnotic suggestion and none of it happened. Josef Krantz slumbers more deeply…clackety-clack…clackety-clack.

At the end of the car is a toilet. Through the seam of his compartment curtain the fat man monitors its traffic. The toilet is small and hardly soundproof, despite the overriding noise of the train, and the stigma of its use produces furtive little trips by one passenger after another. Two and a half hours go by and everyone in the car makes a sojourn in preparation for the night. Everyone but the Jew. The fat man is disgusted. His enemy would have a superior bladder! He himself makes a trip. Then, shortly after twelve-thirty, the Jewish Guardsman ghosts past the fat man's curtain.

As soon as the toilet door closes, the fat man rolls out of his berth and glances up and down the aisle. All the curtains are laced. At least two people are snoring loudly. Without putting on his shoes, he pads softly to a position outside the toilet and pulls out his nickel-plated pistol.

This will be easy. The Jew will be no match. He may even use the knife and just haul the body to the platform between cars afterward. But why should he risk even that momentary spectacle? Make the Jew walk onto the platform himself. Above the roar of train wheels the shot outside the car will scarcely be distinct from an aberration in the track.

The toilet door opens suddenly, and a surprised Mika Lott sullenly obeys the gunman's motion to step out. *Amateur*, fat man repeats to himself. The pistol motions again, and moments later the two of them are on the trembling, swaying platform, exposed on three sides. A ribbed walkway reveals rushing ties and ghostly gravel a meter below their feet. The noise is deafening.

The icy wind braces Mika, and he realizes his mistake now. The Thulist wouldn't have risked shooting him inside. Desperately he lunges. The pistol fires wildly. Still driving, Mika pushes his adversary to the railing, jamming the pistol between them. This time when it fires the bullet rips through the fat man's chest, lodging in his spine. He is dead in the instant, but his momentum carries him over the back of the front car's platform.

Lodging upside down, one leg hooked over a coupling hose, the dead man thumps against the rearward car for several moments until a rough section of track and some sharp curves shake him loose. His body drops onto the track and is immediately severed. Stockinged feet and legs tumble down the embankment to come to rest in a wheat field; the head and torso pass under the train, battered and rolling in its wake for some distance.

Amateur.

Inside the car, Josef Krantz's eyes fly open. He has just been back to Mehring Damm 26 in a nightmare, and he is gripped by an absolute conviction that the force he felt there was real. It is a hackle raising, lung stifling, bowel melting force—an obscene force, a wrong force. Something loose, profane, unnerving. A thing that makes dogs howl, cats spit. And he has seen something else this time. Some sort of negative illusion burst upon his dreams, but as soon as he awoke, the chill and the nausea drove it away. Fully awake, the train whistle shrilling its journey into the Pomeranian night, he understands now that the missing image will tell him what happened and whether or not there is a hell. And he is quite sure he doesn't want to know.

4

The station, mantled in fresh snow, is little more than a facade. Behind it are lakes, marshes and thick forests of ash, pine and birch. The lakes are cuticled with ice and correctly reflect the state of a deepening freeze in the Baltic Corridor. Invisible at four a.m. is the snow-packed road circling bogs to the northeast, where it eventually reaches the coast and wends from fishing village to fishing village along the Hel peninsula. But before it does that, it passes through Niski Kosciol a kilometer or so inland.

Protesting wheel and coupling, the train pauses to relieve itself of Krantz and Lutka before gasping on toward Gdansk in a Gd-awful hurry.

Lutka twirls across the platform, the fur hem of her thin gray coat ballooning, her emerald eyes flashing with airless clarity in the snow bright night. And Krantz, infected by her dance and the confectionery aspect of the snow crested station, follows. Like a cuckoo clock with frosted eaves and an abrupt tenant, the stationhouse door suddenly bursts open.

"Wagon comes in an hour," pipes an elf of a man in archaic Slavonic.

The door slams shut, dislodging snow from the lintel.

The young couple enters into an orange realm of roaring fire, burnished wood, ruddy cheeks, leather, leaves and colored glass. The leaves seem to be a hobby of the old elf's, arranged as they are in dried bunches pressed under glass.

He serves them tea in clay mugs on the hearth and for the foretold hour or better conducts a barter of information for news. His tone is convivial, and it isn't until the driver arrives (an emaciated creature with a fat horse) that they detect the note of prejudgment in his dual introduction: "*Pan* Krantz and *Pani* Gerlak traveling *together*." The stupid driver leers all too transparently.

So that is how it is going to be.

Through an interminable dawn they journey by wagon to Niski Kosciol, and in the phantom play of light off snow Krantz again glimpses the outlines of things past at Mehring Damm 26. Or is it the rhythm of the horse and its syncopating jets of steam, so like the breathing of the train, that brings back the shadows? What has Helmut Dürer stolen from his senses with the rhythm of that mesmerizing voice?

"Icy," the driver informs Krantz, pointing to a long, climbing curve ahead. He reins in. "You have to get off."

For the next six kilometers Krantz is obliged to walk and even push the wagon against the difficult footing, and it isn't until Lutka's twittering brings his weary head up that he beholds her gleaming Shangri-la.

It is nothing like what she described, of course, and he wonders if it lives up to her own childhood memories after Berlin. Maybe if you stay on top of the hill and squint away the smoke, maybe then.

"Where are the gingerbread houses?" he shouts.

She points toward a two-story house of massive black logs stuck together with white mortar that looks like a chocolate torte layered with vanilla crème.

"Not gingerbread!" he yells back, but she is waving at doughy figures moving in the street.

Some of them have sighted the wagon and are running up the hill. Children in leggings and soft boots. Shouting.

Polish laughter is aggressive, the kin to Russian for Krantz, but Lutka hears the warmth she has missed in German merriment. The eldest child, perhaps twelve, recognizes her instantly and adds Krantz to her understanding with an annoying worldliness. The adolescent gathers her less precocious friends for whispers and giggles, and then one of them—a brave harlequin only half aware of her own meaning—dashes alongside to gibber at Krantz: "Are you a German soldier?"

Amid titters of exquisite glee the menagerie tumble off for the village, each child unique in stride and style through the snow according to its height.

German soldier. They didn't invent it. Gossipy women and cruel men invented it. *"Lutka has gone to Berlin to be an actress—and after what the Germans did to her brothers!"* Before they reach the first house, a dozen doors and windows fill with faces. But the one with no faces—the fourth house—that is their destination.

Krantz gives Lutka a look of pure love, flourishes his knuckles, knocks and locks his hands behind his back.

"Must you posture like a German field officer?" she whispers. Stepping to the door, she adds her own signatory taps.

A minute passes. Krantz smiles, glances at the gallery of faces, smile some more. The spectacle of their humiliation is painfully clear. This time Lutka fists the door solidly three times high above her head. It is a knock to end all knocks, and it brings forth a booming response.

"Take your whore and go away, German!"

Meanwhile, a diminutive erg of human flesh is plying down the street. The collective face of the neighborhood softens at her passing. "Lutka, Lutka!" she cries, enveloping the young woman with motherly caresses. "Lutka, child, you've come home!"

"Not *quite*, Auntie."

"Ah-h, that old father of yours. Big a mule as ever. May God un-stiffen him with a bolt of lightning. Don't you believe for a minute there aren't five broken hearts behind that door. All right, maybe only four—your mother and sisters—Feliks is all the little man and thinks his father meets regularly with the Almighty. Who's this?" She thumbs toward Krantz. "The young German soldier whose rumors fly faster than crows and twice as black?"

"He's not a soldier, Aunt Zofia. He's my betrothed."

Krantz jiggles around, preparing for amenities, but Aunt Zofia cuts through his silly grin: "Brave and stupid, I see. Well, true love never had a better test, Pan...?"

"Krantz," he says.

"Ah, yes. *Krantz*." She screws up her eyes. "This village will spit on you before it shakes your hand, do you know that, *Herr* Krantz?"

Cavalier gesture. "My hand will remain extended."

"Words are wind." The elder woman takes Lutka by the shoulders. "You're not much brighter, child. At the very least you should have left him at the station for a bit."

"Pan Krantz," Lutka sighs, "this is Panna Modjeska."

"Pleasure," he nods, ablaze with teeth.

"Well, your manners are all very well and good, young man, but you can't stay here with Lutka. What you should do is go talk to the priest. That won't hurt your reputation any, and it might get you a bed in the rectory. In that event, the whole village will either become heathen or you'll have won your first bit of respect. Come, Lutka."

And with that she snatches her niece's satchel and storms up the street. "Right at the first corner, third house," Lutka imparts over her shoulder. "I love you."

"Auf Wiedersehen," he whispers, fingers twirling.

5

At the far end of the village is a plaza paved with tree stumps at the foot of a weather-beaten church. The church is larchwood, large as such structures go, with a dome, steep roof lines broken by unusual animal carvings at the gables, and a rectory attached.

Niski Kosciol. Translation: *New Church*. It must have been new in pagan times, Krantz reflects.

The rectory door is answered by a short, wiry man in long wool underwear and a pair of dusty trousers. He is at least sixty with a face as dappled and worn as the inside of a shoe, oversized leathery ears, and glasses that smear his pale blue eyes into rheumy grayness. In his gnarled right hand is the stub of a cigarette.

"Sorry to disturb you," Krantz begins. "I was sent by Panna Mod—Modjes…"

"Modjeska," the priest says. "I'm Father Ledochowski. Come in, come in."

"Josef Krantz. Thank you, Father."

In three steps Krantz finds himself well into a simple room with a blazing stove. The furniture is nicely turned but worn. Books and newspapers are strewn about. And sheet music. The sheet music is already a touch of home for Krantz. His father's laurel was briefly playing oboe under Furtwängler in Mannheim, and Krantz is as indifferent to music as his father was to him.

"I was just filling the stove," says the priest. He squats to poke the fire with a stick.

"My name is Josef," Krantz repeats. "I'm German, and I came here with Lutka Gerlak to get married."

The priest glances quickly from the fire, scattering ash from his cigarette. Two final pokes with the stick and he rises to offer his hand. "Congratulations."

"Her parents won't open the door," says Krantz. "Some Aunt Zofia-or-other took her in and told me to come talk to you about finding a place to sleep. But I'm not Catholic."

"If God put up with Martin Luther, Niski Kosciol can put up with someone who isn't Catholic. You're welcome to stay here. I hope you like potatoes and pickled sprats."

Krantz marvels that the priest has smoked the cigarette into oblivion without getting burned—the future patron saint of lips. "I don't have much money," he says. "I'm just a student."

"A student, at your age. You'll find that's an oddity in these rural parts. Most of our young people are through with school by the time they are fourteen. What are you studying, if I may ask?"

"Architecture and archaeology."

Father Ledochowski studies him a little too long. "You speak Polish rather well."

"I learned in Berlin, but I spent a summer here once. Near Gdansk."

The priest removes his glasses for wiping, revealing eyes like overripe grapes slit horizontally. "Well," he says, "we have no archaeology and no architecture to speak of around here. And you won't need any money to stay with me, but if you'd like to earn a few zloty and you can man a broom, old Rudnicki might use you in his dry goods store."

At that hour, far to the west, two farm boys playing with their dog along the railroad right-of-way come upon the lower half of the man from Thule. Shortly before noon the rest of him is discovered by the district police.

The police conclude that the man was shot elsewhere, then thrust under the night express when it slowed on a grade in a clumsy attempt to make it seem like a train accident. But interviews with the engineer and brakeman, and subsequently the conductor, produce the shoes left by the fat man when he padded down the aisle in stockinged feet. Two days later the revised story reaches Niski Kosciol: murder on the night train…a Berliner known for anti-Semitic activities.

Father Ledochowski draws another connection—something an old priest sitting atop a terrifying secret must do. Because any stranger is a threat. Especially a German. Especially a German interested in archaeology. And especially a German interested in archaeology who speaks Polish and arrives on a train with violence in his wake.

And then there is Mika. Suddenly center stage. He has killed now—inadvertently and in self-defense, but he has killed. It makes his heart pound, stuns him, takes away his stomach. As a victim, he has known violence all his life: the cruel awakening in childhood; the ragged street beatings in Vienna; the blasphemous murder of Katya. When has he ever known peace? But this…this is a loss of innocence. *He* has killed.

When the fat man fell between the rail cars, Mika just stared in horror. And after the body slipped onto the tracks, he felt the palpable remains in every lurch and thud of the train for the rest of the interminable night. This was one of the people who had murdered his precious Katya, he told himself, but if revenge is a dish best served cold, he took no nutrition from it.

He crept back to his berth in a cold sweat and thought for a long time. He was a thinker, not a doer. Always he had worked through others, seeing what was necessary, relying on his insight into the occult nature of the enemy—that was his talent. Perhaps it came from his singular escape from death as a child. No matter. That was his role: thinking, understanding, working through others. And now he must return to that, justify it. There was this Krantz fellow, and he was important somehow. Mika, curled womb-like in his berth, rationalizing all this and praying for forgiveness.

He watched the young couple detrain at the station outside Niski Kosciol, and he passed on to the next stop at a place called Blatatak; and now two days later he is back on the outskirt farmlands where he has quartered a discreet distance from Niski Kosciol with an obliging swineherd.

Aunt Zofia has the largest dog in the world. Krantz discovers this by throwing ice chips at her window. The priest then counsels him that if he wants to make headway in this village, he should be sober, chaste and friendly…and wait for Sunday. Sunday is the only day for social advancement. Sunday comes and Krantz finds himself roasting in the sunlight pouring through the church's east window, while around him ranges an emotional geometry of Lutka on the aisle, her older sister, Prakseda, with the choir behind the altar and the rest of the family in a rear pew. Foremost in that family pew is a large bear he fears may someday be his father-in-law. The creature is all hair and fiery eyes—vodka eyes. One fatherly embrace from that at his wedding will guarantee no children right away.

Sunday passes and, as far as Krantz can see, nothing changes.

But in Aunt Zofia's parlor after church Lutka and her three sisters (Prakseda, Cecelia and eleven year old Maria) have a joyful reunion. Prakseda brings the news that her father has relented and invited Lutka home.

"Your father is a pillar of salt," advises Aunt Zofia. "Give him time and he'll wear away. If this Josef is worth a single groszy, your father won't stand in your way for long."

"She's right," chimes Cecelia. "Already the villagers are accepting him. He does magic tricks at Rudnicki's and the children love him. Tell her, Maria."

"With cards," Maria says. "Lucjan saw him."

"I heard the same thing," says Prakseda. "He made a big impression on Panna Swincka when he told her he was the Permanent Chairman of the Friends of Poland Society in Berlin. Imagine, the Permanent Chairman!"

Lutka imagines.

"Go home, child." Aunt Zofia gives her niece's hair a stroke. "Let your father eat his words in little spoonfuls. It would choke him to take big bites."

Sometimes on Krantz's way to the dry goods store, when he skirts the road to the Hel peninsula to avoid snowballs, and when the long winter night seems to hang forever at dawn, and when the wind is blowing off the Baltic with smells that begin in the black depths of a hostile world, he remembers Mehring Damm. He feels his mortality then, recalling the cold fume of that room, colder than this arctic air, ranker than the sea's effluvium, the spectrum of paleness starker than the snow and the sky and the silhouettes. It becomes quite real again and his breathing sounds desperate and frail as he crunches along.

Today he stops in his tracks on the outskirts of the village and tells himself: "I'm a long way from Berlin. There's nothing out here but villages."

Only today there *is* something.

Cued by the German's hesitation, a Polish youth steps out from behind a tree on the edge of the Hel road. He wears a dark coat with faded embroidery, and a fur cap, and he holds his hands behind his back. Enough of his face is visible for Krantz to recognize its paleness as well as the lime green eyes and pixie chin. This is Lutka's fifteen year old brother, Feliks, the only surviving son since the war. Feliks draws within two meters of Krantz and brings out his hands, revealing a tarnished dueling pistol in each.

Krantz breaks into a sweat.

"They're primed," the young man says calmly.

Krantz tries to turn away, only to have one of the pistols drop at his feet. "Why don't you just shoot me in the back, Feliks?"

"Like a German does? Ten paces."

Ten. As a boy, Krantz lost a little finger in a door, and it was a childhood joke that he couldn't count to ten. That comes back to him now. I could run like hell, he thinks. I could leave the little son of a bitch alone. But would Lutka love a coward more than a martyr?

Reluctantly he picks up the pistol. "This is nonsense, young man—"

But Feliks has already turned his back on him and begun to pace. The choice seems to be between ten paces or twenty before a bullet is fired at his head. Josef Krantz spins around and commences rapid, seven-league strides—twelve of them—before Feliks shouts his name. For just a second he hesitates. Would the young man shoot him in the back? Maybe he should just refuse to face him. And then he hears a hammer cock. Pistol still at his side, Krantz turns to face the young man who has no intention of ever becoming his brother-in-law.

A single lime green eye is sighting toward him behind a steady hand. The puff of smoke floats away as the discharge compresses from hill to hill. He thinks he hears the bullet sing by.

And now his young adversary faces fate with the self-righteous assurance of a Samurai.

Today is the anniversary of Adamo's death. Adamo, Henryk Gerlak's oldest son. Adamo his first born. Feliks' and Lutka's brother Adamo, who used to pull them on the sled. How Henryk has preached that to Feliks. And about Tadeusz. And about the Germans who killed them. The Germans who rape their homeland as regularly as locusts, who murder sons and brothers, then come to steal daughters and sisters, and—Mother of God, how upset he was this morning when he saw the dueling pistols gone from the mantel and Feliks nowhere in sight! What kind of foolish old man incites his last remaining son to—

He stops dead on the road, breathless and speechless. There, where the hill dips, he sees Feliks shoot and miss. And the German. The German raises his pistol and…and throws it away!

"Feliks!" Henryk bellows. A tardy cry. A father's cry.

Both duelists turn.

Feliks reads his father's relief. The hated German has shown him mercy and his father is grateful. Ashamed, confused, Feliks throws down his pistol and runs.

Krantz watches him out of sight before taking a lingering look at the old man. There is no surrender in Henryk's eyes, but neither is there anger. Stooping and tying his shoe, he continues on his way to Rudnicki's.

For a long time Henryk Gerlak stands in the road, staring first one way then another, as if waiting for instructions. And, indeed, his lips move as if he may be requesting directions from the Almighty. Twice he takes a step for home, but when at last he overcomes the inertia of his thoughts, he retrieves the dueling pistols and goes to talk to Father Ledochowski.

Krantz, broom in hand, watches through Rudnicki's window as Henryk passes. Slower and slower the broom pokes beneath a crate of cabbages as he leans toward the glass. Henryk is going to the rectory, still carrying the dueling pistols. What is that all about—moral contrition? And Feliks is off sulking in the woods. For the first time since arriving in Niski Kosciol, Josef Krantz feels like something other than a sex-crazed pariah. Well, a pariah anyway. He has been lusting for Lutka more or less nine waking minutes out of ten. And Lutka's mother and sisters are putting up preserves at a neighbor's, if he heard the chatter correctly yesterday in the store. When you get done with all the subtracting, it comes out right. Lutka home alone.

Feigning a sudden toothache, he takes his leave from Rudnicki's, arrives unobserved at Lutka's, and there broadly hints to his lady love that he is risking his life for her in Niski Kosciol.

"The Friends of Poland weep for their Permanent Chairman," she says.

So then he tells her the whole thing, and she glances at the mantel where the dueling pistols were. Real shock registers. Her thin nostrils distend, green fires swirl, her lips puff in outrage.

"Men!" she snorts. "Stupid beasts!"

But moments later she is in his arms on the verge of tears.

He plays it to the hilt, how his life isn't worth a groszy here, and what an irony it will be if he dies without ever having loved her, and of how the marriage ceremony is just a formality. She is so wrought up, that he actually makes headway. They end up arguing about the risk of pregnancy. A fat actress from Hamburg who had three children before she was seventeen once told her the good days and bad, Lutka says, and about all the odds for each and how they don't mean a thing unless you put a walnut between your knees and keep it there.

So then Krantz tries the only way left. Lutka's mouth opens in surprise as he bulls against her with trembling, outrageous caresses on her thighs and breasts. Her face dampens red. She digs her fingers into his arms, but she doesn't try to stop him, and that is enough acceptance for Krantz. He pulls her skirts up by the handful to commence the intimate fumbling which, despite its artlessness, achieves its purpose. In the wake of passionate groans, their faces come together like a pair of hot irons. Somehow they move through the curtain into her room, and then they are beyond faces. Embracing, groping, gasping, they topple moist and molten on the bed. Resistance seems petty. The suffocating clothes are pawed away. He is stiff and bursting; her vaginal lips are extruded, glistening. And so they begin the burning thing which is, after all, so utterly simple.

Except—

Except it isn't so simple when Henryk Gerlak opens the front door and stamps the snow off his feet and calls to one of the participants. Not simple at all.

Nevertheless, done. And explainable, too, even to the fact of the bedroom window being open.

Papa: "You look feverish, Lutka. You must be ill. Keep the window closed."

Lutka: "Yes, Papa. It was just so warm in my room."

Papa (turning away and staring into the fireplace): "I've decided to let you see the German…"

6

"You have a Josef Krantz in your employ, I'm told," Mika blurts, trying to sound officious.

Rudnicki smells of cigars and brine, though he cannot afford the former and he is one of the few Kaszubs who has never fished for a living. Perhaps the illusion is because Mika's nose has been rendered ineffective by his stay on the pig farm.

"Eh?" Rudnicki's wooly head tilts downward to afford his eyes a look over half-shell glasses. "Josef? Why do you want Josef?"

"Just a few questions. I've come all the way from Berlin."

"Are you a relative? You don't look like him."

"Police business, my dear fellow. We're trying to solve a murder."

"Oh." Rudnicki nods thickly, pauses. "The murder was weeks ago, wasn't it—if you mean the train?"

"We're still investigating."

"Oh. Well, Josef just works here, but he's not here now. He'll be here in a little while."

In twenty minutes to be exact. Mika knows this because he has been gathering information painstakingly and discreetly, has returned once to Berlin in fact and become intrigued by what little he found out about Krantz. And because he really has nothing else to pursue, and because he still harbors some guilt over the death on the train, he keeps coming back to try and divine why Krantz is so important to the Thule.

The fact that the young man was being followed the night of the murder says that it is not a cooperative association, but there is nothing very dramatic about Krantz's recent movements. So, Mika, in frustration, has planned this out: first, approach Rudnicki pretending casually to be the police, because that way he won't be challenged for credentials; then, after Krantz hears second-hand from Rudnicki that an investigator is looking for him, he may not ask for proof at all. One of the reasons Mika has waited this long is because of the finite possibility that Krantz—despite his preoccupation with a young lady—will recognize him from the train. Let the memory fade.

"I'll be back," Mika says to Rudnicki.

He leaves before the storekeeper can compose questions and passes around the outside of the building to higher ground away from the rectory and the direction from which Krantz must come. Screened by a stand of spruce, he watches and waits. Denial will be the measure of Krantz's candor when they meet, he decides. He knows so precious little of the young man, other than that he is or was a student at Berlin-Charlottenburg with studies in archaeology and architecture. Unusual combination.

When Krantz arrives, stark against the snow, Mika waits another fifteen minutes, long enough for the slow-witted Rudnicki to inform the young man that the police are looking for him. There is an expectant pause on the parts of both the old storekeeper and the young student when he re-enters the store.

"Herr Krantz? My name is Inspector Weichs. May I have a word with you? Outside, if your employer will permit?"

Rudnicki nods deeply and solemnly. Krantz gets his coat from under the counter and follows Mika into the street. Scarcely have they turned to face each other when Krantz volunteers: "If this is about the murder on the train, no one in our railcar knew about it when it happened."

"We, you say?"

"My fiancée and I. Lutka Gerlak."

The young man shows no guile whatever, his vaporous blue eyes attentive as he relates his unremarkable itinerary.

"The murdered man was indeed in your railcar," Mika informs Krantz at last. "Weren't you aware of being followed?"

Krantz blanches slightly.

"You were followed for at least two days before you boarded the night coach. We were trailing the man who was following you."

"I don't understand. You're not saying the man who was murdered was mistaken for me?"

Mika prolongs the false perception. "Why would anyone follow you, Herr Krantz?"

"My God…following me. It has to be the Thule Gesellschaft. I don't believe this."

"Believe what?"

And suddenly there is wariness in the young man's eyes. "Am I a suspect? Who are you? You look familiar."

"I assure you, you are not a suspect."

"They said…they said there were high-ranking police officials at the séance that night. They threatened me if I told about them. And you say you're the police. Are you testing me?"

"If I was testing you, then why would I admit I'm from the police?" Mika ventures, trying to make sense of Krantz's fears. "There are no police after you. What night are you referring to?"

"The night of the séance," Krantz repeats. "I can't believe they followed me all the way here."

"You must be important to them. Tell me everything."

"But I'm not important!"

"Then you can only help us and yourself by telling me everything."

Krantz studies Mika for a moment, then sighs and begins the Mehring Damm trauma in weary detail.

Mika listens, his insides tightening like an over-wound watch. This is the vaguely defined fear that resonated his interest in Krantz to begin with—that there was some occult connection. Because why should the Thule follow the young student if they didn't think he might be useful? They routinely murder their enemies, surely Krantz would not have survived this long if he wasn't important to them.

How to play it? Before Josef Krantz has even finished, Mika decides to take a chance.

"Listen to me, Herr Krantz," he says earnestly. "You were not the target of the killing on the train. These people want you for something. They are what you said they are: the worst dabblers in black magic and racist politics you could find. Their purpose is long-range political and social upheaval, and they are very powerful. I advise you to stay away from them. You cannot let your guard down, now or ever, until they are destroyed. Do not take this lightly,

Herr Krantz. Remember this now and in the future."

But Krantz's interest is the past and the present, occurs to him as soon as the words are out of his mouth. Is that the young man's value to the Thule?

"How do you know I wasn't the target on the train?"

"Because we know who was killed and why."

"But you don't know who did it. There's still a murderer out there."

I am the killer, Josef. Mika Lott. Congratulate me.

"Given enough justification, there are many murderers out there, Herr Krantz. Remember what I've said...."

Mika is alarmed and relieved. Krantz *is* important, but he is also innocent. Innocent in every sense of the word. While his own soul was fracturing in the clammy vapors of Katya's severed head boiling on the stove of their apartment in Vienna, Josef Krantz was gazing through a classroom window in Berlin at an ice wagon and wondering if school would let out in time for him to watch the local fire brigade train for a race. What the younger man told him of his nightmarish experience on Mehring Damm in Berlin suggests he may sort out the evil for what it is. Then again, he may look the other way as so many have, or live his life in denial, or even become complicit.

Like long-term comets, the two of them may meet again, but now Mika can leave the Hel peninsula and return to Munich. Others will do the fieldwork. He must gather the intelligence, analyze it, keep track of what's going on. No one else can do that as well as he does. The most essential thing in predicting and disrupting the growing menace is to understand it.

7

The Pullman from Berlin sways through the Pomeranian night just as it did when Klieg rode it to his death. Klieg was the fat half of the vicious duo from Mehring Damm. His severed body, identified through papers, eventually wound up back in Berlin, where Thule members of the police force promptly traced the full circumstances and reported them to Mehring Damm. Hence, tonight's passenger: the skeletal half of the vicious duo.

His name is Vouten, and he wants to kill Josef Krantz by cutting him in half. Wants to but probably won't, because his instructions forbid killing him at all. The Thule wouldn't even have sent Vouten, knowing he wants to avenge his partner, except that he speaks Polish. Rosenberg and others are convinced Krantz had nothing to do with Klieg's death, that it was, as it appeared to be, a confrontation with the Jewish underground, but they are intrigued by the fact that Klieg had a ticket to the station nearest the Hel peninsula.

Presumably Krantz went there. Vouten is to find out exactly where, and why, if possible. It may be that Krantz will lead them to the thing they know they *must* someday find—something about which even Vouten doesn't know details.

The Hel peninsula is a hinterland, and it is utterly incomprehensible why Krantz should go there right after the Thule meeting. Eckardt thinks something went wrong with the hypnosis, that when Helmut Dürer questioned him as to his background and then left a post-hypnotic suggestion that someday Krantz might accept an archaeological mission to the Pomeranian coast on behalf of the Thule, Krantz misunderstood. Dürer doubts this. Krantz didn't even know what the mission was. What will he do in Poland?

Vouten has his own theory: Krantz is himself a member of the Temple Guard. A Jewish sympathizer. Maybe he even has Jewish blood. He came to Mehring Damm to spy. Then he went to Poland to discover what is important to the Thule on the Hel peninsula. On the way, he and his kind saw their chance to take Klieg.

The railroad is trying to suppress the story of its infamous night, but the conductor obliges Vouten with specifics. And at the stationhouse, the old elf who sold the young couple tickets fills in the rest: Yes, Krantz is the German's name. The woman is Lutka Gerlak. They went to Niski Kosciol by wagon.

Vouten questions the stationmaster's driver, but the man is from another village north of the stationhouse and either he doesn't know much or he simply won't talk. Vouten offers him a sizable tip to arrange a quiet lodging, and the Kaszub takes him to a farm outside Niski Kosciol where a peasant named Zolkower lives alone.

Zolkower is as thin as Vouten and as reticent as the stones that dot his miserable fields. The farm is within walking distance of the village. Money is exchanged. The Kaszub promises to return tomorrow and drives off. Vouten follows Zolkower inside the dilapidated farmhouse. There he is flabbergasted to see a menorah on the table. Zolkower is a Jew! For a moment he nearly loses control. He has just been thinking how much alike they look, and suddenly to realize—

Pretending to study the carved figurines on the fireplace mantel, he checks his anger. There is a game to be played in this village of Slavs and Jews. And if it is played right, eventually men like him will return here delivering death and bondage to these throwbacks of humanity who deserve no better fate than the way they tend their own animals. But for the moment...

Zolkower knows little more than the stupid Kaszub, it seems. He tells a wild story about some earthquake that supposedly struck the region. The quake is probably in the bottom of a wine jug, thinks Vouten. One thing he does learn: a German stranger is staying at the church.

Vouten gives his thoughts a good airing as he walks through the snow toward the village just after dark. He is helpless in this place. His friend, Klieg, suffered atrocities at the hands of a Jew, and he can do nothing about that. He wants to eliminate Krantz, but Rosenberg and some of the others have this crazy idea that the man is inclined toward Thulist doctrine, that because of his background he may be of inestimable value someday.

Bullshit!

Blond hair and blue eyes don't always make an Aryan. Krantz is at the very least a pacifist sniveling Christian; at worst a Jewish conspirator. If Rosenberg and the others won't tell him specifically why he is valuable, they should get rid of him. They should also eliminate this Lutka Gerlak woman. She is almost certainly a Slav and another Jewish sympathizer. That Krantz and she are lovers was more than hinted at by the stationmaster. Vouten wants to eliminate Zolkower, too. Just for the hell of it.

But for the moment he cannot do any of these things. A murder and a stranger in the village will be instantly connected. He would be easily traced. Better to do as ordered, but present it in such a way that his superiors understand: the sensitive area of the Hel Peninsula is a muddle of Jews and Slavs and Christians; and Krantz is thick with them all.

No mistaking the largest building in the village by moonlight, even without looking up at the small bell tower. The plaza is empty. Not even a stray dog about. It is a cold night. Snow queues across the swept surface. Vouten is not really dressed for this. He has come from Berlin with only a small valise and a leaky pair of buckled gaiters.

Passing in front of the church, he comes to the rectory window. Inside the warmly lit room are an old man and Josef Krantz. For a minute Vouten just stares, thinking how he would do it—kill Krantz.

In his pocket is a knife purse, and in the purse a stag-handled knife with three crocus blades. Each blade has tasted the flesh of an enemy at least once. He also carries a nickeled, hammerless revolver. The more he considers it, the more convinced he is that he can do it and get away. By the time the local constabulary arrives from far-flung parts he will be a mere wisp of smoke. The Jew, the driver and the stationmaster will all come forth to testify, of course, and he will be traced to Berlin. But then he will be a drop of water in an ocean.

Movement inside the room snaps Vouten out of his fantasy. Krantz has gotten up and taken a black Ulster coat from its peg. Melting around the corner, Vouten watches as the door opens, spilling the young man's silhouette onto the snow in a golden rectangle. The coat is thrown loosely over Krantz's shoulders as though he is only stepping out for a moment. He is going to to the woodpile, Vouten realizes. Keeping to the mud in order to cover his footsteps, he darts to the shelter of two slim birches.

Up with the knife…one step…down!

He could haul the body into the woods. Kill the old man, too. Haul them both to the woods. The Kaszub is coming at dawn. A train stops at the station before noon. By the time they trace him to the farm he will be in Berlin. But the Thule will learn about Krantz's murder. And he cannot run from the Thule. Dying at their hands would not be pretty. Not even to avenge Klieg.

Krantz straightens with an armload of wood and crunches back through the snow to the rectory.

Vouten glides to the window again. The Thule and the party know how to handle Jews, Slavs and Christians. Eckardt and this new man, Hitler, are uproarious when they talk about how they will invoke God to advance their cause. Let them decide when and how to eliminate the enemy.

For a few minutes more Vouten leans close to the frosted part of the window, picking up enough scraps of conversation to learn that Krantz was recently given permission to marry someone and that a wedding is forthcoming. Lutka Gerlak, of course. An Aryan and a Slav! So that is why Krantz has come to Poland.

8

The thing about a Polish village is its inertia. Getting married is a slow process with ritual performances by a proposer, *starosta, boyars, woznica ra*j—not to mention months of courtship. And if you're going to do it, what better place than a village on the Pomeranian coast? In summer you can read late because it stays light a good twenty hours a day, and in winter you can catch up on the sleep you lose in summer. And if you get tired of reading there are always the clouds, or the crazy sunsets, or the simply wild tides. And tourist attractions! The barren coast is aflame with them. The curing shed for instance—every village has one—and the fishermen are a howl. You haven't lived until you've seen a Kaszub get fish drunk by dipping dough-balls in alcohol. Others catch 'em bare-handed by channeling the water, or make eel traps called "jacks" out of a bunch of tubes.

Stupefaction.

Salvation is the priest. Intellectual salvation. The rectory has books, and the wispy old cleric has actually read them. Conversation, at least, is possible in Niski Kosciol.

Besides people, Father Ledochowski knows history. After four or five months of listening, Krantz knows the Polish chapters himself—kings and conquerors, Piasts and pagans, monastic orders, Teutonic knights. And prehistory.

This is where they have a genuine exchange. Krantz has a theory that the island in Biskupin Lake will yield Bronze Age settlements. Father Ledochowski smiles when he hears this, like a parent in the presence of a child. At least that far back, he agrees. The cigarette between his lips brightening interminably.

Krantz is surprised that his host is equally well-informed about Germany, even to the current political unrest. Surely the newspapers can't have given him so many insights. The priest, however, is a shrewd analyzer, and maybe the packets he receives each month by courier (from the Vatican, he jokes when Krantz glimpses a triple wax seal) contain official Church summaries of world affairs.

Inevitably in the long evenings Krantz relates his story of Mehring Damm 26.

Outwardly nothing changes. Father Ledochowski listens, puffs his pipe, rocks. Finally he sits forward smiling faintly.

"Those elements aren't unusual for the kind of people you describe," he says. "Sexual perversion, racism, rituals, anti-intellectualism…" Smoke trails from both sides of his mouth. "The ritual is to condition the mind to obedience. The irrationality renounces what *is* and invites new allies—*chaos* and *will*. The sexual perversion is the heart of black magic, the evoking of will, the subjugation of nature. And racism is the arrogance of survival, supremacy unchecked."

"Ledochowski, chapter twelve, verse six?"

"I suppose it is a formula. Not exactly the first time it's come up in human history, though. We priests are smart. We take notes and pass them on."

Spring thaw brings the villagers out in a host of communal projects, and Krantz is obliged to put in three hours a day bricking the road to the Hel peninsula. Occasionally he accompanies Henryk to the coast to help him make boats as well. A carpenter by trade, Henryk has a reputation for balancing such craft better than anyone else on the peninsula. The simple method is time-honored: fell the tree, float it in the water, note the position, scoop it out.

On each of these trips Krantz is struck by the abrupt coastal moraines sculpted out of eternity and garlanded with flora and emerald turf. And one especially…a monolith half sheared off at the sea, surely once a colossal tumor of granite palisades over which glacial giants lapped sediments. On top is a superb sun-through-mist silhouette of ruins. Ruins hold a fascination for Krantz. A medical student studies death, a student of architecture studies ruins.

So why has Father Ledochowski omitted mention of this sarsen pinnacle?

"Ah, pagan shrines," replies the priest when asked, tugging his already oversized ear. "We've talked about them before."

"But not *that* one."

"Nothing there."

"It's been excavated?"

"Nothing to excavate. I should warn you, though, Josef. The locals will shun you if you visit what they consider to be an unholy place."

A dig, a tell, a glacial moraine at least twenty thousand years old with only God knows what under it; high and prominent, and on the edge of the sea; the sun's first touch at dawn and last illumination at dusk? *Nothing there to excavate?*

The Saturday morning he picks to investigate is peculiarly orange and laced with humidity. He bicycles to the coast, leaving the borrowed machine in one of the shadowy hovels called *dols*, which bathers dig in the yellow sand. A brief scrutiny of the moraine's inland approach fails to reveal a path, so he begins to clamber up its steeps, which are slippery with lichens and moss.

A feeling of enchantment palpitates on its slopes. Krantz straightens to look for its cause and to catch his breath. There are black butterflies and tiny purple flowers in crevices and a daguerreotype panorama of the whole area. Squinting away the shimmer of his eyelashes toward the village, he sees a peasant in a cart behind a dappled mare. The horse has a high wooden yoke. Krantz has asked a dozen times what those wooden bows are for, but no one seems to know. The cart isn't moving.

He climbs the final few meters to find himself standing before the dolmens at the summit. He imagines the place to be a favorite for lovers, suicides and peasants hailing the new moon with a triple bow and a wish, but there is no path. How can people visit if there is no path? And now, as if a cloud is passing overhead, the feeling of enchantment begins to fade. In a very few seconds it develops into something stifling, in fact, and the stone is somehow becoming ugly, alarming. Earth, sky and water seem to recoil, leaving him remote within a haze that glistens yellow on the dolmens. Off in the distance, the horse and cart are still waiting as if at a border as he steps within the monolith circle.

A wave of vertigo sweeps over Krantz then. He has never reacted predictably to heights, and the humid climb in the smothering perfume of the little purple flowers and now the force-fed gulps of dank air off the sea conspire to disorient him. He closes his eyes. But the buffeting wind steepens the nausea, and when he looks again his perspective is hopelessly muddled. Tongues of orange sunlight run together off the glistening dolmens, and the whole thing seems to drop away in a series of images. Caves and water and a row of lozenge shapes flicker across his mind—and in his memory—the ones he has seen while touching Dietrich Eckardt's Mecca stone. The ones from Mehring Damm 26.

9

Before mass the next morning Father Ledochowski hands him a note:

Dearest Josef,
Papa says I can't see you anymore. I love you, but to cut off my roots again is impossible. I would be miserable. You would be miserable. We were, to say the least, impetuous. You were quite irresistible. It may be best that we were forced to slow down and weigh our different backgrounds. Forgive me.
  Lutka

"Evidently you went to the pagan site yesterday," the old priest says when Krantz crumples the note. "I tried to warn you, Josef. Someone must have seen you and told Henryk. Going there is an unforgivable blasphemy…unforgivable. You've seen the women bless the bread with a knife. That's pagan, of course. They believe the bread itself is holy. I don't know what happened on the top of that moraine, or when it happened, but the memory of a taint lasts forever among these people. Sometimes I feel very helpless here…"

She comes to mass with her family just like nothing has happened, except that she never once looks his way. How can she do that, he wonders angrily. Her eyes aren't even red. She isn't *that* good an actress. If she feels a thing for him, if she expects him to wait this one out, she damned well better let her lip quiver a little before mass ends. Even captive princesses let their lips quiver a little. Once, anyway.

Heartbroken, he watches her glide out of his life at the end of the service.

And then comes the weariness and a giant overdue helping of disgust. He regrets every moment, every pickled sprat, every brick laid on the road to Hel. Crazy young duelists, feisty Aunt Zofias, thick-headed Henryks and dull as a post Rudnickis! He will laugh all the way to the stationhouse—and damned if he will push the wagon with the fat horse again! He will laugh all the way to Berlin. Laugh and get drunk and find a woman and…and cry.

After Krantz is gone Father Ledochowski sits alone in the darkened rectory. He will miss Josef. But he knew when the young man told him about the Thule in Berlin that he had to end it. A marriage would have tied Niski Kosciol further to the outer world, another step closer to possible renunciation of the superstitions the Church has nurtured for centuries about the moraine in order to protect it from exposure. Besides, the Thule is on the list he gets from the Vatican each month—a list that comes by courier with triple wax seals. The connection between the Thule and Josef Krantz is casual, antagonistic in fact, but the archaeology student is German, and the Thule is gaining control of Germany through a political party with the initials NSDAP. The Party is on the list, too. And so is its firebrand, Adolf Hitler, a man the Holy Roman See says, "…may be allied with the forces of darkness."

It is, perhaps, unjust to connect Josef Krantz with all of this. But the wrong man in the wrong place at the wrong time might forge a link between earth and hell. Somewhere, somehow, there would be coincidences, or worse.

"Father, Mary, Jesus, grant me the foresight to keep the unholy place from coincidences…or worse."

MUNICH

1
1923

The late leader Joel Graafe of the Temple Guard is still warm in the Munich morgue when news of his extreme silence begins to spread throughout the Jewish underground. But by the time the inefficient remnants of his cell—cell six—can be summoned, Graafe is ice cold. Four men and a woman sit in a print shop awaiting their new leader, assigned by Berlin. One is a coward, one a war hero, the other three are quietly in the mainstream.

"I hear he's no Graafe," says the war hero Aaron Wiesel.

The woman—Esther—sighs. "Who could be Graafe? Graafe was a saint, a friend and a humanitarian all at once."

"Damned good man," affirms Rudolf Sneltz, still in his trenchcoat and leaning hard against a mountain of newsprint. Sneltz is the coward.

"Maybe if he was a bit of a bastard, we wouldn't be here," growls the most physically imposing of the five. This is the printer himself, Willi Oberstein. He blends easily in his natural habitat—the damp angularity of objects fitting his movements best, the dim light suited to his eyes alone, the ether of machine oil absorbed nutritionally into his doughy body while seemingly toxic to others. "Graafe was like every leader cell six has ever had—soft as hell. When are we going to stop being nature lovers?"

"Graafe was as gutty as the next one," says Sneltz, snuggling within his coat. "No one can say he wasn't gutty."

"Gutty isn't the same as tough. That's what got him in the end."

"Listen, Willi, the bastard Nazis got him, nothing else. And you'd better show some respect for Graafe around me."

Sneltz is mousy-looking and myopic, and the coat—a Hungarian trench breed of padded leather—makes him look twice his size. Everyone smiles at the charade of Sneltz picking a fight with Willi. Willi fakes a yawn.

Hermann Wyerdoern is the one who remains silent. Good old Hermann. The social insect. He works in the bank, approving or denying loans for the benefit of the whole.

"If Graafe's replacement has any balls, which I doubt, he'll be an improvement around here," says Willi.

"I hear he fought with Ludendorff," Wiesel notes.

Sneltz nods. "Wiesel knew everyone in the war personally. Both sides."

"He was in the navy," says Esther. "On a dreadnought somewhere—the SMS Rheinland, I heard."

It is a game now.

"The way I got it, he sat on his ass in cell one so long that everyone mistook him for a paragon of wisdom," says Willi. "Thinkers are all alike. They saturate you with their quietness and inaction until you suspect that all their energy is going into great thoughts. So, they decided to make him our cell leader and find out."

"At least we know nobody knows a damned thing about him," says Esther. "Except he's late. Graafe was never late."

"Graafe *is* late," a sixth voice intrudes suddenly.

Esther peers at Willi; Wiesel and Hermann look to Sneltz; Sneltz jumps up. With a soft scraping of soles, Mika Lott sidles out from behind the mountain of newsprint.

He is forty but looks fifty. A decade of salt dapples his arcing, ram's horn hair. The once smooth brow is tiered with wrinkles that yoke his unfocused eyes. The eyes are the same—watery cocoa in tarnished cups—but the cocoa is deeper, cooler, and he is more abstract somehow, lost in himself, an unpruned bush.

"The *late* Graafe," he repeats pointedly. "You'll find I'm early for meetings. It gives me time to sniff out traps. Regardless, I haven't used a watch in fifteen years."

Hermann Wyerdoern tries to apologize, but Mika waves him down.

"If Graafe had been early, he might have scented the trap. But, like you said, he was a saint. Saints are innocent. I have absolutely no innocence and far too much cynicism to be a saint. Berlin can't afford any more martyrs, so they've sent me to help you stay alive. Lesson one, search the premises before you meet and re-lock the door each time someone comes in. No, don't bother now. I went up and locked it while you were sitting here."

Willi grins fiercely. "You *have* got balls!"

"Willi is it?" says Mika. "Well, Willi, it was your voice I heard mentioning cell *six* the first time. Now, the enemy may not know there are six cells, so henceforth we will call ourselves *Buttons*. If that seems childish, let me tell you what happened to Graafe. I saw his body, and it's not the first time I've seen a sucked-in belly with horizontal slashes. They drained his entrails while he was still alive. And while that was happening they pounded wooden stakes into his orifices—"

Sneltz retches dryly.

Mika looks away but continues speaking. "You ask yourself what kind of people do such things. The place is Germany, the moment is now. When you scrape away the Party and the SA, you get inner Thule, and they're out to destroy God and order and us. *Us* first, God last. Drawing out Graafe's entrails was nothing. That's a thousand year old trick to them. You've heard them say they're in collusion with a supernatural race. That's the trouble with having an enemy who's irrational; you have to keep remembering he's real. Believe what you want about a world governed by discoverable laws and five tangible senses, but I'm begging you, don't underestimate these creatures at the core. They aren't a fad. They are the oldest and darkest conspiracy on earth."

He takes a reading. Five not particularly compatible types sitting around a printing press. One of them knows how to run it, the others have one thing or another to do with what goes into it.

"All right, Buttons. This cell is going forward. How do you distribute material?"

"Wiesel handles posters and bills," says Willi.

"Fund transfers?"

"Wiesel transfers funds."

"Guarding candidates?"

A pause. "Wiesel."

Mika turns to the veteran. "Are you married?"

"No," says Wiesel.

"Working?"

"I'm a mail clerk."

"Background...Education?"

"I arrived at the Gymnasium thirsting for knowledge but nearly drowned after one sip. Do I get the job?"

The others snicker.

Mika purses his lips, nods. "I asked about marriage because... people who take risks put their wives in danger."

Fifteen years ago this very night a man at least 1000 years younger than this version of Mika Lott came home to a boiling pot and found his wife's head. The rest of Katya's body was in the new cupboards, but he didn't discover that right away. He went downstairs to his workshop and picked apart the watch that had been left there for repairs, gear by gear, to postpone the shock that was roaring out of his soul. Only later did he realize it belonged to her killer and that it had been an excuse to get Katya to open the door. Killers. Two of them, later caught and hanged. Empty vessels, just like his boyhood Prussian soldier. The real evil is in Munich now. Because Hitler is here.

"I limp a little, too," Wiesel adds. "Took a leg wound in 1916— same as Hitler, except his went away. So, I'm pretty good with a tin cup, if we have to beg for funds."

Mika regards the smiling veteran coldly. He knows a little about this one already. Twenty-eight. Tough and disillusioned, scorn for armor. Joined the 2nd Company of the 16th Bavarian Reserve Infantry Regiment a month after Hitler joined the 1st. Fought the dirtiest parts of the war. He claims he used to spell his name with a double "s" but that the British shot one letter out at Ypres.

"You won the Iron Cross, First Class at Somme," Mika says.

"Same as Hitler," Wiesel scoffs softly. "Lost my sight, same as the little bastard, too. Only he got his back after a few days, of course, while I got a glass eye."

And that stops whatever Mika was going for cold. "Hitler... Hitler was blinded?"

Wiesel has a handsome face and an off center smile that varies little with the changing expression of his good eye. "Hitler took some British mustard gas in France at the end of the war," he says.

"They shipped him back to Pasewalk on a hospital train for a few days."

Score another one for magic, stunned Mika thinks. Another hole ripped in the fabric of time. Another vote for Hitler as the messiah. Because these odd details are exactly what Solovyov prophesied before 1900. Right there in any library to read.

Ten years ago Mika stood outside the Vienna Academy of Fine Arts, having just learned the staggering coincidence of Hitler's birth date with Solovyov's prophecy. And in 1921—the year Solovyov said the Antichrist would gain power—Mika saw incontestably that the little ex-corporal "with the funny mustache" had solidified his leadership over the Nazis.

But where was the brief spell of blindness that was to precede it? The Antichrist was to appear after its chosen vessel recovered from a brief spell of blindness. Mika was all too relieved to find even that one tiny error in Solovyov's *AntiChrist*, written at the end of the nineteenth century when Hitler was not yet a teenager. He lumped that detail with the others that were unfulfilled: *"He will be a vegetarian...he will write a book which welds ancient traditions and symbols to an unheard of radicalism...he will rule Europe from Berlin—"*

"Anything else?" from Wiesel.

Mika turns toward the one in the Hungarian trenchcoat. The little mouse sweats enthusiasm and bravado from every pore. His leather coat makes him look like an Ochrana agent, but in reality he is a thirty-one year old math tutor and part-time gardener. He is likable but dangerous to the Guard in any role except printer's devil to Willi Oberstein.

"What do you do, Sneltz?"

"Anything that's asked, Herr Lott."

"You help me run the press, Sneltz," says Willi. "Don't put on airs that you're fit for anything else."

"*I* put on airs? You're the one who thinks he's so special, but you only standout like a fart in the smog of the Ruhr, Willi."

Oberstein is a junkyard dog, and the toughness is genuine. It comes with the wrestler's body and the butcher's hands impregnated with ink and the round, thick skull that reduces life to discerning neutral acts from war-like acts and prescribing retribution for the latter. He was probably the neighborhood bully once, but now, at forty-one (the only cell member older than Mika), he is just a printer with a pumpkin face and bad teeth who sees the Guard as his reluctant destiny. He is tired of and a little embarrassed by his reputation as a scrapper, but life shackles one with habits and now dark clouds are gathering again.

"Is that your wife's picture upstairs under the counter, Willi?"

"By God, Lott, you searched the place!"

"Leaving her picture there makes you vulnerable. It makes her vulnerable."

"Vulnerable?" Wyderdoern interjects. "I've got five children. You don't think we know our families are vulnerable? Being a Jew is vulnerable. That's why we're here, isn't it?"

"Any one of you can go home now and be safe for a long time. Your children could be grown before these Nazis even stand a chance of gaining control."

"Then there would be grandchildren," Wyerdoern says with finality.

So Mika comes to the woman. A girl really. Tenty-five. Esther Masterograncesco. "I won't even try to pronounce your last name," he says.

Sometimes she says that Masterograncesco is the name of the family who adopted her, but her blood father was Spanish. She is dark and could pass for any number of nationalities. Vivid eyes, a cherubic face grown long and beautiful, black hair, white teeth, gapped but somehow attractive. No make-up. A buffed skin, like a piece of sanded balsa. Her shoulders are broad and loose, breasts full and pendulous. Her feet, Mika imagines, are narrow and knuckled-looking. Women's feet are a fetish to him. Don't argue politics or philosophy with her, they say. Don't even mention Kant or Schelling. Her pamphlets are masterpieces of defamation but comprehensible only to scholars. Still, she is reported to be more than adequate at gathering and interpreting information.

"I'm a clerk at Reinhold's emporium and I live on Barerstrasse in Schwabing," she volunteers.

"The artist's quarter? Dietrich Eckardt lives somewhere in Schwabing. Do you ever see him?"

"Only at rallies."

"But you'd recognize him?"

"Yes."

"If you could find out exactly where he lives, it might be useful."

"I'll do that, Herr Lott."

He asks for their addresses, one by one, committing them to memory, and sauntering back a few steps from the direction he came concludes:

"Three things. First, go about your daily business until I reach you. Second, from now on avoid all contact with members of other cells whom you may know. Third...since you have never seen me before and asked for no proof of my identity, how do you know I'm not a member of Thule come to learn all about you, your activities and your addresses?"

Retrieving his light coat from behind the mountain of newsprint, he has the distinct impression that they really do consider him the enemy.

Munich, old and intellectual, has learned to converse with Mika, middle-aged and a good listener. It was quite different before the war. He came to find Hitler, of course, and the Munich he saw then was fervent with radicals. Then the war broke out and Hitler joined the "Lizt" regiment and the radicals seemed distracted, or fulfilled, or preoccupied temporarily.

Ironically, it was a serene period for Mika; he had time to discover Munich's ghosts, architecture, culture. He wasn't the slightest bit concerned over the outcome of the fighting. The war was a welcome storm that interrupted a more sinister flow of events. Because sooner or later the storm would abate and the radicals would sort out the meaning of it in such a way as to advance their cause. Then it wouldn't matter if the stage was a German occupied world, or a world occupied Germany.

When the verdict came in he was waiting, having dug his own personal trenches deeper into Munich. And now when he walks the streets his eyes travel to the Rathaus tower, his nose declares which neighborhood he is in, and he hears Munich's voices—rustling crêpe left over from Oktoberfest, the dull peals of Trinity Church, the ponderous rhythm of Bavarian brass, the long floating calls on the Isar.

Eons hence archaeologists will excavate a dig known as Munich, and there will be the brass and the bell and the bit of crêpe. The river, too—indestructible. But what about the vulgar little armies? The Temple Guard is already dying. Munich seems about to be torn apart by its political riots. Since January the French and the Belgians have occupied the Ruhr basin in order to collect defaulted war reparations out of German resources. The resulting worker strikes and inflation are tearing Munich apart.

Teachers are paid twice a day, their spouses waiting at the schoolhouse door to take the money and spend it before the value evaporates. A woman pushing a wheelbarrow full of cash to the store can save a million marks or so on the price of a chicken if she runs to beat inflation. Yesterday someone stole Mika's knapsack full of money, dumping the marks on the sidewalk and keeping the knapsack. In his pocket now are a handful of *notgeld*—privately printed vegetable marks, sausage marks. In his belly is turnip coffee, stale pastry, synthetic honey. It is nasty, this inflation. But the vulgar little armies thrive on it. The Thule has the whole top floor of the Four Seasons Hotel as headquarters. Hitler struts around with a dog whip made of hippopotamus hide. The little pervert's star is rising. But the Temple Guard is dying amid the breakdown of order.

Meanwhile, assassination and incendiary blame are escalating, as if only madness can end madness. Kurt Eisner, Prime Minister of Bavaria, was shot down in the street. The Thule's biweekly, *Völkischer Beobachter*, runs articles about how the unrest is a masque for the Jewish revolution supposedly in progress. And *Sturm Abteilungen* (storm troopers) march in the street singing Eckardt's composition, *"Sturm! Sturm! Sturm!"*

They can all count. Munich's fifteen cells of the Temple Guard are now six. That is why Mika told the "Buttons" to eliminate contact with the other groups. No need to lower morale even further.

Yes, the bell and the brass and the bit of crêpe may outlive them all, but the troubling thing is that the other little vulgar army will outlast their own.

2

Hermann Wyerdoern registers Mika's arrival casually over the heads of a middle-aged couple sauntering out of his office.

"Mortgages," he says, closing the door. "They pay them off with sums that won't buy a slice of bread today. I represent the failing half of the bank."

"There's a successful half? Your tellers are weighing money on a scale instead of counting it."

Wyerdoern ushers Mika to a red leather chair in front of a monstrous desk with a family photograph under one corner of the glass. The wife is pretty; the oldest child perhaps eleven. Everything else on the desk—stacked In and Out trays, an empty ashtray, ledgers upright in descending order of height, pen parallel to pad—speaks to formality and utility. Wyerdoern settles into a swivel chair and presses his fingertips together.

"What do you have for me, Mika?"

"Manfred Haupte."

The name rebounds smoothly off the banker.

"When a bailiff seizes property and sells it, what does he do with the money? Does he keep his own separate accounts?"

"He could. This Manfred Haupte is a bailiff?"

"And a member of inner Thule and a gambler."

Wyerdoern taps his teeth thoughtfully. "You're saying he delivers writs of execution, sells the property, then pockets the money to pay off gambling debts?"

"Is it possible?"

"I suppose. He'd have to juggle the accounts, of course, paying off the most pressing ones. I can inquire at local banks. But"—the finger circling Wyerdoern's lips freezes in the air—"there's one thing, Mika. With this inflation, paying back yesterday's losses with today's money is a bargain. If the money is being collected, the accounts may reconcile."

Mika rises. "Here's a phone number. Call me when you know."

Wyerdoern takes the scrap of paper. "Is this where you work?"

"Yes. Sometimes I help a watchmaker. If I'm not there, you can leave a message for me to call back."

"Ah, the man who hasn't used a watch in fifteen years is an expert."

"Take care of that family of yours, Hermann."

Out on the street, Mika slides his watch free of an inside pocket—the watch that hasn't been wound in fifteen years—and with his thumb caresses the well-worn inscription, *Love Forever Katya*. It stopped the day of her funeral, and it seemed, somehow, a blasphemy to turn the stem again, to restart its pulse when the most precious heart in his life had stopped. As he has half a hundred times since then, he almost winds it. Almost.

Wiesel is next.

Mika waits for an hour in the street outside the veteran's apartment beside a charred Citroen. The car has been torched simply for being French.

At the end of the hour, he decides to go eat. Wiesel is a young, unmarried postal clerk, why should he come straight home from work? But unable to find a dinner he can afford, Mika returns twenty minutes later with an empty stomach. A neighbor is playing the latest American rage on a gramophone—*Ausgerechnet Bananen* ("Yes! We Have No Bananas"). Another half hour and Wiesel comes limping onto the scene.

"Hello, Lott," he says without warmth.

"Hello, Aaron.

"Can we go inside?"

"We're standing in the damned street in the damned night and the damned Nazis are home listening to their radios."

"There's something I need to discuss with you."

The young veteran's smile hooks like the horizontal bar of a swastika. Mika follows him through the street entrance. Floor by floor they ascend, a ziggurat of licorice banded steps and insubstantial cooking smells.

"Penthouse," Wiesel explains at the top as they pass into a single room with the barest amenities. "I'd offer you something to eat, but you might accept. Some wine?"

"Some."

Wiesel pours a niggardly amount while Mika takes in his meager collection of pen and ink wild animal drawings.

"I drew them before the war," Wiesel explains, as if creativity is no longer possible. "What do you want, Lott?"

"I want you to help me kidnap a member of Thule."

"You're insane."

"Possibly."

"It must be pretty damned important."

"Possibly."

"You don't know?"

"I'm fishing."

"You're nuts, Lott. Stark and raving. I saw it the other night. When I said that about Hitler going blind your face fell a league. You've got some secret mission, or a personal obsession."

Mika swirls his wine clockwise. "You have a mind like a steel trap, Wiesel. But you catch mice in it. I need you to catch lions." The wine stays in Mika's throat and he coughs.

"Why?"

"Is telling you why a condition of your doing it?"

"Doing it for whom?"

"I'm not interested in your warps, Wiesel, so I'm not offering you mine. Suffice it to say there are valid reasons."

"Give me one."

"It's difficult to explain. But there really seems to be something to all this pan-Germanic mysticism. There are coincidences, predictions…parts of legends or traditions, a whole sub-history of mankind that seems to be synchronized—"

"Occultism—dear God, you believe it."

"They believe it, Wiesel! That's the point. It doesn't matter what I believe, they believe in it. Chaos and disorder. Something more than mass hysteria." He brings his handkerchief to his mouth to stay another cough.

"Just for the record, Lott, you do believe in it. That's clear. Admit it."

Mika senses that he will get no cooperation if he lies. "I've seen it all my life. First in Russia, then more clearly in Vienna and now Munich."

Wiesel toys with his glass and oddly enough in his moment of triumph does not look into Mika's face.

"There's a man I think I can coerce for information—a bailiff—if I can get hold of him," Mika imparts rapidly. "He's an active member of Thule. Not the propaganda section for dolts, the satanic part."

"Like I said, Lott, a personal obsession."

"The world isn't flat anymore, Wiesel. Have we ever accepted anything without having the truth rammed down our throats?"

Wiesel wipes his lips once with the back of each hand. "So how are you going to take this bailiff and what will you do to him?"

"I was hoping you had the method. I don't have a car, but if we blindfold him, I have a key to a watchmaker's shop. As for making him talk, I've watched him and I think I know a way short of torture."

Wiesel shakes his head slowly but nevertheless begins an outline of how it might be done.

"The leopards are very good," Mika, whose eyes have been touring the drawings, interrupts presently. "Are they from the zoo here in Munich?"

"Do you want to hear this or not?"

And to Wiesel's astonishment Mika says: "Oh, I trust you, Wiesel. Just tell me what to do, I trust you."

Manfred Haupte. By day a dark brown suit and caramel striped tie; by night a pair of silk pajamas and red robe. The tie occasionally changes. The pajamas are augmented by brown slippers when he is up, a knit sleeping cap when he is down. Whatever is being washed or mended, there are duplicates in his closet or bureau. Beneath his weak expressions, blue eyes and gray hair he disdains the common man and dreams of an aristocracy composed of creatures like himself. He is self-serving, capable of any violence, an expert fencer, a collector of first editions, a passionate gambler. At baptism the minister misunderstood his name and therefore his sex, offering a prayer for "guidance to womanhood," which may somehow explain his homosexuality.

The low, urgent knock comes as he is unsashing his robe for bed. He is instantly alarmed. Since the sacking of Party headquarters by the Reds, he has kept a chain on the door of his apartment. Winding the sash like a garrote, he passes through his rooms.

"Who is it?"

"Your neighbor from upstairs, Herr Haupte. I smell smoke."

Why should anyone upstairs know him? He only knows the supervisor. But there *is* something acrid in the air.

The chain stiffens as he cracks the door. Like himself, the man standing there is wearing a robe.

"Sorry to alarm you, Herr Haupte, but there is definitely smoke. Do you smell it in your room, or is it just here in the hall?"

Room? Haupte has three rooms. Shouldn't the apartments upstairs know that? He doesn't recognize the man with the sweeping hair and watery eyes. But there *is* smoke! Is that why the man's eyes look watery? Some bastard below has set his sofa to smoldering with careless smoking and any moment flames will erupt.

Haupte untethers the door and immediately there is a pistol in his face, held by a second man, grinning, who sidles forth to back him into his apartment. The gun wielder drops an embered, damp rag to the floor and grinds it out with his toe. The first man closes the door and secures it before removing his robe to reveal street clothes.

"You're making a mistake," Haupte protests. "I'm not wealthy."

"Who is? Are you alone?"

"Yes."

Mika crosses to glance into the other two rooms, nods.

"Then we do it here," Wiesel says.

"Your pistol is military issue," notes Haupte. "I have friends in the army—"

"Stop your whimpering. It probably won't be necessary to kill you. As much as you like to gamble, I don't think you want to bet your life."

Haupte's pasty face reveals nothing at this cue, but his fine wire glasses seem somehow more opaque. "I don't owe anyone," he says slowly.

"Only the good citizens of Munich. We have the records of your court accounts—shifts, shortages, dates."

"The court records are a shambles, have been since the war and, even if your wild imaginings were true, my accounts are, I believe, pfennig perfect."

"The magistrates of Munich will be glad to know that owing to inflation you've made up the differences."

"*You* smear *me*?" Haupte trembles angrily. "A couple of Jews—oh, yes, I recognize you now! You want to make a National Socialist martyr of me. How desperate your little underground is getting. But by all means, be my guest! The Party can stand it."

"Not just the Party, Haupte. Of course, it will reflect badly enough on them. Can you hear the catcalls when Hitler starts ranting about the international financial manipulations of the Jews? However, we were thinking more of what you'll be doing to the Thule. And vice-versa."

Haupte's face jars open like a vampire caught in the first rays of dawn.

"The Thule Gesellschaft," Mika pursues. "Not that corp of weekend magicians, but the real below-ground bunch. The reincarnations. Your crowd. You look ill, Haupte."

Wiesel's gaze is glued to the bailiff in amazement. Haupte is trembling, his brow and upper lip bead sweat. Green recruits in the trenches looked that way, and Mika's words have burst over the bailiff's head exactly like shells.

"What do you want?" Haupte whispers huskily.

"Everything you know about the Thule. Everything you know about Hitler." Mika senses calculation as he passes between Haupte and the gun. Already the man they grasp by the soul is coiling into another more devious one. "Be advised, half of what I ask, I already know the answers to. A bluff ends the game for you."

"If I tell you, my bank and court records still exist. I have no assurances."

"Just hope."

"Well, since I can't imagine what good anything I can tell you will do, I have nothing to lose. Quit pointing that pistol at me and get on with your outrage. I'm already blackmailed."

"Tell us about the Spear of Longinus."

Haupte blanches. "Hitler doesn't intend to steal it, like Kaiser Wilhelm, if that's what you're worried about. He says it's of no consequence for the present, that it will come to us."

"Why is it so important to him?"

"For the same reason it was important to the Kaiser."

"When I ask a direct question, I want a direct answer."

"Clearly you're amateurs. You don't know what to ask."

Wiesel cocks the pistol.

Haupte's lashes flutter. "The Kaiser was inflamed by Chamberlain's stories of Fatherland Spear-holders. So a scheme was cooked up to request the loan of German holy relics from Austria, which would naturally include the Spear, to coincide with a State visit by Emperor Franz Josef. After that the Spear would be kept. But General von Moltke, good Christian that he was, betrayed it."

"How?"

"He wrote a secret letter."

"To Franz Josef?"

"Yes. Warning him that if the Kaiser got the Spear it would incite him to war. So, the loan was denied. But war wasn't hard to provoke."

Mika nods. "Well, you had your chaos and disorder and what did it get you? A defeated Germany—"

"Because of Jews and von Moltke."

Haupte is side-tracking him, but Mika really does want to know the history, and besides, he sees that Wiesel is getting an education about the Thule crowd. "Why von Moltke?"

Haupte smiles faintly. "On the eve of the war von Moltke collapsed in OHL. Von Moltke had personally revised the Schlieffen plan and was ordering troops to the Eastern and Western fronts when he fell onto his desk. They thought it was a heart attack. But he revived in ten or twelve minutes and later wrote an account of a trance he had experienced in which he found himself linked between the present and the Dark Ages in the person of Pope Nicholas I. He recognized others, too, both at Supreme Command and in their ninth century incarnations. Do stop me when it gets too unbelievable for you, Herr Jews," he adds merrily, reading their faces.

Wiesel rolls his eyes. "Go on," orders Mika.

"Well, it's all there in black and white. Scores of links, the whole panorama of history from the disintegration of spirit into the phenomenal world to the struggle for mastery. And von Moltke could have tossed his lot with us then—with the German race—but the fool tried to preserve the world rabble by ending the war quickly. Only he failed to consider fate. Everything went wrong. General von Kluck disobeyed orders and ended up attacking on the wrong side of Paris. It seemed like such a sure thing, but there weren't enough troops deployed to fill the gaps, and the British and French couldn't be surrounded. The colonel sent to assess the situation became ill and in near delirium ordered a disastrous regrouping. So, the war became what we wanted, but only for four more years."

"And now your opportunity is over."

Haupte's laugh is disturbingly hearty and, in it, Mika hears the depth of his own despair. Wiesel, too, is moved to bring the pistol back on line.

"Von Moltke knew it wasn't over," Haupte says. "He named Hitler as future Führer of a Third Reich and the next person who will claim the Spear!"

"Von Moltke died in 1916," Wiesel interrupts. "Nobody had even heard of Hitler then."

"That's right," Haupte grins triumphantly.

"Hitler was just a messenger in the Lizt Regiment," Wiesel elaborates. "You're a liar."

"You can read von Moltke's predictions yourself! They were written down by his wife in séances. Several hundred pages. Remarkable stuff. Already coming true."

"What horseshit!" Wiesel soars, looking hard at Mika. "You don't believe this?"

Mika paces deep in thought. He wants no more evidence of predestiny for Hitler, no more intervention of occult forces. The little bastard is a malevolent miracle. *Meldegangers* (messengers) have short lives in war—but not Hitler, who somehow survived. Arrogant down-and-outers from Vienna who have read Lanz von Liebenfels' anti-Semitic pamphlets are not destined to lead. Those who call *The Foundation of the Nineteenth Century* the pan-Germanic Bible can't possibly be understood by the masses. The man who invokes divine guidance for his satanic dream will surely be struck down by lightning. Hitler is an aberrant intellect, a sexual deviate, a black Don Quixote whose excessive readings trigger manic outbursts from some hidden wellspring of words. Such men sooner or later imagine themselves God; and if the circumstances are right, if there is enough disorder, if coincidences and idle prophecies merge—

"What about the Holy Grail?" he demands of Haupte.

Haupte sucks a tooth. "The cup that held Christ's blood at the Last Supper, if you believe it exists."

There is more to the Thule's interest in the Grail than a satanic inversion of Christian principles as a way to power, Mika knows, but Haupte is right—he doesn't even know what questions to ask.

"Does Hitler know Houston Stewart Chamberlain?"

"Alfred Rosenberg introduced them at Wagner's house in Bayreuth just this fall, but Chamberlain is paralyzed and hard to understand—"

"Hitler was at the house of Richard Wagner?"

"Villa Wahnfried. Yes. Cosima, his widow, invited him herself. Chamberlain has sent him a letter since then, telling him he has mighty things to do for Germany."

"Why?"

Haupte grins. "Chamberlain synthesized Wagner and Nietzsche into the concept of the Superman; he went to Vienna and saw both the Spirit and anti-Spirit; he wrote under the guidance of demons—"

"Yes, yes, I've read reports of Abwehr agents who saw him fleeing devils," Mika scoffs. "Chamberlain is a regular German Rasputin. But why did he pick Hitler?"

"You'll have to ask *him*."

For a long moment Mika scrutinizes the bailiff. "You said Rosenberg introduced them."

Haupte nods once.

"How do Hitler and Rosenberg fit together?"

"Rosenberg brought him the *Protocols of the Elders of Zion* in 1918. Through Eckardt."

The *Protocols*. The ones that purport to be notes of a plan for world domination formulated at the World Congress of Jewry in Basel, 1897. It created a stir after the war. Even the British newspapers picked it up.

"And where did Rosenberg get them?"

"He said a stranger delivered them."

"Which no one believes. Where did he actually get them?"

Haupte smiles benignly. The damage is done. What difference

if a couple of Jews know the truth? "The Russian Ochrana had them drummed up by Nilus, a student of the Russian philosopher Solovyov."

"All right, Haupte. Tell us something that will transpire this week and convince us of your candor."

"I'm a member of Thule. Local politics bore me."

Probably true. He isn't the beer hall type.

"Hitler then," Mika says. "What is he up to?"

"Hitler?" Suddenly Haupte throws his arms wide: "Hitler is going to conquer the world!"

Wiesel nearly pulls the trigger. "Sweet Jesus, don't do that again!"

"I told you I had nothing for you," Haupte chortles. "You see, I can be perfectly honest and it won't do you any good, because Hitler can't be stopped."

It is the same thing Mika heard from Hans Lodz, the peasant herbalist in Wachau, ten years ago—*Hitler can't be stopped*. There was a time when he could have killed the foaming little demagogue and didn't. And now the web of intervening figures like Haupte makes it impossible to get near him.

"You don't have to believe these things," he tries to reason with Wiesel later in the streets, "they believe them. And if they come to power, it's going to be hell on earth."

3

Trivia question: What is the funniest night-time entertainment to play Munich in 1923?

Answer: The Beer-Hall Putsch.

But on November 8th, Esther Masterograncesco has a front row seat to Munich's pocket rebellion and it is anything but funny. Coming out of Reinhold's emporium ten minutes after her shift, she immediately notices the unusual number of workers in the street. And then through the swiftly pelting snow she picks out the field-gray windbreakers, the ski caps, the swastika brassards, and she knows. SA. Storm troopers are moving with purpose, though not all in the same direction.

Since Graafe's death she has been nervous as a cat, but this has to mean something. Small groups of them moving up and down the streets. They are canvassing. Mika should hear about this. Reinhold's has a telephone. She ducks back inside.

"Forget something?" The manager is dewy-eyed, unctuous.

"Excuse me, Herr Kessler, but would it be possible for me to use the telephone?"

He has been trying to seduce her for months and, while she calls the number Mika made her memorize, he stands in the doorway, whistling dryly. She asks the operator to keep ringing, but there is no answer.

Through the window she sees a truck filled with fully geared Stossrup Hitler (shock troops) rumble past. Then there is a sound that might be a shot. Too much. She has to find out what is going on.

"Thank you, Herr Kessler," she says, hanging up the earpiece, "thank you very much."

"Your party wasn't available? Can I give you a ride? Or perhaps you would like something to eat. I'm just on my way to dinner."

"No, I have to go. Thank you."

He forces her to brush past him at the door, but she pirouettes successfully and he receives only her elbow as she turns up the collar of her short coat before plunging against the wind.

The snow is flowing faster now. She runs in the street, head down to follow the fresh tire tracks left by the truck. But at the first corner she nearly collides with a gray sortie group of SA. Predator delight lights up their faces. One of them takes her by the chin.

"Don't I know you, Fraülein? Barerstrasse, isn't it? The apartments?"

"No...I'm sorry—"

"Seize the bitch!" another calls as they surround her.

And just like that she is jostled into step. The smell of men and hate and oil from the several guns sets her heart beating wildly. How foolish she has been! These little sorties out for blood. Tomorrow they will go back to their jobs selling shoes and sweeping streets, but tonight, all puffed up in their uniforms, they are capable of anything. This is the madness that murdered Graafe. If she falls down amid their striding legs, they may kick her to death on the spot.

The one who knows her has a phone book, which he examines under a streetlight. "This one...*Borenstein*," he reads. "You can't get more Jewish than that. Two blocks from here." In short order Borenstein, fat and fifty, pads coatless alongside. The outrage is repeated until they are a party of fourteen in full stride. Then one of the SA suggests they take "their Jews" to the Bürgerbräu, and off they go toward the main thoroughfare. But they travel less than a block when a man darts out behind them and, standing feet braced apart, shouts: "Run, comrades, the coup has failed! Regular army are coming up Barerstrasse!"

The storm troopers glance in all directions.

"It's a lie," one of them asserts. "We'd hear trucks."

But they are on hairtrigger now, edging apart.

"Here...here!" Esther shouts, waving gleefully in the direction the army is supposed to come from. And as the SA recoils and swivels, she darts toward her lone would-be rescuer—no mistaking Mika's flaring hair.

The other Jews are as confused as the SA. Borenstein drops to his knees and prays, a woman screams until she is slapped. An SA shouts: "He's a Jew! Get them!"

Esther reaches a sidewalk stairwell before pounding steps overtake her and she is yanked off her feet. And Mika...ah, poor plodding Mika, one of the SA was the best runner in his gymnasium two years earlier.

They are dragged back more or less together, gasping, wheezing, a single look postponing questions between them. One of Mika's bushy brows is dampening darkly with blood. Knotted into the group again, they continue the march, a black engine of humanity with too many armatures and ragged steam flowing out of them.

The snow has flurried away by the time they reach the Bürgerbräu. Munich's largest beer hall—largest hall after the Krone Circus—is now jammed with 3,000 people. Shock troops abound. The local "blue" police on duty for a speech by Commissioner General von Kahr have been expelled en masse. At the open front door of the main hall a machine gun has been set up, pointing in. Steel helmets ring the walls. A man named Hermann Göring has just fired a shot into the ceiling and is trying to make his own speech to the chattering mob.

"Where's Hitler?" one of the SA who have taken Mika and Esther prisoner demands at the entrance.

"Political conference," smirks the guard. "He took Kahr, Seisser and Lossow into another room to convince them they better go along with his coup against Berlin. We sent Scheubner-Richter's car to bring General Ludendorff from his villa." Ludendorff was Quartermaster General in the war and Hitler hopes to trot him out against the government that signed the sell-out Treaty of Versailles.

The SA gestures flimsily to the prisoners. "What do we do with our Jews?"

"Take them around back. We're using the cellars below the dining halls."

And so now the forlorn prisoners are herded around the gardens in view of the Isar River and down a flight of narrow stairs.

The cellar is rank with human fear. But it has a delirious quality, almost laughable, because what is happening is absurd. The SA are like children who have seized power and don't quite know what to do with it. They are surprised at how easy it is. And the prisoners see this comic despotism, and yet, they are prisoners. Who is to say what tyrannical children might do? "Our Jews," they keep calling them. As if they are stray cats.

If they were flies, they might have their wings pulled off. There is feral glee in this. The tyrannical children are still exploring the possibilities. Give them enough time and they will build camps with crematoria and showers with no drains. Already, the sense of that. Satan has been loosed. All rules are suspended.

Each time the door opens, the prisoners below catch their breaths. And when it closes, there are one or two more frightened beings in their midst. Nearly forty now, each bearing a tale of the night's outrage.

"It's that damned Rudolf Hess," mutters a Munich official who is not Jewish at all but was rounded up with a handful of administrators. "We don't even belong here. He's threatening to hang two government ministers. Took them to the mountains with a rope!"

"Shock troops were tearing the *Post* apart when we went by."

"What are they going to do to us?"

"Don't know, but they abused old Erhard Auer's wife. That's his son-in-law over there."

The babble choruses uneasily.

"How's your eye, Mika?" Esther murmurs, dropping down beside a wine rack.

Mika touches his brow and discovers blood. "Listen to them," he says. "The Jewish *Canterbury Tails*."

A metal rack of wine bottles has picked up the resonance from the great hall above and, even without words, it is frighteningly coherent. Righteous verbal volleys uncoil like dragons through the wine. Thunderous applause seems to fizz. The cadence and oscillation resolve into Germany's unambiguous National Anthem: *"Deutschland, Deutschland über alles..."*

Halfway through it an SA appears on the cellar steps to announce that Ludendorff, Kahr, Seisser and Lossow have endorsed the Putsch. A small but rousing shout goes up from the guards, contrasted sharply by the dead silence of the captives, as if a single winner has just been announced in a lottery.

"Is this really happening?" Esther whispers in a white voice.

"It won't spread to Berlin," Mika says.

But inside he is quaking. The circumstances, the extraordinary circumstances he tried to define with Katya so many years ago have come to pass. How did they imagine it would be let loose? Doomsday machines? But instead it is just this probing, schoolyard bullying arising out of post-war humiliation and economic despair spreading to the masses in the street. It is impossible to grasp on a personal level. Aren't these their neighbors and fellow citizens of the same great city?

The anthem is suddenly empowered by a brass band in the distance. The first regular unit of Reichswehr to back the National Socialists is marching before the Bürgerbräu a thousand strong. Victory is in the air!

Brief and dismal reports accompany each influx of prisoners as they settle into the cellar, cowled with melting snow: "The storm troopers are pouring in from everywhere—Garmisch, Weilheim, Tölz, Ingoldstadt, Landshut…""Ernst Röehm—that dirty queer—took the Military District Headquarters an hour ago!"…"I saw shock troops armed with potato-masher grenades, and the Oberlanders" (Bavarian rustics who are a part of Hitler's Fighting Union, the Kampfbund) "have their erasers and matches" (rubber clubs and pistols).

The facts that come out later will paint a much different picture. Kahr, Seisser and Lossow have renounced the pact made with Hitler at gun-point. To cover this defection, Hitler spreads the rumor that the three are being held prisoner by the Reichswehr. Quartermaster General Ludendorff is disillusioned at the renouncing of the Bürgerbräu pact, because it means that an officer of the German Army has broken his word to him.

To bolster confidence, Hitler orders that the SA be paid, and the money, confiscated from a nearby publishing plant belonging to Jewish brothers, is doled out at the rate of two trillion marks a man.

But the crisis in leadership deepens. Contradictory wall posters go up by the half hour—sometimes side by side—announcing and denouncing solidarity. A pathetically funny story circulates about Kahr being bribed by a Jew with seven Persian rugs! A Landshut battalion of SA actually repair a disabled car on the road without realizing that it contains the deposed Ministry of Munich on its way to Regensburg to set up a legitimate government.

And even the Temple Guard delivers a comic stroke to the fiasco. A month earlier they stumbled on a Nazi weapons catch in St. Anna's church. Now the model 98 carbines are put in service by the SA—without firing pins.

And then comes word that the Putsch will be attempted again. A column of two thousand led by Ludendorff, Hitler and eighty shock troops will march through Munich. The captives are to be contained within the column and killed if the Kampfbund suffers a single casualty.

Below ground, frightened babbling breaks out, tightening the acoustics of the cellar. More guards clatter down the steps, swinging machine pistols.

"On your feet, stinking Jews!"

Esther flashes Mika a child's look.

"Stay close," he warns.

Prodded by weapons and kicks, they stumble into line and up through a gauntlet of guns.

The snow has been trampled underfoot and the street is black and glossy. Truncheons and pistols are everywhere. Two red swastika banners nod in opposite directions, while the tri-color black-red-white of Imperial Germany hunkers down in between like an embarrassed fugitive. General Ludendorff is clearly visible, a scowling giant rising above the mob. A truck mounted with a heavy machine gun keeps revving its engine as if to clear a path, but no one moves. The prisoners, who are still popping like hiccoughs from the cellar, begin to jam up.

Then a car edges toward Ludendorff, like a scow making for harbor. Alfred Rosenberg disembarks in order to report directly to Hitler, who stands stone-faced and ashen in a trenchcoat next to the General.

Hitler's hands go up for quiet.

In strident but hoarse tones he announces that there has been a change and the prisoners are to remain behind. The last thing Mika hears before descending the stairs again at the point of a bayonet is a second order for the column to unload its weapons.

The cellar is as clutching and hermetic as a glove now. They are aware that a confrontation is taking place above, that their fate hangs in the balance. Presently a great rumbling reaches them, and they know the column is launched.

As before, reports filter back: the column has reached the Ludwig Bridge…the column has passed through the Isar Gate and onto the Tal…the Marienplatz

…and finally *the Town Hall!*

A new detachment of prisoners arrives just after the Ludwig Bridge report, this one ominous, because they are Green Police—Seisser's State force. The column has taken them without a shot at the bridgehead. And then, for some unknown reason, the column is marching again. Reports say they are approaching the Hall of Field Marshalls.

Reports say there is a platoon of Green Police at the Felderrnhalle.

Reports say there is shooting at the Felderrnhalle.

Hitler (*rejoice, ye pure of heart!*) Is dead! Ludendorff is dead.

Correction. Rumor.

Ludendorff is not dead. Through the brief fire-fight he calmly marched into the enemy's ranks, brushing their weapons aside.

Hitler isn't dead, either. His arm was locked with Scheubner-Richter's, and when the shooting broke out, he hit the pavement so hard he dislocated his shoulder. His bodyguard, Graf, lay over his crumpled form, absorbing six bullets for him.

Update: Hitler has escaped by car, running over a child in the process.

Variation on update: Hitler has escaped by car after braving murderous fire to rescue said child in his arms. Arm.

Less than an hour later, Green Police free the prisoners at the Bürgerbräu and the Beer-Hall Putsch is over, five years to the day after the stab-in-the-back Republic was announced in the Reichstag.

4

Snow.

The all-purpose cleaner. Munich is lathered with it and about to be scrubbed behind the eaves where its Nazis have taken refuge. The trials will do the scrubbing: Hitler, Ludendorff, Röehm, Pohner, Frick, a handful more in the dock.

Hitler was dragged out of a friend's attic in the mountains where he tried to shoot himself but couldn't because of his dislocated shoulder. He was imprisoned at Landsberg Fortress west of Munich and promptly announced that he would starve himself to death. So far—two weeks and counting—he has refused to eat, and the agony of shame makes him look even more ridiculous.

Greater Germany is embarrassed. Munich is its pimple. The world is pointing, laughing. Thousands of presses clack irreverently printing millions of words about the revolution-that-wasn't, which are devoured like ribald gossip with a chuckle over marmalade toast and coffee. A city famous for its beer becomes famous for its brawls.

The Buttons are jubilant and meet six days running. In the ink and machine oil ether of the print shop they convince themselves that the Nazis are irrevocably crushed. Except for Mika. Mika sees it mainly as an emasculating of inner Thule.

But that, at least, was the satanic evil part.

Hitler may indeed have been the chalice of the Antichrist, a budding malevolency, a bit of demonic natural selection that, through its own impetuousness, has fallen on a rock instead of in the virulent mud of Munich. Looking directly at the man, Mika sees what thousands have testified to, that astonishing bursts of contagious energy seem to pass through him, electrifying crowds and leaving him a shredded, sweating rag of a man, empty as a medium. And then there is the un-divine guidance that has preserved him time and again. Even at birth. The fourth child of his parents, he was the first to survive infancy. After that it was the hellish war, near assassination and, at the end, his bodyguard taking bullets meant for him—phenomenal.

But it doesn't matter anymore. The plot to insinuate the Landulf of Capua, to betray the Grail path, to exploit the dual powered Spear of Longinus, to create a substitute for the German messiah, *is done*!

DONE.

A killing frost has nipped the thousand year black rose of the Thule, and as if by divine decree, a second bolt of lightning now scorches the root. Dietrich Eckardt, Hitler's mentor, dies the day after Christmas, his lungs at last burnt out from the long-ago effects of mustard gas.

How white the snows of Munich!

Two arresting details of the death are brought to Mika at the print shop by Aaron Wiesel, who promised to verify the rumor. First, that Eckardt died praying to his Mecca stone. Second, that he told his followers not to mourn him and to look toward Hitler; that Hitler would dance but it would be he, Eckardt, calling the tune; that through Hitler he will change history more than anyone before him!

Disquieting. A little.

Eckardt made it sound like he was dying in labor. But of course the blasphemy is stillborn now. Hitler is all but buried with him.

Mika shades his watery eyes casually at the end of the recitation. "Where did you hear this, Wiesel?"

"From none other than our dear friend Manfred Haupte."

"You took a risk. The whole cell could have been jeopardized."

But the danger seems dead now, and besides that, Mika considered doing the same thing, even though he knew Haupte has had time to think, to plan, and most certainly has decided he must maintain contact with these Jews so that he can pin them down and have them murdered. How else can he be safe?

So Mika lets down his guard, even to the extent of allowing Esther closer to him.

Since their ordeal at the Bürgerbräu she has treated him like a big cuddly panda. "I want you to eat at my apartment at least three times a week," she bullies. "And if you don't come, I'll follow you to your apartment. Oh, and bring your laundry. And the next time you want a hat, let *me* pick it out."

He grumbles but secretly likes the idea. A great many carbines were found smashed against trees in the woods, evidence of storm trooper frustration when they went to bury their weapons following the Putsch collapse. So, what harm can come from a little coziness between a lovely young woman and a middle-aged (insert *lonely*) widower?

Her apartment has a certain planned emptiness. A single, innocuous painting of hyacinths garnishes pale yellow walls, but where are her favorite books, her mementos and bric-a-brac? All drawers, doors and curtains are closed. This is not a matter of neatness, it seems—dust collects behind the radiator, spiders spin unmolested miracles high in opposing corners. Rather it is freedom. Lacking reflections of herself, she can grow, shrink or change without contradiction. At twenty-five she wants no costly commitments.

After all, who is committed to Esther Masterograncesco? She never knew her real parents. And the men in her life are too self-occupied to be her father, though it has never occurred to her to want one. In a sense, the Guard is her guardian, a single commitment she can trust, because it expresses her anger.

The odd friendship with Mika progresses in a series of meals, domestic chores, discussions. The lines between blur. There are compatibilities: art, music boxes, a fondness for certain cheeses and nuts, a mutual intolerance of dripping water. And discords: she detests cards, he hates sports; she is impatient, he sits an hour at a time sucking his pipe and uttering senile clues to his thoughts in the form of solitary words.

"You do everything at a turtle's pace," she scolds. "You walk slowly, talk slowly, laugh slowly. I'll bet you even *cry* slowly!"

And to prove his turtlehood she kicks a soccer ball all around his lumbering feet in the local park.

"I'm older, therefore, I have less time than you," he says one day. "You should be the one with patience."

"Poor old Mika, running down like his watch. You should feel wound up. Now that Hitler is in prison, you're going to have time on your hands."

He tries to amend her metaphor. "One of our enemies chimes may be silenced, but the clock is still ticking."

"You can't fix every tick, Mika."

He puts his hands on her shoulders and attempts to stare down his nose.

"Esther, I know I'm overly cautious. I know I'm scarred and that my life is a caricature of worries, some of which are petty, some of which are beyond doing anything about, but this trial unsettles me. It's not a victory for us. Not yet. This is the wrong time to let up. Let's see what happens. We can't arrest hate, and we can't put anti-Semitism in jail."

She kisses his hand sadly, not knowing yet what she wants their relationship to be or whether he is capable of anything but living out his past.

The trial begins on February 26th under enormous security. Barbed wire and helmeted police are all around the Infantry Officers School chosen for the site. The building is the one from which the thousand Reichswehr cadets marched to join the Putsch. It is, therefore, symbolic of restored order, if not justice.

The crowds outside are also enormous. Inside are some one hundred reporters from the ends of the earth. The rush for remaining seats scarcely dents the mob at the gate each morning. Mika—shunner of crowds—daily elbows and pushes to maintain an early place in the queue. Other Temple Guards are also there from the crack of dawn, and inevitably, one, two, or even three are seated in the courtroom.

But what Mika will remember most when he thinks back to this trial will be the feeling he has the first day as he clings to the cold bars of the gate, his breath warming his knuckles, the crowd pushing at his back like a dynamo of retribution. They have come ostensibly to witness the ritual extermination of all he has opposed since the horrors of his childhood. And yet, even on this first day, he knows it is false. The attraction is not righteousness, not the repudiation of hate and racism, nor even a dim recognition that something evil has been trampled underfoot. The attraction is the contest itself. The hope that there will be a contest.

And there is.

It begins with Hitler speaking. And ends with Hitler speaking. And in between is Hitler speaking.

The press, who come expecting to write a final chapter to the saga of bemedaled Quartermaster General Erich von Ludendorff, become instead the opiated chroniclers of a Chaplinesque firebrand with an Iron Cross First Class pinned to his shirt. The prosecution witnesses—Kahr, Seisser, Lossow—shrivel in triplicate under the scathing indictment of the demagogue. Indeed, when Hitler is done with them, their sin seems less that they strayed from loyalty to Berlin, than that they failed to stand firm with him and National Socialism.

But like Ludendorff, the tainted trio fall quickly out of the limelight while the Fatherland's icons are retrieved one by one from the mud by Hitler and hung from the hooks of his swastika.

It starts Mika's stomach churning like a cement mixer on February 26, and by the end of the trial the cement is set. He has swallowed Hitler's stone. It is fantastic, simply fantastic all the while it is happening. The words stream forth in voluble bursts, raining down on Bavaria, Germany, the world...

That they evoke such righteous conviction out of blasphemy is fantastic to begin with. More fantastic is that the little spellbound judge with the white goatee permits such propaganda. Exceeding fantastic is the irony that the devastating beer-hall revolution turns out to be merely the rent paid for a new platform from which Hitler hurls his voice. What the citizens of Munich have been calling an *Indianerstreich* (Indian strike) is now the holiest of crusades.

The prosecution's summary against Hitler scarcely matters. Hitler's prosecution summary against the State is four hours long and drums up the highest ideals of purity and patriotism, touching on every ill in Germany since the surrender of 1918. The gallery and the nation are awash with tears, and his eighty thousand followers become two million in a fraction of a day.

The sentence is minimal: five years fortress arrest. It is April Fool's day, 1924 and, in Munich, it has stopped snowing.

5

"Goes to prove that if you threaten loud enough, nothing happens to you," the mouse-beast Rudolf Sneltz says, leaning against the walls, glasses glittering, in the basement of Oberstein's print shop. "They're scared to death of the little bastard."

"Shut up," Willi directs.

"'Adolf genuinely loved his mother—I swear it before God and man,'" Wiesel quotes sarcastically. Gustl Kubizek, Hitler's former roommate in Vienna, has said this, and the curious avowal is a catchphrase with them because of its lameness. "Haupte told me Hitler cried when he found one of his canaries dead. I really think we're overstating the threat. Hitler's just an old softie—"

"Stop it," commands Esther.

"What was the name of that Jew who gave him the ragged overcoat when he was down and out?" Wiesel persists. "Come on, Sneltz, you're the expert on fashion, who gave Hitler the rag? You know, that Hungarian Jew—"

"Neumann."

"Neumann! Yes. Now, that's what will save us from extinction. Hitler will remember Neumann and repent."

"Stop it, Wiesel!"

"Dear me, I've offended the lady. She's found a gentler comrade-in-arms and now we're too crude for her."

The reference is to Mika who is sitting in a bentwood chair, smiling for all the world as if he has just heard a polite joke. He is leagues away from the personal and the petty and lost in the plunging despair at what they face. The fire from the small stove flickers over him, cuing him that the silence is expectation.

"There was a man at the trial the last day," he says softly. "Worker type. He called Hitler 'the Drummer.' It stuck in my head. Something historical. I found it in a book this morning. The Drummer of Niklashausen, 1476. He was another non-entity who became a spellbinder of the masses. He had an uncanny way of knowing what they wanted, and he stirred them into a hysteria of revolution against the government."

Willi cracks his knuckles. "So, what are you saying?"

"He thinks this Niklashausen is another incarnation!" Wiesel laughs curtly. "Climbing around Hitler's family tree with the Landulf and Barbarossa!"

He stops mid-inflection to cock his good eye as Mika pops out of the chair as if in response to the sarcasm. Wyerdoern grips his hat, Willi stiffens in the act of wiping a shoe. But Mika has only caught hold of his private train of thought again.

"The Spear," he says, pointing nowhere, "that's where it started—"

And this time when Wiesel smirks, Mika steps grimly into his face.

"Don't laugh, because I haven't said anything funny!"

"You're fogging my glass eye," Wiesel says with restraint.

Mika turns away. "Let me remind you, Hitler has stated flatly that he stood before the Spear of Longinus scores of times for hours on end as he was given a vision of his future and destiny, that he sensed an awesome presence around it, that it was a magical medium between the real world and the powers beyond, and that he saw a Superman—intrepid and cruel—and gave his soul to its will in holy awe. Safe to say, this nobody who now leads two million is serious about the Spear."

"He said a lot of things, Lott. Now he's locked up."

"You want me to admit that I believe what he obviously believes? All right, Wiesel. Let me be the crazy one." The great cocoa cup eyes move from face to face. "I'm more than half convinced, more than half the time. Hitler may actually represent something…supernatural. We're all very scientific here, but my stomach turns whenever I look at the circumstantial evidence. Because it's overwhelming. 'We will create a new race,' he says. And he *thinks* he's a medium. He was born on Braunau-on-the-Inn, a town famous for its mediums—Madame Stokhammes, for example, and the famous Rudi and Willi Schneider; and Willi Schneider's wet nurse was Hitler's wet nurse; and his cousin is a medium, too."

"Germany is full of mystics," Willi says with measured slowness in the long silence that develops. "It really doesn't matter what any of us believes. In desperate times, people rally around desperate ideas. What do you want us to do, Mika?"

"Hitler may be in Landsberg Fortress, but he's damned near a celebrity. I don't see any reason to believe his leadership is in question. He'll continue to run this thing. He's got Rudolf Hess in there with him, of course. But there's no question in my mind that this Karl Haushofer is a key figure on the outside. Thule strongarms made sure there was a seat for him every day at the trial, and a police clerk told me Haushofer accompanied Hess back from Austria when he turned himself in."

"Hess was Haushofer's pupil in geopolitics at the University of Munich," says Wyerdoern. "Won an essay contest under him. Some big prize put up by a rich German in Brazil."

"When?"

"About four years ago. The subject was what the German messiah should be like."

"Like Hitler, of course. What else do we know about Haushofer?"

Wiesel rubs his palms. "I knew about him as a general before he became a professor. He was a nut then. I don't know anything about that theory of his they call geopolitics, but everyone in my outfit knew he was a nut."

"What kind of a nut?"

"A nut's a nut."

"You don't know why?"

Wiesel looks exasperated. "Mystical shit, that's all."

"For instance?"

"They said he could predict attacks, storms, even where shells would fall, that kind of shit."

"Could he?"

"He had a reputation. He must have got lucky a couple of times."

"Anything else?"

The veteran glowers, irritated that the whole subject of occultism can't be dismissed. "He was an asshole that went to the Far East every year or two. Even spoke Japanese. Always talking about how Germans and Japs would rule the world. He was supposed to have joined one of those Buddhist societies and taken a suicide vow. A real nut, a capital *A* asshole."

Mika cups his hands over one knee: "The Thule believes in an Indo-Germanic race that came from a great island that sank in the pre-history of the world. The survivors were supposed to have migrated east and north. No doubt Haushofer believes in reunification of the original human strain. The eastern branch is supposed to have split into two paths. Agarthi and Schamballah of Tibet."

"Be on the look-out for scowling Tibetans," warns Wiesel.

"We're going to keep track of Haushofer," Mika asserts.

The April sky is running with gray wisps that promise icy rain. Mika scoots along, silver ram's horns adding streamlined glints to his passage, and suddenly Esther is there at his shoulder.

"Such a turtle…faster than a Lancia Lambda," she says. "I want to see a rematch between you and that SA rabbit that ran you down the night of the Putsch."

"Who knows, maybe you'll get the chance."

"Will you rescue me again?"

"I didn't rescue you."

"You had good intentions. Why are we galloping?"

"It's everyone for themselves in the Temple Guard, Esther."

She measures the shock in four silent strides. "All right, what's the matter?"

He makes a brief, tight gesture, like an umbrella opening part way and sticking. "We've been careless. Everyone uses their real name, everyone knows where everyone else lives…"

"Everyone knows about us. You don't want emotions in the cell, is that it? Nothing to jeopardize your leadership."

"I'm not worried about my leadership."

"Listen, I understand if you're worried about us. Really I do."

"It has nothing to do with us, Esther."

"What then?"

The hurt settles somehow in the puffiness of her lips. A half frozen raindrop stings his cheek, then another. He doesn't remember leaving her or hearing his name called. He feels and sees and listens to the rain as he soars down earthly streets in a city called Munich, and even though the drops turn to ice now, he doesn't blink.

6

Sneltz vs Hitler
David vs Goliath

There is a chill on the hillside below Landsberg prison, but Sneltz has given up his alter ego trenchcoat for a thin leather vest and hunting jacket common to the countryside.

Hitler is no doubt warm and comfortable inside the Fortress where he has a cell in the Festung block for political prisoners. Cell seven. Spurious ironies occupy Sneltz's mind for the long hours of his watches—cell six in the Temple Guard observing cell seven at Landsberg, for instance, as if they are next-door, which in a way that appeals to Sneltz's number-oriented mind they are. They have moved Count Arco-Valley out of that cell to accommodate Hitler. Arco-Valley is the one who pulled the trigger on Kurt Eisner, launching a blood bath of assassinations. Hitler owes him.

Mika reluctantly agreed to let Sneltz handle the observation post, since the others kept at it for most of a week and grew unbearably bored. The idea is to keep track of Hitler's stream of visitors. A spot watch, Mika calls it. But Wiesel calls it a waste, and it is difficult for Willi, Wyerdoern or Esther to take time off from their jobs to come some fifty kilometers from Munich and count noses in passing cars. So…Sneltz.

Sneltz loves it. It is what he needs to prove himself. Because they all treat him dismissively. No matter that he is practically a mathematical genius. None of them even noticed the cell seven irony. That is what he is good at. Numbers, quantifying, figuring out the odds. He will take this drone task and come up with something, and they will all see that they underestimated him.

A valley sweeps up timbered precipices on either side of his watchpost, and the river Lech giggles past him like some mad poltergeist. The Fortress itself is gray-white and massive behind its studded iron gate. There are two wings. Besides the Festung block for political prisoners, there is the Gefangenenanstalt for common criminals. Cell seven is the large one on the second floor with the view. Mika took a single look and said he was quite certain Hitler would enjoy staring out at the spot where Otto the Great moved armies under the Spear of Longinus a millennium ago, crushing magyars.

Sneltz yawns and stretches his stiff muscles in the chill air. It is nearly five p.m. and nothing has come down the lonely, twisting road from Munich since a group of prisoners before noon. The sun is sluffing off and a wind is picking up. Maybe he should walk back to Landsberg for supper.

Mika is coming to the inn tomorrow morning to find out what he has learned and to take him back to Munich if he wants. He doesn't, of course, but what can he report except that Hitler's lights are permitted to stay on until midnight when everyone else's go off at ten? Sneltz remained on watch one night—right outside the walls—to see. And he heard singing from that direction, one of their Putsch songs. There is singing in the morning, too—storm trooper stuff when the men come out to exercise. The chorus no doubt includes Hess and Dr. Weber and Emil Maurice, Hitler's chauffeur, and Colonel Kriebel of the Bund Oberland, each of whom he has noted in the window. He cannot see them when they go into the court or gardens at eight. A delivery boy from Landsberg told him that the prisoners have gymnastics equipment there and sometimes box or wrestle.

As for visitors, he has seen Haushofer once in a heavy touring car, and Ilse Pröhl, Hess' girlfriend, by bicycle all the way from Munich, and the Friday contingent of strudel-bearers—a group of National Socialist women—and three men he didn't know, though one might have been Hanfstaengl, whose house Hitler was arrested in. Sometimes he hears a typewriter going or sees a cat walking the ledge. Flowers and gifts pile up daily at the window of cell seven.

Seven. A magic number.

Does Mika know that? *I've been thinking, Mika—lots of time for that, you know—I've been thinking and it may be significant that the number seven was—*

A car.

Blue. Percussive. No side screens. Sneltz lifts a pair of field glasses.

Two men in a blue Peugeot are approaching the old wooden bridge across the river, and the passenger…the passenger is Manfred Haupte. Second visit in four days. The car stops at the gate. Haupte disembarks in a dark brown suit and caramel striped tie and is promptly admitted. It looks like he intends to stay awhile, as the blue Peugeot diesels off in the direction of Landsberg. Odd. Visiting hours are nearly over—if any rules still apply to Hitler.

Sneltz decides to stay put and eat his supper later.

Three hours pass while shadows deepen down one orange precipice and up the next. The Lech babbles melodiously. Sneltz ponders. Then, just at dusk, the dark brown suit and caramel striped tie appear outside the gate. Manfred Haupte consults his watch and looks toward Landsberg. Apparently the driver of the blue Peugeot is late.

The nearness of the man, stranded as he is, excites Sneltz. This is it. His Chance. The something he needs to prove he exists. *I could walk right up to him now and engage him in conversation.*

Haupte's hooked upper lip gives him a hawkish expression, but a certain delicacy of dress and manner render him aristocratic to Sneltz. Too refined to offer much resistance in a physical situation.

Mika wasn't happy when Wiesel went back to pump Haupte about Eckardt's death, but the fact is it worked. The blackmail over the embezzled bailiff accounts is still effective. As long as Haupte can't find a way to eliminate the whole cell at once, he can't risk harming any one of them separately.

Haupte, in apparent disgust, begins to walk toward Landsberg. Sneltz, heart pumping wildly, descends the slope from his post and steps out to intercept him at the bridge.

From twenty meters Haupte fathoms the situation. Another of the blackmailing leeches! They slide out of shadows and wait, knock on his door in the middle of the night, follow him in the streets. There will be no end to it until he makes an end to them.

If only he knew how many there are and where they meet! There can't be many. They make no impact on the Munich scene. This one looks especially pathetic. Standing there in oversized clothes, staring at him with marmot eyes—the neurasthenic bastard! The bailiff stops at the foot of the bridge, flicks his tongue over a molar.

"Haupte, you know who I am?"

"The local troll, I expect."

"I was sent to question you."

"Lucky for you you caught me on foot like this. But then, maybe not so lucky." Haupte seems occupied with a hovering mosquito, though it is too cold for insects now.

"We're in control of things. I suggest you cooperate."

"Control? What can a handful of Jews hope to accomplish?"

"A handful of Jews are worth a dozen Nazis."

Poor mathematical Sneltz, putting a denomination to everything. Haupte is astonished to glean this inkling of his enemy's number so easily. Less than a dozen. Neither of the other two Jews who interrogated him let anything slip. He was beginning to fear they are indeed well organized, if not actually intelligent.

"You can't win, Herr...?"

"Hitlerstein. Call me Adolf Hitlerstein."

"Most amusing. Well, Herr Hitlerstein, perhaps we should talk about this over a beer-stein in the village up the road."

"I'd love to piss in your beer, Haupte, but my mother warned me never to drink with the devil."

"It's only a matter of time, you know, and we'll round you up."

Sneltz laughs hollowly. "We hear you marching in the streets. You practically step on us, and you don't even know we're there."

A cellar? Incredible! Less than a dozen meeting in someone's cellar. This one is a gold mine. If I capture him, he'll break in an hour, thinks Haupte. We can round them all up. A few of the SA will do it. Heissen's crowd are bloodthirsty enough. I can let them use the lodge and have some fun. Tape their mouths, though, to keep him from telling Heissen I botched the theft of the funds from my court accounts.

"But we know where *you* are," adds Sneltz. "We know why you're here and just what you're up to."

"Splendid. Then you don't really have any questions?"

"Naturally, I want to hear it from your lips."

"Naturally." Haupte cocks his head and glances back at the

fortress. "It's all rather compromising out in the open like this. They can see me from the prison. No self-respecting victim wants to be seen with his blackmailer as long as he has blood left to suck."

"We can go to the woods."

"You go to the woods. I'm on my way to Landsberg to stay at the inn."

"You think I don't know that you're waiting for your driver?"

"...to take me to the inn. Anyway, I don't care what you do."

Reluctantly Sneltz accompanies him toward the town, whose quaint heights are now the day's last embers. He will be wary. What can Haupte do? Nothing while the others are free to respond. And if Haupte is staying at the inn, he won't go near his own room there.

"I want to know about the prison," he says.

"The prison? Not much goes on inside a prison. Up at six, breakfast at eight—"

"They exercise at eight," Sneltz corrects.

"Yes," beams Haupte. "Absolutely correct. They exercise at eight. They breakfast at seven in the common room. The trustees do the serving. And lunch is at noon, tea at four, dinner—"

"I know the routine. Tell me something else."

"Like what?"

All people have a numerical characteristic, and Sneltz has a fix on him now. Take Mika, a perfect four. Or Esther, two—conflict. Haupte is a nine. Nines are deceivers. He has never dealt well with nines.

"What about security?"

"Oh, very tight. Twenty foot walls. But, of course, you can see that. And then there are the peepholes. They're on all the doors. Even Hitler's. The guards are supposed to spy, to make sure another revolution isn't brewing. Isn't that funny?"

"Why?"

"Because there *is* a revolution brewing."

"*Was*, you mean. That's how your little Napoleon got his ass thrown in jail to begin with!"

"No, no—aren't you listening to what's going on? What on earth does your little group do?"

"We expose people like you."

"Oh, it's all very open. Hitler even talked about it at the trial.

He's writing a book, you know. Dictating to Hess. *Four and a Half Years of Struggle Against Lies Stupidity and Cowardice.* Awful title. Have to be changed when the publisher gets it. What's even funnier is that, through their own spying, the guards have been won over. Hemmrich—and even the warden—is impressed with National Socialism. So, it's all very open. Everyone is sympathetic to political prisoners. They even publish a little propaganda sheet in cell one. And one night—this is really funny, Herr…?"

Sneltz scowls at the second attempt, Haupte smiles apologetically and continues.

"Well, Hitler tells me they came to his room in sheets and lampblack, waving brooms, and restaged the whole trial. They found him guilty and sentenced him to tour Germany by car—"

"What about Haushofer?"

"Who?"

"Karl Haushofer. What does he have to say to Hitler?"

"Haushofer comes to Landsberg?"

"You know he does. Why does he bring books?"

"Maybe it's to give them to Hess. Hess was his student in geopolitics at the University."

Haupte slows his pace and stops as if to emphasize a point. Now in front of him, Sneltz turns his back to the village. And suddenly he hears the car. Such deceivers these nines! Sneltz spins back to catch the last crimson glint from the Schöner Turm spire, and twin blue tongues—the front fenders of the Peugeot—beneath glowing headlights, and, within the broader silhouette, an inconsequential driver, except that he is consequential now, because Haupte grabs Sneltz by the lapels.

They wrestle absurdly in the protracted roar of tires and screech of breaks until four grappling hands become six. Sneltz leaves the ground, kicking, kicked, and is rudely pinned in the rumble seat while the blue Peugeot, an electric phantom in the twilight, ghosts over the winding, deserted road toward Munich.

They tape his hands down first. In some nameless room an hour and a half later Haupte and the consequential driver do the thing, and following that, Sneltz can't even see their faces because the light is in his eyes. All he sees are his hands taped to the chair arms with white strips that start crossing at the first knuckles of his little fingers and work back over his wrists. He doesn't immediately divine the reason for that, because he is too terrified. But then Haupte leans into the gray latitudes between the light and the dark and from a papier-mâché face states matter-of-factly: "I'm going to rip your fingernails off one by one, Herr Jew."

At last Sneltz has his stage, spotlight and all, illuminating every drop sweating from his soul, but the hush of the audience only amplifies the dislocation of his mind in whimpers and groans.

"…unless," adds Haupte, "you answer honestly and fully."

Sneltz registers metallic clicks as if a hammer is ringing off an anvil. A latitude of grayness brightens then. Haupte's cold blue eyes and hooked lip reach into his space.

"I've sent my driver out. No one knows about those bank shortages except you and your friends. And you know I like to gamble. So now I'm gambling that I've caught the right one of your miserable little enclave. If I have, I promise you a peaceful ending. If not, there are anguishes you haven't imagined in your worst nightmares, Herr…?"

"Sss-sneltz."

"Sneltz. Good. Who wants a mess? Now. Your friends. How many?"

…to die utterly without merit, to betray one's companions, to never have done a single worthwhile thing. No. No. No. No.

Again the metallic click.

"Sixx-x," gasps Sneltz, curiously melodic.

"Names. Slowly."

Sneltz begins to whimper.

"Look at your hands," commands Haupte.

Sneltz squeezes his eyes shut.

"I said look at them. Choose a finger."

Into the region of grayness rears the metal thing. Needle-nosed, red handles. Snapping.

"You're probably right-handed," says Haupte, and he lets the cold metal fall across the left fingertips, sending a slight shock through the nails.

The absurdly delicate blow shatters Sneltz's remaining control like a rap on a faucet. He weeps freely and wets his pants.

"Last chance," says Haupte. "No?"

Bending softly to the task, face and jowls quivering with effort, nostrils distending—he lifts and lifts.

For Sneltz all is red. The sound, the blood spurting over the tape, the smell of that tape. But, oh God, despite the swelling in his skull, he resists! Rudolf Sneltz resists! Brave Rudolf Sneltz—

"Names?"

The hand is in spasms when the second nail goes.

"Names…addresses?"

Molecular screams from Sneltz.

The third nail is his limit. Mind bending pain. Intolerable, excruciating pain. A Rudolf Sneltz is made for no more. Writhing, bellowing, retching…he has really done quite well.

Even if it isn't well enough.

One by one the Buttons are collected.

Oberstein is taken early in the day. Five SA enter two minutes after his printing shop opens. "Special on obituaries," Willi offers, picking up a lock wrench as he backs into a corner. The five have two pistols between them but are afraid to shoot out of fear of the neighborhood. Ever since the night of the Putsch, the SA have kept off the streets and there is talk of a cleaned-up coalition. So it comes down to a battle with a junkyard dog, yielding one fractured skull and a broken hand, neither of them Willi's.

Wyerdoern is next, at the end of the day. Quietly hustled off the sidewalk on his way home from the bank.

Then Esther, leaving Reinhold's. A blue Peugeot is waiting.

Mika is tougher to find. Haupte has to pull Sneltz together well enough for him to make a Judas call by telephone. Then they roadblock Mika on the way to Landsberg where he believes the call has originated.

But Aaron Wiesel, for all his apparent casualness, has eyes in the back of his head. You might stand beside a charred Citroen and call to him as he arrives home from work, but you won't get near him with a crowd, or find a route he frequents twice in three days. As soon as he sees the car through the window of the post office where he works and another male-lingerer across the street, he suspects the truth. He tries to phone the other Buttons. Connections with the worried wives of Oberstein and Wyerdoern complete the picture for him. Slipping out of work by the dispatch entrance, he begins his own watch further up the street.

Haupte is annoyed when his henchmen return empty-handed. Wiesel is shrewd and may become the hunter. But Haupte's men assure him they were not seen, and anyway, it is too late to stop things now. Haupte doubles the squad watching Wiesel's apartment and prepares to join the prisoners in the mountains outside Munich.

The closed British Sunbeam that intercepted Mika on the way to Landsberg is waiting for Haupte in the street. In the backseat is Mika with tape over his mouth. Haupte scurries stiffly from the entrance to the car, pausing on the running board to glare triumph and croon: "Ah, Herr Bastard, how good of you to join me."

The windscreen is up and Haupte removes his travel goggles and then his gloves, plucking between the fingers twice around as the Sunbeam percolates away from the curb.

"I hope you can stand pain better than that Sneltz fellow," he says to the prisoner beside him. Reaching across, he strips adhesive from Mika's lips and mustache. "How much do you know about the Thule, Herr Lott? I gather from your flunky that you are interested in Karl Haushofer's visits to Landsberg." A cold, weary glance accompanies this. "That's really quite good. You must have guessed it. Not many in the society realize that Haushofer is its secret master."

Mika leans against the leaky side screen, cool air soothing his raw lips.

"And now Hitler is his pupil," says Haupte, "learning the origins of the Aryan race in Atlantis. About the sub-races and their blasphemies, I mean. Isn't that what you wanted to know? About their magical faculties and the perversions of the holy fertility cults and the degenerations that put the Aryans in exile. You knew that much, of course? No? Ah, Herr Lott, you're not looking well. Yes, I'm sure you knew that. After all, the Old Testament tells about it, more or less, if you can solve its allegorical style. But you didn't read it in the Torah, did you?"

The pause is genuine and expectant, and Mika knows Haupte intends to pry the sources of his occult awareness out of him one way or another and that he will never believe it came from reading the same heresies Hitler read, or from living in the endemic pits of magic and racism in Vienna.

"There's no reason we can't talk, Herr Lott. It's all over now. Would I be so candid if it wasn't?"

Haupte makes a suave offering from a gold cigarette case. Mika looks away.

"I must say, you impress me, Herr Lott. Very resourceful. I'd really like to know where you learned about the Spear and Haushofer. You're certainly not an adept. Someone must have told you. Or you bribed someone, or tortured them, or infiltrated, or blackmailed...who?" Haupte taps both ends of the cigarette on his knee. "Really, there's no point in this, Herr Lott. I'm quite convinced that your Sneltz told me everything regarding the threat to myself. I fear nothing more from any Jews, and I'm willing to talk to you about whatever you like. I've already told you what you wanted to know about Haushofer's visits to Landsberg Fortress. Is it too much to ask how you knew these things?"

"Hitler won't be able to use it," Mika says dully.

"I see. You want to talk about Hitler. Hitler, then. You mean because he's in Landsberg? Landsberg is a haven. Everyone knows it won't last long. Not five years. One at the most. Long enough for the professor to refine him. He's ready for it now—always talking about the *Cyclops eye* and using his pineal gland to fathom the time spirit of the Spear. How beautiful to reach out to a civilization in remission and call down demigods! Such a voice—"

"No one in heaven or hell is listening to Hitler. A few eccentrics and a mob."

"Listening to him?" erupts Haupte. "*Hitler* does the listening."

For the first time, Mika is attentive. "What do you mean? You mean to Haushofer?"

"*Through* Haushofer, you miserable Jew! Can't you get it through your head that what's happening has been trying to happen for thousands of years? You said in my apartment you knew about our reincarnations, presumably you know it's almost happened before. A thousand years ago the last time. All that history, do you think it just lies down in graves?"

"We all have histories. If your history has powers, there are counter powers."

"Let me tell you something, Lott. Let me offer you knowledge this side of the grave, since you stand on the brink of it. No ritual adept, no initiate or novice, no ally of Satan in any form denies the existence of God and Christ. But what do you think is knocking at the gates Hitler is going to open? A new mutation is coming, at your expense. Wherever a drop of pure blood exists, the surrounding taint is going to be spilled. You know that's coming, don't you? The millennium is ours."

The road has been winding and rising but now levels off. One of the two men in front, neither of whom has followed the conversation owing to the roar of the engine, sings out their arrival. The Sunbeam's lights pick out a rutted lane and the parked blue Peugeot. They grind to a halt in the drive of a two-story lodge.

"What remains for you," says Haupte, "is to choose the manner of your death and the death of your friends. The choice will hinge on whether or not you answer me. I would like to know who told you about the 'below ground' Thule, as you put it to me once."

"Any fool can see that your street Party is made up of cretins," Mika murmurs. "The Thule is a bit of gloss for those who consider themselves honest thinkers. So there had to be an elite level for the really sick ones—like you Haupte. I've known your type since my Vienna days. All puffed up with your new orders and levels and degrees."

"That's it?"

"Gospel."

"From a Jew." He lights his cigarette swiftly. "You'll be pleased to know another order is going to open. The Vril. An Eastern name for psychic energy. Haushofer will introduce it soon. It will be solely for those who understand the origins of the race and are dedicated to its magical restoration."

From behind the lodge a dog starts to howl.

"Bring them all out to the pit!" orders Haupte.

The driver crunches up the path to the lodge and within thirty seconds Esther, Wyerdoern, Willi and Sneltz bob forth in the company of a half dozen SA. Their mouths are covered with white tape, their hands tied behind them. In the faint light they look like weathered Roman statues with chipped lips and truncated arms.

"Quite a round-up, eh, Lott? Just like a Karl May western. Hitler will be delighted to hear the details. He has a whole shelf of Karl May in Landsberg."

Mika is prodded toward the floodlit rear of the lodge where his stomach tightens at clear sight of Willi bruised and cut, trig Wyerdoern disheveled, Esther haggard and Sneltz—dear God, what is wrong with Sneltz?

The guards push them to the brink of a square pit excavated against the foundation and breached at the bottom by a framed shutter connected to a rope. On cue somebody gives the rope a yank, triggering a dusky streak through the passageway below.

The breed is barely distinguishable from a wolf. Someone claps sharply, and it hurls itself at the seven-foot embankment, a rapacious blur of muscles, silver hackles and saber teeth. Its steady yellow eyes never leave the figures above, despite predacious circling.

"We call him 'Gladiator,'" Haupte informs the prisoners. "And, of course, this is our coliseum."

He signals toward Sneltz. Guns are brought on line. Sneltz is wrestled crying out of his hunting jacket and leather vest.

"Haupte, I told you the truth!" bellows Mika. "Haupte!"

Unholiest of scenes. Sneltz, stripped and lowered screaming, over the edge. Impossible not to look, to indelibly imprint the spectacle of death and dominion, even when one knows it will be no more forgettable than forgivable. Nailless fingers, stark buttocks, lathered assassin. The few seconds it takes are interminable, and in their collective awe and outrage, no one hears nor sees the approaching car. Enter the scornful altruist.

Aaron Wiesel at the wheel of a stolen Austin, carrying no fewer than three loaded pistols—which, like Wiesel, are war relics. He has never really left the war, and this is just another battle to try and kill the enemy he missed at Somme and a hundred other places.

The Austin spins around the other two cars, skidding sideways, as through the open window Wiesel begins shooting. "Down!" he shouts, though his four comrades have already gleaned what is happening and have rolled beside the running board. Wiesel jumps out. The SA scramble for higher ground, affording him time to haul everyone to the lee side of the car, extract a screw driver from the fender box and slash the tape from Oberstein's wrists.

By then the flanking SA are firing back. A gas line on the Austin is hit. Flames spurt up to the canvas roof, and Wiesel shoots blindly through the glare.

"You got Haupte!" Wyerdoern shouts.

Thanks to Willi, they are all freed of the tape now.

"Go...go—get the hell out of here!" Wiesel hollers.

Cynical, death-loving Wiesel. They are trespassing on his profession. Unlike Sneltz, he will not be cheated.

Mika takes the first step, and all at once, the four of them are dropping stride by jump down the mountainside...until suddenly Wyerdoern isn't there anymore. And when they hesitate, Esther is hit, and Willi and Mika have to brace her up. They cross the road, stumbling down the lower slope, Esther groaning at each step. The desk photo of Wyerdoern's family keeps popping up in Mika's mind, and then they hear the Austin go up in a great searing breath and they know...the Buttons are just three now.

7

"I'm dying, Mika. Don't let me die."

Esther holds him by the wrist, and her strength is the strength of ten. The doctor has removed the bullet that struck her side and somehow followed a rib around. "Bones like a dreadnought's spars," is the verdict.

"You're not dying, Esther," Mika murmurs. "Enough have died already."

"Wyerdoern?"

"Wyerdoern."

"And Wiesel?"

"Yes."

"And Willi?"

"Willi's moving to Hanover. We all have to move."

"I can't. I'm dying."

"They say you'll be discharged in three days."

"I'm dying inside. I've been dying since that day you walked away from me in the street. I thought then maybe it was necessary. Mika wouldn't hurt me, I said, so it must be necessary. I thought I could do without us being so close, as long as we shared the same goals. But I can't. I need you, Mika."

She looks vulnerable, cherub face all holy with love. Still holding his wrist, she flings her other hand up, pulling his face into hers. The kiss on his raw lips is both painful and euphoric. And the hand she holds is drawn into the covers between her thighs. But Wyerdoern's family photograph keeps coming between them. Mika pulls away.

She looks hurt, incredulous.

"I had a wife, Esther." His cheeks tremble, his eyes glimmer like sunsets. "They cut her head off."

He tells her he is going away to Hamburg. Then he says goodbye. Then he starts for the door.

"Mika!"
He stops, eyes averted.
"Where will I send letters?"
"The Edenhaus Hotel," he says after a pause.

"Not another!" says the desk clerk at the Edenhaus. In his hand is a pale blue envelope with no return address. "Who the hell is this Mika Lott?"

Six hundred kilometers to the south, outside Landsberg Fortress, Mika stands in the cold where Rudolf Sneltz stood five months earlier, pondering ironies Sneltz never pondered. He is occupied in particular with a short story he recently read.

The plot features a gang of heinous criminals who terrorize Europe, butchering and burning whole families who—say the criminals—are blocking the development of the human race. It reminds Mika of the SA, and it strikes his prophecy-prone fancy because it was written in 1896, by an Englishman named M. P. Shiel. One of the similarities is the title and the name of the gang. Not that it is called the SA. That would indeed be a shattering coincidence if a mob of Hitler's making had the same name. But the names are close. The title of Shiel's short story is *The S.S.*

Suddenly the fortress gate opens and a man in a trenchcoat and floppy hat emerges. Two other men, waiting in a black touring car, hurry to take his belongings.

One of them is a printer, Adolf Müller, who is going to publish Hitler's book, now called *Mein Kampf*. Mika has no doubt that it will win fame and that it will "weld ancient traditions and symbols to an unheard of radicalism," because that is what Solovyov predicted of the Antichrist.

The second man is Heinrich Hoffmann, a photographer, and he is trying to snap a picture of Hitler posing at the gate for posterity but the prison guards are waving him off. Undaunted, the party drives toward Landsberg to pose by the town's ancient gate.

It is nine months since Hitler was imprisoned here. Nine is a deceitful number, according to the late Rudolf Sneltz. And if he were here, he would notice.

WEWELSBURG CASTLE

1
1933

Clackety-clack.

Lutka on her way to Berlin by night coach from Niski Kosciol. The joke has been twelve years in the making, she reflects.

Tell it all, *clackety-clack*: how Pani Gerlak forsook a career and true love with Josef Krantz for the inscrutable mystique of Niski Kosciol, married the village blacksmith in order to console herself with motherhood, turned out to be barren, and then, when husband Jan died in anaphylactic shock from a bee sting, blithely abandoned that for which she had sacrificed so much.

Quite a laugh, eh, *clackety-clack*? Pardon me for not laughing with you, but old jokes are only nostalgic to me. And don't mispronounce the name. Lednicki. It is *Panna* Lednicki now. Talk about being late for a train.

Laugh on, *clackety-clack*...

At Eberswald, the first stop over the border, she picks up a thin-lipped bird of prey with hungry eyes and a bowler hat. It brings back the mustard and the marching and everything else she left behind in wicked Berlin.

"May I assist you in any way?" he begins, calling her Fräulein, to which she replies she is Frau somebody-or-other, the wife of the famous marksman. He offers a cigarette, then advice, and when she continues to gaze steadfastly out the window of the train, he begins a chronicle of horrors in Berlin.

The depression has hit hard, he says, and if she wants a job she will have to get in line behind six million unemployed. Not to mention there are the brawls, strikes and riots, beggars on every corner and crazed veterans shooting at poster columns. Not a place for a woman alone (it certainly is good that she is married, and to a marksman, too!). She will need his protection until Chancellor Hitler has time to end all the chaos.

Hitler? Chancellor?

Hindenburg just appointed him on January 30th, she learns. Quite a story there. Gregor Strasser, the second most powerful man in the Party, split with Hitler in December, calling him and his circle—pardon the quote—"satanic perverts." Things looked bad, but a certain seer, Erik Jan Hanussen, published a poem New Year's Day which accurately foretold certain secret meetings and included the unlikely prediction that Hitler would be named Chancellor on January 30th. The thing was lampooned, but of course when it actually happened...would the Frau like a peppermint?

"Politics are always stupid, and politicians—who are always men—are also stupid," she says, adding pointedly that she hates peppermints.

The train pulls into the station, and the bird of prey flaps leadenly away.

Light snow creates a fade-out of the visible city, whose massive and involved architecture recedes behind progressively thicker veils, but there are more automobiles than she has ever seen in any one place before, and the Berliners look shabbier than the ones in her memory. Workers in capes, idlers in doorways, women with bags and satchels.

The taxi driver charges a shameful rate of exchange and looks remorseful when she doesn't argue. She has to go to the bank as soon as she unpacks, she decides. If she is prudent, the money she got from the sale of the livery and the tools and the house in Niski Kosciol will last until she finds a job.

The main thing is to stay away from the Schiller Theater where she met Krantz. That would be too much like trying to go back to the past.

So the first theater she tries is the Repertoire. But they already have an understudy, and the rest of the cast is disgustingly healthy. Next she tries a tragedy six blocks away, uncovering a case of paranoia. The prima donna feels threatened by understudies. The last replacement, kept secret by the director until Madame Diva showed signs of contracting a cold, quit after a hair-pulling row.

Lutka moves on. And on. Until she gets an appointment for a Thursday reading of a new production.

Love, love, love...life is love! she scans from the manuscript at the Kaiserdamm. *Let me live to overflowing!*

Hideous, but who's complaining? Thursday is three days away. "Love, love, love..." Lament it, Lutka. Limp, listless. Luke warm, low-voiced, lassitudinous. That's a lie. Get the alliteration, though. Lilting and lyrical maybe. "Love, love, love..." Sing it, child. Oh, yes. "Love, love, love..." in the elevator, at breakfast, in the shower, lying in bed, on the way to the dentist—

The dentist.

Niski Kosciol's dentist lived in Warsaw. In twelve years Lutka opened her mouth for vivisection only twice. While that was good, it was also bad. So many cavities! The Berlin dentist is kind enough to squeeze her in on Thursday morning.

"Love, love, love..."

But six fillings! He stands on her shoulder, climbs in her mouth.

"Love, love, love..."

No lunch. The reading at one. Stage lights. Yawning, empty seats. Director and cronies in row six. Mouth hurts like hell.

"W-wove, w-wove, w-wove..." she winces woefully, "w-wife is w-wove. W-wet me w-wive to ow-werfw-woing."

Her lips a knot, she stares Neanderthally into the darkness of the sixth row. Then she drops the script and drifts weightlessly past the indifferent huddle and out of the theater.

But two hours in a cafe, listening to talk about whether or not the Reds are responsible for burning down the Reichstag in February, and how wonderful this dreadful little man Hitler is, and how his admirers have even painted swastikas on his cows at Haus Wachenfeld in the Obersalzberg, give her the urge to go job hunting again. She tries the Renaissance, and then the Komödie, where foreign talent is featured, and finally the cabaret theaters. And in one of these she lands a small role.

The place is opaque with smoke and she has to shout her lines, but remarkably nearly every speech brings applause. Especially the one that quotes the poet Heinrich Heine: "'German thunder is truly German...but it will come, and when it crashes it will crash like nothing in history has crashed before…never doubt it; the hour will come.'"

No thank you. Lutka closes tonight. Exit stage right.

So that leaves the Schiller, where she met Josef Krantz. Who can blame her? She doesn't know why she reads so well for that one. And did I mention, she doesn't know why she reads so well for that one? The producer makes up new posters: "Lutka—fresh from triumphs abroad."

And however did she read so well for that one?

Each night she scans the audience through the hole in the curtain, and on the evening of her fourteenth performance she sees a man very much like Josef Krantz. There is the calm, unreadable face, the blue gaze, the aquiline set of the lips, the impression of ball socket shoulders and long muscles beneath the coat. But the man's skin is bronzed rather than satin pale, and the blond hair is too thin at the temples, and there is a certain hardness impossible to put to one feature. Not Josef. Too old for Josef. Still, twelve years—

At the last curtain she bolts off-stage, through the crowded tunnel and out the stage door. Lifting her skirts, breath steaming in the late March chill, she negotiates the slush to the street and there cranes in either direction.

"Josef!"

He turns and twelve years shrink to twelve steps. A taxi brushes by, honking, and suddenly they are holding hands. Again.

2
A DRAMA IN FOUR SCENES

Scene 1:

"I'm late, Lutka," he says, kneeling over her in the nude one morning. "*Late* as in fired-from-the-faculty."

"You're always late, Josef. Whenever we make love you have a million things to do. By actual count we have done the act twenty-two times in the last month for a total mattress clocking of twenty-three minutes."

"I keep thinking your father is going to interrupt us."

"Oh, that's hysterical. *Pater interruptus*." She flings an arm over her eyes and snuggles fiercely into the covers where the muffled lament continues: "Sixty second Lutka, that's me. We could do it to The Minute Waltz."

"I really do feel that way about your father, darling. Sure it's funny, but it also happens to be true, because that was my first sexual experience, you know—your father practically standing over us."

"Poor bird."

He swings out of bed, grumbling.

"Papa's mellowed," she says as he inserts himself hopping into his trousers. "When Jan died, Papa said I should marry again. Really, he actually said that. So, you haven't got anything to worry about."

Marriage? Nothing to worry about? Marriage is a sealed trunk in his attic.

He thrums the newel post at the bottom of the stairs, considers going back to tell her how he feels about marriage, decides to tell himself instead, and brisks off for the Institute where he teaches. No, there will be no marriage, no matter what. No more Niski

Kosciols, no matter what. He is a Berliner all the way. No matter what. Because he has nothing to do with politics.

They talk politics all the time at the Institute, but he only has to listen to it when he plays cards with a few of the faculty men. The worst is Bolgardt, who gestures with one of those unctuous Havana ropes while he rants, leaving toxic dead spots in the air that always seem to waft toward Krantz.

"This fellow Einstein"—gesture, waft—"they seized his bank deposits on a violation of the Jewish lethal weapon act because he had a bread knife in the kitchen!" Gesture, waft.

Krantz plays cards silently, and once in awhile these insipid political anecdotes trigger his Mehring Damm fugue to insistency. Such as when Gustl Tromblein, another professor with whom he shares an office, relates the Hanussen thing. Hanussen, who regularly casts Hitler's horoscope, was consulted by Hitler after Strasser split the Party in December. Hanussen told him that the only way to mend his fortunes was to secure a mandrake root from the yard of a butcher in Hitler's hometown under a full moon. At the Chancellor-to-be's behest, Hanussen carried out this nonsense, and of course, the fortunes changed dramatically just as he said they would. Tromblein swears it is true, having heard it himself from Hanussen after his famous prophecy that Hitler would be named Chancellor on January 30th was published New Year's Day.

Krantz believes it is true simply because it brings back the dizzying surrealism of Mehring Damm. But he is more interested in the fact that this Hitler is a lover of architecture. Berlin might yet have a future in stone. No, Krantz is a Berliner now, and he will never leave the city again for the likes of Niski Kosciol. Or the love of a woman.

Scene 2:
"I want you to know that I didn't forget it was our third anniversary together, Lutka," he says. "As a matter of fact, I've been trying for weeks to get you the crown jewels of England. The royal family absolutely refuses to give them up. I considered a Mercedes, but you don't want to drive the same auto as Hitler, do you? And Paris is so gloomy this time of year. Therefore, I ask you: what do you want?"

"Marry me, Josef."

Scene 3:

"*Mein Gott!*" She says it three more times, once in Polish, over the headlines in her lap. "They're arresting everyone right and left."

"Not everyone." Krantz kicks off his shoes. "Jews and Communists."

"…and even Social Democrats."

"Did you leave a towel in the shower?"

"Don't you care about these people, Josef?"

"They're political agitators."

"The Jews? They don't even have a party."

"Jews will ride it out. They've done it before. Anyway, lots of them were Social Democrats. You've got to expect some scalp-taking."

He unwinds his shirt, moves to the next room alongside the tub, drops his trousers. She rattles the paper.

"Scalp-taking," she repeats. "You mean like making them eat old socks or gulp castor oil—"

"No towel!" he hollers.

"Look behind the door. Well?"

"Castor oil's pretty awful, all right."

"It's degrading, Josef. What are you going to do when they get around to arresting Poles?"

"Hey." He appears in the doorway, towel around his waist. "You've been reading too much Kafka."

"I've been reading newspapers. They arrested Virtz, you know. Illegally, of course. In the middle of the night."

"Virtz? Oh, yes, Virtz. The one who drinks and sings Russian songs in your play."

"They took him to their SA barracks and made him spit on a picture of Lenin."

"Now, that's really terrible."

He retreats to the shower, tosses the towel in the sink, grasps the faucets.

"Why don't we get away from all this?" she shouts above the shower.

Flee to Niski Kosciol, she means.

He takes her to the movies instead.

"This is what you brought me to see," she asks, "Triumph of the Will"?

"It's a documentary. See it. *Then* be ungrateful."

"Lead on, Spirit."

The theater smells of beer and sauerbraten. They sit halfway back from the screen. Someone smokes in the dark, a small child cries, an SA with his girlfriend keeps getting his hand slapped.

Lutka slumps down in her seat. "Certainly has brought out Berlin's cultural elite, hasn't it?"

"That's the screen in front of us," he points out to her. "We needn't concern ourselves with the audience."

To begin with, there is Zeppelin Field, a vast stone plateau encircled by thousands of banners. At one end looms what can only be called an altar some four hundred meters long and thirty high. And above that an eagle clutching a swastika in its talons rises on wings spread another thirty meters. Even more impressive are the night shots of the six-day Nuremberg rally. A stunning array of 130 anti-aircraft searchlights fire columns of light some five kilometers straight up into the darkness. The effect is to draw a ring around the legions, a "cathedral of ice."

The panorama is played out from unique camera angles: aerial views, shots taken from a crane and from an elevator platform mounted on the tallest flagpole. One perspective even reveals clouds drifting through pillars of light.

But the soundtrack of Hitler's raucous diatribes, punctuated by awesome swells from as many as 200,000 regimented Party faithful, the flickering torchlight, the titanic white columns, the swaying banners, the delirium of the masses in unison, chill Lutka to the bone. Quietly sickened, she leaves the cinema during the final scenes.

Perplexed, Krantz sits another moment before following her to the street.

"Well?" he asks.

"Someday," she says softly, struggling for self-mastery, "those people you admire so much will force you to choose between them and me."

Scene 4:

"'The Law for the Protection of German Blood and Honor,'" she reads slowly from the newspaper, adding a declarative, "So."

"So?"

"So, it's only a matter of time now."

Krantz begins tapping his lecture notes with a pencil. "A matter of time till *what?*"

"Until it's illegal for *us* to marry."

The pencil plops to the drawing board. He swivels on the stool, grasps one knee in both hands, and leans back.

"Lutka. It says 'Jews and citizens of German or related blood' are forbidden to intermarry. Neither of us is Jewish."

"It won't stop there. Anyway, I don't want to live in a country that bans, boycotts and beats up little groups of its own citizens. Ex-citizens."

He dances his notes together in a sheaf. "We've been over this before."

"Apparently you missed the fine print." She offers him the newspaper. "It says 'extramarital intercourse is also forbidden.'"

"Oh, well, that will certainly stop us."

"You don't think living together speaks for itself? You think this kind of a government will stop at creating witnesses?"

"What the hell, it'll be like old times. The Gestapo standing over us like your father while we fuck."

She emasculates him with a look.

He nods. "Okay. Forgive my crudeness. I postulated something ridiculous to make a point. Only, remember this—and I don't mean to hurt you—*but you can't have babies*. So do you really believe this hypothetical Gestapo representing a hypothetical law of a hypothetical Reichstag is going to care about a Polish actress who can't have babies?"

"Sometimes you can be cruel, Josef. Maybe it's a German trait. Maybe I've never really understood you before."

He rubs his brow. "I didn't want to say it, Lutka. If it wasn't necessary, I'm sorry." He swivels slowly around. "And I'm sorry for what's happening to the Jews and the Reds and the rest of them. I don't endorse any of it. But it isn't my road, Lutka. Or yours. And life is full of roads. You can't walk them all. Pick one and stay on it. There's no point in trying to repair the ones that don't go in our direction."

"Maybe our roads aren't the same anymore," she says wearily.

"Maybe I detoured for you when I saw where Germany is going. My road says 'marriage,' Josef, what does yours say?"

"Is that an ultimatum?"

"No, it's a compromise. I'll stay in Germany…if you'll marry me."

3

Enter Fritz Ender. Chauffeured. Immaculate. There is no doubt he is the one. The note inviting Krantz to the biergarten at two in the afternoon was signed by Reichsführer-SS Heinrich Himmler's adjutant. If this is a joke, it now takes on elaborate proportions, because the prevailing drabness of the gray street and its gray people is incised by the gleam of an open tourer (courtesy of Daimler-Benz to the Reich) and a penguin of a man who alights as freshly dressed as a hatchling stepped out of its shell.

He is small and slow and silent. And innocuous. To be sure, he wears the black tunic of the SS with its silver clusters and buttons and crimson swastika brassard. But the glittering jackboots seem to inhale him, and the visored cap with the death's head insignia remains on the back seat of the tourer. He walks rather than struts, hands cupped slightly away from his sides, rather like a little boy who has just discovered frosting on his fingers and no place to wipe. Any minute now he will wipe them on his Sunday suit. Actually it is his older brother's Sunday suit, and he is struggling to stay afloat in it, except at the collar, where his skin bulges out like cookie dough, teeing up a round face with raisin eyes and lips as pale and puffy as orange slices.

"Herr Krantz, Fritz Ender," he introduces himself, slightly out of breath. "Reichsführer Himmler sends his regards."

Krantz half rises, mouths a platitude, and offers the adjutant a glass of beer. Ender drops down gratefully, mopping his nose with a neatly squared handkerchief.

"You don't know what a pleasure it is for me to sit in a place like this and drink a beer these days." He promptly sneezes. "An open tourer." He gestures to the car. "Practically winter, and they loan me an open tourer. It was very kind of you to agree to this meeting on such short notice, Herr Krantz."

"Josef."

"Josef. Fritz, then. That makes the beer even better. I'm an informal man in a formal job. Informal but quiet. Someone has mistaken my shyness for tact, and so whenever they imagine diplomacy is required in the private sector, they send me."

Tact. The man reeks with it.

"Private sector," Krantz repeats. "You've come to me because I'm an architect?"

"I keep forgetting it scares the hell out of people to be contacted by the SS or the SD. Yes, an architect. Sorry."

"The SS is interested in architecture?"

Ender sighs, and his raisin eyes and cookie-dough face expand as though baking.

"Unlike Göring or Bormann, Himmler isn't noted for building projects, that's true," he says, "but this is a very special building that will require very special architects."

A smile from Krantz. Himmler is finally embarrassed by a personal reputation for building wooden barracks and labor camps. And Josef Krantz has just been dealt the hand he deserves and has expected for years.

"What kind of building?"

Ender's cookie-dough face firms. "A medieval castle."

"I beg your pardon?"

"Yes, yes, it sounds strange. No doubt you expected me to announce a new colossus on Wilhelmstrasse with the Brandenburg Gate in the background, some marble repository for his files and bureaus. But the project is, in fact, a medieval castle."

"In Berlin?"

"Westphalia. Near Paderborn. We have a chief architect. But he needs assistance."

"Speer?"

"Bartels." Trying hard to catch the reaction, Ender stoically delays another sneeze.

"May I ask why I was chosen?"

"Your reputation for history and archaeology is well known." Ender doctors his nose, each dab using a fresh section of the handkerchief. "You studied under Tessenow, the same as Speer, you admired Troost and the Führer himself has praised your 'esthetic engineering' principles."

"I'm flattered. But how do you know I admired Troost?"

"You came to his funeral."

Mild alarm. Krantz sits back, draping an arm right, straightening his leg left, as if to throw himself open. "May I ask how long you've kept track of me?"

Ender looks melancholy. "Your file goes back to 1921."

A chill wafts over Krantz. The memory of a murder on a train and a warning delivered to him begins to tingle. "The Thule meeting," he says.

"Yes."

"Am I being forgiven?"

"If you want to look at it that way. Everyone isn't meant for the Thule. You didn't try to scandalize them—that's good enough for the Reich. It really isn't much of a file."

"Does it say what happened to me that night? I never did figure it out."

Ender's shrug rises through his tunic like a trapped bubble, passing up his face and flattening his wrinkled brow. "You shouldn't feel threatened," he says. "Himmler is an inveterate file collector. He has one on everyone. Myself included. Yours is just scraps gathered together in retrospect."

"Retrospect? From what?"

"As I said, your thinking on the subject of architecture has been admired by the Führer himself. And you do have a knowledge of history, an appreciation for the past and an understanding of how and why other cultures built as they did, and perhaps…where." The little adjutant stops talking to his glass, raising his eyes in a question. "The Reich is bursting with plans, Josef. Commissions are being formed. We have need of reliable architects with vision."

"Vision? For a medieval castle?"

"Not all the Reich's buildings will be castles, Josef."

"I'm not even a National Socialist."

"Every German is a National Socialist at heart. In your case, the Party is a formality—"

"But I don't want to join."

Over a brief silence they drift to new positions and there is an odd sense of sanctioning coming from Ender.

"Most people in your position would simply default into joining," he says. "I respect your feelings."

"Please, don't make a virtue out of it. Look, I don't think this will work out. I appreciate the offer, but—"

"It worked out for Leni Riefenstahl. She made the film 'Triumph of the Will' without joining the Party. She told Hitler to his face exactly what you're telling me. Imagine that."

Krantz absorbs this for a moment. The Nuremberg rally film has stuck in his mind along with admiration for Speer, who is, after all, the Reich's architect.

"Concern yourself with the project, Josef," says Ender. "The politics will work themselves out. If not, you can always quit. The Institute will free you up for a leave, I'm sure. And we're prepared to offer you your salary plus expenses…plus one hundred Reichsmarks a month."

The sum is generous. "I couldn't leave before the end of the term," Krantz says.

"Understood. But the concept of the castle needs some initiation. We hoped you might familiarize yourself with that in the meantime. I would act as a resource for you."

"Is this to be a residence for the Reichsführer?"

"Oh, much more than that. A center for the SS Command, actually."

"And I'd work there under Bartels?"

"Independently. You would submit your own designs and suggestions, both before and during construction."

"In an advisory capacity?"

"Not at all. If you're asking does Bartels have the last say, the answer is no. Himmler does. I can't be any more candid than to tell you that your qualifications have been painstakingly measured and earnestly sought after. You are unique, Josef. We need you."

"I'll think about it, but frankly I'm not very enthused at this point."

A Nazi castle! The idea is absurd. *There goes poor Josef. He built that crazy medieval place in Westphalia. Hasn't worked since.* Even Speer shied away from this one. Or is there a little rivalry between the

Reich's masters that keeps their architects separate? In that case he would be cast as Himmler's.

"Take your time, then," Ender says, somehow creating a second impression of his purpose—an ambiguity: the penguin adjutant, dutiful, loyal; but under the uniform, an owl of a man, peering, thinking for himself.

The receding tourer bears him away like a rich and unhappy child in the back of the family limousine, and Krantz detects a second sanctioning look from the owl half of the man just before he sneezes.

"A medieval castle," he tells Lutka. "They want me to build a medieval castle."

"Everyone should be allowed one castle," she says.

She is filled with Delphic asides these days. Why is it that when two people want most to talk to each other they resort to clues, he complains, and she answers with a two-day silence. The day after that is lethargic. And the one after that sad. And all the ones after that. Sad.

"The Princess is sad!" he decrees, and the Crown Prince of Bastardy arrives (looking very much like Josef Krantz riding a mop with a fruit bowl on his head) to break the spell. But love's sweet kiss fails. Then Cagliostro flaps a hearth rug summoning Bacchus with a bottle of Liebfraumilch to no avail. Lutka gets annoyed with Seneca in a bed sheet, and Krantz claims victory. "At least you aren't sad anymore," he declares. The reward? A faltboat excursion down the Naab with the Princess.

She agrees. But sadly.

Saturday. A day born wet whose afterbirth hangs above the river in shredded mists, whose marble clouds show threads of iridescence. A day in which sound travels effortlessly and the river is a room, empty save for this odd couple in their boat and out of their season. Is the swan that glides mutely on the edges of the mist a symbol?

The paddle dips. *Plash, plash!* Get thee hence, swan. Singer of leaving.

Lutka is still sad but no longer annoyed. This isn't Germany. This is a way station between two moments. One gone, one coming.

Krantz is involved with greenness. Sedge and sentiment, gluey currents and plush stands of fir, luminous boulders, Lutka's lime eyes...

"I'm going back to Niski Kosciol," she says.

They are moving on a river and he can't be sure he heard her correctly. Words are not possible in a wordless setting. Sounds maybe. The soul relieving itself. Limberlost. He will commit an act on her to contradict the pseudo words. He will commit love.

Laboring gently, he draws her supple form to the bottom of the boat where he makes a nest of her clothes, so that her torso lies naked from neck to knees, bedded in silk and wool. Around her throat is a choker of black velvet with a piece of green jade in the center. He can't look in her eyes, so he concentrates on the jade. Drifting on glass, they reach the exquisite intimacy quickly and intensely, and afterward lie melted and steaming in the chill air. And all the while her gaze remains sad—first watching him dissipate his swollen energy, then cushioning euphorically, finally fixing translucently on the gray sky running overhead.

Down, curtain.

On Sunday she is docile and thoughtful. But still sad. They spend the day talking quietly, caressing, watching a languid snowfall of large, aimless flakes.

On Monday he teaches two classes.

On Monday evening he returns to the apartment and finds it empty.

4

Dummy.
    He says it to himself as he opens his eyes.
Dummy. You let her go.

His head is roaring, but he gets up and concocts the latest substitute for coffee and snaps on the radio. They are playing marches interspersed with propaganda about the French-occupied Rhineland. He leans on the pantry shelf. Blue mold on the pumpernickel.

Dummy. What do you do now?

Get out of the Institute, out of Berlin, grow a mustache, buy a car, have an affair, gamble, drink, carouse, ski...*go to Westphalia near Paderborn and build a medieval castle.*

The scrap of paper with the name and phone number is at the Institute. Fritz Ender. Cookie dough. Penguin. Owl. Some people invite caricature, attracting nicknames like lint. Like teddy bears. There is another one. Teddy bear. With a death's head ring.

Tromblein is already in the office. Krantz carries the phone as far as it will go between the file cabinet and the wall to let Gustl know this is a private conversation. He smells apples. There behind the file, one of Tromblein's rotting cores—"Hello, Fritz Ender?"

"Speaking."

"This is Josef Krantz at the Institute of Technology. I've given your proposition some thought and decided to accept."

"Excellent." Ender repeats the word as if to make it stick. "Can we meet tonight? In my office at the Prinz Albrechtstrasse? Or would you be more comfortable in my apartment? No politics or bureaucracy in my apartment."

"Your apartment," Krantz says, repeating the rest: "...seven, yes. Across from the bank. Apartment G."

"'Youth—large, lusty, loving,'" Tromblein quotes when the phone is recraddled.

"Goethe?" Krantz guesses. Tromblein is always quoting Goethe.

"Whitman."

"I'm going to take a leave at the end of the term, Gustl. Will you watch that Kempler returns all the books he borrows from my shelf?"

"My dear boy, you'll never be a full professor if you keep taking leaves. What is it this time, travel or commission?"

"A castle in Spain."

Tromblein shakes his head. "'The fate of the architect is the strangest of all…to produce buildings he may never enter in.'"

"Euripides?"

"Goethe."

In his natural habitat Ender is the owl-like caricature Krantz glimpsed at their first meeting. And the setting this time is nocturnal—dim light, a clock that emits soft clicks—but the man himself is fresh, preened, calculated in appearance. No sign of the jackboots when he opens the closet to hang up Krantz's coat, no tunic or cap flung carelessly on the shelf. The obligatory swastika is straw size and stuck in a pencil caddy. There are signs of asceticism: the absence of a phonograph, liquor or ashtrays. Pastoral yearnings whisper from a series of quaint landscapes and in the predominantly poetic choices on the bookshelf.

"Modest vintage," Fritz apologizes, bringing out a bottle of wine. "I'm the pauper among adjutants. The bootie accumulated by Göring's aides is legendary. Even the Führer's staff has its scandals. But as you can see, I live strictly within my means. Reichsführer Himmler himself is also quite frugal. I myself have loaned him a mark or two on occasion. He always pays it back with interest."

If the confidences are meant to melt any ice, they do.

"But he indulges in medieval castles," Krantz replies bluntly of Himmler.

"One castle." He hands Krantz a goblet full of red wine. "This will be the only charge Himmler has ever put to the State. Between eleven and fourteen million marks, we estimate. And that's only for reconstruction, technically."

"Reconstruction?"

"The ruins of a castle are already there—Schloss Wewelsburg. Swedish soldiers destroyed it centuries ago. But its foundation is so strong that it's been partially rebuilt several times, as a prison among other things. Himmler feels that its many reincarnations make it appropriate for what he has in mind."

He searches Krantz's face for enthusiasm.

"It's very good," Krantz says about the wine.

Ender retires momentarily to a desk, returning with charts and papers.

"This," he says, spreading the first map over the coffee table, "is Wewelsburg Castle, or what's left of it. And this is Sudostwestfalen airfield, a few minutes away and almost completed. The road is good; and the Alme River here is adequately bridged and inconsequential to moving materials. Schloss Wewelsburg itself is laid out on a gigantic thrust of triangular rock, so that it overlooks everything."

Here Ender produces photographs of a gaunt, gray mass of stone whose round towers and remaining hollow windows conjure up institutional horrors to Krantz. He is intrigued by its muteness; gaping ruins always seem to be screaming history at him.

"Rough cut," Ender says. "Like a quarried block of granite waiting for the hands of Michelangelo. Wewelsburg's centuries may only have been an initiation for its ultimate purpose. A very special purpose few will understand. It lies there on its rock like a shed dragon skin, waiting to be resurrected. You'll breathe life into it, Josef. You, with your knowledge of historical structures and appointments. Wewelsburg will rise out of its ashes bearing history on its wings, a living, unbroken link of heritage and tradition specific to Himmler's design."

"You said it was to be a center for the SS Command."

"A center, a retreat, a citadel. The SS is an order of Teutonic knights...in Himmler's design. The Ahnenerbe has verified many of the origins you may have heard about at the Thule meeting in 1921. Those Obergruppenführers of the SS who are eligible to use Wewelsburg will have a room directly relating to their ancestry."

Reincarnations, he means.

Something wise passes between them. Silence is a sentry gliding in and around the Wewelsburg project already. Reincarnation will not be questioned.

"You won't be required to pass judgment on any of it," Fritz continues. "And there will be a great deal that may strike you as irrational. I only urge you—privately—not to laugh at it. That would be a mistake on two grounds: ignorance and personal welfare. Please don't feel threatened by this. Himmler is well aware of your expertise and knowledge of structures. He expects nothing more than that. However, you will have to know the rudiments of symbolism and tradition behind Wewelsburg. It is also expected that you will be discreet in your comments after Wewelsburg is built, just as you were discreet after your encounter with the Thule."

Krantz sips his wine. "What rudiments?"

"All the German emperors from the ninth to the nineteenth century for a start. Charlemagne through the collapse of the Old Empire when the Spear of Longinus was taken from Nuremberg to Vienna to keep it out of Napoleon's clutches. Exactly a thousand years."

"Spear of *who*?"

"Longinus. The Spear that pierced Christ's side. It's a talisman. All the emperors possessed it. It will have a special place at Wewelsburg."

"But you said it was in Vienna."

"It belongs to Germany. Someday we expect it to be returned. In the meantime, a replica has been made to be kept in Himmler's room—the room of the Fowler Emperor, Heinrich I."

Krantz looks puzzled. "Himmler's previous incarnation?"

"The Reichsführer-SS has made a study of theosophy and is of that opinion, yes. He believes he himself may one day be responsible for turning back an invasion from the East at Wewelsburg. There was a Saxon prophecy in the reign of Heinrich the Fowler that predicted such a holocaust coming out of the East and overpowering the Germanic peoples if it wasn't turned back in what is now the area of Birkenwald, Westphalia—another reason for the location at Wewelsburg of the SS citadel. At any rate, the Spear was the inspiration for the founding of the original Teutonic knights, and it was carried by Heinrich at the battle of Unstrut."

Ender relates this without fervor, almost gloomily and with a loss of lucidity in his gaze.

"Since each room will represent a different segment of the millennium, it will be up to you to shape its design and construction," he continues. "Agents have already been selected to acquire tapestries, paintings, carvings, furniture, period artifacts and personal possessions of the emperor claimants from collections all across Europe. Through Bartels you will be able to hire whatever craftsmen you think necessary and authorize purchases of art objects and court regalia."

"What about construction firms?"

"Bartels will handle labor."

"Bartels and Himmler will have final decisions above me?"

"And Hitler, of course."

Fritz smiles as if to remind him that Hitler *is* the Führer. But what Krantz is wondering, of course, is how deep the Führer's commitment to this ancestral heritage nonsense is.

"There will be a room at Wewelsburg for Hitler, too," says Fritz. "Frederick I. Barbarossa. The Spear fell from his hand just before he died."

"Cause and effect?"

"Charlemagne dropped it, too, just before he died."

"Must be slippery."

"The shaft is disintegrated now. Only the metal is left. Anyway, I wasn't trying to make a case out of circumstantial evidence. There are much harder portents for those things. Comets and torn temple veils and ravens…" Ender takes an astringent gulp of wine. "You'll want the list of rooms. Also the Ahnenerbe research into the claimants."

He moves the papers in front of Krantz.

"What is this Ahnenerbe?" asks Krantz.

"Our bureau of research into ancestral heritage."

"Racial make-up?"

"That's a factor. The Wewelsburg elite must be made up of SS free of race-shame for at least five generations."

Krantz rubs his brow. "The Thule, as I remember, only demanded three."

"Do you have any qualms?"

"No. But I don't know who my ancestors were past my grandparents. Maybe you should run a check on me."

"I'm sure Himmler has. Josef, the future doesn't have to impinge on the present."

He says this earnestly, with an apologetic smile, and Krantz files it aside for later consideration. He feels genuine warmth coming from Fritz, and loneliness, and something else. The hidden sanction he sensed at their first meeting each time he balked?

Whatever it is, they spend a good part of the evening discussing Rembrandt and architecture and poets. Fritz knows Goethe as well as Tromblein, quoting one little delight, that "architecture is frozen music," which Krantz has never heard before. The little adjutant must be starved for intellectual stimulation working in Himmler's offices at the Prinz Albrechtstrasse, he thinks. What a pity that he hasn't the personality to rule instead of just taking orders.

5

At least Fritz didn't lie about the reason for the thing, Krantz reflects Wednesday morning. He could have told him it was going to be a museum, a monument, or even a private endeavor, but no, the bloody Reich is building a bloody medieval castle to house its bloody séances.

He reasons thus, intent on the water closet mirror and the possibility of growing a mustache. He has reached the age where hair is a crisis, no longer renewable at the temples but sprouting from his nostrils and occasionally sending up six gauge shoots in solitary contrariness from his brow, neck and other disconcerting spots. Age, it seems, has its little jokes.

A mustache is a bow tie for the nose. Why do revolutionaries wear them? Lenin, an ascot from nostrils to chin. Hitler, a snide cravat. The smoothies—Alexander the Great, Napoleon, Caesar—they weren't wordsmiths or insurrectionists, just conquerors.

A car is to pick him up at ten for Tempelhof airfield where Fritz and a twin-engined Junkers will be waiting to fly him to Westphalia, but Lutka's ghost drives him out of the apartment at eight-thirty.
Across the street the ethnic decor reads like a wall map. The Jews have their book and antique dealers behind the larger window scribed in flecked gold. The Serbs sit in scowling clusters just down the street, playing cards in a storefront. Above them is a row of Swiss professionals: investment broker, dentist, lawyer, and a coin dealer whose casements gleam with mint sets in cardboard frames. Adjacent to the Swiss peninsula begin the Scandinavian penthouses where window boxes are attended by plump, wholesome women—flowers in summer, ceramics in winter. Below that and above the Jews, a knot of German families have prematurely strung their sill with Christmas decorations. Finally, there is the candy shop,

neutral, declared solely by a cloying aroma and the word "Sweets" in nonpareil. He always meant to buy Lutka a kilogram of chocolates but somehow never did.

There is a park down Kreugerstrasse, a little knoll of land with three maypoles that look like the day after Calvary. He goes there and sits at the foot of the central pole and agonizes over Lutka. At ten o'clock he returns to the apartment.

Krantz has never flown in an airplane. The experience seems somehow to begin with the chauffeured ride to Tempelhof where Fritz is waiting, scarved and gloved. The Junkers, a hunchbacked shaft of corrugated metal with double wheels beneath the tail, inspires no confidence whatsoever, but he allows himself to be capped and goggled, and, feeling like a vulcanized fire hydrant, climbs into a seat. The engines kick in with a vengeance. Down the runway they course, ever swifter, until the earth drops away and they soar to unforgiving heights.

There is nothing bird-like in this kind of travel, Krantz discovers, rather they are astride something angry and bolted together whose occasional hiccups hint at disaster. Reluctantly he forces his eyes to encounter the horizon. There are only fir trees, hoop skirted in deep green, as far as he can see. The flight seems endless, but finally white runways and a tower appear.

At a signal from Ender, the pilot banks east and half a minute later Krantz sees the triangular plateau rising out of the earth. Stuck to it, like a piece of chewed gum, is Wewelsburg Castle. Quite unnecessarily, the pilot stands the Junkers on a wing to circle the ruins, causing Krantz to clutch the canvas grips and close his eyes. When he opens them again the airfield is in sight.

They land with a skip and a lurch before rolling to a stop.

"Finest plane Junkers made before they closed the factory," the pilot boasts to Ender, rapping the fuselage with his fist. "What do you think?"

Krantz refrains from asking why the factory closed.

On foot they pass the control tower, Fritz waving off an SS-Mann who appears at the lower level, presumably to drive them in the sedan parked near the gate.

"Beautiful country, isn't it, Josef? Do you ever hike?"

"A little."

He hikes a lot. Lutka despised it, so he accepted charge of a youth group that met at the Institute and once a week he took them on an excursion into the mountains. It got to be distasteful when more and more he had to fend off the political indoctrination of the boys, who were also members of the Hitler youth. *Yes, Erich, the Jews control commerce, but look at the Larkspur!*

"Boating on the Naab is my specialty," Ender confesses.

Krantz cocks his head. What are the odds of running into someone who mentions boating on the Naab four days after you have done exactly that? Is Fritz trying to warn him he is being watched?

"Have you ever been to the Bayreuth Festival, Josef?"

"I don't like classical music."

"And I thought I'd cleverly found the key to explaining both talismans to you." Fritz gropes for his handkerchief. "Richard Wagner, I thought. Who would suspect that the son of Furtwängler's oboist hates Wagner?"

"My father had more time for Wagner than he did for me. But… Talismans?"

"The Spear and the Grail."

"The Spear of Longinus?"

"And the Holy Grail." Ender shakes out the handkerchief, blows his nose. "Wagner has woven the whole Germanic era of the Spear and the Grail into a profound allegory beginning with *Lohengrin* and ending with *Parsifal*. They're both works of Templar Catharism, if you happen to know anything about Templars and Cathars."

"Templars went on crusades in the Middle Ages. Cathars were… heretics?"

"Labels aren't important. But please understand…there is a coherent history going back before the current world order, and the Reich traces a true Germanic bloodline through it. I'm speaking of a religion now, Josef, and as a religion, these doctrines enhance and unify the bastardized versions of creation and order in all global cultures." A cock pheasant whirs out of the brush to the right of the road. "It will be enough for you to understand the general origins, the directions they took, the symbols that arose from them, I think. Especially the symbols. Because it will be your job to provide for them in the architecture of Wewelsburg."

Ender is sane and intelligent, and it bothers Krantz that he speaks like one of the Thule's gloating mystics. Or rather that he doesn't sound gloating and mystical when he speaks. Where does the thinking owl half of the man leave off and the obedient SS penguin begin?

Suddenly, as if reading his thoughts, Fritz turns to face him. "Is it likely that all early cultures would make up myths to the complete exclusion of their true histories?" he poses as if asking the question for himself.

"Most myths have a grain of truth."

"History begins with a few grains." The scripted voice is back. "Literal truth has a way of sounding fictional, like a child's story."

"What literal truth are you talking about?"

"The beginnings."

"Snakes and apples? Turtles carrying universes on their backs?"

"Races and places."

"Thule?"

"Hyperborea, the White Isle, whose capitol was Thule," Fritz says precisely.

"It's not in the atlas."

"Not in the current edition. There are plenty of witnesses who say it was in the old one." Seeing Krantz's expectation, he recites: "Seneca, Virgil, Pindar, Herodotus, Pliny the Elder, Diodorus."

"...and it sank without an oil slick," scoffs Krantz. "Captain and crew. Like Atlantis."

"Some of the crew made it to shore. Atlantis sank later. Part of the same archipelago. Add Solon, Plato, Proclus and Strabo to the testimonies for that one."

"They heard stories," Krantz says unenthusiastically.

"Lots of stories. And the Greeks and Romans understood myths, wouldn't you say? Still they accepted Atlantis and Thule as fact."

"Thule?"

"'The mighty island will be found...and Thule will no longer be called Earth's end'—Seneca's *Medea*," Fritz quotes mechanically.

"All right. The issue isn't whether or not there were beginnings. There were. And one myth or another—maybe all of them—point in a general direction to look for traces. But this stuff about superior pre-races smacks of the storytellers art."

"Does it?"

"Oral traditions are always embroidered. It would be strange if you found one that wasn't exaggerated."

"Exaggerated, perhaps. But discredited? Naturalists, like Germain, have noted the similarities of Canary Island and Cape Verdi fossils with those of archipelagos all over the Atlantic. And Canary Island mummies have been found averaging nearly two and a half meters tall with very large brain cases and locks of blond hair. The stories of giants in Thule and Atlantis are, of course, common to all the sources. That they should be considered demigods by lesser races is understandable."

Krantz pockets his hands. "Understandable but wrong."

"Don't make hasty judgments, Josef."

"Hasty?" He stops dead still, but Fritz strolls on. "If the evidence isn't in now, when will it be in?"

"It is in."

Krantz catches up. "Oh. Well, then it's clear. A few primitive midgets looked at a few primitive giants and called them gods."

Unperturbed, the little adjutant walks a half minute in silence. "Granted, the term 'giant' is relative, Josef. Take a victory lap, if you like. We need not contest their size. The *Book of Henoch* says they descended from otherworldly intelligences, Herodotus says they were transparent, the Egyptians—who represent a degenerated and assimilated remnant of one racial branch—trace their gods Min and Hathor and themselves to the sunken archipelago. Echoes of it abound in the Eddas, the cyclops stories, the Bible, the Hindu Vedas, Tibetan writings, in the stories of migrations, in colossal terraces and structures around the earth, in myth and legend and folklore."

Krantz smiles foolishly.

"Say it," Ender invites without looking at him.

"It's crazy. I don't believe it."

"That's a good attitude to have, if you don't want to get involved in what's coming in Germany, Josef." Ender's tone is somber, his chin down as if he is concentrating very hard on the best advice he can give. "A good attitude *if* you don't want to take sides. By all means ignore the evidence. But understand it. Hear the arguments, so that they can't surprise you later on—then shut off your mind."

"I don't have to shut off my mind. It was clear to me the first time

I heard about this Thule—this…this 'island in the extreme north'—that all its so-called advanced civilization was just somebody's way of dealing with the boredom of surviving on an iceberg."

Fritz absorbs the argument with pained familiarity. "You should know that the White Isle's warm interior isn't so much laughed at now that tropical remains and coal have been discovered at Spitzbergen. And that the Celts and the Vikings knew of titans with brass-colored hair who came from 'the fog-bound island where Hyperboreans drew power from the secrets of the world.' Tibetan frescoes tell the same tale. So do some South American legends. The demigods were supposed to be clairvoyant and magical, and their scientists and priests lived at Thule with twelve members of a Supreme Rite. Plato describes their fall as a gradual diluting of the demigods to human frailty through interbreeding."

They pause again to face each other.

"Do you understand now, Josef? The Führer wants to bring them back. The main business of the Reich is to collect the pure blood of the Aryan race—in a kind of Grail, if you will—and restore the original order."

"Demigods and all?"

"The Superman has been defined," Ender says grimly.

Overhead, the Westphalian forest interlaces tightly, a vascular structure respiring in the wind. The light is blue-gray and swims with minnow-like flashes.

"The thing of it is that there are and have been a lot of people who are very, very serious about this, Josef. For twelve thousand years they've been serious about it—since the Deluge. So many people for so long…things happen, Josef."

The blue-gray bathes his doughy face, heightened in luminosity by the sea of black cloth cresting in pockets and silver insignia.

"What things?"

"I don't know," the adjutant croaks softly, starting to walk again, aware that a discarded weakness from childhood has crept back into his voice. "The human spirit has real power. Give it time to develop rituals and…and whatever it is we call magic gets organized."

An astonishing statement to Krantz.

"There's always a Grail," Fritz says then, achieving a settled voice. "Usually in the form of a chalice, but always with a ritual meaning. The gold cup of ambrosia is one. Plato says the gods of Atlantis collected the blood of a young bull in a cup as a symbol of renewal. Iris drew water from the river Styx for the gods in a gold cup. *Iris* means *rainbow*. The race born of the rainbow was the Nordic race to the ancients. The Aryan race."

Fritz steals an earnest glance at his companion.

"The same cup?" Krantz responds dryly.

"The same idea. A vessel of knowledge."

Krantz avoids Ender's face by peering at the chimera of gray through the trees where Wewelsburg Castle lies.

"I won't go through all the etymological significance of the word Grail, but it's come to stand for a path to ultimate knowledge," says Fritz. "The Reich believes there is an object as well."

Ender is reaching out to him beyond the dictates of an assignment, Krantz is certain now. The Reich has imposed a strain on him. He needs someone outside Himmler's compassionless crowd to talk to, someone more cosmopolitan, more humanitarian. And that first day in the biergarten, even then, Fritz was sizing him up as a man from the academic community, softer than SS, intelligent, sensitive. That sanctioning look. Fritz was trying to tell him two opposing things. Since then they have taken off their architect and adjutant coats. Now Fritz is vulnerable, letting his own doubts show, but trying to draw Krantz up to some hidden level of objectionable truth. Objectionable to both of them. But still true, it seems. Somehow he has to trust him, if only until he can see for himself.

"A chalice?"

"Or a stone, a scroll, tablets. Maybe even a book."

"The vessel of knowledge?"

"Yes. The secrets of the Aryans from Thule. The object, or the tradition, seems to have traveled east after the Deluge, returning thousands of years later to the Druid priests of the Celts."

"The Holy Grail."

"The Holy Grail," Ender affirms. "Here it does become a chalice, the cup used by Jesus Christ at the Last Supper, subsequently used to catch holy blood when the Spear of Longinus pierced Christ's side."

"So the Spear and the Grail are talismans together."

"With long independent histories already, of course." Ender

pulls a burr from his sleeve. "The chalice is supposed to be cut from the emerald eye which fell from Lucifer's forehead when he was banished from heaven. 144 facets. The story may be rooted in the Hyperborean legend of the third eye—the pineal gland, an organ of special knowledge that supposedly degenerated when the demigods were tainted with human blood. The giant Cyclops myths again come to mind. Grains of truth, Josef."

"Where do the Knights of the Grail get into it?"

"King Arthur and the Round Table is the Templar inspiration for the Reichsführer's Teutonic Castle." He gestures ahead. Wewelsburg's ruins lie before them. "The guardians of the Grail. Templar Catharism again. Eschenbach, who wrote *Parzival* from the poem *Perceval* and called the Grail a precious stone, was a Templar, too. Guyot, the author of *Perceval*, was a Cathar. Eschenbach traces the Grail from its possession by Solomon, to its seizure by Alaric, to its sequestering by Albigensian Cathars in the Grotto of Sabarthez at Montségur."

"France? And that's the end of the line?"

"No. The end of the line is Wewelsburg."

"Are you saying you expect to bring the Grail here?"

"It's expected to come to the Reich." Ender waits for the shock of that to sink in. "You're to prepare a place for it, Josef."

They stand among the ruins, the SS adjutant and the architect, dwarfed by the enormity of a legend and the chaos of the age and the momentum of the Reich and the shallowness of civilization and their own moral inertia. A cold wind whistles through the rubble, elevated as though on an altar, forcing them to half shout. They speak of towers and halls and shrines for fantastic things while whirlwinds of dust rise up from the graveyard close by the castle. High above them an eagle wheels slowly in search of the unwary, and off to the north a raven vents ugly jeers.

This is real, Krantz tells himself. Real because he is standing in a dry moat making sketches, real because he is measuring off its breadth and width, real because back at Sudostwestfalen airfield he meets chief architect Bartels, who has just arrived, and receives from him a sheaf of photos and graphics of the site.

Uneasy as he is about returning by plane to Berlin, there is genuine relief in getting off the ground. Three times he has felt this sense of dislocation, he recalls as he weathers the shudders of the Junkers when it strikes air changes above the river. The first time was at Mehring Damm 26, the second at the pagan site on the coast above Niski Kosciol, and now Wewelsburg. Maybe 'the magic *is* getting organized.' Magic. That, too, is becoming real.

6

Like a snow queen in the silver dawn, Lutka stands at the foot of a frozen pond outside Niski Kosciol. Once she was a princess at this very spot, gathering her garlands from among the high grasses of spring and summer. Now she has come here to commit suicide.

Moving like a skater she starts out onto the ice: *push-glide, push-glide, push-glide.* Currier & Ives. *Push-glide, push-glide—crack!* Arms sweeping up in a pale ballet.

A bone-shattering chill grips her as she accelerates through the hole, the hem of her dress closing over her like the petals of a flower. Bubbles rise in short strings, white as pearls, and disappear as though corruptible in the air of the living. Seconds pass, and then she sprouts up again, gasping and draining like a leaky rain barrel. She has straightened her legs and found the bottom not much more than waist deep.

Her extremities are cruelly pinched, her clothes already beginning to stiffen with ice. Not thinking to tear anything off, she flounders to the edge of the pond and from there across the brittle snow to the first street, second house down. Almost too numb to feel the jarring of her fist, she pounds on the door.

In the few seconds it takes her Aunt Zofia to leave a chair, Lutka is sputtering out like a guttering candle. But then the door is open and a zephyr of hot air floats over her like a web, and her aunt's enlightened gasp against the irregular wheeze of a tea kettle presupposes rescue. Strong hands clasp her like a block of ice, for she can no longer move, or even fall down now that the supporting door is open.

"Mother of God! Mother of God!" the old lady keeps repeating. She is still an erg of human flesh when the task requires, but age has wrinkled her skin the way waves wrinkle a beach. "What happened to you? Mother of God!"

Before the fire, she unwinds her niece like a mummy. The clothes pile up, stiff as plaster casts, looking much bigger than Lutka herself, who stands knock-kneed, slump-shouldered and eventually naked. Towels come out; a comforter is slung over her. The old lady brisks her as immodestly as she might have three decades earlier after a hot tub bath.

Lutka's purple lips move, but the words remain locked up. Pink and saved and miserable, she sits on the hearth, swaddled in comforters and cupping a bowl of broth.

"Now, how did you get so drenched?" Zofia demands, re-enthroned in her chair an arm's length away.

"The pond," Lutka gets out, sipping broth. "I tried to drown myself."

Old Zofia never misses a beat but continues to rock as if she has already figured everything out.

"Your brother Tadeusz went through the ice, did you know that? Christmas Eve, it was. You must have been two or three then. Right through on a sled. Henryk was there and had him out in a flash. Got himself soaked, too. They looked like a pair of cod packed in ice for Warsaw. Henryk, he wouldn't undress. As if anyone cared to see his holy bare bottom." She laughs shockingly loud. "Never complained about thawing out, but he didn't father another baby for six years!"

Lutka smiles wanly in spite of herself.

"You didn't want to drown yourself, dear. The pond is much too shallow for that. If you had wanted to drown yourself, there's the lake half a kilometer further."

"I forgot."

Zofia stops rocking. "Is there a man worth hating yourself for?"

Lutka stares vacantly at the ascending sparks. "I'm preg—I'm pregnant. All that time married to Jan and he thought it was me. That I was the one who couldn't...couldn't—"

Leaving her chair without actually straightening, Zofia lifts another log onto the fire.

Lutka slowly shakes her head. "...unforgivable."

Zofia grunts. "What's unforgivable? Nature doesn't much care where her seeds get sown. It was the German, I take it, and so now you've decided to do the noble thing, is that it? Spare your parents the shame. They certainly would have been grateful."

"Papa would."

"But he wouldn't know about the baby, would he? Just that his daughter committed suicide."

Silence.

"And the baby, you'd be willing to kill it?" asks Zofia.

"What kind of life will an illegitimate child have in Niski Kosciol?" Lutka says leadenly.

Her aunt leans toward her with a crone's scowl. "What kind of life will it have dead?"

Lutka winces and bursts into tears. Zofia nods in satisfaction and resumes rocking.

"You're sorry, I take it," the old woman says a minute or two later.

"I'm sorry, I'm sorry…so sorry. I've never done anything right in my whole life. I couldn't stay in the village when I was a girl, and I'm sorry for that. I went away to Germany against my father's wishes, and I'm sorry for that. I fell in love with the wrong man and brought him home to defy my father, and when I should've married him, I married the wrong man instead. I'm sorry for all those things. I'm sorry for not having a baby when I should have and for having one when I shouldn't have, and now I'm sorry because I tried to do a terrible thing to it, and I'm sorry because of the life I'm going to give it—"

"That's much too sorry, even though you didn't mention becoming an *actress!* Just as well. Now you have a real role to play."

"What do you mean?"

"Maybe you should wait and see about that life you're going to give your child. How far along are you?"

"Three months, I think."

"Well, I can't give the baby a father, but I can make it all right with your parents and the village."

"But how?"

"Never mind the details. Trust me. I'm like an old clam lying on the beach. There may be sea moss growing on my shell, but when I open my mouth it's still smooth as silk. Maybe I even have a pearl or two inside. The family will be together soon for Easter. Trust me until then."

"*Pisanki!*" cry the children, rushing for the wooden bowl containing hard-boiled Easter eggs.

"I did this one—see the stag?" Zbigniew boasts.

"Grazyna's is the best," asserts Bogdan.

"No fighting!" Prakseda warns, leveling a finger. "Let Grandmamma choose first."

Helena Gerlak—Grandmamma—waves the honor aside. "Without my glasses I can't even see the designs."

"Take the brown one, Grandmamma," advises diminutive Jagna, who boiled that particular egg in onion skins.

Zofia is accorded a similar choice, followed by Henryk and each of his four daughters in descending order of age—Prakseda, Lutka, Cecelia, Maria—then the three husbands and unmarried Feliks, and finally, the eight children. Nineteen in all. Henryk rumbles the prayer. Loaves of hot *babka*, a sweet yellow bread, are brought out. A plump chicken follows, goat's cheese, cold sour milk, cherry vodka, a wine which Feliks says was "made in Hungary but aged in Poland," and suddenly there is a knock at the door.

"It's Father Ledochowski," Helena predicts as Feliks goes to answer.

But the young man who edges in beside Feliks with his pant cuffs tied in the manner of bikers is a stranger.

"Telegram for Lutka *Krantz*," he reads from the envelope.

The long table falls silent.

"People up the street said it must mean here," the young messenger chirps hopefully.

Aunt Zofia's eyes weigh heavily on her niece, and Lutka rises like a sleepwalker to accept the telegram, after which Feliks gives the delivery boy a slice of babka and closes the door. The shudder of the bike frame is audible against the crackle of the fire. Something fragile in the way Lutka holds the slip of paper as she reads demands interpretation, and when it flutters to the floor and she bursts into tears, the pang of raw sympathy that flashes round the room misses no one.

Aunt Zofia, having brazenly read over her niece's shoulder, pushes Lutka into her parents' bedroom and slams the door. An indecisive moment follows before the general rush to recover the telegram. Prakseda has it, raising it above all hands before slowly lowering it to eye level and reading aloud: "'REGRET TO INFORM YOU HUSBAND DIED SATURDAY LAST IN AFTERMATH OF EXPLOSION YOUR APARTMENT -- stop -- DEATHBED WISH WAS FOR BABY TO BE NAMED AFTER MATERNAL GRANDFATHER -- stop -- FUNERAL TUESDAY 2 PM ST JAMES CHAPEL BERLIN.'"

Behind the closed door, Zofia has her niece by the arms as she whispers urgently, "Of course he isn't dead. *I* sent the telegram. I had to surprise you and hope you'd cry. And so you did. Wonderful crying, and no *acting* at all. Now it's struck everyone at once, so it comes out right and not twisted along the way. And you can be sure the messenger alerted half the village trying to find Lutka *Krantz*— he is the father, isn't he? You never answered me."

"Yes."

"No matter. You and Josef were married, and when you found out you were pregnant, you came home to rest a few months. You were going to break it to your parents gently, and Josef was going to come in the spring when he could leave whatever work he does. You'll have to go away a few days to attend the funeral, of course. I've made arrangements for you to stay at Leba—that's where I went last week to pay the money and telegraph the Berlin office to send the telegram you got today. But you must insist on going alone. As for your belongings in Berlin, there will be nothing left. The explosion ruined everything, you'll say. Do you understand? I've made it all right for your baby in Niski Kosciol, Lutka, and now you have the longest running performance of your life."

"They'll never believe it."

"Are you telling me I'm not clever? Of course they'll believe it. They saw it happen, didn't they? Listen, when I think of a ruse it's no common turnips. Why, you cried yourself, didn't you? You have no idea how fancy this is. Did you see the way we sat? That was no accident, you know. Bogdan, who can't read, on your left. Myself on your right so I could pretend to read the telegram first. That damned cart all the way to Leba. I'm an old lady, don't tell me I made that trip for nothing. I even tucked an onion in my shoe to make you cry in here if necessary. Did you see the cat when I walked by? You feel guilty and you can't imagine this thing working out, that's all. Go confess to Father Ledochowski, if you want to feel guilty, but in the meantime look upset—"

A low knock trembles through the door. Helena's voice.

"Well?" from Zofia softly. "Here's your mother, ready to tell you how much everyone loves you, and how the baby will have a grandfather to replace his father. Can you act like a widow again?"

Lutka barely nods before the door opens and the whole family crowds around them.

Zofia lets herself be edged out of the room. Yes, indeed, they believe it. Hasn't she always been able to manipulate old Henryk? And if you turn the mule the cart will follow. He is too simple and she has been too elaborate for him to suspect a deception. All the way to Leba to send a telegram!

Stooping to remove the slice of onion from her shoe, she winks at the cat.

Later, when everyone has gone to church to pray, Henryk sits alone cracking the last hard-boiled egg.

"Who does that old meddler think she's flattering?" he asks the same cat. "Naming the baby after me if it's a boy! Zofia, you never were as smart as you gave yourself credit for. And Henryk Gerlak is not as stupid as he used to be…"

7

"I was hoping I wouldn't find you here," Fritz Ender says in the doorway of Krantz's apartment.

"Bartels has my sketches," Krantz replies. "There was nothing else for me to do."

"You have to supervise, Josef. They're not skilled laborers. They'll build turrets upside down and put a drawbridge where you have a door."

Krantz frowns. "What kind of laborers *are* they? They look like zombies. When do they eat? I saw two of them collapse myself. I think one of them was dead. I don't like knowing some poor bastard might drop in his tracks because I added a few meters on a blueprint."

"I'm sure you've heard there are political prisoners here. The SS ordered them to work on the project."

"If that's the way they're treated, why don't they just hang them?"

Fritz closes his eyes. "That would certainly take all the fun out of being alive, wouldn't it? Especially for the ninety-five percent who will survive Wewelsburg. They're criminals, Josef. Don't ask me what they've done, I don't know. But there *are* criminals in Germany." He rotates the visor on his cap to contemplate the death's head. "Is that me? Do I look like a man with a whip?"

"You want some coffee, Fritz?"

"The SS is lots of people: cooks, tailors, clerks…civilian architects under contract. They shouldn't pass judgment on each other."

"Do you want some coffee?"

"Are you coming back?"

"In a few days."

"Tomorrow."

"It's boring out there. No newspapers, no restaurants."

"You can go to Paderborn."

"The story of my sex life could be called *Twelfth Night*."

"Do you want me to requisition a couple of whores for you?"

"Two days," Krantz says. "Give me two more days."

"I really don't like showing up here like the Gestapo, you know," says Fritz. "Two days, you said, and it's been four. You've done a marvelous job so far, Himmler is pleased with the plans, no doubt the Führer himself feels generously disposed toward you, but Heydrich thinks you should belong to the Party. Are you listening? Reinhold Heydrich, Himmler's deputy in the Gestapo and head of the SD. He's nobody to fool with, Josef, and he wants your immortal soul on the dotted line. I've told him that you don't have a political judgment in your head, that you live solely for form and design. That's why it's so embarrassing for me to try and explain why you keep coming back to Berlin. Well, this time I've got good news for you. The heavy work is done except for the north tower dome, and that should be finished by the end of the week. There are only a few political prisoners on hand—well-fed and underworked—and they'll be gone by Friday. Hired craftsmen are working inside, the firm of Liebler-Hintz is handling wood interiors, and bids from private glaziers have been taken. Your services are henceforth mandatory, your absences indefensible. Don't make it sticky, Josef."

He was going back anyway.

He doesn't know why he keeps the apartment in Berlin. He will live at Schloss Wewelsburg until the project is completed. No SS barracks for him, no garrulous village widow with spare room. Lutka Lednicki is a village widow. (He doesn't know why he keeps the apartment.) There really isn't any reason for keeping the apartment. He is going to stay at Wewelsburg this time. And he doesn't know why he keeps the apartment, or leaves the key above the lintel. After all, Lutka is probably very happy in Niski Kosciol.

So he goes back to Wewelsburg and strolls through the crazy castle gate imprinted with the twelve ancient circles of the diocese of the Bishops of Paderborn—twelve is important, as in twelve members of the Supreme Rite at Thule—and over the stones of the lower hall, and up to the wood floors of the higher levels to the upper chamber in the north tower where sits the Round Table—as in King Arthur's Knights—whose twelve thrones for twelve SS elite are in the crafting, and whose twelve pillars to support their twelve coats of arms are already in place—as in *twelve*, Ibid., Op. Cit., et al.

There are glaziers glaziering on the east face and masons masonrying on the steps of the Treppenturm. A matched set of skeletal beings in gray workmen's uniforms remind him of the other reason he didn't want to leave Berlin as they bear rolled tapestries from room to room as rigidly as pallbearers. He makes a few notes and inquires if the mosquitoes are bad in the castle after sunset, then asks an SS-Mann to place some blankets and wood in the un-windowed lower chamber of the north tower. This particular room is to be used for rituals, including the burning of a knight's arms. Twelve knights arms. There are twelve plinths for holding funerary urns around the walls. An eternal flame will be lit here, but eternity hasn't started yet for Himmler's knights, and so the wood...

Later he eats in the village, and when he returns to the castle the other workmen are gone, except for one of the glaziers tap-tapping on a casement in the distance and swearing in thick, slow syllables. After awhile that stops too, leaving Krantz to sense the castle's solitude. If solitude is the word. He has resurrected this structure from foundation to roof, and yet it shuts him out somehow. The newest masonry seems to respire with the old, as if hidden capillaries have worked their way up through stone and mortar, pumping an ancient vitality out of the ruins. Goethe was right: *"The fate of the architect...to produce buildings he may never enter in."*

Heat lightning shimmers on the horizon and a sudden wind comes furrowing across the tops of the Westphalian forest like an armada of galleons. A storm is imminent. From a second floor window opening he watches an SS sentry struggle with his rain cape against gusts in the courtyard. Not far away a cigarette sheds embers beneath the silhouette of another sculpted helmet. Knights.

The next flicker of lightning is closer, and he makes his way to the north tower by intermittent flashes. There he uses a flashlight to enter the lower chamber, arrange his blankets and seat himself against the wall. A ventilation system—like the Vatican's—for removing smoke from the burning of a knight's arms allows the lower chamber air to circulate.

The Vatican.

There are many Catholic parallels to Wewelsburg. Himmler is Jesuitical. But the theme has been twisted. It is antipapal. One of the models that had to be studied for Wewelsburg was the octagonal Castel de Monte in Sicily. The Emperor Frederick II Hohenstaufen, himself a Templar mystic struck down by the Church, built it according to a sacred numerology to be the seat of his New Empire. A man of considerable genius and legendary occult powers, Frederick II prized the Spear of Longinus above all things and sought the esoteric knowledge of the Grail in order to become Emperor of the world. Ah, Himmler, so ambitious, so dutiful to the past, so…so devout! But who is his God?

Krantz turns his flashlight off. Thunder rumbles and rain thrums at the top of the ventilation shaft, but nothing can be felt through the four-meter thickness of the north tower's walls. He has used this chamber before to sort out what is happening to him. Lutka, Mehring Damm 26, the castle, the haunting eyes of starving prisoners he wishes he had never seen—a place to meditate. It seems fitting, because directly above him is another chamber with bizarre implications.

Overhead, is the colossal meditation room for SS retreats, some five hundred meters square, and level with that, in its own vaulted setting, lies the black marble alter of the Holy Grail struck with its silver double rune: the twin lightning bolts of the SS. Runes are another area of research necessary to Wewelsburg. The Grail is supposedly inscribed with runes from the White Isle—Thule. This is why the Cathars could never decipher it. Even before the Church effectively destroyed runic artifacts as Satan's writing, Hyperborean symbols were lost except as sources for the Greek and Latin alphabets.

Krantz doesn't believe in a literal Grail, of course. Despite what Fritz says and the Reich believes, no chalice, emerald or tablets will be found. Symbolic, yes, he can accept that. The Gospel according to Krantz is in agreement: the stone (or emerald), which supposedly dropped from Lucifer's forehead at the time of the Fall, merely symbolizes ultimate knowledge.

Much easier to swallow something vaguely consistent with his Christian upbringing—*Man's* knowledge lost through sin.

In metaphysics, the stone has become an organ of knowledge and magical power—the 'third eye'—which *Man* lost in the Fall. Krantz has trouble following this because he has little interest in life sciences. But he understands that discovery of the pineal gland, apparently a vestigial organ in the brain, was quite naturally a plus for third eye enthusiasts. Moreover, there actually is a primitive lizard, still surviving as a species, called the Tuatara which the Führer is deeply interested in because it has a third eye in the center of its head. The eye is functionless and imbedded in the skin. But since lizards are the ancestors of mammals, Hitler believes that the third eye is evolving in the Tuatara and that its remnant pineal gland in modern man represents its decline.

Somewhere along the line, the emerald from Lucifer's forehead was dreamed into a 144-facet chalice, and priests, from whatever cultures, no doubt kept the cup manufacturers busy. So, if there was a civilization at Thule, maybe some sacrificial blood did get collected in a cup, as Plato said, and that became a symbol of pure racial heritage and ultimate knowledge.

The cup got passed, so to speak, and everyone jumped into the act. At the crucifixion, the modern era of the Grail began with the cup collecting the blood of Christ. It is also the cup from the Last Supper. Same symbolism. The Church washed the legends to get the pagan stains out, of course, and that made things confusing for all kinds of surviving traditions.

The Reich's account is rather comprehensive. Krantz spent days studying its many aspects and gained a respect for Himmler's dogmatic energy, if not his philosophy. As much as anyone, Krantz understands the intention of the Reichsführer-SS to found a Teutonic Order here at Wewelsburg with himself as grand master.

Amid these reflections, the young architect dozes off. When he awakens, the rain has stopped. At first he thinks it is this change that disturbed him, but lyrical laughter and a contrasting male voice reach him from the adjacent chamber. Rising stiffly, he gropes to the tower doorway.

In the moonlight beyond is a pair of officers and two women. The women are coiffed and gowned, obviously not village fare. The officers are strangers to him but high-ranking SS. They would have to be high ranking to get past the gate. He thinks he makes out Brigadeführer insignia on one, but the light through the narrow windows only flickers over them as they move. They have wine glasses and at least one bottle.

"You can't see them," the blond woman complains, looking out. "I want to see the unicorns. You promised we'd see unicorns!"

"Karl, you didn't!" scolds the Brigadeführer. "Karl is such a liar when he's drunk."

"I thought I said *satyrs*," the other man replies. "Which would you rather not see, satyrs or unicorns?"

"Unicorns." The blond tosses her head.

"Oh, there!" the second woman exclaims, jumping up on her toes. "There's the airfield. I see our plane."

"Impossible." The Brigadeführer drapes himself over her at the window. "It must be a unicorn."

Krantz is on the verge of coughing politely, but instead he quite recklessly settles down beside the slightly opened door in the presence of a toast to unicorns.

The intrigue moves predictably to brash talk, the men making bolder caresses and intimations, the fraüleins feigning shock and pretending to be drunker than they are.

"Where's the powder room? I want to go to the powder room," says the blond, moving close enough to the north tower for Krantz to smell lavender and alcohol.

The man called Karl groans. "There are no powder rooms in castles. Why do you think they build them near forests?"

"Karl!" she says disapprovingly. "Where is it?"

"Come with me, Magda." The dark haired woman disengages from the Brigadeführer, and in spite of protests they clatter off to the staircase.

"Whoever designed the female bladder ought to be shot," Karl grunts, pouring himself another drink.

"Why can't a woman go to the toilet alone?" The Brigadeführer lights a cigarette, coughs, moves to the unglazed window. "So this is Himmler's castle."

Karl stoops and raps his knuckles on the floor. "Oak, I'll warrant. The tally's running toward fourteen million. Have you ever known Himmler to spend marks like that?"

"Never. He darns his own socks."

"It's worthy of Göring."

"Not his style." The Brigadeführer draws on his cigarette. "Göring would make better use of all this space, you can be sure of that. An orchestra in every room, Greek statues doing what Greeks do best, and unapologetic art on every wall. Have you seen his new table?"

"Oh, yes. The one with the cocks holding up the top? Women's breasts for testicles?"

The Brigadeführer laughs silently, attested by ribbons of smoke from his nostrils. "Twenty thousand marks, they say. Twenty thousand to have it carved."

"The Führer will have a fit if he sees the bill."

"After what he spends on entertainment?" The Brigadeführer holds his cigarette at arm's length and flicks the ash. "I hear stories of what goes on up at Berchtesgaden."

"You mean the blue movies they shoot right there?"

"And other things…really filthy stuff."

"Quite a heavy guard around here," Karl says after a moment, crossing his legs on the floor. "You'd think the Grail was already here."

His companion takes another long draw. "Is Otto Rahn still looking for it in that tangle at Montségur?"

"For a fact. In the Grotto of Sabarthez to be precise. But it's *Standartenführer* Rahn now—they finally forgave him for publishing *Crusade Against the Grail* after his first expedition."

Again smoke plumes out the Brigadeführer's nostrils. "If he does find it, the Führer will never permit it to be brought here first. Mengele will get it, if the biological cells are intact. After the cells are safely removed, then the Grail will come to Wewelsburg."

Karl draws his legs under himself. "Should we be talking about this?"

"Why not? We're in the castle, aren't we? Our oaths aren't binding here; Wewelsburg is being built for contemplation of such mysteries."

Karl gets up and dusts the back of his thigh.

"Yes, Mengele will get it first, if the Thule cells are there. After he successfully extracts them, no doubt Himmler will get his chalice."

The Brigadeführer flicks his cigarette out the window. "What do you think Mengele's chances of restoring them are?"

"I haven't the faintest idea. None of it makes sense to me. You take parts of two cells and put them together. It works with carrots and frogs. That's all I know. I don't suppose Mengele himself has much of an idea what to expect. I believe what I swore to uphold—that the Aryan race will be restored to supremacy."

"You needn't sound so patriotic, Karl. I'm not testing you. We have a right to talk about such things. Even the Führer talks about them. Hasn't he said creation isn't finished yet and that we're in metamorphosis? I heard him myself describe the forthcoming new species as infinitely greater than ourselves—"

"I think I hear the ladies."

The women return and the banter resumes—they have missed the unicorn, they are told—and then the four of them are petting and undressing. The Brigadeführer mounts his conquest on one of the rolled tapestries; Karl spreads his tunic on the wood floor and inserts himself into Magda.

To the voyeur at the foot of a doorway in the north tower there is nothing erotic about it. Once again Krantz is overwhelmed by a sense of dislocation, something utterly irrational. How can you feel erotic when you have just learned that you are sitting in a medieval castle you helped build to house the magic weapons of a civilization returning from extinction?

8

"Push," the midwife says.
Pardon me while I scream.
"She's tiring," Father Ledochowski whispers from outside the circle of lamplight.

On the other side of the bed Aunt Zofia's puckered lips seem to be chewing. "Typical first labor," she coos.

First labor? Oh, no. Dear God, no. Last labor! Twice-widowed, once-married Lutka is not going to do this again. Consider it a sacred oath. I shall find me a walnut and hold it between my knees forever.

"Don't stop!" says the midwife.
She stops.
It's my baby, and I'll have it when I'm ready, thank you…I'm ready.
"This time," Aunt Zofia says. "Breathe deep, build your strength."
Lutka takes deep, exhausted breaths.

She could have been in a cold, Berlin hospital now, surrounded by Nazi doctors.

"Pss-t, Doctor, this woman is a Slav."
"What! A Slav?"
"Yes. Right here below the navel. It says Slav. See?"
"Call Hitler, nurse."

"Oh," pleads Lutka, "don't call Hitler. The father is Aryan. Half a good-little-German is better than none."

"Even half a Slav is unacceptable."

"But I'm a famous Slav. Helen of Troy on stage. And I invented the famous wise old Polish saying: It is easier to become a widow than a wife."

"What does that mean?"

"Well, we're not really married, but back in my hometown I'm considered his widow—"

"Call Hitler, nurse."

"Push," says the midwife.

Instinct challenges pain a final time, and the baby's head emerges.

Lutka, in her own bed in Niski Kosciol, the bed she lost her virginity on, appropriately gives birth to her first child from a joining with that first lover. Nothing between those two events matters now. The link is forged in the image of a human being, and it is Zofia who whispers in delight: "It's a girl. Now you don't have to name it after Henryk."

Halfway across Europe the rebirth of Schloss Wewelsburg is underway, and the father of a baby girl in Niski Kosciol has less than paternal feelings at the moment. For as he passes alone from the north tower upper chamber, where a Round Table sits surrounded by twelve chairs bearing silver nameplates of SS elite, into the bedroom of thousand year old Emperor Heinrich I—reincarnated now as Heinrich Himmler, Reichsführer-SS—his gaze is arrested by a newly placed object on the desk. And as he continues to stare at it, he remembers:

Mehring Damm 26...a cold, malodorous draft...obscene phantoms emanating from the vagina of a nude peasant...dead voices...quaking fear, dense as ice...himself opening the door...the whole scene vanishing.

He wanted to believe it was an illusion then, that when Helmut Dürer hypnotized him it was somehow suggested. Dürer had indeed suggested something. He had given him the illusion that when he opened the door, the room would be empty, when it wasn't! And through all those years Krantz has caught flashes of what could not be suppressed, the feeling of evil, the sense of dislocation.

Now that he sees the object on the desk he believes for a certainty that Mehring Damm 26 really happened and that everything visible through the keyhole was actually there when he opened the door—the faces, the table, the object. Because he has seen the thing on the desk before. That night. In Mehring Damm. And the suppressed memory of it now links up with the reality on the desk: Himmler's replica of the *Spear of Longinus*.

EAGLE'S EYRIE

1
1938

You don't need a messenger to the next door neighbor's house if you're going to knock down the wall anyway. That's what Mika thinks when he hears that Franz von Papen, Reich Minister to Austria, has been recalled.

"*Anschluss*," he says to himself, sitting in his Berlin basement room. Annexation.

Of course, it isn't that simple. Austrian Chancellor Schuschnigg will offer nearly any appeasement in order to keep German jackboots off the Heldenplatz. So Mika isn't surprised when fellow Guard member Magnus comes to him with the rumor.

Magnus the ear. Gimpy. Slender as Sneltz was. A marvel of infiltrative ability. Magnus the magnificent. One of the roller bearings that keep the Temple Guard going.

The rumor is from Vienna. Coffeehouses there are buzzing with gossip about a secret meeting between Hitler and Schuschnigg. There, above the border town of Berchtesgaden, in Hitler's Obersalzberg mountain lair, the Berghof, the Führer reportedly browbeat gentle Schuschnigg to his metaphorical knees. Shaken by threats and melodramatic tactics, Schuschnigg finally signed an "agreement" that placed Austrian Nazis in charge of everything but virginity (though that too, in a sense). The police, the defense and the interior ministry will all be headed by National Socialists. The Nazi assassins who shot the previous chancellor (Dollfus) in the throat are to be freed from prison.

The agreement has not yet been announced—except in the coffeehouses of Vienna, as witnessed by the flood of Jews trying to emigrate. Schilling notes are leaving Austria so fast that her securities take a dive in London and Switzerland.

"*Anschluss,*" Mika repeats to himself.

At the border, the 2nd Panzer Division of Germany executes maneuvers. And then Hitler's voice is hurled across Austria by radio from the Kroll Opera House, where the Reichstag has temporary headquarters. "*Sieg heil!*" responds the muddy trickle of Brownshirts on Vienna's streets, and a swastika is raised over the town hall in Graz.

Four days later Schuschnigg broadcasts his own impassioned speech.

"*Rot-Weiss-Rot! Bis in den Todd!*" (Red-white-Red until death!) roar Austrian patriots.

"I'm going to Vienna," Mika tells Klaus, the baker under whose shop he lives. "The annexation is coming, and I want to be in Vienna when Hitler arrives."

Klaus looks at him through muzzy old eyes. "No Jew will be safe in Vienna," he says, breath shrieking through gaps in his teeth.

"I should stay in Berlin maybe, where Jews are coddled?"

"At least you know where to hide in Berlin."

Klaus has learned to move slowly and not to gesture, so as to minimize the aura of flour that puffs out of his pores and makes him look ghostly. His first wife left him for being a ghost.

"Klaus, you have absolutely no need for the living," she said.

But he has his causes. He took in Mika, didn't he? And allowed him to turn the cellar into an archive of anti-Nazism.

When he talks, Klaus leans slightly toward the listener. Mika imitates this, the two of them like a pair of yellowed ivory tusks bowed together. Mika is grateful to God for letting him find a companion along the way to wherever he is going.

Once, a long time ago, he imagined he was going to the Promised Land. Not an extravagant piece of real estate, mind you, just some place safe for he and Katya. But now he stands like David before an immense Goliath, looking for an opening, hoping that the opportunity will arise to do some crushing thing, if only he can keep abreast of the occult motives behind the Reich.

"How do you know Hitler will go to Vienna?" Klaus poses, sprinkling water with a baptismal motion on a lump of dough.

"I know."

"The files?"

"The files."

To Klaus, the files in the cellar have acquired comprehensiveness beyond their parts. Want to know if Hitler farts? Ask Mika and he will show you a page of anecdotes about Hitler's uncontrolled stomach problems and flatulence. Or you can read the fact that the Führer hates Christmas decorations, or has nightmares, or about his water phobia, or his vegetarianism.

Any of these things could be learned by chance, but Mika has thought about them, interpreted them. Take the vegetarianism. Mika will tell you it could be just fear of cancer, or the repugnance for eating dead flesh Hitler often cites, or because vegetarianism is one of Wagner's themes, or as a consequence of Geli Raubal's death, or—he will speculate reluctantly—part of the Cathar doctrine of purification.

The files. And Mika. Oracular stuff.

"So what do I do with your files if you don't come back?" asks Klaus, grasping one end of the dough roll and slamming it like a gavel.

"Try to understand them."

"And what good will that do?"

"I don't know."

"You've spent your life collecting them, and you don't know? You've lived for nothing, Mika, you know that? Why don't you let me teach you to bake bread?"

"Guard them with your life, Klaus," Mika says solemnly about the files.

"With my life," Klaus promises, wondering how effective throwing pastries at the Gestapo would be.

Mika packs a small satchel for his journey.

The British, French and Italians are worried about Austria, that much is clear from newspaper reports of diplomatic activity and propaganda speeches. Hitler dispatches Ribbentrop to meet with Mussolini. Ambassadors flick back and forth between capitols like sparks igniting fuses. The shortest fuse is Berlin.

When word comes that Schuschnigg has called for a national plebiscite on the question of a free and independent Austria, Mika leaves the apartment. The new fuse is four days long. At the end of that time Austrians will vote. Hitler has to stamp out the fuse before their voices explode.

Carrying forged papers supplied through the underground, Mika takes the night express across the border of Salzberg and from there another train to Vienna.

Underground.

The name annoys him. When he first followed Hitler to Berlin the Temple Guard still maintained an offense. Information gathering, fund collecting, bribery, extortion, propaganda—the same weapons they used in Munich were still viable then. But now the business is defensive—buying releases from prison and passports for emigration right off the thriving street. Ironically, the once poor Temple Guard has all the subscribers it needs now. "Your money or your life," has become a clear choice.

But if money is no object, time is running out. Three hours behind Mika, German police close the border and all trains stop running.

He is in Vienna by then and overwhelmed by echoes of his past. For just a moment standing on the train platform a faint whiff of cabbage broth drifts to his nostrils and it is Friday again. *Friday, Friday—I must not be late!* Katya will be hurt if he is late. She has timed the bread so that it will be warm and everything just right when he walks through the doorway at 5 o'clock as promised.

But he is twenty-five years too late.

He begins walking aimlessly because the few people on the street this early are staring at him as if his memories are shouting out loud. For the moment he does not want to silence them. Let the politics fade while he listens to Viennese waltzes synchronized to a flood of images: the night they strolled home from Demel's Cafe; climbing slopes in the woods; an afternoon at the Spanish Riding School. It all comes back, burning behind his eyes and then in his chest, leaving him quite breathless apart from the pace of walking.

But at last he comes to the memory of that final day and his heart seems to stop. And suddenly he realizes that he has been expecting this moment, because he has postponed it for years. Coming back to Vienna had to trigger it. He is standing still now, his breathing charged, ready to face it. Ready to remember the horror one last time of that boiling pot. Ready to sob his heart out right there in the street with Vienna, the City of Music, for a witness.

Except that it isn't happening.

He remembers the stroll and the woods and the Spanish Riding School, but not the kitchen. The kitchen is a still life painting in his mind, done in gray, the cupboards closed, the pot refusing to boil. He feels cold and settled all at once. And he cannot remember the names of her murderers. Just that they were hanged.

Taking a deep shuddering breath, he begins to walk again. How simple life is. You think it's over, and time passes, and here you are.

He wonders if Katya hasn't reached out to him to fulfill his mandate, because coming back to Vienna for that too was inescapable. If Hitler—if Satan—ruled Berlin, the first thing he would do would be to conquer Austria, and then he would come in person to Vienna, and then he would go to the Hapsburg Treasure House in the dead of night and claim the Spear of Longinus away from the blood of the Grail family. All the emperors from Charlemagne to the last Hapsburg have descended from this bloodline according to the history of the Odilienberg. In Hitler's twisted thinking, following the tradition will sanctify his reign.

And Mika must know, must confirm the insanity that justifies the evil and the hate. Because if he can't stop this, someone else can. But how can they be persuaded to stop it, if they don't know why?

Just ahead in the dawn he sees that the inner city is blocked off. A police cordon has been thrown around it to keep the Nazis from demonstrating. It won't stop them, of course. Half the police are Nazis. But it stops Mika from reaching the address Magnus gave him for safe haven. An apartment not far from the chancellery near Ballhausplatz. Someone named Gabriel is waiting for him.

As night lifts, truck columns of "Fatherland Front" patriots move in opposition to Hitler through the streets. From windows and doorways handkerchiefs wave. *"Osterreich!"* is shouted bravely. *"Osterreich!"* Mika shouts back, as if this is still his Austria, his Vienna.

But even the street names are different. So many cars and scarcely a horse in sight. How odd of Vienna to have abandoned her coachmen and her graces. She has become a tawdry whore dancing to her own waltzes played from an array of radios block by block and interspersed with patriotic marches. Overhead a plane circles, releasing clouds of leaflets urging a *"Ja!"* vote on Sunday's plebiscite for a free Austria.

Skirting the cordon as best he can for almost an hour, Mika drifts along residential streets until—quite by accident—he recognizes Katya's old neighborhood. How many times has he passed this green lamppost and the house with the flower boxes half a dozen doors down? It hasn't changed—wood-framed, squat, two narrow stories, lead-camed glass in the door—but her parents must be dead now. His knock is answered by a stout, albino woman who scrutinizes him expressionlessly.

"I'm looking for the Popovs. My name is Mika Lott, and I married their daughter…Katerina."

The woman's porcine face takes on a vague, unreadable twist as she steps back through the foyer. "Ilya is dead," she answers softly. "Vera is inside."

The old woman sits in a faded chair, wrapped in quilts, her pinched face tilted into her frail palm as if caught in the act of falling. What little hair she has stands out in patches and her eyes are drowning in whirlpools of flesh.

Hat in hand, Mika bows pointlessly. "Frau Popov?"

The response is slow, her eyes flicking wide a few seconds late as her head lifts. "Mika?"

"Twenty-five years," he says for no reason.

Now the tears, slow trickles down her cheeks.

"You look wonderful, Frau Popov."

"Mika…Mika Lott. Katerina's choice."

He sets his hat aside and takes her hand. "How have you been?"

"A long time dying."

"We're all a long time dying."

"Did you talk to Ilya?"

He licks his lips, but then she apologizes, telling him Ilya is dead and that sometimes she forgets.

"Today I forgot that Vienna is a quarter of a century older than the last time I was here," Mika says. "Have you had any trouble with this German thing—I mean personal trouble?"

There is a disconcerting pause. "Oh, oh…they hanged those men, didn't they?"

"What men?"

"Yes, they hanged them. I remember."

Betz and Hein, she means. Mika remembers the names now. Katerina's killers. He purses his lips at the mantel clock. The same clock. Still broken. Little wonder Vera Popov gets lost in time.

"I've come to Vienna at a bad moment, it seems, Frau Popov. The police have blockaded the city, and there's no place for me to go. I was wondering if I might stay here a day or two. Your sofa would be fine, if that's possible. If not, I understand perfectly. Frankly it's not safe on the streets for a Jew at night."

"Stay? Yes, Katerina's husband can stay. Marta?" The stout woman steps forward instantly from the arch. "Marta, Herr Lott is going to stay with us. Set another plate for dinner, will you? Put him across from Ilya."

For the rest of the day Mika listens to the radio with Marta and chats at lucid intervals with Vera. The Plebiscite is canceled, and shortly after noon an announcer breaks into the music with a call for all unmarried reservists of the 1915 class to report for duty.

Trucks again rumble through the streets toward the border while 100,000 Austrian Nazis begin to gather at the chancellery on Ballhausplatz. Sometime early in the evening, Schuschnigg comes on the radio and in a choked voice announces that the government is stepping aside after recalling its troops from the frontier.

Marta cries, Vera reminisces about a cat, Mika waits.

Early the next morning—but not too early (yawn)—Wehrmacht troops begin their casual invasion of Austria. The only delays down the main highway are caused by welcoming crowds and mechanical failures within the 2nd Panzer Division, which refuels at gas stations along the way. A light snow lends a confetti atmosphere to the pilgrimage-like caravan as it winds through the Führer's past: Braunau, his birthplace and the birthplace of mediums; Lambach Abbey where he went to school at age ten; Hitler's boyhood home of Linz.

Mika sits near the object shrine in Vienna to which he is convinced the Führer of the third Germany is coming and wonders how many in the oncoming invasion understand the personal significance of each station in that pilgrimage. Who but he has an archives in Berlin devoted to that single creature and his demonic retainers?

Creature.

The word is precise. Goebbels himself said as much. That he would not want to swear Hitler is human, that the Führer gives him chills at times. Goebbels has spoken this more than once to men of conscience. Mika extracted it with candor, with sleight-of-words, with bribery. All in the files.

And Lambach Abbey.

Who will understand the radio reports of Hitler's solemn visit there? Will reporters note the monastery's coat of arms carved on the stone arch at the gate and its primary feature, a gamma cross— the swastika? Those who enter will find that same gamma cross carved everywhere. And if they inquire diligently, as Mika has, they may learn that Father Theodoric Hagen, a Benedictine with a scholar's interest in Cathar heresy and astrology, returned to Lambach Abbey in 1868 after a twelve year trip to the Near East and immediately had that swastika carved all over Lambach.

Ah, the astute observer will say, the Führer went to school here at age ten and never forgot his swastikas! But who will fathom the universality of that sign and its German (hooked left!) distortion? Who will see beyond its solar wheel origins to an occult continuity through the Druids of Thule's magic shores? Or more recent connections.

Tibet, for instance.

Good old Karl Haushofer, clairvoyant ex-general of World War I, renowned professor of geopolitics at the University of Munich, mentor of Rudolf Hess, initiator of Adolf Hitler into the Secret Doctrine during Hitler's imprisonment at Landsberg Fortress, has a passion for Tibet. Who, besides Mika, has checked Haushofer's leaves of absence from the University, or carefully collected the minor newspaper notices telling of his annual expeditions to Tibet since 1925 with other members of the Vril Society—the Vril, founded by Haushofer himself as an elite branch of the Thule?

And if you didn't notice the appearance of a Tibetan colony in Berlin (and Munich and Nuremberg, according to Temple Guard reports), you wouldn't make a connection. But the Tibetan contingents continue to grow annually. Greening, so to speak. Green is what they call themselves. The Society of Green Men.

Seven members of the Japanese Green Dragon Society also live in the Berlin colony. One of the Tibetans is called "the man with the green gloves." He is a monk who three times startled the press before Hitler became Chancellor by predicting the correct number of National Socialist votes in the Reichstag. He is also said to be "the keeper of the keys to the Kingdom of Agarthi." Agarthi is the left hand way of the cave adepts of Tibet whose powers came from Thule. The left hand are Lucifer's allies. Agarthi is also called The Verdant Society. The swastika is their sign, too, said to be the remnant of the green gem from heaven.

A green emerald, Mika speculates. Like the one that fell from Lucifer's brow when he was cast down. The one the Holy Grail is supposed to have been cut from. In the 20's, Hitler was often seen with "the keeper of the keys to the Kingdom of Agarthi."

But who will connect Lambach Abbey's swastikas?

Mika's files. It is all in Mika's files. Just one example of the universality of Thule and the swastika. And if an observer knew of Tibet, what about China, or Egypt, or India? What about South America? Has anyone else saved the news item that reported an uprising of Cuna Indians against Panamanian militia in 1925? They founded a republic: the Independent Republic of Thule. Its flag is orange with a red border, and in its center is a swastika. Mika's files.

And there is something else about Lambach Abbey the observer of its swastikas will not know. Something that happened when Hitler was there as a boy of ten.

A Cistercian monk named Adolf Joseph Lanz came for several weeks of research. Mika has never been able to discover what he researched. Neither the prior nor the librarian could or would tell him. But whatever it was, it was important, because it was connected somehow with Father Hagen's abrupt introduction of the gamma cross thirty years earlier.

Connected with Hitler, too. Because Hitler sought Lanz out again years later. Only not as a monk.

Shortly after the time at Lambach, Adolf Lanz was defrocked, or gave up his frock, and went to Vienna where he founded a new Templar order in 1900. He then became Lanz von Liebenfels (to keep others from plotting his horoscope, Mika believes) and founded the notorious *Ostara*, whose issues were avidly read by Hitler and Dietrich Eckardt. How well Mika remembers those anti-Semitic tracts with their Aryan propaganda about Thule on the White Isle of Hyperborea, and of Lanz's sign, the swastika.

Lanz was a member of Guido von List's blood lodge then, the sect Mika helped uncover in the Vienna press. And List was one of Lanz's Templars. Before his death in 1919, List endorsed the rune—the SS double lightning strike—as a forthcoming symbol of a pure Reich. That Reich would begin in 1932, he said, and thereafter vanquish Jewry and democracy. One year off.

"What are we going to do, Herr Lott?" Marta whispers anxiously when both evening and the Germans are approaching the city.

"Stay indoors and sit tight, Marta. Listen to the radio."

"Aren't you staying?"

"I may be back. If I can, I'll come back."

Tanks from the advance guard do not reach Vienna until midnight, but even at that late hour boisterous crowds are on hand to greet them. The atmosphere of victory bestows a temporary sanctuary Mika takes advantage of to reach Ballhausplatz. Moving freely along the Ringstrasse among the celebrants, he cannot hear himself, though his lips are moving in a vain prayer. Divine lightning, it seems, is in short supply. Five minutes later he has reached the contact named Gabriel, whose apartment overlooks the plaza.

"I tried to get here yesterday morning, but they had checkpoints set up," Mika tells him.

"You shouldn't have come at all," says the young spindle of a man. "It's over for Vienna."

"Maybe for Vienna, but it won't stop in Austria. We have to think of ourselves as citizens of the world now."

"Yes, I've heard of you Berliners. Well, as the Jew who would save the world, then, you couldn't have picked a worse time to come. There's a rumor that Gestapo Chief Heydrich is expected to land at Aspern any moment. The local Nazi scum opened an office for him on Morzinplatz."

"Heydrich isn't new to me," Mika replies. "I was beginning to miss him."

"You may find him more of a beast here than in Berlin. Does Hitler hate any Jews more than Vienna's Jews?"

Gabriel peers out the window. This Lott's appearance in Vienna just when everyone fears for their lives is a pain in the ass, he is thinking. Aloud he tries to keep it all business.

"The Gestapo has been active here for months," he says. "The same people who have been telling us the Germans were coming say the local Nazis are talking about another Dachau here in Austria. At Mauthausen."

Suddenly drawing back from the window, Gabriel tracks an SS figure in the street below with a rapier finger for Mika's benefit.

"You see that? He's been coming back to check on his men for three days. A German colonel in uniform, bold as you please. And there are others in uniforms. They showed up fully armed, taking positions outside the Treasure house of the Hofburg."

"It's Sievers," Mika says grimly to his host's astonishment.

"You know him?"

"Oh, I've never had the pleasure of his company in a beer garden, but it's Wolfram von Sievers, no doubt about it. He's head of the Ahnenerbe, Himmler's occult bureau."

"Impressive, Lott. They say you know more about the fucking Nazis than the Nazis. So what the hell is this Colonel Sievers doing guarding the Treasure House? They almost shot it out with the police cordon yesterday."

"Hitler is afraid the same thing will happen that happened to Napoleon when he conquered Austria."

Gabriel touches his scarf. "You're going to lose me again, Lott. Please don't say anything crazy again."

"The Spear was smuggled out before Napoleon could claim it."

"The spear?"

"The Holy Lance there in the Treasure House."

"Just what we need, an imitation Napoleon who comes in behind tanks and suffers paranoia over a spear." Gabriel moves closer to the window to get a better look at the colonel in the street. "This Sievers scared the shit out of some museum officials. They defected and turned the keys over to him before the Wehrmacht even crossed the border."

"Is there any place where I can watch the entrance to the Treasure House at night?"

Gabriel shrugs. "The Heldenplatz."

"All out in the open?"

"The Volksgarten beside it has trees, the plaza itself has statues, but—"

Mika recalls statues of rearing horsemen on pedestals. Massive. "Statues will do. Can you get me a pair of field glasses?"

Smiling emptily at this eccentric from Berlin, Gabriel reaches behind a shelf of baking tins and withdraws binoculars with worn grips. "German made," he says. "Very powerful."

"Good. I'd like to go to the Heldenplatz."

Dismay withers Gabriel's thin features. "Right now? God himself wouldn't go out there tonight, Lott!"

"I did."

"That was an hour ago. It's worse now. They're organizing. They'll come looking for us soon enough."

"It won't get safer. I'll go alone."

"Heard you were hard-headed." Gabriel flings on jacket and cap.

"It really isn't necessary for you to come."

"You do know what you're doing, Lott? I mean this *is* important?"

"It is."

"Like I said, they say you know more about the Nazis than the Nazis."

Magnus must have said that. It angers Mika. What he doesn't need is a reputation as the Reich's enemy. Call him hard-headed, but don't hang medals on him for everyone to see!

The smell of diesel fuel and the clank of panzers now poison the air of Vienna. And as if the jewel of the Danube isn't bright enough, torches have been lit. Up Graben along the darker stretches of the Kohlmarkt they flicker off the gaping, toothless glee of a mob.

Gabriel and Mika do their best to look elated despite feeling like fatted calves. Around the Hofburg they go and onto the crowded Heldenplatz where globular lights brighten the faces of the Austrians but seem to be absorbed by the Wehrmacht's sheenless steel and drab silhouettes. German troops have spread like a massive stain over the plaza.

"Close enough?" Gabriel pleads beneath a line of chestnut trees.

Mika buries his chin. "A little closer…that statue at the other end."

"It's Prince Eugene on a horse. Just like any other fucking prince and horse in Europe."

"How high is it?"

"In the name of God, Lott, is that all you've come for? I've got books that tell you that. Books with pictures taken in daylight—"

"Can I climb the pedestal?"

"If you want to get shot."

"I don't mean now."

Gabriel leans stiffly against one of the chestnut trees and blinks uncomprehendingly into Mika's sad, coffee-cup eyes. "Lott," he says patiently, "if Hitler comes anywhere near that statue, a dozen SS and Gestapo will crawl all over it with magnifying glasses. If you're thinking of shooting him, forget it."

"Unfortunately I'm not a good shot. But I could probably aim a pair of German field glasses at the Treasure House steps. And that's where Hitler is going to be."

Gabriel straightens. "All right. I don't know exactly what you're doing or why you're doing it, and I don't know if you can climb that pedestal or not. You're not a young kid or a pigeon—a squirrel, I'm not so sure. But if you have to see, let's go. Only, for God's sake, be discreet!"

They could be Abraham and Isaac, but they stroll through the Wehrmacht ranks like Fatherland patriots and somehow make it to the statue of Prince Eugene, where Mika actually tries a few handholds on the coat of arms at the rear of the pedestal before a contingent of local storm troopers bully up to their elbows.

"Skinny bastard, Gabriel!" one jeers with recognition. "Where are your pamphlets now?"

"This one must be a Jew swine, too!"

And just like that they are taken captive.

Up Lowelstrasse they are dragged to a National Socialist office and herded into a back room where a dozen other Jews stand anxious and silent. Outside, the city of music resounds with "Today we have Germany, tomorrow the world!" to the accompaniment of clanking panzers.

"You are incredibly stupid, Lott," Gabriel murmurs darkly. "I can't imagine how you survived in Berlin."

"Yes, yes, you would've been safe in your apartment forever."

"What do you think they're going to do with us?"

"I don't know. I doubt if they know. But this is very much like Munich fifteen years ago."

"What did they do then?"

"Nothing. They were defeated."

"Well, they aren't going to be defeated this time. Shit. I can't believe how much joy you've brought into my life."

"How much joy do you think you had left, Gabriel?"

Mika settles down in his coat against the wall as he did with Esther Masterofrancesco long ago in the cellars of the Bürgerbräu in Munich. Can he hope for a second miracle rescue like the one back then? They were on the winning side that night. No longer. This Gabriel is so typical of what's wrong with the Temple Guard. And yet he took the risk of going out in the madness on the plaza. He reminds Mika of Wiesel—all negative talk but capable of action. Heroic, martyred Wiesel.

At dawn a fat Sturmabteilungleiter with an incandescent face comes in to announce cheerily: "We've brought you some acid!"

The prisoners crowd away but are dragged one by one into the street, some crying, some in sullen silence, all quaking with fear. The acid is in buckets, to which the Sturmabteilungleiter gestures.

"Pity you had to deface our beautiful Vienna with your plebiscite slogans," he says with barely contained glee. "Now you'll have to get rid of it."

A wave of cautious relief softens the prisoners' fear that acid is going to be thrown into their faces.

Mika and Gabriel stay shoulder to shoulder while the huddle is kicked and pushed into small detachments. When their group is singled out, they are escorted along with two old women and a trembling banker with broken glasses across the Ringstrasse to Lichtenfelsgasse beside the old town hall. There the five of them are given brushes—but no gloves—and told to scrub away the political graffiti on the walls and street.

Eyes watering, fingers burning, they commence the thing on hands and knees. A crowd quickly gathers. The acid hissing over the pavement drowns the sounds of spitting and harsh laughter, but in any event Mika keeps his head down until Gabriel grunts in his ear, "Look at the butcher shop."

A dozen Wehrmacht officers mill around impatiently waiting for the door of a small shop to open so that they can stock up on what is unavailable or too expensive in Germany.

"The major," Gabriel says.

And Mika sees, indeed, a German soldier with a major's blue insignia frowning in disgust or irritation at the scene with the Jews. He seems about to get involved, but just at that moment the butcher unlocks his door and the Wehrmacht file in. One by one the sausages in the window come down. Another minute and the first officers begin to trickle out bearing bags and boxes. As they pass the scrub detail the major suddenly advances toward the two Jewish women. Cursing loudly, he kicks their buckets over.

"Get out of here!" he shouts, extending the order to the other three prisoners with a sweeping glance.

Gabriel rubs his wrist; Mika wipes his nose. One of the astonished storm troopers starts to protest, but the major turns on him with the fury of an admonishing parent and the five prisoners scramble to their feet and hurry away.

"You see, not all of Germany has to be defeated," Mika says when they slow to a walk.

Gabriel doesn't answer.

Back at the apartment there is more good news over Gabriel's old Mende radio. Hitler did not arrive at the Treasure House the night before. The "invading" column is long and ceremonious, and the Führer's pilgrimage has resumed from the Hotel Weinzinger in Linz this morning.

If the Austrian eagle were not chained to a Nazi perch, it would see an insect procession wheeling against an overcast sky. The villages teem like anthills. Between them stretches an unbroken queue of febrile humanity and disabled vehicles all along the old Niebelungenstrasse to the capitol. And crawling up the line like some dragged piece of carnal debris comes yesterday's vagabond from Vienna, standing in his open car and saluting stiff-arm to welcoming crowds in every village.

Young peasant girls in dirndl dresses rush forth to throw boughs in front of his vehicle. German flags wave from windows and doors where two days earlier Austrian banners flew. On the outskirts of Vienna, late in the day, genuine hothouse flowers join the tributes. Hitler rises up in the open car, arm outstretched almost constantly now. Church bells are rung by order of Cardinal Innitzer. On the wider Ringstrasse, SS escort vehicles once more flank the

Führer and Wehrmacht in cloche helmets stand arm to shoulder against the cheering throngs. The procession winds its way to the Hotel Imperial where, on a night when the Hapsburgs entertained twenty-five years earlier, Hitler earned a few hellers shoveling snow off the entranceway as Karl and Zita arrived.

At this hour, the 50,000 man Austrian Army is swearing allegiance to Führer and Reich. 125 refuse. Only three of these are not Jews.

The radio carries reports within minutes of events. Hitler sees X, Hitler sees Y. Hitler is speaking from the balcony of the Hotel Imperial. Mika listens while playing solitaire in Gabriel's apartment. Gabriel leans on the windowsill trying to smoke, though his throat is still raw from the acid fumes.

"Two nights in a row," he says. "They've got to go home soon."

Mika drops the king of clubs. "They're standing watch for us. As long as they keep track of Hitler, we can just listen to it on your radio."

"Glad to see you're showing some sense, Lott. They could make us drink the acid next time. It was insane going out there."

Mika whistles airily. "I see you have an orchid catalog," he says to change the subject.

"What happens," Gabriel begins undistracted, "when they stop watching?"

"I go sit on my statue."

"For God's sake, Lott, why?"

"You don't have to understand, and you don't have to come this time. In fact, I insist you do not."

"Fucking ridiculous." Gabriel puffs hard on the cigarette, coughs. "Does Berlin make everyone stupid?"

"Berlin makes you happy if you're a Nazi…depressed if you're a true Berliner…terrified if you're a Jew." The pauses are to play out the deck of cards. "And if you stay terrified long enough, either you become an emotional cripple or you fight back. I'm fighting back."

"By skulking around statues?"

"By trying to understand what's happening."

"Fucking strange." Gabriel shifts his cigarette, having made himself conscious of the raw spots on his fingers. "All you Germans are strange. You believe anything so long as it's strange enough.

One foot in Atlantis, someone said. Every German has one foot in Atlantis. You believe in Wagners and Nietzsches and Horbigers—"

"Horbiger is an Austrian. And I was born in Russia."

"Well, he may be an Austrian, but he had to go to Germany to be regarded as a genius."

Some truth to that, thinks Mika. It is Hitler's endorsement that gained millions of followers for Horbiger's eccentric scientific theories.

"You think we don't know what's going on in Berlin?" Gabriel says with accusation. "We know perfectly well, we just don't pretend to understand it. We're not stupid, Lott, and we're not gullible. You can be sure of that. I've tried to fathom this anti-intellectual stuff, because there must be more to it than the diversions of a bunch of bored mystics, but it always comes up nonsense."

"I don't think Austrians are stupid, Gabriel, and I'm impressed that you know about Horbiger."

The hoary pseudo scientist with his flowing white beard explains the solar system as fire and ice in eternal conflict. According to Horbiger, a super mass of ice originally penetrated the sun and caused an explosion whose fragments now constitute the solar system. All the planets are frozen except Earth, which is in ongoing struggle between fire and ice. The theory is complex and even compelling in its coincidence with glacial ages, Aryan racial myths, destruction of fabulous cultures and implications for biological mutations. Hitler talks of building monuments to Ptolemy, Copernicus and Horbiger. Horbiger has become his champion of a Nordic-National Socialist science in opposition to Judaeo-Christian science.

"And then there's this Bender?" Gabriel scoffs. "Is *he* Austrian? Göring's distinguished pet in the Luftwaffe? And that one says the earth is hollow and we're living inside it. What's more, the sun and the moon and the universe are also inside it. Slight discrepancy there, Lott. I mean all that shit crowded inside, and either we come out of the sun and the sun's not inside, or the sun is inside and we don't come out of it, right? But not according to Hitler. When they ask him to pick and choose, he just says: 'Well, our perceptions don't have to be logical, they may both be right.' Now, what the hell kind of a statement is that? Germans! Fucking strange…"

"'Coherent,'" Mika corrects. "Hitler said 'our views of the universe need not be coherent.' And Bender called it a 'phantom universe' inside the earth. It's not such a crazy idea really, if you look at the details. Not new either. And not German. Bender is an Englishman, I think. I'm going out now," he adds suddenly.

"I hope the pigeons shit on your head instead of on that statue, Lott. I hope they shit so much you think it's snowing."

It is nearly ten o'clock. A handful of people remain in the streets. Not a pigeon in sight. Mika skirts the Heldenplatz. Strapped around his neck and hidden by his coat are the German made field glasses. The Hofburg Palace stretches L-shaped around him, its central facade gracefully indented in a twin tiered bow etched with columns on the higher level. There are lampposts on the Heldenplatz and globular clusters of lights on the palace walls. Some tufts of vegetation lay on the edges of the greens.

Best to stay in the open, he tells himself. Good Reich patriots walk in the light now. Take it slow. Be yourself. Old and stiff. He is stiff from scrubbing pavement as well as from age, stiff from sleeping four hours on Gabriel's sofa. The SS are there on the steps. Sit down at the foot of the pedestal, Mika. Wait till they've forgotten you. You've been waiting all your life. Wait some more.

The cold seeps from the stone through his thin trousers and makes him stiffer. To his right, a single bulb flickers in one of the lamps.

You should have brought a gun, Mika. Let God do the aiming. Close your eyes and fire when Hitler arrives as you know he will. He must. Another three quarters of an hour pass and the Heldenplatz is virtually empty. The SS are bored and looking at something one of them is sharing.

Rising slowly, Mika begins to climb. Like a sloth. Hand. Foot. Hand. Foot. The first ledge juts out. He has to belly over it. But the field glasses beneath his coat catch, and he hangs there like a sea lion on a rock waiting for the next wave. Gathering strength, he rolls up and onto his hip, clearing the glasses. The second ledge is narrower, and he hauls himself up by the metal horse's fetlock. There he nestles beneath the rearing animal's hindquarters, puffing and nursing his shins. Finally, he undoes the top two buttons of his coat and pulls the field glasses out.

The vigil continues until he begins to feel like part of the stone and bronze himself. Gabriel was right. Fucking strange. He was wrong, and this is stupid. Despite the risk, what is there to gain? Is it just to confirm something within himself? But the years have confirmed him in his gathering of esoteric information in esoteric ways, and so he sits—an old man on a statue—waiting for something he both wants and fears to know will happen.

Well after midnight a car arrives before the narrow staircase leading into the Hofburg Treasure House. Three men get out: Wolfram von Sievers, chief of the Occult Bureau better known as the Ahnenerbe, Ernst Kaltenbrunner, freshly anointed SS Führer of Austria, and Major Walter Buch, Nazi legal expert.

But no Hitler.

A grand tour of the city, a dinner and a reception were all declined by Hitler earlier in the day. The Führer then retired to his suite in the Hotel Imperial. To wait, Mika believes.

And now a second car sweeps with assurance around the Heldenplatz. Mika's heart pounds. The Prince of Darkness is coming. Triumphal swoop in the dead of night. Coming to claim power. *God in heaven, do not let this happen!* Klingsor…the Landulf of Capua…Adolf Hitler, meeting in time and space. The Holy Lance lies waiting. Out of the car steps Hitler, followed by his servant Heinrich Himmler.

Nothing is spoken. The others watch like so many ceremonial ravens while Hitler and Himmler march into the shadows of the Treasure House. A few minutes later Himmler returns.

Adolf Hitler remains alone with the Spear of Longinus for over two hours.

2

There is no lucidity in the heights whatever above Niski Kosciol, and the old larchwood church seems to bear the weight of the sky like a wedge under a door. An orange suffusion begins at dawn, racing like St. Elmo's fire along certain damp surfaces—metal eaves, wet slate tiles, a pair of lightning rods. Tucked behind the rectory is a nether glow that seems unrelated to the orange, and in this principality grow beets, potatoes, carrots, cabbages and half a dozen other vegetables.

Here Father Ledochowski performs his only miracles. The soil is responsive. His beets are so fat they have to be dug out, and his cabbages might be tapping an underground stream. He would have made a prosperous farmer had he taken his share of the land when his father died instead of going into the monastery. But that was fifty years ago.

There on his knees between furrows of green beans he is confronted by the shoes.

Above the shoes are wide trousers with turn-ups, a double-breasted coat, striped tie, an intense square face and a trilby hat. The hat comes off to join wash-leather gloves in the man's left hand, and Father Ledochowski notes the incongruity between the brim mark and the tan-line on the forehead.

"My name is Anthony Simmons, Father. I'm a visiting professor at Jagellon University in Cracow, from Great Britain."

Phrase book manner and overstatement. *Great* Britain, and of course Jagellon University is in Cracow. The man is rehearsed.

Father Ledochowski struggles to his feet, but his black biretta comes only to the stranger's shoulders. He gestures with two handfuls of beans to the professor towering over him.

"Ten minutes and they lose their flavor, so I steam them right away. Nothing like it if you steam them right away. You get fussy when you eat green beans and pickled sprats for a steady diet."

The professor smiles without grace. "By all means, I'm in no hurry. I'm only here because I've been trying to track down a certain site of Teutonic origins. They say you know the history of the area better than anyone else."

"Do they? Most of it is mythology, I'm afraid. But come along then. Try some of my sprats."

He leads him around to the front of the rectory where an Austin Ten is parked. Green and dusty. Rain spots on the windscreen.

"Such a fine car. The University must value you highly. Do you have a family, Professor Simmons?"

The professor's eyes flow to the car's ample interior. "My... sister's automobile," he says.

"They came with you from England?" Father Ledochowski nudges the rectory door open.

"My sister lives in Cracow. That's one of the reasons I accepted the temporary post."

"Ah." The priest drops the beans in a basin of water and places a colander over a pot which is already coming to a boil on the stove. "So you're looking for some sort of site, you say?"

"Teutonic."

"…referring to the conquering of Conrad of Masovia by Teutonic knights in the eleventh century?"

The "yes" is briefly hesitant as the stranger takes a chair. His clothes are like retainers holding him back. The smell of pomade rises from his calid brow like a tropic vapor. He reminds Father Ledochowski of some newly ascended champion boxer on tour, displaying his wealth for the first time, overdressed, trying to be obliging but hopelessly outmatched and longing to throw a roundhouse.

The priest uncaps a jar of sprats. "Try these."

The stranger plucks a sample out with thick fingers, chews quickly, swallows hard, smiles his graceless smile. "About the ruins on the coast—"

"The coast? Oh, yes. The tract just north of Torun, you must mean."

"North of Torun?"

"Just north."

Father Ledochowski rinses the beans and transfers them to the colander.

The professor's intensity radiates like hot iron. "Torun is inland," he says. "Isn't it? I said on the coast."

"There is no Teutonic site on the coast that I know of. None at all."

"Maybe I should have said pagan site. I only meant Teutonic in the sense of the origins of Teutonic peoples."

He has finally caught his error. Father Ledochowski knew what he meant, of course. And he has trapped the professor. There was no conquering of Conrad of Masovia by Teutonic knights in the eleventh century. Teutonic knights were not even invited to the north until the thirteenth century. The professor professes lies.

The rheumy grayness of Father Ledochowski's eyes disappears when he takes off his glasses. Now they are pale blue, and they herd the stranger and his question into an empty room where there aren't any answers.

"The pagans were supposed to have migrated from a land that sank into the sea," the man says. "They were giants, or came from giants—"

"Ah, giants beneath the sea," chuckles Father Ledochowski. "I love those myths. Have you ever read the Eddas? Wonderful tales, but wholly—"

"I'm told you're quite a scholar on the subject, Father. And on pagan sites. They say you were censured by the Vatican during World War I. They say you secretly visited a place against the wishes of the Pope."

"*Mea culpa*. I spent a summer running around archaeological digs and ignored my flock. The censure politely referred to only one."

"Which one?"

If the man knew which one, he wouldn't be here. "Biskupin, I think."

It starts to rain, large, gluey drops pelting the roof tiles and windows. The steam from the boiling pot is suddenly clammy, and there is no relief when father Ledochowski opens the door for the stranger to leave a few minutes later. The old priest watches until the man wipes the mist from the windscreen with his sleeve and drives off. Then he retrieves his worn leather Bible.

Professor!

The pomade smelled of Berlin and Gestapo. Should he risk a courier to Rome? The man knew about the censure, which means he has sources close to the Church—better to wait until the Bishop comes through in three days. And how did the stranger know about the pagan shrine on the coast in the first place? Certainly not through the secret manuscript in the Vatican library.

Then Father Ledochowski recalls the young German from long ago—Josef Krantz—who actually went to the moraine. But he is supposed to be dead. Lutka Krantz is raising their daughter, Zosia, in her parents' home. The child must be nearly six. No, if Josef Krantz had revealed the site, the Gestapo would have been interested sooner and known exactly where the glacial moraine is. And the stranger mentioned the giants and the migrations and the sunken cities. Of course, the Nazis would know about those. The Thule is still on the Vatican list.

Stopping in the book of Job the old priest reads aloud: "'Dead things are formed from under the waters and the inhabitants thereof...'"

He stays in the rectory all day and all night. And the next day. Waiting for the Bishop. And he would have stayed the whole three days, even though he is out of cigarettes, except that a boy comes in the evening with a note. The note says that Jasio Skarbek is dying. The boy isn't Catholic but the son of a whore and a hard-drinking farmer below the Skarbek fields. Nevertheless, Father Ledochowski gathers up the viaticum and a phial of oil for Last Rites and starts for the farm.

But he is barely out of the village when he hears the car. No need to turn around. He tries to run, but the scent of pomade is already there. And the Luger.

"Get in," says the professor from Cracow.

He prays throughout the long drive, but God seems remote. Tape covers his eyes, and the only thing he can feel is the wrist shackled to his own. Every priest should welcome such an end, he tells himself. A chance to die for Christ. But in his heart he knows he is too weak for what lies ahead. The magnitude of his pending betrayal chills his soul.

At the end of the drive they rip the tape from his eyes, taking half his brows. Then they lead him into a small farmhouse. The first session lasts six hours and they do no more than burn him with cigarettes and break his thumbs. The second session is unspeakable. And when they threaten to break a glass rod they have inserted in his penis, he babbles the location of the giant moraine where the pagan thing is.

Afterward, lying naked amid his clothes on the floor of a damp cellar, he sees a window. If his strength comes back, he might be able to squeeze through, he thinks.

If he wants to.

Beneath the window is a shelf. On the shelf are boxes and cans. Still faint, he fumbles through his cassock for the viaticum and the oil. The Gestapo agents find him hours later. He has eaten several fistfuls of rat poison from one of the boxes. The last communion and the oil lie beside him. Untouched.

3

Face tight with sleep, Krantz gets up and goes to the window. Where is the smoke coming from? A thick gray rope of it hangs dead above the street. He has heard no sirens. With pent-up alacrity, the alarm clock goes off behind him.

Aside from two minor commissions and a few consulting fees he has done nothing since Wewelsburg. If you call thinking nothing.

Who the hell is he kidding? If anything, he has been busy *not* thinking. Lots of Germans are doing that. You can walk down the Kurfurstendamm and shudder at Berlin's dominant street art on featured walls—Jews being tortured, Jews hanged, Jews beheaded, Jews maimed—appropriately inscribed with deathless prose celebrating sodomy, sadism, coprophagy. The heart quails. "Regrettable turmoil," Fritz Ender describes it. "The excesses of a few."

He and Fritz have remained friends. Meeting Ender is the reason for the alarm. Ten o'clock. New Chancellery. Hitler's monument to the Reich, a place where the world will come on its knees ambassador by ambassador, is still unfolding under architect Albert Speer's magic. Fritz promised him a preview.

Krantz drinks some coffee, dresses and discovers he is out of toothpaste. Toothpaste is essential to the public good because his breath is staler than sour socks in the morning. In desperation he gargles wine and sucks a hard candy. It was *her* toothpaste, he remembers then, hailing a cab. His latest fling's. Ex-fling's. They don't last long these days, but this one has struck a low blow. Getting him to depend on her toothpaste and—presto!—gone.

He leans out the taxi window. More smoke. Acrid and burning. And they are beginning to pass shops with broken panes. The taxi driver has to pick his way through shattered glass.

"What's going on?" Krantz murmurs.

"Damn Jews causing trouble again, but this time they got what they asked for."

Chief among the casualties are the synagogues. Site after site. Smoke and fire lap pockets of fallen beams. Charred transversals, collapsed walls, the air warping hot over gray stones like ugly saunas. Altars of rubble.

And no sirens...

What failed to move him with Rosenberg's articles of the National Reich Church now stabs Krantz to the heart. The Rosenberg articles banned the Bible, superseded the cross with the Swastika and placed the sword and *Mein Kampf* on every altar in Berlin, but now smoldering ghosts all along the Fasanenstrasse begin to haunt his architect's soul.

"Stop!" he shouts to the taxi driver.

Thrusting his fare over the front seat, he hurries back a block to the still heated ruins of a synagogue he has often admired.

What stupidity this is! What ignorant, crass, blasphemous, twisted, arrogant, deviant, unbounded stupidity! The SA bullies have had their last fling. Josef Krantz will protest. Berliners will protest. Good Germans will protest and Hitler will step in.

In indignation he clambers over the ruins in search of a pulse, but the heat penetrates the soles of his shoes, forcing him to an open path between collapsed sections. And that is how he comes face-to-face with sad, tarnished eyes and a brow yoked with wrinkles and silvering hair swept back in unruly shocks.

"Are you the rabbi?" he blurts.

The sad face turns away with a flicker of mistrust.

"No—wait! All Berlin is mourning today. The government won't stand for this sort of thing. Restitution will be made. I'm an architect, and I intend to help. I'll donate my skills."

Mika Lott seems to listen a moment longer than necessary before his eyes widen with recognition. Seventeen years since they met outside Rudnicki's in Niski Kosciol. Not surprising Krantz doesn't remember him. Ironic, however, since the last thing Mika said to him was a warning about where Germany was heading.

"You think this was done without the government's consent?" he asks softly.

"No, no…of course the government didn't do this. I'm not naïve, and I'm not an apologist, but I can assure you the government had nothing to do with this, Rabbi. This was barbarian blood, not Aryan blood."

"You hear that, God?" Mika addresses the sky. "I can't be all bad if I'm mistaken for a rabbi." His eyes come down slowly.

"Hitler loves architecture," Krantz says with conviction. "He's surrounded by architects and people who commission buildings."

"So…this is about architecture."

"I just meant—"

"I know what you meant. Göring has his Karinhall, Bormann his Obersalzberg, Himmler his Wewelsburg…"

The final example comes like a dart, Mika's eyes flicking after it to Krantz's face. Bull's-eye. The architect is looking steadily at him now.

"So, of course, the government loves its architecture," Mika continues. "*Its* architecture. But then all this"—he waves fussily—"this burning and breaking of glass, this is *degenerate* architecture. The synagogues are burned. And so are miserable little shops and homes. Jews are dead, and the looting is still going on, and the crowds just watch quietly, and the police"—he laughs gently—"the police are arresting us 'for our own protection.' No, I think the government only loves *its* architecture. And Hitler was well aware of last night. November ninth. He has a sense of history, you know. November ninth was a day of betrayal for him in 1918—the day the Reichstag announced the Republic. And in 1923, November ninth was to be a vindication. The Beer Hall Putsch, they called it. You know what happened then. So November ninth needed even more vindication last night—"

An acerbic alarm clock is ringing again in Krantz's head. "You know me. Who are you?" Smoke thickens copiously in a pocket to their left. "What do you want?"

The pocket of smoke bursts into flame. "There are very few like you in the Reich."

"I'm not in the Reich."

"You were important to Wewelsburg."

"Wewelsburg was an eccentricity."

Someone on the sidewalk aims a camera at the ruins. Mika turns away. "The Spear of Longinus and the Holy Grail are powerful symbols to the Reich. You created a citadel for them."

"Myths."

"I didn't want to believe it either."

Their eyes meet in a bond neither understands but each wants to trust. Somehow encountering each other in the surreal smoking ruins of this synagogue cannot be chance, and yet Mika cannot have followed Krantz on this morning and Krantz cannot have followed Mika.

"You may be interested to know the Spear is no longer in Austria," Mika informs him. "It was returned by armored train to St. Katherine's in Nuremberg last month. Against Himmler's wishes, of course. Apparently Hitler doesn't want to share its power."

Krantz licks his lips. The shock of the night's carnage and of the bizarre candor cuts through his resistance and persuades him to confidentiality, but he cannot bring himself to speak. Not so the Jew before him who seems quite certain of what he must say.

"The SS are still looking for the Grail." Mika gestures to the smoldering ruins. "Its discovery will inspire more of this, of course, because Himmler will claim it held the blood of the original Aryan race."

"What...if it isn't blood?" Krantz hears himself ask as if he is back at Wewelsburg pondering the conversation of two SS officers in a darkened chamber that holds an empty altar.

A deep, searching look comes back from Mika. "Not blood in the Reich's Holy Grail? What, then?"

"Cells."

"One hundred and fifty meters," says Fritz Ender as they enter the great gallery of the new Chancellery. "Pity the ambassadors who have to walk it on the way to face the Führer."

Krantz lags, touching the marble like a child, unable to disengage from his meeting with the Jew in the ruins.

"You're not paying attention, Josef. I thought you were interested. Some day Hitler will say to you, 'build me another Chancellery like Speer's,' and you'll say 'whose?'"

"Plenty of empty sites around this morning. Is the Reich's business tearing down or building up, Fritz?"

"I'm not here to apologize for ashes, Josef. There are things underway that strain credibility."

"That's exactly what I'm talking about."

Heat lightning flashes in Ender's eyes. "I knew Hitler in 1920," he says, and beads of sweat are actually forming on his brow. "I *knew* him. He was an insignificant little Reichswehr corporal with small dreams. Then he met Eckardt and Rosenberg. They were among the seven who founded National Socialism. Eckardt was a man who…who died praying to that Mecca stone of his, Josef—it was a meteorite. And Haushofer was a clairvoyant who could predict where shells fell in the war. Those were Hitler's teachers. They recognized something in him. He was to be their medium. They were looking for a man like Hitler. The German messiah. By 1923 he was changed. When Eckardt lay dying he told the Party elite that by teaching Hitler to communicate with *Them* he had influenced the world more than any other German."

He pauses, softening to incandescence. "After that, Hitler began to talk of storms of steel and a new evolution. He used to tell us we didn't know anything about him, that something greater than a new religion was coming. I felt then that he was possessed. And ever since, it's been one stunning success after another. He is what he says he is, Josef. A medium…a high priest from subterranean Germany. There isn't any doubt. If you've ever been near him at those moments, you know. You don't hear or even see the Führer speak, you *feel* him. I believe it, Josef. What I meant was straining credibility was just how far toward a new world order things will go." The incandescence is dead now. Ender's stare is dead. His voice is dead. "Josef," he says, "Hitler wants to see you."

4

What are the dreams of a medium? Are they his, in the case of Hitler, the airing of a ragged mind belonging to a terrible little corporal with pernicious hates, who cocks his head and withdraws his chin in a peculiarly sneering way? How awful the repercussions of that snide look. How disturbing the venting of his dreams and nightmares.

At precisely one a.m. the small staff at the Führer's Munich apartment is awakened by his screams. If it were Obersalzberg or Berlin, the episode would trigger practical responses, but here the crisis has never been witnessed first hand. Aides rush in and out of the bedroom, registering horror or alarm. Whispered footnotes shock those who remain outside: "The Führer is paralyzed...the bed is shaking...he's convulsing...his lips are blue."

"There—over there!" hoarse cries erupt through the door. "He's in the corner! He's here for me! Don't let him touch me!"

At last Dr. Morrell is reached in Berlin. Instructions are issued. The terrified garbling ceases. Hearts pounding, the staff sit up the remaining night through, and in the morning the Führer leaves for Berlin seemingly refreshed and eager to go about his mission.

"I follow destiny with the confidence of a sleepwalker," he says.

Late that day Krantz is summoned to the nearly finished Chancellery in Berlin. It is the last time he will see the monument unscathed by bombs, but now he strides slowly along the great gallery guarded by SS as still as statues. Fritz Ender was right. Pity the ambassadors who have to walk it on the way to face the Führer. Pity Josef Krantz.

Escorted into Hitler's unheated office, the door booms shut

and there he is, alone with the legend in the gloom. Expect the unexpected from the Führer, he has been told, but nobody mentioned the uncanny gray-blue eyes, or the fact that they will stand there without speaking for at least a decade, exhaling plumes of frosty air like a couple of stallions. The plumes are as blue as Hitler's eyes in the faintly illuminated room. And they are apt little betrayals of each man's inner state—in the Führer's case, twin streams of stable respiration; in Krantz's own, a flutter of cosmic steam, eddied, ragged. To top it off, the massive desk behind which Hitler stands is inlaid with what looks to be a fallen cross but gradually resolves itself into a half unsheathed sword.

And then the Führer's voice touches the room, seeming to try out its acoustics, slowly at first, telling Krantz how discreet he has been in the past, how successful in the present, how important to the future. The voice picks up speed from surface to surface, listing Krantz's skills like a soccer player's statistics. Now the stream of words flows in excited bursts, now it soars in smooth arcs round the walls. And finally the voice returns to Hitler, becoming harsh, broken. Jagged sentences stab at world realities. And again it builds, but this time there are no ventriloquist tricks. The Führer is the absolute centrality. His words come out like arrows.

There follows a full half hour of histrionics and magnetism. The pale column of a face is suffused with vigor. Slashing hands cleave empires and destinies out of the air with trembling ecstasy. Truths and magic are revealed in bits and pieces, then upgorged like lava—*the cyclical nature of civilization…an ultra-race in remission…Germany the plain, Hitler the gateway to return…reservoirs of power in the form of biological cells buried in the earth…a site that must be excavated at all costs.*

A site for Josef Krantz to excavate. Because he understands ancient structures and archaeology and the Hel peninsula near Niski Kosciol. Because that is where the site is. On the coast of Poland. Beneath a glacial moraine. There he will uncover that reservoir which the survivors of the White Isle of Hyperborea have left. The White Isle.

Josef Krantz will be one of the few who understand the significance of the code name for the invasion of Poland: *Case White.*

Later that evening, while passing through a crowd, an incident happens that greatly disturbs the Führer. A woman admirer grasps him by the arm and says: "My Führer, do not touch black magic. The white is still open to you. If you accept the quick successes, your destiny will be dominated and held to this earth."

That night, spent in Berlin, Dr. Morrell is again summoned to chase away a nightmare.

5

"Did you accept?"

Listening to Fritz Ender in the doorway of his apartment, Krantz has a sinking feeling. Did he really have a choice? The Reich made graduated assumptions about his reliability because he has never protested above a whisper. Now he knows too much to refuse. Fritz understands that. Fritz wants him to have accepted. Doesn't he?

"You accepted," Fritz concludes, closing the door behind him.

"I'm going to Prenzlau when they set up the team. In about a month. Hitler was vague about that. Political unknowns. It's pretty clear, Poland is on the block."

"There will be provocations."

"Whose?"

Fritz drops into a chair. "Stalin has designs on Poland, too. If she fell into our hands, it would amount to protective custody."

"You don't really believe that, Fritz. She's more like a piece of meat suspended between snapping dogs."

"Ah, Josef, I worried less about you when you were politically innocent."

"I'm still politically innocent."

"Good." Himmler's unlikely adjutant says it twice without feeling. "That's your armor. Stay out of political conversations at Prenzlau. Your candor is like a dormant disease. It flares up now and then."

Suddenly the clock and the radiator and the elephantine beat of a Bavarian concert coming from a distant radio are very loud, and Ender shrugs ponderously for no reason at all beneath his uniform. The SS black tunic seems to wear him, as usual. More and more it makes him look convalescent, as if he has lost weight, or energy, a precise and theoretical man drowning in waves of raw reality.

"You know Heydrich disapproves of you," he says.

"I lie awake nights."

Fritz's smooth face seems to thicken with the effort of communicating. "You may not know that the Spear was among the Hapsburg treasures transferred to Nuremberg last month. Himmler is angry that it didn't go to Wewelsburg. Cooperation between his office and the Führer's is at low ebb. He *will* listen to Heydrich."

"Because I'm not a member of the Party?"

"That's a start."

"Hitler said it was of 'no consequence' to me yesterday. I brought it up. I told him I wasn't political and I wasn't hypocritical. I said I had no plans to join the Party. He said what you once said to me, Fritz. That Leni Riefenstahl had said the same thing to him. He said it was of no consequence, that the important thing is that I'm German and want to serve the Fatherland."

Ender seems to drown a little more. "It may soon be impossible to stand outside the Party," he murmurs. "You should prepare for that. Prepare for everything…"

"Someday," Krantz says, "you'll be given the honor of announcing the end of the world."

"You're going to get more than dirt on your hands digging in Poland, Josef."

"Meaning?"

"Meaning you didn't like political prisoners building your castle, and you didn't like being German on 'crystal night,' how in the name of God are you going to function in occupied territory?" Following a thoughtful pause, Ender goes back to murmuring. "You're like me, Josef. You have your microcosm of *things*, and you don't have the wisdom or the foresight or the heart to deal expeditiously with people."

"I won't have to deal with people."

"You didn't have to at Wewelsburg. But it bothered you. You came close to disaster with Heydrich, whether you knew it or not. Himmler was your guardian angel."

"That was different. *I'm* different."

"Yes, now Hitler is your guardian angel."

"He told me what I had to do. If it means some greater good

too far down the road for me to see, that's fine. I'll take his word for it. I'm tougher now. What the hell, I've been asked to head an archaeological expedition, that's all. Why are we arguing about it? You're the one who's been convincing me it's all for the best."

"I believe what I've been trying to do is convince you that it's all *real*," Fritz says carefully, and Krantz senses that the little adjutant is trying to clarify his own thoughts. Outside, the beat of the Bavarian band becomes leaden as Ender continues: "Of course it's for the best. We can't all see it, though…some greater good, like you said. But we have to try. We…have to understand our leaders. They're the ones who can see it, and if we understand their motives, if we… trust their intentions, why, then we can be sure it's all for the best, because…it means such a change in everything, I mean a whole new world order—my God!—everything. You have no idea what's coming, Josef. Really. Total change. Everything. We can understand that, Josef. We have to understand that."

The fascinating vehicle of inner Fritz completely distracts Krantz. A still life is in motion. He peers hard through the barrel of a microscope at the muddle of emerging self—Fritz Ender *in vitro*.

But the flow of truth is cut off with a little cough. The known timbre returns to Ender's voice and the SS penguin reaggregates. He issues an invitation that Krantz barely hears.

Yes, he would like to see more of the Reich's architecture, Krantz gets out tardily. Obersalzberg? No, he has never seen Hitler's Berghof. Or his Eagle's Eyrie—the amazing retreat Bormann has set atop the Kehlstein for the Führer, who calls it "Barbarossa." Tomorrow? Yes. Tomorrow.

They travel to Munich by train and there rent a car for Berchtesgaden near the Austrian border. Ender, it turns out, is one of those enigmas of the open road: a soft, retiring personality who drives like a Valkyrie in a fiery chariot. He aims the car with apparent vagueness toward the middle of the road, allowing it to drift all the way to either shoulder before making corrections. Speed is irrelevant. Motion is motion, and he makes no distinction beyond the abiding faith that if he pushes the brake, the car will stop. Eventually.

"Bormann is an *ant*!" Fritz shouts above the roar. "He's raped Obersalzberg. A berghof here, a hotel for Hitler's visitors there—all at the cost of the loveliest country you've ever seen. He's put a fence around the whole mountain. Two fences! The outer one is fifteen kilometers long. And everything inside is paved. Even the forest paths. Bormann is a blind, bulldozing ant!"

Just out of Munich they sideswipe a horse and cart. Krantz hasn't been this thrilled since the airplane ride in the Junkers to Wewelsburg. Arms outspread, he braces himself at the juncture of door and seat, casting grave looks from the onrushing road to freewheeling Fritz.

The topic of Bormann's rape is much too stimulating, he perceives. He tries to introduce banalities about the weather, his favorite puddings and some hardy winter foliage he would like to identify if only it wasn't blurring by so fast. If only it wasn't blurring by so fast, is repeated. But Ender speeds on as if the matter is entirely out of his control, and Krantz worries that it is.

On the outskirts of Berchtesgaden they reach the foot of the Obersalzberg and take a turn, literally for the worse, up a road more suited to half-tracks. A few farmhouses are visible and a church and, finally, clusters of barracks for construction workers.

"Ant hill!" Ender disdains, gesturing to the plethora of building sites.

It starts to snow. The little overhead wipers on the windscreen slash quadrants in gray mush.

And now, quite oblivious to his passenger's alarm, Fritz begins to describe a history of treachery for the network of roads. Trucks loaded with building materials have gone over precipices, brakes have failed. The eight kilometers-plus route from the Berghof to the nearly two thousand meter high Kehlstein peak where Eagle's Eyrie perches is especially tricky. It cost nearly thirty million Reichsmarks (that Bormann!), so difficult was it to build.

"If you think Himmler was a stern taskmaster at Wewelsburg, you should see Bormann dealing with private contractors," Fritz recounts, "docking pay, suspending ration cards. He actually jailed a couple of them!"

On that indignant note, they veer perilously close to a sheer drop of some sixty meters. Krantz, rising half a head taller, experiences a premonition of his impact into the grandeur of the valley.

"Fritz…"

"Don't worry, Josef. I know these roads. If I do a little circling, it's to avoid the checkpoints. I'll tell the guards at the tunnel you're just here as one of our architects getting background on the Führer's tastes."

But that *is* why they are here, isn't it?

The snow ceases as abruptly as it began. Dull sunlight splashes down the face of the mountain. Fritz points out several well-hidden machine gun nests and talks of the elaborate smoke machine that can actually obscure the crest of the Kehlstein and Eagle's Eyrie from air reconnaissance.

Reconnaissance? What is the Führer expecting? This island in the sky is surely quite useless. What could ever penetrate the Reich here in the Fatherland?

But Fritz Ender goes on about the incredible defenses of the place and of how a Troop Carrier plane practiced snatching a glider off the peak with slow passes and an elastic towline. Modifications made after two lives were lost now insure the ultimate escape plan, should the Führer require it.

Topping the next crest, they are suddenly struck by a burning apparition in the setting sun. They have reached a parking lot blasted out of the rock of the Kehlstein and the glare arises from two massive bronze doors in the face of the peak. SS sentries, their machine pistols at the ready, instantly flank the car.

"Stay put," says Ender.

The little adjutant maneuvers into the back seat with surprising agility as one of the SS leans his weapon against the dashboard and slides behind the wheel. No detectable signal is given, but the bronze doors swing open on a high domed tunnel with two lanes receding into the Kehlstein. Krantz is awed. The surreal magnitude of the thing in such a resistant setting!

"No other cars, Kurt?" asks Ender.

"Just the cook and staff up there," replies the sentry, slowly accelerating into the mountain. "Goebbels sent up a special wine for later."

"Mistress," Ender explains, and Krantz receives an icy appraisal from the SS driver.

The point of the tunnel's extinction broadens into a circular room and another pair of bronze doors, these being merely huge.

Ender regards Krantz keenly as they step from the car, but again his words are vapid, under-colored: "There are poison gas jets the length of the tunnel and in here."

Here? The second set of bronze doors open on a luxurious square room with walls of polished copper, a carpet, phone, mirrors, upholstered furniture and benches. Ender follows Krantz inside where they settle into overstuffed leather chairs as the doors close.

"Do you know where you are?"

Krantz feels the pressure change in his ears. "We're moving."

Ender nods. "It's very quiet for an elevator. The power comes from Berchtesgaden, with a back-up submarine generator in case there is a failure. Albert Hellmuth, the electrician, is the only one who understands it. He tells an amusing story about Hitler confining him to quarters for drinking, then sending for him when the elevator stopped running. He refused to leave his room until the Führer gave him permission personally, and since they were separated by the elevator, a phone line had to be strung up the Kehlstein, which is mined, to Hellmuth's quarters. Hitler gave him permission to come out of his room, Hellmuth got the thing going in an hour, and the next day there was a bottle on his bed. Hitler told his generals that if they followed orders as faithfully as Hellmuth, he could take a vacation."

All this is related without a trace of humor. And as the doors re-open, Ender adds a dreary note. "There are gas masks hidden here and in the Eyrie, in case the poison has to be triggered, though I've never been able to find the compartments."

But Krantz is deaf to the last words as he rises from his leather chair in awe of the biggest fireplace he has ever seen. Circular, glassed-in, bronze-tiled, Roman-pillared, the grate holds what can only be described as a burning tree. This is the Führer's tearoom, with its round table and thirty chairs surrounded by Cararic and Untersberg marble walls and encircling bay windows.

The panorama drops down snow-veined mountains to textured valleys and a river and, on one side, an abrupt rock face that looks molten in the eerie play of sunset. Caught between these final rays and a deep violet twilight, the snowstorm they have just fled seems to hang suspended in a vast ocean of air.

Krantz laughs in boyish astonishment, but when he turns, Fritz is standing in the same spot, the peculiar deadness still in his eyes.

"We can't stay long," the little adjutant says and guides Krantz through the various adjoining rooms, all the while narrating facts about the stone-lined walls inset with panels of pine and elm.

And suddenly they are standing at a descending flight of steps. Slowly, almost surreptitiously, Ender leads him down to a lower chamber where the tearoom's enormous fireplace cannot reach and a deep chill prevails. The mechanical detailing resumes—background of the construction engineer, Fritz Todt—but this time Krantz interrupts to ask why it is so cold. The look Ender gives him is so utterly sterile that when it rises above his head and locks on the wall behind him, Krantz is compelled to turn around.

And there, springing vividly off the surface, are the most unbelievable obscenities he has ever seen or imagined. Fantastic paintings of women in detailed perversions with snakes, horrendous sodomies, mutilations, excremental defilements, torture sadism—Krantz is stupefied. And all the while, Fritz continues explaining in a sucked dry voice how Hitler's workrooms are kept ten degrees colder than normal, that the Führer has decreed eleven degrees Celsius to be his optimum working temperature.

Hitler in the frosted gloom of his new Chancellery bursts upon Krantz's memory, but the voice-over is Ender's: *We have to understand our leaders...if we understand their motives...if we trust their intentions... you have no idea what's coming, Josef....*

They drive back in silence, and the hairpin descent leaves the young architect indifferent this time. Is it possible that the particular dislocation of morality he saw at a séance on Mehring Damm eighteen years ago now guides an empire? What has he gotten himself into?

What did Father Ledochowski say that long-ago winter evening? *"...sexual perversion is the heart of black magic, the evoking of will, the subjugation of nature."*

Maybe they will share a quiet laugh when the mission fails in Niski Kosciol. Because when the momentous, spectacular, mind-boggling non-event non-happens, the whole deck of cards will come tumbling down into non-sense forever and a-non. The Nazis will quietly turn a-non-y-mous.

After all, the economy has improved with wage and price

controls, unemployment is down to zero, *Autobahnen* are springing up everywhere, a factory is making a "people's car"—the *Volkswagen*—for the common man, and even the Ruhr basin has started to clean up its pollution. On the other hand, the everyday German might find out what is on a wall in Eagle's Eyrie. That is why Hitler has a crazy plan to escape by glider. In case of a general revolt. In case of general *revulsion*.

But what if the house of cards does not come tumbling down? Suppose for a moment that this...this superman mutation is real. What kind of nature must it have to ally with those things on the wall?

Moment's up.

Josef Krantz, you are ill. Get out of the car now. Get away from Fritz. Taste a little life. Fuck someone—opposite sex, missionary position. Eat a good meal. Drink a bottle of schnapps. Go to a soccer game. Sit with ten thousand people who are roaring something besides *"Sieg heil!"*

"I'm going to stay over in Munich," he says.

"Where?"

"I don't know. The hotel on Theresienstrasse maybe."

Fritz has been trying to warn him. Only, Fritz hasn't been able to make up his mind on the moral issues either. The thing is, Fritz believes the ultra-race in remission thing is really going to happen. Did not the two officers in Wewelsburg's north tower say that parts of cells would combine? It worked for carrots and frogs, they said. Mengele would restore them. Who the hell is Mengele? Some Nazi quack who will end up with a green carrot that hops, most likely.

Outside the soccer stadium in Munich the next afternoon Krantz is approached by a fraülein. Her brother is playing, she says, but she doesn't understand all the penalties and stoppages, so she probably won't go in. He takes the hint, even though he knows her brother isn't playing, and buys her a ticket, and they sit cozily twenty rows up at mid-field.

The player she identifies as her brother keeps changing numbers. She has selected him by his blond hair, not noticing the other two fair-haired Aryans on the bench. Eventually all three are in the game at once and she gets confused, and Krantz puts his hand inside her brown coat as she sucks her cheek and lets him fondle away. But instead of feeling sexual he feels a little dismayed at his own degeneracy, and suddenly he invites her to dinner, whereupon she bursts out laughing. "What were you doing, feeling my ribs?"

They go to the Osteria Bavaria and drink a quantity of schnapps well beyond a bottle, and some brandy, too. She chatters obsessively about the job she has been promised as some magnate's secretary, her collection of glass animals and of how her real and true brother was once knocked out by Max Schmeling in the fourth round. She used to hate boxing, her brother being pummeled in the head and all that, until someone pointed out to her that it doesn't seem to hurt woodpeckers. "Woodpeckers bang their heads on trees all day," she avers solemnly. So now she doesn't mind her brother getting pummeled in the head and all that.

Inexplicably, the waiter comes to tell Krantz he has a phone call then, and he excuses himself to receive a very agitated Fritz Ender.

"Josef, I've been trying to reach you for hours."

"I went to a soccer game."

"I've alerted half of Munich trying to find you. The hotel said try Carlton's Tearoom, Carlton's suggested the Cafe Heck." Fritz's tone remains tight above the phantom whistle of a bad connection. "You have to return to Berlin right away."

"Why?"

But Fritz's voice is suddenly unintelligible as if he is addressing a third party. "I'll call you back," he says presently. "Stay put."

What the hell does that mean? Krantz replaces the receiver. Fritz is having his strings pulled, that's what it means.

He glances across the restaurant at the fraülein sucking her cheek, her long fingers playing with the rim of a brandy snifter. Returning to the table, he sighs heavily. "They've sent for me from Berlin."

For the first time in their brief encounter her eyes meet his in a steady gaze. "Who, your wife and family?" she says a little wistfully and rises slowly to her feet.

The last thing he sees of her is the brown coat through the window, and then the waiter is at his elbow with another call.

No mystery about who it will be, but this time Fritz's voice has the same airless precision as on the day they visited Eagle's Eyrie:

"I'm instructed to tell you that a private plane will be waiting at four a.m., Herr Krantz. The pilot will fly you to Tempelhof. You must identify yourself to the military dispatcher at the Munich airport." There is a pause. "SS Obergruppenführer *Heydrich* has seen to the details."

Abruptly the line goes dead.

More than a little troubling. Krantz hangs up, pays the bill and walks out into the twilight.

Heydrich has seen to the details.

The train depot isn't far. He could take a night coach to Berlin. Report to Fritz in the morning. Say the phone connection was bad.

Suddenly uneasy, he glances around. There have been times since Wewelsburg when he thought the Gestapo was watching him. Or maybe it was the curious old Jew with the sad eyes who told him to follow his conscience that day in the ruins.

All the way to Berlin the imperfections in the track click double notes: *Sieg heil!...Sieg heil!...Sieg heil!*

At six-thirty the next morning he is sitting in a cafe half a kilometer from Fritz's apartment debating whether to call. The cafe is surprisingly busy. Beginnings and endings are evident. A soldier drapes himself across intervening chairs to render two female students charmed, but the puffy matron two tables away seems left over from the night before. Krantz munches a pastry. *Heydrich has seen to the details* tightens his stomach until the pastry begins to chew like a sponge. Dropping it to the plate, he asks to use the telephone.

"Hello, Fritz?"

"Josef?" comes back in a rush with a note of something Krantz cannot identify—relief? In the background are noises like books falling. And the next words are devoid of spontaneity. "Herr Krantz, you are ordered to report to Reichsführer-SS Himmler's office for further instructions. The plane you missed this morning crashed two hours ago. How fortunate that you weren't on it."

A dull boom comes over the phone.

"Fritz? What's going on?"

"The Gestapo is here," is spoken softly before the phone is cradled.

Krantz dashes wildly from the cafe. Traffic is light and he runs the half kilometer in three, maybe four minutes; but he knows already he will be too late. Which is a healthy thing for him, of course. Because the Gestapo has been and gone by then, along with his odd little friend. Odd, too, that the notion they are—or were—friends only takes root as he charges up the stairs.

Ender's room is methodically upended. The pile in the middle of the beige and madder brown carpet is of functional items; the other is books and papers and slit picture frames. They must have been desperate to find anything they could use. Which means Fritz has been arrested for nothing substantive.

This was because of me! stirs out of Krantz's conscience with a mixture of outrage and fear. *My foot dragging…Fritz was protecting me and I pushed it too far.*

The intimidating elements that were there the night of Mehring Damm are in Heydrich's office now, if not Himmler's himself. He is too important to Hitler to be arrested, but not too important to have an airplane accident. They have him in a maze, and he will run the way they tell him. He will go to Prenzlau and then to Poland. And he will join the Party. Were that he had as much courage as Fritz in the end.

The last thing he notices, leaving the apartment, is the obligatory but undersized swastika stuck in a pencil caddy.

6

Mika has trouble getting into the library. First the frail woman behind the desk moves the yellow NEIN JUDEN sign so that it faces him, and then she gets a timid-looking male to come out of the stacks and discreetly ask him for papers. The man studies the forgeries an inordinate length of time, as if to materialize a stigmatic "J" stamped thereon, and finally hands them back with an uncertain apology. Twice spoken, doubly insincere.

This is what I need for my archives in Klaus' basement, thinks Mika. *A sign. NO ARYANS. Scarlet letter "A's" distributed to all Aryans.*

The timid-looking man retires to his stacks as to a jungle through whose printed leaves he peers nervously. It isn't as thick a jungle as once. Thousands of Jews have been removed from the shelves. NEIN JUDEN. Anthologies have been maimed with razor blades. Bonfires have blazed in the street outside. Spinoza and Einstein suffered first degree burns but still maintain tendrils of wisdom through countless branches in the tree of knowledge. The encyclopedias and reference works—already paper sieves—need further raping. Denuded as the place is, the pruning will never be complete. Half empty shelves are still well endowed with half-Jews, undiscovered Jews, Jewish thought and influence.

Just like the Nazi Party.

Mika has uncovered Heydrich's quarter-Jewishness directly from the evidence. And Hitler—dear God, forgive his Jewish blood! In 1927 Mika himself traveled to the parish of Döllersheim to see the baptismal records of the Führer's father, rumored to be half Jewish. And there it was, Alois Hitler, born illegitimate as Alois Schiklgruber, later to take on a stepfather's surname. His mother was a cook from a family riddled with mental instability who became pregnant while working for a Jewish family named Frankenberger.

Other records showed that Maria Schiklgruber received a paternity allowance from the Frankenbergers. Adolf Hitler's sire, it turns out, was a cross between a Jew and a mentally unstable Austrian.

Three years later Mika heard that Hitler's lawyer, Hans Frank, also checked the records at Döllersheim. Which explains why, following the *anschluss*, the German army evacuated Döllersheim and used it for artillery practice.

Heil, mein Führer Schiklgruber-Frankenberger!

For a time Mika tried to expose the hypocrisy of heritage in Nazi ranks, but his anonymous letters to the local Press were never printed, and the foreign Press was ignored in Germany, of course. Later, he actually sent summaries to Himmler and Otto Strasser. Had he known then that he was only adding to their leverage, he would have suffered pangs of remorse. Because suspicion and spying by the Reich on the Reich was already endemic. Strasser himself once traced down what he imagined was a death threat only to unearth his own garbled memorandum referring to *strasse* (street) deaths due to speeding cars.

It was months before Mika realized he was actually helping them, that they welcomed information and held it against each other for future blackmail. There is a certain balance in this. If Himmler knows of Heydrich's Jewish blood, Heydrich knows that Himmler is protecting a Jewish cattle dealer who married into his family.

No, the Reich is like this library trying to expunge its very roots. They can purge it forever and hypocrisy will still win.

But the subject is cells. This is why Mika has come to the library.

Cells are electric devices.

Cells are containers.

Cells are homes for nuns and monks.

Cells are groups, like Munich's Temple Guard once was.

Cells are small prisons that men build to contain lives.

Cells are small bits of life God uses to build men.

And this last is why Hitler thinks he can play God. Because he has some genetic cells. Raw material. Elixirs of life are nothing new to mad Germans, and he thinks he has a Grail-ful. If they can find it. Some clever interpreter like SS Colonel Otto Rahn has decided that the Grail never held blood at all. That it was cells. And wherever it is, it still holds them.

Hitler talks about mutations—a Superman mutation—and if you know his background, you know he means Aryan demigods returning from Thule. But you can't stuff a demigod in a chalice, can you? Besides, the cells would be dead, all done replicating. But what if they aren't done replicating? What if Hitler bleeds on them or something, reconstituting a new batch? Then you have soup in the chalice. *My cup runneth over...*

In the next half hour Mika hauls fourteen biology texts, an equal number of journals and a handful of loose articles into his corner, while *homo librarius* continues to stalk him through the stacks in a veritable tizzy. Hours more pass before he absorbs enough terms, processes and theories to grasp what he is looking for.

It is rudimentary: all living things grow from the doubling of cells. The Reich, in its pseudo scientific way, might believe that they need only join them under womb-like conditions and let them grow in order to restore the donors. *Or* maybe Hitler's Supermen mutations will be the result of inseminating Aryan women with such cells. *Or*—and this is really strange—induced *parthenogenesis*. Spontaneous doubling. Non-sex. Virgin birth. Some plants, it seems, actually reproduce this way. But human beings...?

Ridiculous! If this is what the bastards are shooting for, you can almost feel relieved.

The trouble is an article in the science journal three months old which describes how a *human* ovum has been caused to cleave by a pinprick. The thing died, but not before it started to grow. Mika has to wonder why somebody wanted to try *that* particular experiment at *this* particular time?

Trouble two: the name Mengele. Dr. Mengele. Mika has heard that name in connection with the Reich. And here in an interview from the *Deutsche Republik*, a Munich weekly, Mengele is quoted as saying it might be possible, just possible, to stimulate animal cells into doubling mitotically to the blastocyst stage where they can be nurtured full term.

One can get lost in a library. A library is a very cold place. Mika wonders what it is like to be Aryan and in fashion. It must be frightening, he decides, if it makes you hide behind shelves to watch old men shuffle by, or stamp cards at a desk as nervously as a stamping horse, or to prick cells with a pin in order to release relatives.

But he doesn't have to be Aryan to be frightened. He has just realized something that chills him to the bone. The Thule Gesellschaft and its elitist Nazi auxiliary, the Vril, believe there are reservoirs of force buried in the earth. Cells, Mika. Cells are buried in the earth. And its *reservoirs*. Plural. As in more than one Holy Grail.

It is a quantum jump for an old gray man. He should have realized it before. At Sabarthez for instance. The grotto is a reservoir. Rahn knew it and searched there rather than the nearby Castle of Montségur.

And in his files Mika has an account from a manuscript circulated among occult groups maintaining that the Holy Grail was found by Barbarossa in the twelfth century and damaged. Why did Rahn keep searching if the Nazis believed the Grail had been found? *Because there are other Grails!* Just the fact that the Grail has been claimed to be in so many places is a tip-off. He should have connected it with reservoirs that day standing in the ruins when Josef Krantz posed the thought that it wasn't blood but biological cells in the mythical cup. And what is the troubled young man to the Reich besides an architect?

The answer is all too clear now. Because Krantz's file, begun seventeen years ago in Poland, has grown steadily ever since Mika trailed Himmler's adjutant to Wewelsburg Castle. He has talked to students and professors at Berlin-Charlottenburg, misrepresented himself over the phone, and used mail-forwarding ruses to trace the architect's movements and leaves of absence. He knows that Krantz worked on a dig near Gdansk, as a student. And when you match that with a plural Grail and the fact that Krantz seems to know what is in them, and with an invasion of Poland imminent, and with a certain coincidence of Hitler's car arriving at the new Chancellery just after Krantz went there last week, you make that quantum jump in what you know...and what you fear.

At six o'clock, Klaus the baker leans against the showcase and stares out the window. He has stood thus for more or less thirty-six years, a fixture to passers-by, gloomy despite the dusting of flour over his apron and his sleeves that makes him look like a stand of birches.

There was a time when Klaus loved many people, and a time

when he loved just his wife, and a time when he loved no one at all. Now he loves Mika Lott. Mika is a good man trying to do a great thing. He will not succeed, of course. Even a great man probably wouldn't succeed. But it is commendable that a good man should try.

For a few days after "crystal night," Klaus worried that he would lose his friend. Some brazen young SA toughs smashed the window and the showcase that night. One of them went upstairs and down looking for cash, while the others painted slogans on his walls. When the thief got to the cellar, Mika went at him with a bread knife and that sent the lot of them back to the streets. But the file cabinets were seen, and Mika was afraid the SA would become suspicious and pass their information on to the Gestapo. He talked about moving and actually began to pack things in boxes. But where could he go? Not to mention that a move in itself is dangerous.

"No one will come for your files, Mika," Klaus insisted. "The little bastard SA just wanted to steal. What would a room full of cabinets and boxes mean to him? And if they did, I would defend them with my life. I would feed them all this pastry they ruined."

"Do you really know what these files are worth?" Mika answered. And to further impress Klaus, he related another of the grim Hitler anecdotes the baker finds so fascinating.

This time they were about the Führer's suicidal paramours. There was Suzi Liptauer who tried to hang herself in a Munich hotel, and Mimi Reiter the same, and Renaté Mueller who succeeded, and Inge Ley who also succeeded, and his niece Geli Raubal, and it wasn't until Eva Braun shot herself in the chest over him that he took her seriously. Central to such despair, Mika said, was Hitler's need to be kicked, defecated on and urinated on by women.

A compromising letter in that vein, which Hitler wrote to Geli in 1929, was stolen by his landlady's son and bought by an odd collector named Rehse. "Rehse," Mika repeated fondly—because Rehse has an archive from floor to ceiling of his room, and because, by revealing himself as a collector, Mika was able to exchange a few items for a number of delicious afternoons spent in Rehse's "cartons."

At any rate, a certain Father Stempfle, who helped edit *Mein Kampf* and was a friend of Rehse's, negotiated to have Hitler underwrite preservation of the collection in exchange for the intimidating letter. And so it ended. Except that very soon after that Father Stempfle was found shot three times through the heart in the forest of Herlaching outside Munich.

Ah, that Mika and his files! "With my life," Klaus promised. "I'll guard them with my life." And Mika delayed fatally.

Because today at five minutes past six, just as Klaus is closing his bakery, the death's head comes calling with its agents to test his promise. And Klaus-lover-of-Mika, foolish Klaus, attempts to do what Mika would have done. That is, he takes up a bread knife.

But these are the trained legions of hatred, and they do not run back out into the streets. They shoot their guns. And the old man—the aged and sunless old man as white as a birch—staggers back, upsetting a barrel of flour. There he falls, gushing life from a dozen wounds. In a little while he is bloodless and whiter still, but the flour that bleached him to his very soul is ironically a spectrum of red.

By then the SS have searched the premises with the utmost efficiency, kicking doors open, zigzagging from wall to wall, even calling Himmler himself. "Hartke wasn't exaggerating," is spoken over the phone, and soon the Reichsführer-SS is seen through the cracked front window disembarking from a staff car.

Thin wire glasses aglitter, Himmler pauses over the form sprawled in the flour long enough to give a soft but disdainful order. By the time he reaches the bottom step of the cellar, Klaus' broken body has been dragged out the door.

The cellar is small and piled high with crates and files. Flour sifts down through the ceiling, clearly marking the spot where the body had lain upstairs. Himmler circles among the stacks, sampling items. Three minutes convince him it is worth hauling away to his own vaults. Heydrich will scream when he hears about this one. Too bad his men have drawn such a crowd outside. The other man that Hartke mentioned had come at them on "crystal night" will be warned now; no point in setting a trap.

And in fact, at that very moment Mika is standing across the street under a corner colonnade. If Esther Masterograncesco were here from the old Temple Guard in Munich she would notice that he cries slowly, thoughtfully. And if it were Katya beside him, she would be aghast at his tattered coat, his gauntness. Neither would understand that the real damage lies across the street. Because that is where their beloved Mika is being amputated.

Klaus. God in heaven, Klaus.

And after the body, up come his archives. The SS load everything on a single truck in less than fifteen minutes. Fifteen minutes for what took years to carry in. And he wants to enter the bakery, but everything that survives is inside him now. The whole Hitlerian concept. A magical civilization, a demigod race degenerating through world cataclysms and mutation into the current world order.

The inhabitants of Thule are always described as having continuous memory; presumably their knowledge is intact somehow in their genes. At least Hitler believes this. And the occultist Nazis with their mystical societies regressing unbroken through centuries, they believe it. And they believe Hitler is the medium. But what makes them believe a civilization in remission would want an alliance with them? Sheer gratitude to Hitler for bringing them back?

The answer, Mika fears, lies in a red velvet case in Nuremberg. The Spear of Longinus, whose mystical traditions entwine with the Thule ancestry, whose legend that a claimant who understands its power can change the world for good or evil, will be recognized for what it is by the ultra-race. They will know that Hitler used it for conquest and genocide of elements of his own species. The genocide will demonstrate that the surviving Aryans are worthy of reunification.

Without his files, Mika will convince no one. But at least he knows.

So he walks away from yet another large chunk of his life and tears up his identification papers. Which is ironic. Because two hours later he is arrested for vagrancy. And Jewish vagrants go to camps.

THE ROAD TO HEL

1
1939

War. A form of mass hysteria. Your millions have offended our millions, so we're going to go get our costumes on. Rattle, rattle. This will be an audience participation event, unpaid extras. One take. Old script. Press releases: "National honor...inalienable rights... protection of interests...unrecognized boundaries...provocations... in the name of God...reunification...natural superiority..."

Shooting schedule.

In Prenzlau, where he goes to train for his advance reconnaissance into Poland, Krantz records the chilling first casualty. Fritz Ender. Shot for plotting against the Führer and the Fatherland, so say the newspapers. Fritz Ender, unpaid extra.

Prenzlau has barracks and a movie house. Krantz spends as little time in the former and as much in the latter as possible. Sometimes he and Lutz Hoffmann walk the dusty road from the base to the town together.

Lutz is a tall ironing board with a broken cracker profile, sleepy green eyes, beautiful arrowhead lips and a loose cowlick. When Krantz first saw him—barefoot, chewing a toothpick, long prehensile fingers coaxing human notes out of a ravaged piano— he mistook him for an Entertainment Corp specialist. That he is in reality a mining engineer from Halberstadt assigned as Krantz's chief advisor is infinitely better than having an SS assistant.

The introduction of a second civilian, Joachim von Ultmeir, logistics (excluding equipment), furthers Krantz's sense of relief. Ultmeir, it is confided, once ran a whorehouse in the West Indies and therefore can run anything. And even Ernst Schaub, equipment specialist, is gloriously pedestrian. Always talking about sex. It is the one thing that annoys Lutz, who informs Schaub crisply one afternoon, as he tries to read his science magazine, that he is more interested in protons and electrons than hard-ons.

Schaub, a short, stocky bullet of a man with gapped teeth, has a nose like a bloodhound's. The capacity of motor oil, the strain on a coil, underdone potatoes, pending rains—all fall within the jurisdiction of that marvelous nose. Just his presence alarms security expert Gustav Gebbler who suffers from a mysterious and unconquerable body odor until Schaub tells him that the stink is coming from his wedding ring. Gebbler is insulted but desperate and secretly soaks the ring in vinegar until the microcosmic encrustations disappear and he leaps forth a cleansed man. Now Schaub smells vinegar when they meet.

Then there are the zombies.

Three of them. All security specialists, obviously SS, obviously part watchdog. Himmler-Heydrich breeds. A three-headed dog. The Bruckner-Lugert-Wolff dog. They are supposedly under Gebbler, though the latter is a quiet little man who smokes his pipe and trains his dogs and takes pains to remain outwardly detached from them.

Besondere Gruppe-Weiss, the eight at Prenzlau are called—Special Group White.

On the afternoon when they leave for Koslin an infestation of flies breaks out. In the back of the truck, Schaub is affected most. His pig-like nostrils, long and shaped like tears, somehow attract entry. The lethal intensity of Schaub's round eyes and gapped teeth as he slaps his nose provides comic relief.

"It's those damned dogs of Gebbler's," Schaub says, groping for a handkerchief.

Gebbler, whose oversized head and short torso make him dwarfish, nods with amusement, and then the truck is shrieking through its gears and the flies go wherever flies go in a moving truck.

They reach Koslin at dusk with two hours to kill. An E boat is supposed to take them east on the Baltic to the Hel peninsula inside Poland. The reconnaissance is considered safe under cover of darkness. In the very worst case, Polish resistance will be adequately handled by the E boat's twin .50 caliber machine guns and torpedo tubes. But Polish resistance isn't going to happen. The expedition will make a quick survey of the moraine to map out a base and decide on an engineering approach, then return to Prenzlau to ready equipment for the excavation. Supplies and personnel will be moved in on the heels of the Wehrmacht after Germany invades Poland.

The three zombies unfold from the long drive like circus tents, staking out their own private triangle in the narrow beach below the naval base. Ultmeir skims a stone over the water, making three pits.

"It's going to rain," Schaub says. "Smell the water?"

"Of course I smell the water," Hoffmann replies, "we're practically standing in it."

"When do we eat?" Lugert hollers. His grin is more or less permanent and means nothing. He would as readily urinate in the street as rescue a puppy from traffic.

Krantz signs toward the half-hex barracks on the bluff and climbs the painted wooden steps from the beach to the command office. The commandant's vivid embarrassment at having missed their arrival hints at the high priority given them. The truck, it seems, was supposed to have been directed onto the base instead of the beach. They eat in a private room, as the rain Schaub predicted arrives in two intense bursts of ten minutes. Afterward they file out into a night washed clean and lit by floodlights. The walkway is littered with worms floating like long, thin barges in shallow puddles. Schaub sips the air by spoonfuls, east and north, declaring the rain past.

In the commandant's quarters they are introduced to the captain of the E boat, a young *Leutnant* with an unvarying stare and a slight head cold. The commandant is obviously under a delusion about their mission, believing it is some heroic enterprise and not just a sneak under the fence by a bunch of civilians. The Leutnant keeps glancing at his watch until finally they board the E boat.

Thirty meters long, sleek and fast, she heels well into the water, kicking spume high in the air. At a speed of thirty knots conversation is reduced to blunt declarations cupped against the wind. Shipping lanes wink distantly; a meteor scratches the night. It seems to Krantz that they are going nowhere and that the vastness of the sea belittles them. Somewhere between Stolpe Bank and Leba on the coast they begin running without lights.

Presently, the sky makes a quarter turn and the E boat lists starboard. The titanic moraine looms forth bigger than Krantz remembers, a bulky cancer among lesser rises. Behind him, one of the crew trains anti-aircraft guns on the summit, and then the engines are cut and waves begin to slap the hull. The sound of surf on rocks reaches them.

Reconnaissance photos earlier revealed three caves at low tide. They are hoping that the middle one with the highest arch is accessible. But the northern lights are visible this time of year, and Krantz can clearly see that the granite face upon which the moraine rests is smooth at the water line.

So he will have to use the underwater breathing apparatus borrowed from the Italian navy. The Prenzlau training was all abstract and the apparatus is new and barely tested. Fortunately his dive won't be more than three of four meters. Any more and he is instructed to surface.

The Leutnant searches the precipice through field glasses. "Bare as a baby's bottom," he announces.

Gebbler will want to size up the heights for the future security that will be needed after an excavation site is established, Krantz has been told. Ultmeir, too, needs to estimate operational requirements on top of the moraine.

"Take Bruckner and Lugert for cover," he tells them.

This leaves Hoffmann, Schaub and Wolff. Goliath, Gothic Wolff with his chill dark eyes from craggy heights, mute lips and marble hands makes Krantz uneasy, but when you need a trained killer you don't want to have just a mechanic and an engineer on hand.

Krantz squeaks into the Italian rubber suit while Schaub and Hoffmann deploy a cork and canvas raft. Wolff kneels, big as a bowsprit, at one end, grasping the paddle like a toy in his massive hands. With a few quick surges he drives them into the current where the Baltic takes over. Moments more and they are sucked through the jagged outcroppings at the foot of the towering rise.

Schaub stabs his light up and down, and the sight of the detailed hardness leaves Krantz momentarily empty. An object as small as a chalice, buried before the last ice age in a cliff under a moraine could take years to excavate, however large the project. Even after the territory is secured they won't be able to blast or use any method that might damage the reservoir.

"Over there," Hoffmann says, and Schaub returns the light to a black cuticle in the rock above the water line.

Wolff back-paddles.

"Damn good current going in," Schaub notes.

"Go easy on my line," warns Krantz. "I don't want it sawed off on the rocks."

Biting down on the mouthpiece, he rolls into the joint-locking chill of the Baltic.

In dead water, he might immediately return to announce his unabashed fear of the several kinds of terror lurking beneath the surface. But the matter of direction and velocity are instantly resolved by the draw of the cliff. He merely strikes a fetal pose. If it was possible to feel ridiculous, he would; but soaring under a forbidding moraine into a black gluey void permits only a feeling of dread.

He hits the cave ceiling head on and begins to roll in the darkness, oxygen tanks ringing off the rock like slow motion garbage cans. No one anticipated a current this strong. At this rate, they will find him raked to pieces in a sewer in Warsaw. And then his outstretched hands encounter a projection of some kind, enough to press a vulcanized shoulder against while he fumbles for an underwater flare.

The flares are phosphorous or magnesium or something. He never got a chance to ignite one at Prenzlau, and now when he pulls the cap he makes the mistake of looking squarely at the burst of light. Disoriented, he lets go of the flare and claws against the saber-toothed blackness. His stomach is inverting and his breathing becomes a faucal roar through the respirator. Thick braids of water tumble him as easily as a leaf in a storm. There is no use fighting it now. The fumbled flare recedes like a pale sun in deep space.

Blackness rushes in, rushes out. It seems interminable, because how do you measure distance with the blindness of time? And then as suddenly as he was swept up, the pushing stops and he spins slowly to a halt. Weightless, his breathing steadies to a vascular murmur. But now a new dread takes over, a feeling that he has entered this void before—at Mehring Damm, and on the soaring palisades of this very moraine, and standing before the Spear's replica at Wewelsburg, and again gazing upon an insane wall at Eagle's Eyrie. In this nether place in the sea, the skin of a planet is of no consequence. Under here...this is what it is like in the rest of the universe.

The first sensations that bring him back to the present are sparks of warmth on his cheeks. Either he has gone insane or he has surfaced. But surfaced into what? He spits out his mouthpiece and takes a shallow breath. *Breathable*, he deems, though the air tastes alive with rankness and spores. Feathering one hand, he frees the waterproof lantern from his belt and raises it above the surface.

The beam seems to travel forever along a great granite hemisphere whose ends are lost in grayness. Playing the lantern slowly along the closest wall, the beam catches the wet curl of a ledge. Sculling wearily with one hand, head remaining up, Krantz fins to its level edge and hoists himself out. And that is when he notices that the safety rope tied to his belt plunges straight down.

Suddenly the surrounding immensity seems to hammer him like a fist. Because setting the lantern aside, he pulls the rope in hand over hand—a very long tether—and at the end there is no fraying, no abrasion...*just a clean cut.*

Outside, Gebbler's group has reached the eastern flank of the moraine and started to climb. The two SS zombies, Bruckner and Lugert, go up like skaters taking long strides and swinging their arms. Behind them Ultmeir and Gebbler trail like a pair of lowland gorillas, prancing two or three steps with their elbows bowed as if encircling dance partners, then straightening to see how much elevation remains.

The night is bright over the open coast and there are disadvantages to being in the lead. A rifle shot pings wide of Bruckner, followed by a flurry of single shots splattering randomly.

Lugert charges, firing steadily. Bruckner weaves level on the left, spraying bullets every third or fourth step. At twenty meters one of the Poles springs to his feet and Bruckner cuts him in half. Two others make their move then, one to flee through the sarsen stones dotting the slope, the other throwing up his arms. Unable to sight cleanly on the escaping Pole, Lugert does the expeditious thing. A quick burst from his weapon decapitates the surrendering man. Bruckner joins him in riddling the stone slope with ineffectual volleys as the third Pole's running steps fill the pauses.

"Enough!" shouts Gebbler behind them.

Bruckner's gaze turns slowly downward.

Gebbler is chalk-faced in the gloom. Ultmeir, less chalk-faced because of his flowing burnsides mustache, arrives alongside him, puffing, "Let's get out of here!"

"Fuckers," says Lugert, still looking up the slope. But he means Gebbler and Ultmeir.

Bruckner notices now that the decapitated Pole is quietly pumping dark blood over his boot. As if brushing away a fly, he kicks the corpse down the slope.

However laughable the Polish resistance, their bullets are real, and Gebbler and Ultmeir set about their survey at the top of the moraine with deliberate speed while the two SS flank them from either end of the plateau. Aerial reconnaissance photos have produced rough survey sketches which they annotate by flashlight, examining the soil, measuring highlighted areas with tapes, pacing others. In twenty minutes, each is convinced that a more sophisticated site inspection after the invasion will confirm the impression that a base is feasible here.

The descent to the dank and slippery rocks on the shore takes half as long as it took to climb up, but before they can free the raft, a score of rifles are cross-firing from the heights and the eastern flank. Potent return bursts from the E boat near at hand produce brief silences and showers of stone. From their right, the other raft is coming. Erich Wolff's powerful thrusts bring it even just as the E boat glides abreast of Gebbler's group.

"Where's Krantz?" shouts the Leutnant above the anti-aircraft tattoo and the engines.

"Drowned," Wolff says bluntly.

And they are hauled aboard like a human molecule, amid the stench of gunpowder, gasoline and machine oil.

"His safety line snapped," adds Hoffmann, managing a lame note of grief. "He didn't come up."

"There aren't any caves," Schaub rasps, his slight lean meant to convey confidentiality to the Leutnant. "The entrances are just erosions at the tide mark."

"No caves and he drowned?"

Suddenly one of the crew calls a warning. A bulky motor launch is rapidly approaching from the east. The Leutnant has orders to take any measures necessary for the safety of the special team, but waiting now is useless, and anyway, he has the testimony of two witnesses that Krantz is dead. With rifle fire still popping impotently from the coast, the Leutnant gives the order to run.

Underway once again with a surge of engines and the flow of a briny breeze in their faces, Hoffmann fixes his green eyes on Ultmeir. He has always thought of him as a kind of gentleman bartender, the sort who listens sympathetically while trying to remember if he fed the cat that morning. With Krantz gone, Ultmeir might be the only one he can talk to. "Wolff was feeding out the safety line and it snapped," he shouts.

"Snapped? Where's the rest of it?"

Ultmeir follows Hoffmann's glance to the raft on deck where the holding strap is still intact but the rope end they all clearly saw after Wolff shouted that it snapped is now missing. Hoffmann isn't offering an answer, he is asking a question, Ultmeir realizes. Wolff, he said—Wolff was feeding out the line. But before either man can comment further, the Leutnant shouts for the forward torpedo tubes to be uncapped. All eyes strain ahead.

Against the closely matched fabrics of sky and sea at the horizon, a white flaw is quickly becoming a second onrushing patrol boat. This one will cut them off no matter how they maneuver; and the Leutnant is not turning. His lips move as if murmuring to himself, and a moment later, with the meter of a poem in his voice, he shouts the commands, "Fire one…fire two!"

A thud detonates to the left, and the first oil-slicked casing rushes out of its tube with a whoosh. But what happens after the second thud is heart-stopping. Because instead of leaping ahead in a long white dive, the roaring, hissing thing pokes its nose halfway out of the launch tube and stops.

"Hot run!" bellows one of the crew.

Occupational hazard. Like throwing out the anchor with your leg wrapped in the last fathom of chain. The weapon will arm automatically after its impeller blades reach a set number of revolutions.

Almost before the words are out of the sailor's mouth, the torpedo man pounces onto the deadly casing and begins frantically spinning the air valve leading to the combustion chamber. The E boat has picked up speed with the first firing and now, off-weighted, it has a tendency to bounce. Each dip turns the impeller blades closer to detonation. Astride the whistling thing, the torpedo man leans far out and rams a rag between the blades.

The turning stops and a dozen human pulses resume.

Meanwhile, at the tip of the first torpedo's wake, a crimson flash now lifts the Polish patrol boat and breaks it into pieces. They pass seaward, hearing the cry of men, feeling the heat of burning fuel. The Leutnant is worried about political repercussions. They will have to claim they were attacked outside territorial limits. Perhaps the Polish government will not protest for fear of forcing Berlin's hand.

And in Berlin, hours later, the Führer is enraged. Josef Krantz cannot be lost, he insists, and the excavation must not be delayed. Case White, the invasion of Poland, will be moved up to early September.

Not far away, at his headquarters in the Prinz Albrechstrasse, Himmler is also enraged. Where is Krantz's body, he demands. It isn't Krantz's continued existence that is essential, but the absolute certainty of his death.

2

Glassy swells rise and fall in the cavern as the moraine breathes. Stalactites drip like ulcers, growing while seeming to melt. Digestion is possible here. Josef Krantz is digestible. In a little while, if the cave mouths don't open with the receding tide, he will plunge back into the current and try to find them. That will be a better death than digestion.

The darkness is almost unbearable. And the silence. Except that the silence is better than the ebullient drips from the ceiling, which are almost indistinguishable from laughter. If this is dying, it is quite mesmerizing. A study in slow surrender really. First you panic, then you are quieted by the slow sensory dirge of your own doom, and when you are quite sure of the outcome, you give up with as little fuss as possible. *I will not go quietly*, he vows to himself. And then, because the eerie oppression of the cavern is already making him doubt his existence, he shouts it out loud.

"I will not go quietly!"

Silence mocks him, followed by the one-note laughter of a dripping stalactite.

Bits of phosphorescence move far below the surface of the water, but Krantz pays no attention until a thought as subtle as the points of light he is watching occurs to him. Could a current be stirring small glowing organisms congregating for sustenance flowing out of the mouth of a shaft? Fatalistically he watches the on-off pattern until the persistence of his own vision is able to define a faint neon line.

The current has to be coming from the larger of the cavern entrances—the middle one, he guesses. With the lantern, he picks his way to the end of the ledge. A few seconds of darkness are needed to relocate the pale lime crescent submerged on the outer wall. Then, tying his cut safety line around the base of a stalagmite, he bites down on his mouthpiece and eases back into the chill.

As deep as his foot can reach he feels no phantom undertow or riptide that might drag him deeper into the labyrinth of caves. Nevertheless, he tries to follow the submerged slope of the roof. It is slow and disorienting as he crawls rather like a crayfish along the curve of the cavern ceiling. In the blackness, he is not even certain his progress is seaward. Perhaps he is only going deeper into the moraine. The tanks knelling against the rock are as mournful as the tolling of a funeral bell.

A dozen times he clings to an outcropping long enough to assess the direction of tidal surges. But when his safety line feeding back to the stalagmite in the inner cave suddenly pulls taut, the last hope for escape flickers out. Because if the line was cut by someone in the raft, the remainder that he tied off on the stalagmite should still have been long enough to get him out of this watery hell. Obviously something has been added, and the words seem to form in his mind exactly as if he heard them aloud: *This isn't the way you got in here, Josef...you are still under the moraine!*

The only solution is to pull himself back to the inner cave. Correction. The only solution was to pull himself back, because suddenly the line goes slack.

An impulse somewhere between panic and the will to survive seizes him. Flutter kicking hard, fending off collisions with the narrow passage, he drives and drives—drives blindly through the blackness. Unknowable things are raining down all around him. Lime deposits crumble at his touch, and stalagmites and stalactites seem to gnash together like teeth as he scrapes past. So be it! He will live or he will die in this last effort. Fins propelling, fingers scrabbling, tanks tolling wildly off the narrowing walls like the bells of Tchaikovsky's *1812 Overture,* he claws his way forward, expecting the final constrictions of his dwindling air at any moment.

Except...the gloom is actually beginning to dissipate. Isn't it? In seconds he is sure. Blessedly, the paleness broadens into a translucent sea, light as lemonade. Forward becomes up, and he begins to take full pulls. One, two—on the sixth catch he bursts through the surface and spits out his mouthpiece. The sky, which even at dawn's first light blinds him for several blinks, seems to fluoresce. Tearing off his mask, the moraine itself steadies before his eyes into a rich velvet against the yellow sands west and east. And at that very moment of recognition, he hears the shout. A Polish shout.

There is a small red boat less than fifty meters away. Three or four figures aboard. The one standing in the bow has a black steel carbine. And all the while he is aiming, Krantz stares back as if this is only a ceremonial act meant to challenge his sanity. Life cannot be this cruel. But then a geyser kicks up and a bullet buzzes through the water to his right. Promptly he raises his hands in surrender. The next shot sounds like a stomach growling, and by the third one he has rolled back under.

Fumbling for his mouthpiece, he kicks deeper than before. The chill blasts him like a wind funneling him deeper still into the sluicing, sinewy current. There is nothing to hang onto this time—no walls, no ceiling. Nevertheless, in some tactile way he senses the openness around him. A vast torrent is flowing here, and utterly without hope, he will ride it to the end until he lodges in some blind narrows or drowns in a sealed room.

But he has forgotten about the safety line. Still dragging behind him, it is now flowing with the current, undulating and looping each time he is slowed. Inevitably it must snag on something. And when at last a coil is pinched between fingers of granite, it upends him and tears loose from his belt. Whipped out of the flow like a cast-off meteor, Josef Krantz spins into the vastness of empty space. Only this time he does not surface in a coastal cavern adjacent to the open sea. This time the chamber is black and silent and sulfurous.

He can smell its deadness, taste its decay. And he dreads turning on the lantern, because he fears that what he is about to see he has seen before. Summoning his courage, he thumbs the switch. Instantly fatalism mixes with awe as the beam falls precisely on the macabre, nerve wracking vision he shared with Dietrich Eckardt the night of Mehring Damm 26.

Something rather like a temple looms over him—rough-hewn, except for the front wall. The granite there is actually polished, reflecting his light and the glitter of the pool like some consecrated resting place in a crematorium. But the really disturbing thing is the regal row of steles in the polished granite that blight his sense of an ordered universe. Because if the smooth facing is some sort of memorial, the inscribed steles look like nothing so much as cartouches covering niches for funerary urns.

There are three huge steps leading up from the water that run the length of the chamber. Ponderously he sculls to the first and hoists himself out. His breathing seems to fill the cavern as he climbs like a child on oversized steps to the foot of the wall. There he traces two fingers over the symbol on the middle stele. A patch of black mold distorts the coloring, but there can be no doubt that the raised surface is in the shape of the yang and yin. Slanting the beam of light down the row in each direction, he recognizes the Christian fish and a swastika turned left, another right. The remaining three signs are unknown to him. But there are *seven* altogether. Hyperborea had seven sub-races. Eckardt reeled them off the night of the séance.

Welcome to the reservoir, Josef!

Until this moment some anchoring part of him was able to deny what he was doing, what he was becoming a part of. But now here it is. Insane but utterly real. And so he must decide for real. Even if he is to die, his state of mind—state of soul—is important. How much further can he go into this madness?

The resemblance of the inner cave to a mausoleum is unmistakable. There are seams between the steles and the wall. Behind them, in all probability, lie the forces of Thule, presumably seven Grails each containing the genetic essence of an ancient race. Or is it one race reaching out to the descendants of any of the seven?

A shell game. Whichever descendants uncover this and conquer the biological engineering, the result will be Aryan demigods. Destroy any six and you still get Aryans. Bungle the restoration of one and you have a half dozen more tries. Not to mention, there are other reservoirs. Under his rubber fins are scores of "Mecca stones," and as he grates over them, Josef Krantz has a Lilliputian presentiment of what is waiting in the Grails.

A world he thought was his and of his kind, checkered with his fields, bound by his roads, patrolled by his ships and planes, a world from whose sands and jungles his kind have pulled cities, whose very time is ordered, measured and spent by his species—that world is a pale ruin of an older one. Until this moment he thought he knew ruins. Ruins are transitions. But the idea that hybridized humanity is merely the ruin of another race is choking him now.

What counts in evolution is survival. To reverse the order of survival—to go backward—would be an enormous betrayal, a blasphemy of incalculable magnitude. Fritz Ender balked at it.

Adjust your reception one hundred eighty degrees and insidious Adolf Hitler comes into focus—a demonic voice with finality in every syllable, a machine gun voice full of exclamation points, yet prowling, flowing with a blunt inescapable rhythm. For a few moments, in a cold, dark room of the new Chancellery, Krantz was conquered by it. But now he understands the true goal.

Ruins. Can he be part of that? Better that he should die in this place, if only the reservoir can remain dead with him. But they will probably find it and his body, eventually.

Sitting down on the top step, he plays the lantern beam over the water. Even though there is a mist, the floor is dry to his touch. It actually seems to suck his palm dry. The metaphor is *breathing*. Running the light back around the walls sends shadows ducking into an oatmeal of granite. He flicks the lantern off, and to his surprise, there is a faint echo of the click. He flicks it on again.

No echo.

The illumination stabs here and there at the edges of the steles, and his heart kicks mightily for a moment as shadows seem to yawn open. But the movement of the seams is only from the changing angle of the light, he tells himself. Crouching behind the trembling beam, he studies them intently. The steles are sealed like hatch plates.

How are they released?

Bending forward, he runs a finger down the left seam of the middle stele. There is definitely a separation where the seal meets the wall. The steles are not bas relief cut into the wall. They are fitted. Leaning closer still, his back is to the water when he hears the ripple.

Whirling around, he is just in time to glimpse something white sinking beneath the surface. The lantern light passes back and forth over black agitation as he retreats a step against one of the steles. Mecca stones slide underfoot. He stoops cautiously and gropes for one of them, never lowering his eyes from the pool. Slowly he stands, the Mecca stone molded between his thumb and forefinger.

Suddenly a slim, serpentine shape lashes out of the water.

Krantz's right hand comes up, but he doesn't throw the stone. The chimera of green scales and lathering serpent jaws in his imagination resolves itself into something wholly unthreatening, if bizarre. Half unglued, he recognizes his own rope moving to the whim of the current. Whatever snagged and spun him loose in the slack he created, the other end of the lengthy tether must still be tied off in the outer cavern.

Fins slapping awkwardly, he tries to leap down the broad steps to the brink of the pool. There are outrages here. He will take his chances in the undertow.

His plunge at the rope's end is done with the light on, but in grasping it, the lantern dislodges to go the way of the flare. Praying that the anchoring stalagmite will hold, he moves hand over hand against the current. Hot lead seems to fill his forearms, despite the chill. Like a mountain climber, he braces against the rock wall for brief respites while holding the line as though rappelling. He is near exhaustion when he finally surfaces in the outer cavern.

Ahead, faint as foxfire, lies the green crescent. He has no idea how much time has elapsed, but the red boat will probably be there. No matter. He will try again to surrender to the Poles. Surrender to keep the reservoir from falling to the Fatherland.

The thought itself brings strength, and when, for the second time, he breaks into open water, hands raised and spits out his mouthpiece, he cries, "Don't shoot!" in Polish. But the sun squinting through doughy clouds shatters an empty pane of sea into slate gray shards. There is no one else there.

Where is the little red boat that will absolve him of treason? He is almost disappointed not to be taken prisoner. Almost. But how sweet it is to breathe air in a world he has doubted for only one hour. How easy to return to life as it *is*. Humble architects should not be placed in such moral dilemmas. There are men who are good at nothing but staying alive, and if they do that at any cost, is that a crime? One can only be responsible for personal survival. Let history make its own mud. The destinies of individuals have no effect in the long run.

3

All decked out in his natty Italian rubber suit, he would look silly coming out of the woods if it wasn't raining. He abandoned the rest of the apparatus in the Baltic hours ago. And the fins. So here he is standing on the edge of a potato field in a rubber suit in the rain.

He might get noticed and he might not.

If he takes the thing off, why, then he will be noticed for sure. Nothing stands out like a naked man in a potato field during a storm. But if he runs across that field to the farmer's shed, chances are no one will see him, or if they do—say, looking out the upper window of the farmhouse—he might pass in the rain for someone with soaked, dark clothes on.

The field is a quagmire sucking at his feet. A single blink of lightning frames him when he is almost across, and by the time he ducks inside the shed, its low cough of thunder has died away. As an afterthought, he darts back out to retrieve a potato. This he offers up to the sky to be washed, and after taking a bite, he steps into the colorless but much detailed interior of the shed again.

The smell is warm and close, tainted with vintage oil emanating through grime and rust. A crack in the lone window catches white light on its sheared edge like frozen lightning. And then a trio of authentic flashes bleaches out the darkness, illuminating a collection of implements, baskets, a disassembled motor and a leather harness on one side of the shed. But in the microsecond before gloom rushes back, he also sees a drab red pair of long underwear and a leather apron and tattered trousers hanging on a four-sided nail.

The rubber diving suit peels off like an immense pair of wet galoshes, and in the next burst of lightning he gets an appalling glimpse of himself. His legs are marbled with bruises and his skin is like the imbibed white tissues of those drowned worms at Koslin.

Something thuds to the dirt floor. He retrieves the Mecca stone he had tucked in his cuff and shoves it into the pocket of the trousers. The flannel undershirt hisses over his body with all the elasticity of a newspaper as he pulls it down over his head, holding his breath. If he were a dog, he would roll in such garments. The smell of ancient sweat is ghastly—buttery ammonia. Rain is welcome as he returns to the woods.

Exhaustion has accumulated like sediment in his muscles, and finding a bed of dry pine needles, he stretches out on the ground. But as soon as his eyes close, ceding control to his other senses, a memory is stirred. The gentle tympani of rain, the yielding bower, the fragrant air in this place…Not the first time he has experienced this on the Pomeranian coast. *Lutka is nearby.* How good that seems. He didn't plan this. Destiny has put him here, hasn't it? And he has left Germany at last, as she wanted.

It is absurd, of course. Too much has happened. He is simply trying to turn his back on the madness that is coming. And anyway, she has moved on. But the dream won't let him sleep.

If she were somehow still in love with him, they could go to Sweden or Denmark and have an obscene number of children. Except that she can't have children. But it is not too late to be married. Put their bickering aside and get the hell out of the way of everything that's coming. Why postpone life any longer?

She was right about the Nazis. He will tell her that. Right, right, right, Lutka! And what if she has remarried, or no longer lives with her parents, or even in Niski Kosciol?

Then you can go to sleep in the woods, Josef.

From its larchwood church to its double row of peaked houses lashing southwest, Niski Kosciol lands on his eye unchanged. There are perhaps more geese huddling under Pan Mazaryk's porch now, and a column of new yellow telephone poles passes stealthily east, touching the village at Rudnicki's store; but otherwise it looks the same.

He gives the failing light another twenty minutes before picking his way across the garden to the window he once fled through after making love to her the first time. The curtains now are a deep ocher and hang like rusted pillars, parted by a sliver of light. He twists his head in an effort to collect the sense of what lies beyond—browns, yellows, whites. The bedroom itself is dark, and he is seeing through to the parlor through the open door. There is tall broad-backed Henryk himself. And more than two voices. The orchestration goes from flute to bass viol in several human ranges.

Something gray flows under the curtain, liquid fur filling the lower third of the window directly in front of his face. A cat widens its colorless gaze as it blocks the sliver of light. Krantz pantomimes its strangulation, but it merely cushions its eyes shut. He taps lightly on the glass, evoking an even stiller "still life." Ceramic cat.

And suddenly the iron pillars of the curtain buckle outward as a pair of hands close on ceramic cat, and a face comes very close. And another pair of eyes now even closer. Lime eyes. Even in the gloom, a stir of lime. Paper pale. Nakedly sad. And vulnerable. Poland personified.

The look they exchange is surprisingly calm. A museum look of twin exhibits behind glass. But the next thing he reads is sternness. The cat pours out of her hands and she retreats. Two minutes later she is hurrying by him in a thin gray coat. At the foot of the embankment beside one of the yellow telephone poles she stops and turns. White moonlight and purple shadows divide her delicate face, grappling for her eyes.

"Lutka," is all he can say.

She shoves her hands in her pockets, ruling out an embrace.

He takes a deep breath, alleviating something. She is really here. It is almost as surreal as what he just left beneath a moraine in the Baltic. But this is a magic he can shape—must shape—if they are to have a chance.

"Stop by again sometime," she says.

"Do we have to stand on these rocks? My feet are killing me."

"You Aryans really ought to discover shoes."

"Considering the importance of my mission, I didn't think I should wear my uniform. I'm here to steal the library of Jagellon University."

She affects a smile. "Whatever would Nazis do with a library?"

"I never liked politics, Lutka. You know that. I'm running from them."

For just a second she softens, and he seizes the moment to

memorize her: rubescent lips that simulate in the admirer a feeling of being kissed by a child, too large eyes, too small jaw, thin prominent ears that make soft mounds in her auburn hair. Homely. Beautiful.

"You certainly picked the wrong direction to run," she says.

"I had to find you."

"You're cyclical, you know that, Josef? I haven't even recovered from our last stand. You must think I'm a masochist. If Aunt Zofia hadn't told everyone I was your widow, I'd be living in a shanty on the shore."

"My widow?"

"I forget how you died. Horribly, though. No one was sorry."

"Not even you?"

"*Especially* not me."

"To think you still care enough to be indifferent toward me. Our lives can be filled with love again, Lutka."

"If you only knew how full of love I was when I left you."

She wraps the coat around her more tightly, and he could swear it was the same coat she had in Berlin. He has held her in that coat in his arms at a train station in Kiel, on a sleighing party at Rostock... where else?

"You're traveling first class," she notes, leaning back against the telephone pole. "But judging from your hair, it looks like the boat sank."

"I want *us* to go to Denmark," he says evenly.

She becomes absolutely still. Like her cat in the window, she tries to look disinterested, but the look suddenly fails in a burst of laughter.

"Josef, Josef, you're such a child. Just...run away whenever you feel like it. An arrogant little boy. You think the world is waiting for your next whim. Well, I'm grown up now, and I've got at least one adult's responsibilities, so I can't come out and play. It's just not that simple."

"All right. All right, I'm arrogant about our relationship. I've always been arrogant about it. Arrogance brought us together, arrogance kept us going, so maybe arrogance can reunite us."

"You don't know what you're talking about."

"At least *leave* with me. Poland is going to get ugly with Nazis."

Moonlight washes the lime hues out of her eyes but intensifies their limpid gloss. "Did it ever occur to you that I might love someone else, Josef? That I might have obligations?"

"It occurred to me." He glances at her ring finger. "If you're not married, you're not obligated."

"Wisdom from Berlin's leading soloist. There are other obligations. Have a good 'solo' to Denmark, Josef."

On that she turns and walks away.

Something inside him stretches like taffy, but it is perilously close to snapping. Suddenly he feels silly. She is absolutely right about everything. What is he doing here? He must get clear of the past and the present before there can be a future.

Help me, Father Ledochowski.

The rectory is dark and so quiet that he hears a clock ticking through the open window, which his knock seems somehow to silence. The man who answers is fiftyish with a thinning circle around his forelock. He has a cirrhosed, rosebud mouth that Krantz finds repulsively anal.

"May I speak to Father Ledochowski?" he asks.

"Father Ledochowski is dead."

Krantz sags.

"I'm sorry. My name is Father Kovacki. And you are...?"

"German," Krantz says bluntly. "And I'm fleeing the Reich."

"But you're in Poland."

"So is the Gestapo."

Father Kovacki peers hard at him.

"I wanted to go to Denmark," Krantz says.

"Denmark," Kovacki repeats thoughtfully. "Bornholm?"

"You could get me to Bornholm?"

Kovacki gives him another long look. What reason would this stranger have to lie about fleeing the Reich?

"There are fishermen near Danzig with large enough boats," he says. "But they'll want to be paid in advance."

"I don't have any money. I was hoping Father Ledochowski..." Krantz gestures lamely.

"No money. Well, I don't have a fund for this sort of thing, but I suppose you could reimburse me by mail. Eventually?"

Krantz swallows in relief. The priest seems genuinely reluctant.

That means he can be trusted.

"I've got an old car," Kovacki imparts. "You can stay here until I get back. Danzig is crawling with Germans and sympathizers. If things work out, you'll board the boat north of here on the coast. Heat up some soup if you're hungry."

The priest goes off to change, and Krantz looks into the icebox. Matches and a pan are in a cupboard exactly where they were years ago. And pickled sprats. Impossible that Father Ledochowski is gone. But, of course, he was old. When Krantz turns back to light the stove Father Kovacki is watching from the doorway.

"You'll need these shoes and some decent clothes," the priest says, laying the items across a chair.

"I'll add a surcharge to the loan."

Five minutes later Father Kovacki leaves in an asthmatic car with one headlight, and Krantz greedily devours the warm soup. The ticking clock reasserts itself, but gently, and fatigue guides him to lie down on the rectory sofa.

There is no doubt that the two cars that bring him out of his sleep are trouble. They arrive simultaneously on either side of the church, doors banging shut like drawers in a rifled bureau. The occupants are already at the step before Krantz is off the sofa, springing barefoot for the annex. Behind him panels splinter and a latch yields.

He reaches the darkened church through a curtain and dashes among the pews. There isn't time to try a window. Whatever is closing on him is quick, efficient. Ahead of him the church doors rattle. Doubling back past his pursuers in the dark is his only hope. He falls forward to the cold, stone floor just as two pair of shoes come slicking through the annex.

And now there is silence, the keen, probing kind that defines space and holds its breath. Into that, after a second or two, come the control notes. Measured footsteps. Slow, fanning out. A row by row search. Krantz smells pomade and even leather as he slithers gingerly under a pew.

When the leather passes, he slides back out and carefully removes a hymnal from the rack. This he hurls deep into the church. It lands with a slap. Two flashlight beams probe after it, crossing as Krantz drops to the floor and crawls for the annex.

"Decoy!" is shouted in German.

The first light sweeps the church, passing directly over the annex curtain, or rather where it should be, because a third man is holding it aside now, squinting. The second beam ripples beneath the pews, leaving Krantz no choice but to grab the nearest hymnal, rise and sling it with all his might.

This time the pages whip open before it staggers the target, who discharges his gun. A roar and a spurt of flame envelope Krantz. He leaps for the annex. Amid the concussion and the smell of gunpowder, he collides with the man holding the curtain. Krantz buries an ineffectual punch in the man's midriff. Immediately a Luger is at his temple.

"Make your next move slowly, Herr Architect. We could kill you now and receive medals."

Father Kovacki returns a half hour before dawn, having struck a bargain with a young fisherman north of Danzig.

"Gestapo!" he groans aloud, seeing the splintered door.

The events are easy enough to read—sofa cushion on the floor, annex curtain wrenched off four rings, hymnals scattered, a large chip of wood shot off the altar—but it isn't until he lifts Krantz's discarded trousers and reaches in the pocket to discover what the weighty object is that the blood freezes in his veins. Because the black stone he withdraws is familiar to him. There are several like it in the Vatican. They are associated with the sites of Thule, with the transgressing life forms, with demonic powers and the resurgence of pagan rites to enthrone them on earth. The thing he was sent here to guard against is happening. *Someone has found a way into the reservoir.*

He said his name is Josef Krantz. And the Nazis are after him. So he knows something about the reservoir. The Gestapo tortured Father Ledochowski to pinpoint it. This German, Krantz, has breached it somehow—which is where the stone came from—and then he panicked. He knew Father Ledochowski, the Gestapo knew he knew, hence...

God almighty, forgive me. He was here and I let him get away. Here, in this very room.

Dropping to his knees, the priest searches for a drop of blood or any sign that Josef Krantz—he prays—may already be dead.

4

The bricks on the road to Hel translate through the car's suspension on his poor pounded body. He smells pomade on his right, well-oiled Luger on his left. He is tired—so damned tired.

There will come a point when he just won't care anymore, when survival will be a pain in the ass. But that is fear talking. The weaker he gets, the more he is afraid of dying. And he wants to survive. Enough of this nearly dying. Keep him out of caves and chases. Whatever is worth dying for won't be worth anything to him dead. Just let him crawl back to Berlin and be known as an insignificant cowardly architect. The nice dentist on the Fasanenstrasse should be the one testing his bravery. But then he remembers that his dentist is Jewish and out of business.

"I didn't realize you were Gestapo," he says to the one who smells of pomade. "I thought you were Poles. They shot at me in the water, and I've been hiding from them all day. So, of course, I thought you were Poles. Let me tell you, I'm not much for heroics. When I got out and realized the team had abandoned me, I thought it was all over. I mean it was too far to swim back to Koslin, right? Shit. Listen, I hope you aren't going to hold what happened in the church against me. I didn't know who you were. You should've just knocked instead of breaking the door down—"

"We knew you'd come looking for your old priest friend," the pomade-wearer, whose name is Wilhelm, says. "And your little Slav whore."

A very effective reply. It tells Krantz a lot. That it won't matter what he says now, for instance. These are Heydrich-Himmler men. They won't hesitate to kill him. His rope was cut when he was underwater, wasn't it? Producing a traitor's body for Hitler will keep peace in the family. They could say they shot him trying to escape, or fleeing to a neutral country.

"Look, before you make an unforgivable mistake, you'd better tell Berlin I've been inside the moraine," he says. "Tell them I know how to go about the thing now. Tell them that with my expertise there's a likelihood of success and without it their best chance is the mother of all earthquakes."

Wilhelm looks troubled. The one holding the Luger purses his lips.

"Of course you would say that," says Wilhelm. "But Germany has many qualified engineers and archaeologists."

They have reached a farmhouse squatting darkly at the end of narrow ruts.

"Maybe Herr Architect found something on his adventure," says the one with the Luger.

"I report only to the Führer," snaps Krantz.

"You can't see the Führer."

"Then let me get back to my group."

The car stops behind the farmhouse. A skein of sparrows flies into and through a hedge in the early light.

"Himmler won't hear of that," says Wilhelm, more to his companion than to their prisoner.

"He will if you tell him what I said about the site. I'm essential. Tell him that. The future of the Fatherland depends on me. If you shoot me, it won't be Himmler who evaluates the two of you."

Wilhelm opens the door. "Get out."

They usher him into a cellar with newly barred windows. Thumbs up, for the moment, he decides. They don't know what to do with him.

The cellar is stocked with bottled fruit and cans. A box of rat poison lies torn and spilled on its side. Just before he falls asleep on an old tarpaulin, Krantz catches the glint of glass on the floor. But he is tired, so tired, and, of course, he doesn't recognize Father Ledochowski's discarded phial of oil for Last Rites.

Four days pass before the man from Berlin comes. He is tall and gray and mirthless, and his faintly blue eyes study Krantz a long while without commitment. The Gestapo agents crane after him in the doorway like thumb puppets, and it scares the hell out of

Krantz—this sphinx come to contemplate him, he sitting between its paws. A stone tirade. With riddle.

"My name is Vouten," he says slowly. "We met once in Berlin, nearly twenty years ago, at a meeting of the Thule." He pauses, but Krantz shows no recognition. "I saw you again one night in Niski Kosciol outside the church. You were close enough to kill. We've killed your girlfriend. Reichsführer-SS Himmler says you're a traitor."

Krantz closes his eyes. When he opens them again, his face is wet with tears. "And what does the Führer say?"

The mirthless stare now relents. The tall gray man scrapes to his feet.

"Herr Krantz," he directs in a loud official voice, "upon arrival at Niski Kosciol, you are ordered to take command of Einsatzgruppe D. There you will seize and examine every child under ten years of age in the manner prescribed by your group specialists. When they have been properly examined and sorted, you will send suitable candidates to the collection point outside Danzig. The remainder will be dealt with according to sealed orders already in the present group leader's hands. If you balk or fail to carry out these orders to the last detail, you will be sent to a special extermination camp. If, on the other hand, your loyalty proves stronger than your instincts, you will be permitted to rejoin Special Group White on the coast. *Heil Hitler!*"

We've killed your girlfriend. The rest is postscript.

Berlin boots strut away. An unschooled trait, this strutting. The whole Reich struts. Take off their boots and they will patter around like little old men. Who will fear them then?

Later, after he has buried Lutka in a dead corner of his heart, he thinks about the children thing. What did he mean "sort children"? Whatever it is, he will have to do it. He *must* do it. The man from Berlin assigns numbers to people. And Krantz is tired and weak, and he wants to survive. Whatever it is, he will simply be circumstantial to the act.

Ageless exculpation.

There is great relief on the part of the three Gestapo agents. They still watch him, and there are questions they ignore, but the atmosphere is one of stranded fellow travelers rather than captors and captive. He is permitted to eat with them upstairs and to exercise a bit outside in company with one or another and even to play cards. And he is so miserably frightened that he never once tries to escape.

Wilhelm makes a joke out of his servility. The other two, Jan and Ludwig, are sober as coroners. If Wilhelm tells a story about wadding paper into the holes of a bowling ball so that an old comrade thinks his fingers have grown, Ludwig merely cracks his knuckles and Jan chain smokes. Then Wilhelm might turn to Krantz out of frustration.

Over Polish radio the men in the farmhouse follow events. On August 24th there is the announcement of a German-Soviet pact, along with the bravura commentary that this is a sign of German weakness. This is followed by Foreign Minister Beck's outrage and indignation, while behind-the-scene there is clawing for the limply extended hands of Britain and France.

There are undercurrents from German sources as well. On August 27th a Gestapo agent arrives on a bicycle he has stolen after his car broke down halfway from Danzig. Two days earlier he was in the Chancellery when Hitler studied pictures Hoffmann made at the Ribbentrop-Stalin talks leading to the pact, he reveals to his listeners in the farmhouse. The purpose of the photos was to discover whether Stalin's ear lobes were "attached like a Jew's or separate like an Aryan's."

"Well?" Wilhelm demands.

"They were separate," says the stranger. "But Stalin was smoking in the photos of the signing, and Hitler had the cigarette painted out before release."

All very therapeutic.

Until the day the distant pounding begins—like Hitler's fist on a desk top in Berlin inlaid with a half unsheathed sword. Now, Friday, September 1st, the news is all invasion. Great clouds of Luftwaffe bombers carry pre-arranged storms to the north. The *Schleswig Holstein*, a German cruiser in Danzig harbor, shells the peninsula.

Soon the radio is drowned by the mechanized roar of panzer divisions diverting around them like a stream. In a matter of hours it passes south and east, and in its wake, stepping gingerly through puddles of blood, comes the man from Berlin again.

The best part of Krantz's war is over.

He follows General von Bock's Army Group North through the Corridor. Screaming Stukas, endless chains of heavy guns on rutted roads, panzers annihilating cavalry—the blitzkrieg soon bottles up the thirty-five Polish divisions and strafes its earthbound five hundred planes. In transit, he hears of the Heydrich plan that launched the invasion. SD men disguised as Polish soldiers "attacked" German border installations, briefly taking a radio station at Gleiwitz and broadcasting provocations. They left bodies dressed in German uniforms behind.

Where had the bodies come from?

There were plenty of "canned goods" in concentration camps, the well-informed soldier answers. By the evening of September 4th, General von Kluge's Fourth Army meets General von Kuechler's Third, transferring possession of the Corridor to the Reich.

Krantz still has no idea what the *Einsatzgruppen*—"sortie groups"— do, but they are an anathema to the regular army. There is grumbling among the Wehrmacht that they themselves will be blamed for what the Einsatzgruppen do.

"Einsatzgruppen?" says the corporal who knew of the border ruse that triggered the invasion. "They're a bunch of sadists from the SS and SD."

When Krantz confides that he is to lead such a group, the corporal actually runs away for fear of having compromised himself.

Twenty kilometers outside Niski Kosciol a weakened country bridge collapses under the weight of an armored personnel carrier, bringing the column to a halt. Soldiers slide like mud off fenders as truck by truck the engines shut down and the smell of exhaust dissipates.

It is then that Krantz notices the train. Westbound it creeps along until finally stopping thirty meters short of the hopeless jam-up. A single whistle produces the usual confusion and haggling across its tracks, and beneath that, audible in the relative stillness of the shut-down, comes an uncanny lowing of cattle. Up and down its flank a tawny mongrel canters, barking. The stench is revolting.

Dead and wounded aboard, thinks Krantz. He scans the length but sees only freight cars. And then, perhaps fifty meters away, something red and blue emerges through the tiny, wired window high up the side of a boxcar. It falls in the weeds, shapeless, palpably soft even at that distance. A stanza of womanly cries from the same direction startles him.

He slips off the back of the truck he is riding and walks, runs, walks to the spot, there to fall on his knees and retch. The train performs a sickening lurch that transfers to his bowels, and the human lowing choruses fearfully. The mongrel circles hungrily until it arrives at the thing that has fallen in the weeds. Trembling, Krantz kicks at the beast, widening its circle. He regards the awful train with horror and loathing, a thing filled with the doomed and dying, a premature cortege, a hell from which newborn babies are extruded through wired windows.

Behind him comes the soldier assigned to make sure the man in new fatigues with no weapon reports to the Einsatzgruppenführer in Niski Kosciol. He is young and dutiful; he doesn't question trains. But the abomination in the weeds shakes him.

Krantz gazes up purblind, his mouth twisting grotesquely, and makes a helpless gesture.

The soldier licks his lips. "They're Slavs," he says. "Sub-human."

Krantz wags his head.

The soldier becomes unnerved. "Get up!" he shrills. "Get back in the truck!"

Round and round the mongrel whirls, growling. The soldier aims, shoots. The dog drops like a stone.

Krantz staggers up. *I will be circumstantial to the act...*

"Damned demoralizing to herd women and children out of their homes," the soldier says. Dozens of men have heard the shot and are watching their return. "Even if they are Slavs and Jews. But this is war, isn't it?"

Krantz regards him with bewilderment. This is the Hitler youth grown up; this is a precocious propagandist on a nature hike of young boys. It all came to this.

"You'll get used to it," pipes the soldier. "We've all got to get used to it."

I will be circumstantial to the...

The smell of fear is in Krantz's nostrils, and it doesn't smell like death. Death is decay. This smells like dying. Dying is a liquid odor—sweat, blood, urine, the contents of the stomach, tartar on teeth—an ungroomed, worried smell, a loss of bodily integrity. Humans into cattle. Lowing. White-eyed. There are moments when death is a gift. One resists dying more than death. The method is to ignore it.

He arrives in Niski Kosciol as mechanized and lame as the column. The first half dozen houses on the western approach are leveled and smoldering. Including the fourth house. Lutka's house. But he doesn't notice, of course, because he is circumstantial. He must not care a row of pins for foregone conclusions.

Whatever we do to the children, it is automatic...orders of the Führer.

The truck stops before the public hall. Soldiers move precisely here, a series of human gates. He is ushered inside, introduced. Einsatzgruppe D. Men and orders. Token sovereignty is handed him in dossier form. He listens, hearing nothing. The Gruppenführer does not understand the significance of all this, but he is glad to hand the children's exams over.

"Pull yourself together, Krantz, we're doing a necessary job. It's hard to do this and remain decent fellows, but that's what makes us so tough. Only a few really enjoy it. Once this business is over, the future will be bright, I assure you. Do what? Read your orders, Krantz!"

FROM SUPREME COMMAND...

Actually, he has nothing to do at all. The Einsatzgruppen. They will do it. And he isn't *giving* commands. He is *reading* them. How simple. Just one or two decisions.

Decision one: a farmhouse.

There is a small one on the east end that will do. A Jew used to live there. Zolkower. He will be gone now, the house abandoned.

Decision two: the children.

He can fake relocation. Get all the families together at a collection point. They won't leave anyone behind that way. A house-to-house search would create panic. Word would spread ahead of them, some of the children escaping. *Yes, that will do! The house-to-house search. The less effective measure.*

Decision three: the examination.

I will have nothing to do with the choices. I am not an expert. The specialists are the experts.

Decision four: the children who fail.

Summer's dust is a cataract on the window. The stand of slender willows south of town where he and Lutka sometimes went will be turning colors now. *The children who fail...* Some of the villagers recognized him coming into town. Dead Lutka's dead husband. *The children who fail...*

He stands stiffly in the street while the search is conducted, eyeing the upper stories, the roofs, the gray frightened sky. Wherever the turmoil comes from, he is looking the other way, an awkward detached figure with summer's dust in his windows.

But the crying. He hears that. His mind produces children with white faces, women in babushkas. There are two children who used to come in Rudnicki's store way back then. A brother and sister. Very young. About three and six. The three year-old couldn't say "sausages," the six-year old tied up on "parlor." So each one said the other's tongue-twister when it came up. Except that the three-year old mispronounced "parlor," too, and neither child realized it. Cute. He thinks he saw them today, before the search, but of course they are grown now.

"Search carefully," advises the Gruppenführer suddenly at his elbow. "Children are the bluejays of war. When they're not screaming, it's because their parents are hiding them."

The village men have been ordered to one end of Niski Kosciol on the pretext of registration.

"Kinder gehtweg!" a soldier bellows, and the tremulous patter of scores of light feet reaches Krantz.

They run in crowded lines, holding their arms straight, like birds with broken wings. It sickens him. He wants to let them go, to strike down this black, oily machine he is part of. *Run, children, run!* But he is inside the machine.

The farm is small. There are six fields, an unpainted house, some out-buildings. The children, obedient and terrified, are herded into a small barn.

Three "specialists" immediately set to work on them with calipers, raising their supple limbs, photographing a select few. Checklists are hastily tallied—a point for an eye fold, a point for an ear lobe. The Aryan standard established by Mongol-smooth Himmler and swarthy Goebbels is rigid. Few of the children of Niski Kosciol pass.

When the hideous lottery is over, a paralysis seizes Krantz. He cannot move his lips.

The Gruppenführer, who stood idly by during the examinations, locks his hands behind his back. "Say it!" he rasps thickly.

Utterly stricken, Krantz raises the orders. His lips twist, the paper shakes furiously.

"Say it!"

"Bury them!" he blurts and begins to sob.

Behind them the Gruppenführer nods to his men and smooths a palm over his short, black hair.

"It's impossible to justify here and now, of course," he says, "but I respect you for it. Really—Krantz?" He runs after him, seizing the shuddering man by the shoulders. "Don't be a fool. You are under orders to see it through, and I am under orders to report your behavior."

The night is bitter cold, moonless. In the open field the children whimper until they are numb. Then the pit is filled in.

Suffocation is quicker than exposure but more terrifying. Together the two methods might work to dull each other. These thoughts, bizarre and listless, occupy Krantz's trauma. It isn't until well after dawn, when the sun has been up an hour, that the full cruelty of the act overwhelms him. Because as the porous earth over the shallow graves warms, it begins to move.

5

Some time after the last car roars away from the farm, a scrawny man crawls out from under a pile of sugar beets in a broken crib. This is Zolkower, the Jewish farmer with whom the Thule agent Vouten stayed almost twenty years ago while tracing Krantz to the church in Niski Kosciol.

Zolkower's onyx eyes dart frantically about and his black hair and beard stick out in tufts moistened by beet scraps. He moves with alacrity but disjointedly, in undecided haste. His black, tattered clothes unfurl with the flapping of his bony limbs, making him look like a cricket. At last he scurries into the field where the children lie and begins to dig.

He digs and digs, half finishing one disinterment, abandoning it for another. He digs with his hands, making little cries to himself. He has tended these fields a score of years, and now, such a harvest! He probes the soil tenderly, then furiously, like a demented mother trying to rouse a stillborn infant.

Down the road a knot of ravenous dogs is coming. Abandoned several days, they are scavenging in a pack. An old hound, sniffing in semicircles, catches the scent of the field and lunges ahead.

At first Zolkower thinks the Germans have come back with patrol dogs, but then he recognizes one or two in the mongrel pack (are these the children's pets?). He shouts, waves his arms like a scarecrow, kicks wildly at a lathered muzzle and gets his leg raked by flashing teeth.

And then—because some of the Einsatzgruppe have remained in the house to see that no one comes for the children—a door slams. Zolkower looks across the field to the uniforms on the porch and starts to run.

Rifles crack. Sharp successions. A single bullet plunges into his shoulder, knocking him flat. He crawls several meters into the weeds, half stands, then lopes along the fringes of the trees. As soon as the soldiers split up to cover either end of the small woods, he flees back across the field toward the house. The grisly carnage of feeding dogs whirls around his feet now. His slashed leg is cold, his shoulder hot. They have him. He knows they have him.

In desperation he hides himself in the outdoor privy, raising the wood shelf with the hole cut in it, lowering himself down. He tries to cling to the sides, his eyes watering, the stench nearly overpowering him. He almost wishes to die. It would be easier.

Ahead of him lies Treblinka, Chelmno, Sobibor, an unending list of concentration camps not yet built. He knows only that he must decide now whether to try to survive.

And then he thinks of the man responsible. *Krantz*, they called him. A man with blond hair and vaporous blue eyes in a melancholy face. And an amputated little finger. He studied him from beneath the beet crib an afternoon and a night. And though God in heaven may forgive that German viper, Saul Zolkower will ride dragons out of hell to find him!

Suddenly the whole toilet seems to explode. Wood chips and dust rain through the hole as the door is shot off. A German command is issued and Zolkower worms out. He is on his way to hell, but he already knows what Satan looks like.

6

It is raining softly out of a white sky. No lights in the houses. The men have not come back. The children have not come back. Just women left. Wailing. A train is coming for them. Outwardly Niski Kosciol looks arranged, like death.

Krantz walks up one street, down another, thinking he is one of *them* now, a giver of orders, an insignificant passage in the translation of abstract theory into culpable horror. At one point an old woman on Bor Street totters out of her dwelling and beats on his chest until she falls exhausted and sobbing in the street. He tries to help her up, but she crawls away in the mud, cursing him.

Rain roars. He turns the corner. More sentries. More of himself. Regular as signposts. Two of him playing cards under a canvas. One of him thumbing his rifle strap and monitoring windows. Hasn't he seen that one sailing a toy boat with his son in a park once. My God, how far they are from home. Who made the machines that brought them here? Who put gas in them? Who tanned the leather for their boots?

He remembers playing war in a vacant field once. His playmate, Gunther, fell from a tree and broke his wrist. Gunther's half of the war went home in tears. War called on account of a broken wrist. Gunther's mother was mad and complained that Josef "shot him out of the tree," which was true enough, though the gun was a stick and the discharge came from fluctuations of his cheeks. Grandfather Krantz shrugged it off. Boys should toughen themselves. Why had Gunther cried? Grandfather never forgave Kaiser Bill. Grandfather should have fought for the Führer.

He passes Lutka's burned and gutted house, sweating with remorse. And Rudnicki's, where he stops cold suddenly as it all floods back over him. The Jew from the burned out ruins of the synagogue—they stood here together almost twenty years ago! The memory is vivid now. He said his name was Inspector Weichs. Only that was a lie, a benevolent lie, because in reality he had come to warn him.

These people want you for something...stay away from them, Herr Krantz.

How is it he failed to understand, to see it coming? A vow to redeem himself sticks in his throat too worthless to be uttered.

He lurches on toward the church where white splinters and mortar chips lie scattered around the entrance. The heavy doors create a Gothic mouth that exhales must and plaster dust as it swallows him. Inside, his eyes are drawn to the single stained glass oval spidered by bullets, and to the east window, completely shattered except for a crust of glass around the cames. As he adjusts to the gloom, flecks of white emerge along the pews and black motes appear upon the walls. A few blinks more and he discovers the figure no more than ten meters from him.

"Father Kovacki?"

The cassock blends perfectly with the pew, the priest's head floating above both like a balloon tied off at the anal mouth. Krantz senses intensity, or some other extreme marked by rigidity. It occurs to him in the brief silence that the priest is wounded, or dead, and, even after he speaks, the impression penetrates Krantz's torpor that there is a kind of ceremony in progress.

"I'm glad you came back," Father Kovacki says.

But he hasn't come back. The church was just here. He hasn't *come* back, has he?

Krantz sinks onto the end of the pew, a wave of maudlin grief sweeping over him. He would like to believe in divine guidance at this moment. The Nazi fiend wandering in the long shadows of his day of infamy, struck by the sun's last rays glinting off a church cupola.

"Do you know what I've done? Do you know what God let me do?"

"What have you done, Josef?"

Krantz shudders and gasps but cannot bring forth tears.

"Is it the children? Is that why you're crying?"

My God! What else? Of course it's the children.

"I'm going to hell, Father. I'm in hell now."

"Because of the children?"

Krantz stares at him. The top of the priest's head catches what light there is. Bald. A tonsure. Why is he sitting like that? As ceremoniously as a cat?

"You're sorry for what you did," Kovacki says for him.

"I can never be sorry enough."

"Even great crimes can be forgiven, Josef. *Great* crimes."

"I didn't want it to happen. They said…they said—"

"We can all be made cowards. The important thing is to repent. Repent and *confess*. Go back to the beginning, Josef. Say it for God. Say it for yourself."

The priest reeks of ulterior motive, but Krantz craves guidance. Nothing looks right to him now. The whole thing is turmoil. Lutka, Niski Kosciol, Poland: concentric rings on a target.

"Why did you come in the first place, Josef?"

"To find Lutka and escape."

"But why did you come to Poland?"

"I was supposed to excavate a site on the coast."

"Yes, the moraine."

"You know about the moraine?"

"I know more than you think. About you, about what you were looking for. But you have to say it."

Don't ask questions, Josef. This is a priest. In the name of Christ, tell him!

"I…was supposed to find traces of original Aryans from a pre-Atlantean era."

"And you did."

"Yes."

"You found the reservoir?"

"Yes!" rings tightly off the walls. "The thing exists. The damn thing exists…seven steles…"

He tells all of it—about the Spear, the Grail, Wewelsburg, Eagle's Eyrie—and it comes to him easily now that the priest already knows. The oldest intelligence gathering network in the world is the Vatican.

"You balked at all this, Josef," says the priest. "That is why you will be forgiven. It offended your morality."

"Did it?"

"Oh, yes."

"It offended my reason."

"Hitler has said it is certain that by nature he belongs to another species."

"He meant *Aryan*."

"Perhaps. But you found that blasphemous."

"I thought it was irrational."

"Until you saw the reservoir." There is a rifle shot in the distance, followed by the spitting of a machine pistol. "Yes, until you saw the reservoir," Father Kovacki repeats for him. "That was when you decided to run away to Denmark. Because you believed it then. And it was blasphemous."

Krantz laughs, and it isn't very different from sobbing.

"You see, you didn't want to excavate the site," says the priest. "You only went because you thought it wouldn't come to anything."

Why is he talking about the site? What about the children?

"And you did the right thing," Kovacki continues. "As soon as you realized what you uncovered, you tried to keep it a secret. But the Gestapo caught you. They tortured you. They made you tell them about the reservoir." He gives Krantz a moment before extending the hook again: "You *had* to tell them about the reservoir."

"No."

"No? You didn't *have* to. But you did."

"No. I didn't tell anyone."

"No one?"

"No one."

"What *did* you tell them, then?"

"Nothing. They didn't ask."

"But they kidnapped you. I saw the door and the bullet hole in the altar—"

"They wanted me dead because of what I know. Himmler and Heydrich want me dead. Hitler wants me to rejoin the special group. I told them I knew how to excavate the inside. I said it to save my life. So they put me through this test…they made me—" He breaks into a cold sweat. (*"Sausages,"* a three-year old tries to say in his memory, and a six-year old rescues him with the self-righteousness that comes from knowing there is a proper world full of proper ways.)

"So now you're going to rejoin your group and excavate the moraine," says Father Kovacki.

"We won't find the reservoir," Krantz promises. "I'll make sure of that."

"It may be inevitable. Or you may change your mind. They may become impatient, and your life would be on the line—"

"No. I won't let them do that to me again. It would be better to die…I—" A proven coward should keep his mouth shut.

"Life has its cardinal rules, Josef, but there are burdens we cannot escape. Make your peace with God and pray that you choose right to the best of your strength and ability. Are you at peace?"

"I don't know."

"Nor do I. God help me."

And with that Father Kovacki slides sideways along the pew and raises his hand in apparent blessing. But from his grasp bursts flame and a roar. Twice. One bullet tears a chunk out of Krantz's neck, splattering blood like a fountain pen. The second strikes him in the chest, bouncing him off the corner of the pew with a pronounced looseness that speaks of ultimate freedom.

The order of the sentinel priests of Niski Kosciol has not failed. A man who knows for certain the location of the reservoir is dead and only one other knows what he knew. But that, too, must be secured. Turning the barrel of the revolver to his own temple, Father Kovacki pulls the trigger for the third time. Priests who kill and priests who commit suicide in the name of the current world order may be at the bottom of hell, and then again, they may be martyrs.

7

Krantz can feel tunnels inside himself. Dead spots. But the first glimmer of actual consciousness intrudes like a sliver, and he cements his eyes shut, retreating amid the respiring tubes and bags around his head. He dreams he is back in the undertow of the moraine, spinning, his breath hissing and bubbling in his ears.

The next time, he awakens sharply, popping clear of the surface where the ugly memory waits. For a few lucid seconds he catches it all—the hospital room webbed with apparatus, himself half-digested in linen and gauze, Niski Kosciol's children standing forlorn and ghoulish in the shadows. And someone else. A woman. That is as much as he wants to see. Grasping these facts like stones, he lets their dead weight carry him back into oblivion.

He returns at intervals after that. The tunnels become rusted bolts inside him. The bullets have torn up the trachea, one lung. He will mend. He doesn't want to mend. Dawns overwhelm him, a child's cry from the ward above lances his dilated soul, kind words produce a sudden sadness.

When he is well enough to talk, the Gestapo arrives with questions, revealing that the priest is dead. Exaggerating his weakness and aided by a genuine hoarseness, Krantz presents the twin frailty that Father Kovacki became fanatic in the wake of the EinsatzGruppen, shot him, and then, overcome with grief, must have killed himself. And why did Krantz go back to the church? To find Lutka's burial site, he answers. "Ah, what fools women make of us," says the Gestapo.

Early in December they move him to the psychiatric wing. Gone are the impartial mists, the antiseptic white, the impersonal measuring of him by what goes in and out of bottles. Here there are colors, choices, informal people with nothing to do but talk. And

Geli Strucker. Buxom. Puffy-lipped. The woman in the room when he came to.

She is one of a class of things he now hates for being catalysts—clocks, phones, puzzles, anthems, enthusiastic radio announcers. She tries to draw him back, but he tells her outrageous lies, voluble anecdotes about World War I, lyrical descriptions of his villa in the Black Forest. Gradually the lies merge with authentic memories. Like mnemonic tinker toys, the scraps of his past build into something bigger than its parts. He is not that frozen moment in time in Niski Kosciol but something that existed before then—a builder of tree forts; a young man crying alone in the showers after a soccer match. Three months of mothering, of kiss-and-make-up with life, and therapist Geli Strucker has reassembled him for duty.

And then, like a snowfall in spring, Lutz Hoffmann appears one day. *"Heil Hitler,"* he murmurs apologetically. "You're going back."

Krantz draws his knees up to his chest. "How wonderful."

"Well, it's our territory now. No more reconnaissance. Just what you trained for."

"I trained to be an architect."

"None of us are purebreds, Josef." Hoffmann sits down, hoists the leather briefcase onto the bed, unlocks the cuff.

Krantz watches Lutz's hands, thin and white, like a pair of ivory letter openers. Diving, swooping, courting swans in tandem. All the while performing mid-wifery on the leather womb, delivering bundles of photos and diagrams.

The site has been split into an upper and lower base. And it is all there on paper: four shifts of drillers, three angled shafts, a tidal lock, details. The most expeditious way of looking for a needle in a granite haystack lies in Krantz's lap.

"A decision has to be made on the linking patterns of cross shafts," says Lutz.

Krantz replies that it is simple geometry, vertical shafts are needed. Amazed at such an inefficient solution, Hoffmann argues. Vertical shafts are a waste and almost insure years of excavating, whereas diagonals could produce a breakthrough in months. Vertical shafts might be slow but they will prevent a large scale collapse, says Krantz. And anyway, the reservoir might be as tiny as a capsule, and in that case they will have to carve up the interior bit by bit, so therefore the basic thrust should be a progressive sectioning rather than wild transversals.

Lutz pinches the bridge of his nose. "They all think you're a traitor, Josef."

"Vertical shafts, Lutz. Vertical shafts."

Two days later he boards a train for Stolp, Poland. The engine keeps slowing to accommodate troop movements, and Krantz is struck by the contrasting countryside. West of the border is the social insect: cutting timber, tending plots, guiding barges. And to the east is occupied Poland where the same species of insect is broken, stunned, crawling. Nothing is ever really conquered. Wars are for the sake of maps.

At Stolp he transfers to the rear seat of a staff car and begins to steel himself for Niski Kosciol. In his mind it is still ruins, a village without children. But he need not fear facing the survivors. When the open staff car brazenly motors down the main street, only a handful of Poles remain, the token indigenous. Soldiers are quartered everywhere. The fine hot-houses south of town have been corrugated into barracks, the tannery is a motor pool, and the schoolhouse—what good is a schoolhouse in Niski Kosciol—has its name struck and is flying the red swastika banners of General Headquarters.

Someone has stopped the scrolled hands on the clock in Rudnicki's window, and that seems appropriate. Niski Kosciol is no more. Krantz feels an unmistakable pang of regret that there is no penance to be served. But then from among a toothless crowd of peasants near the church he glimpses a pair of large amber eyes and beetle brows following him. He has not been forgotten, not forgiven, he thinks almost with relief as he stares straight ahead on the road to the coast.

They arrive at a single checkpoint at the moraine with its sign, "Hospital," a quarter of an hour later. The base purports to be a staging area for medical supplies and patients. Beneath that cover is another deception: *U-boat base.* To the thoughtful, this explains the second fence—electrified—and the sentries who patrol with dogs at night.

The checkpoint guard calls ahead, and Gebbler himself comes, nodding his oversized head, gray eyes icing the distance between himself and Krantz. "Are you fit?" he asks bluntly.

"Berlin thinks so."

"I've cleared the largest office in the administrative wing for you." He leads the way into a blockhouse corridor and with shooting fingers ticks off the blueprint. "Four wings: northeast, Schaub's machine shop; northwest, Ultmeir's logistics; southeast, quarters; southwest, administrative wing. There is a separate mess hall and receiving depot. A few of the villagers have overcome their superstitions to deliver supplies. We keep them out of the main building."

"Skip the offices, Gustav. I want to see the site."

Gebbler ushers him back out the corridor and across the grounds to a cage on the edge of the cliff where a heavy wooden lift on a winch eases them to the frothy rocks below. Through the cage mesh in the final stages of descent, Krantz confronts the upturned faces of the zombies. They are standing on a newly built pier: granite faced Bruckner, grinning Lugert, Gothic Wolff. By the time the cage clangs home on a catwalk they have their backs to him in studied contempt, and Gebbler leads him down a flight of nine steps into the damp, corroding lock that breaches the outer cavern. A dimly lit neck of tunnel connects another nine steps going up.

And then they cross the threshold where physics seems to break down.

He has forgotten the feeling. Enervating. As if the body becomes a sieve for the energy under the dome. The air tastes hot, smells oily, and seems to stick in his throat where the bullet wound healed. Even with lights and shafts and scaffolds, the sense of trespass is the same. Gebbler's face reflects it, too, a light gloss, deepened breathing. A distinct cloud lies over the water and rainbows gird the lights spiked into the walls on snaking cables. And even these—the lights—seem to illuminate nothing but the geometry of scaffolds, as if their energy is also manipulated.

Somewhere in one of the three shafts vaguely illuminated by more lights on the scaffolding, a drill erupts briefly, dropping powdery meteors into the black water.

"Damn it, take a chunk out!" Ernst Schaub's gravelly voice materializes above them.

An answer floats out of one of three shafts. "Big rocks might break the scaffolding! I can't swim!"

"Gebbler's sending lifeguards, take out chunks!"

"Schaub!" hollers Krantz. "Let him be careful!"

Schaub's stocky form leans out, white face pressing down. "Krantz?" He moves along the catwalk. "Is that you?"

"We don't want the whole roof in our laps, Ernst, just bits and pieces!"

"Damn, it is you!"

"Schaub-y's found his element as a petty tyrant," Gebbler says. "Hoffmann told him you intend to excavate a pebble at a time. But there's no stopping a natural born driver."

They wait in chill silence for Schaub to climb down and emerge from the graininess like a photograph out of a negative, grinning his gapped-tooth grin.

"Welcome to the inside of the whale. It's like the Ruhr without the smell."

"At this rate the whale's going to be gutted without being examined," says Krantz.

"Ulcers, just ulcers." Schaub dismisses the dome with a wave. "It's like talking to the fucking moon up there...like talking to an oracle. You say something to one of those three holes and out pops a fucking answer."

Schaub smells of beer, Gebbler reeks of his pipe; it occurs to Krantz that they are all struggling for an identity.

"The one thing Berlin won't tolerate is failure," he says. "We have to find the reservoir *eventually*, and that's all that matters. Speed is secondary. Did Hoffmann tell you we're going to vertical shafts?"

"Begging your pardon, sir, but vertical shafts seem like a waste. We should keep angling through the largest untouched areas."

Sir. A new formality. *You're full of shit, sir.*

"The angles were a justifiable gamble," Krantz sighs. "If the reservoir was a large room, we would have hit it right away and all gone back to Berlin drunk on champagne. But it isn't a large room, and therefore, it is probably no bigger than a capsule—a chalice—something we could easily lose in a 'chunk.' So permit me my educated guess, Ernst, that it's centrally located above the dome and in the lowest layers of the moraine. Verticals."

The drill interrupts, trailing debris like rain.

"Verticals," Krantz repeats when the echoes die.

"Angles, verticals—all the same to me." Schaub grins. "Hell, I can't even put my socks on in the dark, let alone figure angles. Hoffmann will be the one to bitch. His men will have to crawl like flies up there. But if Michelangelo painted ceilings that way, I guess the master race can drill."

Hoffmann indeed bitches. Spitting his s's crisply, sucking his m's like mints. Krantz listens patiently at dinnertime.

"The men aren't magnets, Josef. We'll have to anchor slings every meter. The place will look like an aerial circus!"

The man passing behind Krantz at that moment is a merchant delivering potatoes from the village. He has passed twice already. Lots of potatoes.

"You can't *sculpt* the thing, you've got to *mine* it," Lutz is saying.

And suddenly the feeling of opaqueness behind Krantz is strong enough to make him jerk left just as the clouded steel of a butcher knife blurs past. But the moment he gains is now lost as he stares at the jigsaw puzzle his plate has become. The white undulation of a man's knuckles rip the knife free, breaking the spell.

Krantz whirls.

The blade flicks back and forth, and around them the room expands. On the second lunge, Krantz catches the man's wrist, wincing when his elbow smashes the wall. Large amber eyes and beetle brows fall over his face like an eclipse as the blade presses downward. Hot breath sears him. Then, quite unexplainably, the assassin rears back. There is a sickening snap, his cheeks spasm, the knife clatters away. Otherworldly Erich Wolff, with his bulbous brow, thicket of jet black hair, hypertrophic physique and cyanic pallor, stands over the fallen body.

"That's what we get for dealing with Poles," wheezes Hoffmann, pinching his coffee-stained pantleg away from his thigh.

A father, Krantz thinks, gasping for air. His wounds are throbbing. It has to be a father. Who can blame a father? Who can blame any decent human being for wanting to kill him? Forgiveness is out of the question.

The months at the base become a year, then almost two, and the wonderfully mammoth moraine shows endless reserve. Anathema to Niski Kosciol, it complements Krantz's penance. The decent population in the village will not come near the moraine; and of course the village is forever banned to him now, even if he was permitted to leave the base, which he is not. It is not just the mistrust, though. They fear his assassination. A well-founded fear. Because there are assassins and one in particular, who, though he has been dragged off to a prison camp, is preparing the final penance for Josef Krantz....

8

Along the border of the commandant's office at Treblinka, valiant deceits poke boldly from the soil. It is said the commandant waters them with the blood of Jews, for they are singularly red, these tulips. Red but odorless. There is only one odor at Treblinka. Burnt bodies. Half a thousand each day. 90,000 in six months.

On this particular day, in the spring of 1941, an SS sergeant drags a scrawny prisoner across the compound to the commandant's door, taking care not to disturb the red tulips. The prisoner is Zolkower, and it has to be said that for all the rigors of a concentration camp he looks essentially the same as he did that September night two years ago when the children of Niski Kosciol were buried alive on his farm. He has survived like a piece of spring steel in a scrap heap of humanity, rusted but strong. He has survived as he swore he would, by hating the man called Krantz and plotting the crossing of their futures. So much has he thought on this that he is now convinced it is inevitable, and that he, therefore, is immune to death until just that time.

Was immune.

The miserable wretch is having second thoughts in the sergeant's grasp. Almost certainly he is seeing his last sunshine, last flowers. A shot of phenol in the heart, maybe benzene, is minutes away. He has heard that at other camps incoming children are given a toy balloon to distract them before the injection. Maybe they will give him a toy balloon.

The titan sergeant hammers on the commandant's door, receives permission to enter and hoists Zolkower across the threshold like a sack of potatoes.

"Dipping his mop in the officers toilet to clean the seats!" he proclaims.

Zolkower bows his head, hearing the chair, the boots, the jangling keys. Authoritarian figures terrify him.

The commandant's voice is flat and calm. "What is your name?"

Zolkower gazes at the commandant's snowy temples and tells him his name.

"Don't you have a bucket, Zolkower?"

The sergeant kicks him to his knees. "He's the one that's been shitting on the floor, sir, I'm sure of it!"

"Have you been defecating on the floor, Zolkower?"

Zolkower lies at their feet in blood-flecked spittle. There are hot stones inside him. Yes, he shits on their floors and dips his mop in their toilets. The bastards trapped him in his outhouse, didn't they?

Another kick flattens him. The sergeant's heel comes down between his shoulder blades while the commandant rages.

"I'm overwhelmed with stinking Jews from the Warsaw ghetto! There's no end to them. They breed like flies. Thousands and thousands. Stinking, sub-human flies!"

"He should be made an example of," agrees the sergeant.

"It's not enough I have to liquidate five hundred a day and sort out the rest." The commandant's hand spirals eccentrically. "I have to send the best labor to Farben and Krupp as well! Nothing left but defectives—Zolkowers, stinking Zolkowers! Your name will be in my *Totenbuch* today, Zolkower. We'll see if that stops these defecations."

Totenbuch. The death ledger. The sergeant wrenches Zolkower upright by the hair.

"Just a moment," orders the commandant. "Yesterday I had a visit from Rudolf Höss. Have you heard of Höss, Sergeant?"

"The Death Head's Group, Herr Commandant?"

"Yes. Ambitious son of a bitch from Sachsenhausen." He leans back on his desk. "He's been ordered to establish facilities at Auschwitz, and he had the audacity to criticize my methods on his inspection tour."

"A little experience will make him appreciative," ventures the sergeant.

"I said I'd supply him with Jewish volunteers to train Sonderkommandos, but I hate to waste the few good workers I have." The commandant palms the hair smooth at his temples. "It occurs to me that Zolkower here could teach Höss a good deal about camp *in*efficiency."

The sergeant laughs.

"Want to be a Sonderkommando, Zolkower?"

Zolkower's head lolls sideways. He has only heard rumors of these teams, Jewry's untouchables. "Cleaning the dead...out of showers?"

"Yes."

"Pulling gold...?"

"From teeth, yes!"

To refuse means to die in the monoxide chambers of Treblinka. Zolkower nods faintly.

"You'll be an important man at Auschwitz," says the commandant. "Höss is ambitious. He'll have chambers that hold two thousand Jews apiece. Imagine! Ours hold only two hundred. You must practice diligently. Herr Höss will expect an experienced hand with a strong stomach."

"You were lucky, you know that?" whispers the prisoner beside Zolkower in the dark of the barracks. "I warned you. By the hair of the prophet, I warned you. Hating does no good."

"You don't hate enough," Zolkower murmurs. "It's sheep like you who make this possible."

"It's useless to fight Goliaths. We're Davids without slings. Let them at least not rob us of our souls. I'll die with dignity. I will not hate out of fear the way they do. I tell you it's not this Nazi supremacy nonsense that brought us here. It's their fear and insecurity. You think this could happen only in Germany? No, Zolkower. Anywhere. Wherever there's hate like yours."

Maybe so. But he must survive. "Go to hell," he says and summons forth his nightly vision of vaporous blue eyes, melancholy face and an amputated finger.

9

Guarding a moraine on the Baltic has become wearisome to the sentries. Lichter especially hates it. He was trained at Krössinsee to dispatch enemies of the Reich. Now, while his unit dispatches them on the eastern front, he performs a worthless watch on a catwalk at the foot of a rock. He can't imagine, and neither does anyone seem to know, what is so important about this "reservoir."

Bruckner, Lugert and Wolff might know, but they are as secretive as the non-SS staff. Wolff in particular probably grasps why they are here, because he underwent political and spiritual training at Vogelsang, the special castle in the Rheinland.

As far as Lichter can see, none of them seem to be in any particular hurry, because not a damned thing is going right. Supplies are always screwed up, equipment damage is phenomenal, morale is low. They argue and that makes it worse. This Josef Krantz is a horse's ass. Ever since he was wounded in the throat, he speaks with a hoarseness that makes him think he's the Führer.

Suddenly Lichter stops. He is thoroughly used to the coursing wind that moans in the tidal lock and booms in the cavern, but what is the other sound? The slithering. Baltic waves crash at the footings of the catwalk, smoothing away the impression.

"Mannerheim!" he calls to the guard on the pier.

A helmeted silhouette disengages from the shadow of a piling, cigarette smoke ribboning on the wind. Moonlight catches the glint of a machine pistol coming to ready.

"I'm leaving my post!" calls Lichter, pointing to the tidal lock.

Mannerheim waves.

Lichter slogs through the puddles of the corroded lock, deafened by the shrill of a sudden gust. When it dies, and his foot is on the first of the nine ascending steps, he hears the slither again. This time he unshoulders his weapon. For two days the shifts have been canceled because of another improbable accident—stored drills tipping off one of the scaffolds—that has left them short-supplied. The cavern should be empty.

There are only two lights burning, one by the generator, the other on the central scaffold that straddles the water like a cargo unloader squatting over a freighter. It all looks rather theatrical to Lichter with its gaping holes in the dome and machinery dangling like gargantuan spiders in black steel webs.

Lichter shoots a beam across the gluey pool in time to witness two sets of dissipating rings. He nudges the light upward, but there is no powder such as falling debris invariably leaves in the air. Back to the motionless surface goes the beam. An eerie feeling takes hold of Lichter. The drillers claim there is energy in the cavern. A hot wind. They say it makes them irritable.

He strides slowly to the tower anchoring the central scaffold and places a hand on the first rung. Deliberately he climbs, pausing every few meters to listen. But the booming is like oil drums banging together now, and he doesn't catch the harsh slither again until halfway up. There the flashlight beam skitters from strut to strut and down to the pool, faintly phosphorescent at this height.

Nothing…

Resuming his climb, he reaches the top and walks the main horizontal, shooting the light upward where it is swallowed by one shaft after another. Angles bend the beam. Fully half the dome's supporting material has been removed. The thing is now a massive chiffon of arches and buttresses.

Lichter is only just beginning to comprehend this fact when the air seems to swell and turn hot against his skin. Simultaneously the slithering increases to a rushing, grating sound that he tries in vain to pinpoint with his light. Back and forth the beam flows over the ceiling as the scaffold trembles.

Suddenly Lichter is staring at an insidious fault line. He braces himself, horror-stricken as the fault line yawns into a grin and cabbage size boulders begin to cascade out of the vault. With the first hits the scaffold jars and begins to buckle.

Lichter falls to his knees and grabs the rail. The flashlight tumbling into the void opens a viscous, green incision in the skin of the pool. Then comes the tumultuous roar as great sections of the dome break loose. Like a mechanical dragon, the whole interlocked tail of catwalks lash stiffly in the rain of debris and plummet into the water.

Bleating emergency horns bring the base to full alert in thirty seconds. Searchlights scissor the coastal sky, anti-aircraft batteries poke free of camouflage, scores of Waffen SS take strategic positions.

But, except for the patrol dogs barking back at the horns, a stillness prevails above ground. Only the troops deploying like a chain of ants to the lower base know the extent of the emergency. Among them Gebbler, Krantz and Hoffmann come down the lift together.

"The roof has collapsed," Hoffmann predicts with a glance at Krantz. "It was inevitable."

"Dynamite!" Gebbler keeps repeating. "Some swine got in with dynamite."

The lock is choked with dust and soldiers making their way up and down the twin flights by flashlight. Inside, the generator has been knocked out.

"Sir?" The sentry who speaks to Krantz beams a light into his own face. "I'm Corporal Mannerheim, sir. I was the sentry on the pier. Lichter was outside the lock. He signaled he was going in just before this happened." The corporal shifts his light to the grainy interior, emphasizing what a dozen other beams are exploring. "The roof just fell in."

"Was there an explosion?"

"I heard a rumble."

"We all heard a rumble, Corporal."

"Lichter didn't come out, sir." Mannerheim's light licks the twisted rails of the scaffold, now half sunk in the pool.

Hoffmann draws Krantz aside. "It may be on the bottom now, you realize. It could be locked in stone down there. We'll have to dredge."

"Eventually," says Krantz. "But the odds have been increasing that it's higher in the moraine. We'll excavate from the upper base."

In the faint rebound of light, Hoffmann's arrowhead lips poise as if he has just gotten a joke.

And then Ernst Schaub's "Oh, shit!" announces his arrival in the company of Ultmeir, whose looping burnsides mustache hides half his expression.

"It'll take me six months to replace some of this stuff," anguishes Schaub, "even at our priority, six months! Some son of a bitch in Speer's office is already complaining to the Führer about my requisitions. Wait'll I ask them to replace this!"

A shout from the ledge of the pool draws everyone's attention. One of the SS has spotted Lichter's body impaled on a strut. The soldiers fan out along the water's edge so that their beams produce spokes of light to the middle. A jumble of iron fingers are cupped around Lichter, who arches out of the water on a thin prong of iron protruding from his chest.

Krantz circles behind the Waffen SS as they prepare the small barge used in joining the center scaffolds to retrieve their comrade's body, and the silence at his passing feels a lot like indictment. Lichter is the third death. Seven months ago a driller fell. Three months later another died screaming when a shaft pinched together. The first two might have happened anyway. But how, in fact, *could* the dome collapse?

Gustav Gebbler has his own theory, which states simply that neither Krantz nor Hoffmann have a competent grasp of the moraine's structure. The granite cliff supporting it must have an uneven surface. Constant drilling isolated and weakened those sections where the softer moraine made pockets in the cliff.

Gebbler has always believed the reservoir is in the moraine itself, because the last ice age predates it. Nevertheless, he accepted Krantz's judgment at first because he was pleased with the security the inner cavern offered. But what good is security when you isolate the wrong area? Colossal incompetence, he was heard complaining at officers' mess just last week. "It boils down to that." And in Krantz's case, a lack of nerve. But now…

"Maybe we'll get somewhere," he tells Ultmeir at lunch. "Excavating from the surface is sure to produce results."

"My dear Gustav," says Ultmeir, stroking his mustache, "it would have been much simpler if the reservoir had turned up in a tunnel or a cave below the moraine. If you think we've spent a long time doing nothing, wait till you see how unpiling a mountain of sediment goes."

Gebbler makes the arrangements for Lichter's body to be shipped home and meets briefly with Krantz to discuss security on the above-ground site. He will have to file a report on the collapse, he says, since it might involve sabotage. Krantz says he is already filing a report and that drill vibrations linking fault lines was the most likely cause, but that Gebbler can file anything he damn pleases.

Afterward, Gebbler visits the kennels to see that the patrol dogs are well fed, checks on a searchlight that malfunctioned at the height of the alert, and offers his commendation to the SS unit for their quick response. Then he writes his report, placing a copy on Krantz's desk, keeping another, sending the original to Berlin.

Following a quiet dinner, he retires to his quarters and his secret passion: translating Gaelic poems. He has a shoebox full of index cards each containing a line of Irish verse, followed by German permutations written in a fine, cramped hand. When all the lines are translated they will be weighed for litheness and balance and regathered lovingly. What he gets out of this, he imagines, isn't far from creativity. But tonight he barely begins when Ernst Schaub calls from the doorway.

"Begging your pardon, Gustav, may I speak with you?"

Schaub is mere prose yet equally as untranslatable as the Gaelic verse. Gebbler scrutinizes him as his visitor carefully closes the door, pulls a chair up tight to the desk, and nervously draws two fingers over his lips.

"We never see much of each other, Gustav. I mean you're a quiet kind of guy, and when you say something, it's important. No bullshit, if you know what I mean."

Gebbler leans forward as if to hear what is beneath the flattery.

"So I don't know just how to say this," Schaub continues, "but me and the men we respect you, if you know what I mean. We don't pretend to understand any of this administrative crap, but we can see you've got a tough job—a *tough* job—and we think you should know we're behind you one hundred percent."

Gebbler continues to lean, his oversized head implying proportions that don't exist beneath the line of the desk.

"So it's plain to us you need our support," Schaub says, "because…because of this situation."

"Situation?"

"This *situation*, Gustav, all this...this screw-up."

"Screw-up?"

"Like I said, we don't pretend to understand administrative things, but when I order drill bits and get back cable, and everything is breaking or missing, and three men are killed—*three*, Gustav—and two of them are mine, well hell, I can smell something. Do you realize what would've happened if we had a full shift up there when the roof came down?"

"Are you telling me this has something to do with security, Ernst?"

"You're damn right it does!" Schaub gives his bullet head a hard scratch. "Security. Absolutely."

"What security?"

"Damn it, Gebbler...damn it, this can't all be accidental."

"Who then? Krantz?"

"That's not for me to say. But me and the men, we're behind you. You understand? If it comes down to a security thing, we're behind you, that's all." He stands up. "We just wanted you to know, that's all. It could've been a lot worse last night. No one wants to get killed."

Alone, Gebbler turns it over. Sabotage. Krantz. Traitor. Not a new theme. But far too bold for the cowardly architect. He might once have had the courage to try to run, to overcome personal inertia—that much courage. But moral martyrdom? If there is any of that in him, it went out with Einsatzgruppe D in Niski Kosciol.

It always works that way. Assigning an abominable task is an old SS trick. Dehumanization. He has heard of SS recruits being ordered to kill Jewish babies in front of their mothers, the idea being to break a social taboo, to create a moral separation. Once done, there is no turning back. The recruit embraces his special role in order to be absolved.

Krantz made his separation at Niski Kosciol.

So the architect's culpability stops at incompetence and a lack of nerve. What does Schaub expect, criminal charges? Things have to get better now. But if they don't, it may come to open accusations...maybe. *Maybe*, he repeats to himself, leafing through his shoebox.

Out on the pier, Schaub is working on a different solution: "Too bad it wasn't Krantz instead of Lichter on the strut," he says to Bruckner.

And inside the cavern Krantz himself sits on the docked barge, staring at the wreckage by the light of a dry cell lantern. Drill vibrations linked fault lines and caused the collapse, he told Gebbler. But perhaps fifty meters beyond the interior wall lies the reservoir he once visited. And there is a kind of energy under this dome almost as strong as in that sub-cave.

A little while ago they found Lichter's body, and that was surreal, too. All those SS around the pool, the metal spire stabbing out of the middle. Teutonic knights and the sword coming out of the lake. Perverted King Arthur. Like Wewelsburg. Like Mehring Damm. Vibrations linked fault lines for certain. But *whose* vibrations?

Carefully he moves his light up the inner wall. Every bump and depression is familiar to him, every highlight and shadow, chink and cranny, crack and crevice, cleft and fissure. The evolving interior of the dome as the Case White special team drills upward through the moraine comes under his examination every day, haunts his nightmares. Because he cannot be sure invisible fractures aren't expanding laterally. And what if the cavern just above pool level begins to sheer away in the direction of the reservoir? What if a fault line brings fifty meters of ancient rock splashing down in some ill-fated way, exposing an obscene little temple with its seven doomsday grails behind seven doomsday seals?

So Josef Krantz does not merely survey the dome beneath the moraine, he meditates upon each change on its surface, large or small.

And now the beam of his dry cell lantern catches a new shadow on the slope closest to the reservoir. The small swathe of darkness is fresh, he is quite certain. But reverberations from the collapsed area could have caused it. No immediate cause for concern.

Except that as he studies the sculpted darkness, *two stones pop out.*

For thirty seconds he stares in fascination. They did pop out, he assures himself. Or was it the wind through the lock, the pressure of shifting rock?

A pair of towers and a catwalk remain upright on that side of the pool. It will not do to ignore any breach of the inner wall. If tunnels or more caves are opened behind it, the excavation must logically extend on that track.

In that case, he would have no more excuse to go in the wrong direction. And he must go in the wrong direction—must continue to stall! The war is faltering. Rumors have the Wehrmacht overextended in Russia and Africa. Rommel is taking a beating at a place called El Alamein. How much longer can it last? Krantz dares hope for a turning point, a settlement, even defeat.

Picking up the lantern by its wire handle and jumping from the barge, he paces slowly to the foot of the scaffold. Heights are not his thing. A step ladder is his limit. Don't look down, he tells himself, and hand over hand, begins the climb.

But looking down isn't the problem. Looking up is. Because the wire handle looped over two of his fingers as he climbs causes the light to sweep wildly over the dome's interior. He tries to focus on the steel pipe at each reach, but already his eyes are swimming. Vertigo fills him. He stops. Closes his eyes. Takes four steadying breaths.

Children play on things like this, he tells himself. And the thought of children playing—the children of Niski Kosciol—chills him with horror, then anger at himself. Opening his eyes, he climbs steadily now, even recklessly, ignoring the humidity that makes his hands slip…ignoring the thrumming in the steel pipe—

Thrumming?

He runs the light across the catwalk and up and down the opposite tower. Sees nothing. The thrumming is on his side.

Something is crawling up after him!

Pulling himself the final couple of feet onto the catwalk, he shoots the lantern beam straight down.

"Schaub?"

The weaving body swarms up the final few rungs like a monkey, and Ernst Schaub swings onto the walk beside him.

Krantz drops the lantern beam to Schaub's chest.

"This is probably what Lichter did," Schaub says, turning his palms up. "If you don't mind my saying, sir, you should stay out of the cavern. Away from the excavation entirely."

"The excavation is my responsibility."

"Lichter must have hit that strut at 120 kilometers an hour. The scaffold stopped collapsing, and there he was." Schaub makes a sucking sound that breaks off suddenly, and then he jabs his finger into Krantz. "Dangerous. Leave the excavating to us, sir."

Unable to keep from looking down, Krantz gauges the fall. A thirty-meter drop, another fifteen from the tower base to the water. The wreckage of the other scaffold leaves little room. He imagines himself plummeting, blood cramming into his skull, fingers spreading, stomach rising—

"You don't like the way I'm running things? Is that what's bothering you, Schaub?"

"Dying. Dying's bothering me."

"This kind of excavation is high risk. It's unavoidable."

"Mistakes are making it higher."

From across the pool comes a transversal of light and Mannerheim's voice.

"We're excavating from the top now," Krantz says to Schaub. "That should make it easier."

He brushes past and climbs down, feeling the thrum of Schaub's descent coming after him.

10

His arrest for vagrancy scarcely registers on Mika Lott. Klaus the baker is dead and his archives are confiscated. What is left? Like Josef Krantz, he has a reason to live—a purpose far larger than himself—and like the young German architect, the stench of death is all around him and his world is gray. But unlike Krantz, Mika's world has a formal name.

Buchenwald.

The horrors here are arbitrary. Life is a pretense. Everyone knows this and that hope is an obscenity. You almost want to die out of shame and revulsion for what your species is capable of perpetrating. But there is a path to survival, also arbitrary.

For Mika, the path begins in July of 1943 when a certain German lawyer named Konrad Morgen travels to Buchenwald to investigate Commandant Karl Koch. Morgen works for the SD's Financial Crimes Office, and Koch is suspected of racketeering in food and selling labor for personal profit. Koch's wife, Ilse, known universally as the Bitch of Buchenwald, is said to fashion household articles from the skin, bone and hair of Jews.

Morgen has already served in a front-line SS division for investigating prisoner mistreatment with too much zeal. But he is brilliant, and Himmler demands the highest personal ethics of his commandants, and so Morgen is here with his assistants to ferret out greed and to ignore "political" matters.

He is surprised at the grounds of Buchenwald. Curried, freshly painted, they include a multi-lingual library, regular mail service, movies, a brothel. Holed up in Hitler's favorite stopover in Weimar, the Elephant Hotel, Morgen begins his search of camp and bank records, as well as interviewing and collecting affidavits. He knows better than to believe in Buchenwald's grass and flowers.

Grass and flowers grow on graves.

The third prisoner he interviews is Mika Lott.

"You work in the kitchen, is that right?" he asks promptly.

"Yes."

"I'd like you to tell me how food supplies are handled. Do not fear for your answer, Herr Lott."

Mika tells him, but to subsequent questions he is careful to omit any mention of the regular profiteering by camp officials in the black market. The interview ends abruptly and he returns to his job not knowing if he has escaped damnation or been compromised simply for being interviewed.

Just before dawn on a warm, humid night some two weeks after Morgen's arrival, three SS guards enter his barracks.

"Epstein…Nausbaum…Lott!" one of them recites, while the others aim lights into terrified, black-ringed eyes.

The three designated prisoners crawl shaking out of their racks amid whispered good-bys. Nausbaum, devout in a curiously original way, swears as he prays—"Dear God, I was a son of a bitch most my life, forgive me and these poor bastards"—until the SS guard who called the names tells him with crisp urgency to shut-up.

It seems to Mika then that the SS are afraid. This is not the brutally efficient manner seen in the daily culling, nor the sardonic humoring of a tattooed prisoner invited into Ilse Koch's parlor where his skin is to be turned into a lamp shade (*just as Solovyov predicted some forty years ago!*). Murder is no secret here. So Mika concludes they are not to die. Some other purpose is being served.

They scurry obediently across the yard, like three bald and loosely garbed novices in a monastery, and into the back of a truck. One of the two SS clambering in behind them indicates a pile of street clothes with his light and orders Mika to put them on. The lantern adds half a meter of shadow to their statures, making them look peculiarly alert.

If it weren't for the street clothes, Mika would believe he is destined for slave labor nearby at a profit to Commandant Koch. Or, since the SD's Financial Crimes Office has been interviewing prisoners, the commandant may be removing him from circulation. But there is no special reason for this. He is a very ordinary prisoner. And why haven't Nausbaum and Epstein been given civilian clothes?

The answers begin to emerge after a short drive to a sawmill on the outskirts of Weimar. He sees only a glimpse of wood frames piled high with boards, but there is the smell of fresh-cut lumber, and Epstein and Nausbaum are prodded out. So they, at least, have been sold. But who buys a Mika Lott—in civilian clothes yet? The truck continues on into the heart of Weimar, and when it stops the second time, the SS guard says simply, "Get out."

So there he is, standing in the middle of Weimar in the middle of the war in the middle of the night, astonished that the truck is driving off. It occurs to him that he will now be shot as an escaped prisoner. The truck will come round the block and the guard will open up on him.

Even though the whine of the truck is already receding in the distance.

He strolls slowly into the street, locking his hands behind him. A pair of cats, white and black, cascade off a ledge beside an alley, and he looks there for the trick. True to form, headlights ignite, and he pulls off the cap they gave him, as if in supplication. The lights reveal his bare head, shorn of silver ram's horns, and his shaved eyebrows. A slight cough introduces the engine behind the lights, twin beams dimming. Then the car starts forward, pinning him in its glare until, three meters shy, it veers and the door swings open.

"Get in!"

Get out...get in. A reasonable balance. He does as he is told.

The lone occupant is perhaps sixty, the flabby ruin of a big man. His hands on the crest of the wheel are better illuminated than his face—big hands, broad-nailed, stained and smelling of ink. There is something familiar about them. But even when the man turns and greets him by name, the face eludes Mika.

"I wouldn't have picked you out of a crowd either," says Willi Oberstein. "But we regularly buy lists from the guards at Buchenwald and other camps. And there you were: Mika Lott, vagrant. The commandant is a bribe-taker, as long as he thinks the prisoner is harmless."

"Willi!" Mika gasps.

Willi grins. "Welcome back to the Temple Guard, Mika."

He is driven to a farmhouse between Bamberg and Bayreuth where a very brave elderly couple has made provision for him. The house has served more than one refugee in the past several years, but Willi assures him it isn't compromised. Still digesting freedom, Mika takes it in slowly. Where has Willi been since their Munich days? How active is the Temple Guard? Who is still alive? Who is free? Esther Masterograncesco...?

Esther is dead. Ravensbruck.

The elderly woman recognizes confusion and guilt and insists Oberstein leave Mika alone. She has seen these things before, an internee suddenly freed after expecting to die, after dying in every spiritual and esthetic sense, burdened with moral debt to the luckless living left behind. She gives him simple food and the sparest room. The radio is kept low; the house breathes order and serenity.

Once, Mika asks for wine and tries to get drunk but only gets sick. Then, just a week after his arrival, he suddenly wants to see Willi.

Willi is summoned like a faithful hound, and the two of them sit facing each other in the sparsely furnished room.

"Willi, they took my files."

"I know."

"All those years collecting...they took my files."

"You can start new ones. Lots of things have been gathered."

"I've still got most of it in my head," says Mika. "And I know what it means. That's something. Someone might go through them and never really grasp the point. But I know. I understand Hitler... the Reich."

"Better than anyone, Mika. That's why you're so important to the Temple Guard."

"What's been done, Willi? We heard rumors that the war is going badly. What's been done?"

Willi licks his lips and his right hand comes up, stiff as a scimitar, to emphasize a point. "We think the British understand a little. The occult instability, I mean. They know Berlin is wobbly. For certain they know that."

"That Intelligence isn't new to them. War is madness built on irrational moments. It doesn't tell them *what's* in charge in Berlin."

"We may have changed that a little when we smuggled out

evidence that the Reich's records were annotated astrologically."

"What evidence?"

"Copies bribed from a senior official. You have no idea how our finances have improved. Jewelry, gold, cash, art objects—"

"And these astrological records are supposed to convince England that the Reich is tapping into something more dangerous than myths?"

"Not just the records. Did you know that Rudolf Hess flew to England to try to arrange a peace through members of the Golden Dawn? He told the British he was directed in a dream to do it, and Churchill had him locked up. *Hess*, Mika! Hitler's heir and initiator at Landsberg prison."

"Churchill locked him up?"

"We think it may have been to avoid a public panic."

"Why?"

Willi shrugs. "All this...Satanic science—whatever you want to call it. There's something to it whether you believe in the black magic part or just the part about other races from the past. If Hess reveals the occult foundations of the Reich—"

"Listen to me, Willi. You've got that wrong if you think the Allies will see this as anything but proof that the Reich is insane. No one will believe what's happening here. Not the tenth of it. They didn't believe thirty years ago, and they won't believe now. All these things, they're just quirks, oddities. The Allies will never see them as a coherent threat."

"But you can give them enough evidence."

Mika smiles sadly. "Quirks and oddities. C'mon, Willi, how long did it take you to be convinced? It took me years to even accept the possibility that there was something besides the twisted mindset of a bunch of sociopaths behind it, and there are still days when I'm in denial. Let the Allies fight the physical war. If there's any role left us, Willi, it's to interfere with the powers behind the politics."

"How?"

"To start with, find a man named Josef Krantz."

The hope that vanished at Buchenwald is rekindling inside Mika. Despite what he said to Willi, he wonders if he—his archive—is more important than he thought. Is there such a thing as a war between good and evil? Are there apocalyptic forces beyond the manipulations of men? Destiny and fate are proven principles to him now. Could a spear now resting in Nuremberg have reached out to subdue him? Was he even worth subduing? The Spear's role historically played on grand stages. How could Mika Lott be a threat?

But now he is free again. Whose magic is that? *Are you listening, God?*

For the next several weeks he assimilates fragments and reports that Willi Oberstein brings him. He is chilled at what has been gathered during his four-year internment. There is the Führer's interest in Atlantean suicide cults, whose members lay their heads together like the spokes of a wheel from which evolved the swastika form, and the congruency of the Reich's pattern of conquest with Professor Haushofer's mystic geopolitics, and another mission to Tibet to trace a connection with the White Isle, and one more suicidal woman in Hitler's life, Unity Mitford—an English aristocrat!

Two accounts of a bizarre war-time mission to the Caucasus capture his attention. Mt. Elbrus (the sacred mountain where the white Aryans settled after the first deluge) was summited in order to plant a swastika consecrated by rites of the Black Order. Is this why Hitler so desperately wants Stalingrad and the area, and why so much has been sacrificed to hold it? He has no doubt whatever that Horbiger's doctrine of fire and ice in opposition is playing a role in Germany's foolish winter campaign there.

And somebody must have found an informant on Göring's staff, because the Reichsmarshall is frequently mentioned and quoted. Göring now brags that he has always been reincarnated beside the Führer. His heroin addiction is clearly taking its toll, but that can hardly be blamed for another fascinating report of an expedition to Rugen Island in the Baltic led by Dr. Heinz Fisher. This one was signed off on by Hitler and Himmler as well as Göring.

The primary goal of the mission was to verify Bender's theory that we are living on the inside of a hollow earth. This was to be done by bouncing infrared (the German equivalent of radar and a priority on the front lines) off the sphere, forty-five degrees opposite the side Rugen Island was on. A secondary purpose was to spy on the British fleet at Scapa Flow by reflection. Can German scientists actually believe this, or does it simply reveal the terrible gulf between an accomplished nation and its irrational leaders?

Still another twist in the Reich's bizarre mind-set in opposition to Judeo-Christian science compels Mika's attention: that there is or once was an SS cadre called the Knights of Poseidon. For some inexplicable reason, its volunteers allowed themselves to be castrated and have their thoracic cavities plasticized. They died horribly.

"That," Mika observes solemnly, "is the most incredible attempt yet."

"Attempt at what?" Willi puzzles.

"To return to Atlantis and Hyperborea."

Oberstein shakes his head.

"To return to the sea, Willi. Hyperboreans from Thule lived in an ether and then underwater. We heard of similar experiments on inmates at Buchenwald. They must have decided Aryan blood might make the difference. You can't expect a bunch of poor Jews to have such extraordinary ancestors, can you?"

11

When Josef Krantz sees a sunrise or hears waves, the earth seems to be as it was before the madness, and its obscenities become only vain strivings. Can a chicken farmer actually run the SS, and a heroin addict lead the Reich's armed forces, and a one-testicled vessel of powers beyond the human race be dictator of mighty Germany?

Away from the base he can walk the stony coast and breathe the sea air and dare to believe that the world order is not changing for his species—even if it now excludes him for what he did in Niski Kosciol. Half a century from now Jews will still light their menorahs, Masi warriors will herd their cattle, Bolivian women will bundle firewood on their backs up mountain trails, and children... Slav children will laugh again in a Polish village. Cultures will wax and wane, tyrants will come and go. But sitting in that alien cavern beneath the moraine on the Baltic he senses the upheaval that might turn civilization inside out, and he can think of nothing except how to betray it....

The Allies are too far away to risk bombing targets on the relatively worthless Pomeranian coast. Especially targets based on Nazi quackery. Zeppelins could dot the sky with arrows pointing to the moraine, blaring "Demonic Holy Grail, please bomb!" from loudspeakers, and it wouldn't matter. Which is why Krantz opts for circulating the rumor that beneath a certain moraine on the Hel peninsula is a German U-boat base.

It sounds so much more credible than the truth.

The rumor travels much too slowly, but eventually it does reach Allied air command. Reconnaissance follows, aerial photos, secondary reports from ground Intelligence. And finally, the Allies are convinced.

Cloud cover is good, and the British squadron leader is confident the Americans will get through. RAF bombers reached Danzig in 1942 without escort, returning successfully. And now, in 1944, the only difference is the target. "A damned hillock hiding a U-boat base," the major described it at briefing. The Americans replied it would be a canyon by late morning.

Cocky Yanks.

The British squadron leader glances across at the lead B-29 Superfortress. They are accurate, he will give them that. But then they have time to train. British lads barely get off the ground before they are on their first missions. Consequently, the RAF has been assigned night saturation bombings and the Americans the day precision runs. Daylight means fighter escorts. Normally, the British can provide that with Spitfires and Hurricanes. But a target in Poland? No fighter can reach that far. It will be a sticky last half for the Yanks as they go it alone.

"Messerschmitts, four o'clock!" crackles over the squadron leader's radio.

Three German ME-109s. Gutty. Desperate.

The squadron leader stands on his wing and dives, followed by five others.

The Messerschmitts split. Spurts of light erupt in sequence from the tailgunner in the near Superfortress. Deadly fire from the homing ME-109 puts him out. The squadron leader catches the Messerschmitt climbing, holding him in tandem long enough for one murderous pass along the fuselage.

Enough.

He looks back. German number two spirals out of the swarm, a scorched moth with flaming fenestra on his wings. Two Spitfires chase the third craft for ten seconds before breaking off.

The enemy's defense is thin, and the Americans are a small bomber group. These two facts might shield the B-29s until they reach target. Then it will be a different story. If the moraine is as important as the major says, there will be hell to pay in the perimeter.

The escort squadron flies ten minutes more, then veers for home.

Klaxon horns mean nothing at the reservoir site. Three, four, five times a week they intrude on sleep, on meals, on the faltering operations. Inevitably it turns out to be a stray from the Luftwaffe or a weather plane. But not this time.

The first bomb knocks Krantz out of bed. He lands on his hip and elbow, half swaddled in bedding. The shock sets his old wounds throbbing and stuns him. Even though he, of all people, should have known this was coming.

In the last desperate months he has been trying to get messages through to Britain's MI6 by talking freely within hearing of supply merchants from Niski Kosciol. Three nights ago, the sentries reported a single parachute flare. He dared hope then that the Allies had decided to act.

Much closer, at the Vistula opposite Warsaw, Russian hordes are poised for a final drive to Berlin. The newly created German Army Group Vistula is to fall back against the Hel Peninsula, ceding the Pomeranian coast to the First Belorussian Front all the way to the Oder. That way, the Russians won't bother with the coast in their frenzy for Berlin. Krantz fears the site falling into Russian hands as much as he fears uncovering it for the Führer.

Hopping into his trousers, Krantz glances out the window. Already the anti-aircraft batteries are pounding the sky. He gains the doorway just as a deafening concussion sprays glass across the room. The corridor flows with men and dust and heat. They vent into the dawn like lemmings running for the edge of a cliff—only, this cliff has a lift and flak towers. Despite the frailty of the honeycombed dome, the cavern is thought to be deep enough under the moraine to serve as a bomb shelter. And even if it weren't, that is where Krantz would go. Because he has a plan.

But just as he faces around in the lift, the main building takes a direct hit. Spinning boards and shingles rain past the lift cage as it grinds nervously down the cliff. The bomber that scored flashes briefly and breaks up. By the time it ditches in the Baltic, the cage is clanging to a halt.

The colloidal atmosphere of the cavern spreads to the lock like a cloud. Each thud above translates into puffs of sootiness below, turning the line of bobbing men into a grainy daguerreotype. And within the cavern the shocks trigger waves and flashes—blue flashes, microseconds long. High overhead, the gouged dome trembles and pops like a worm-eaten coffin.

Written on each watery face in the light of a failing generator is a more subtle awareness, because the cavern is resonating with quantums of energy that all knew were there but none have felt before. And it helps Krantz give the orders to set charges around the cavern. No one will fault him in retrospect. How can this be anything but the end?

It is suddenly incredulous that they are here. The jeweler's apprentice fondles his shaking hands. The young boy who once wanted to be a priest prays. Even the seasoned veteran blanches, because he has seen death before but not in a place like this, not in a place with hot, middle-earth odors and queasy air. He doesn't want to die this way.

Commands echoing hoarsely, Krantz strides along the lip of the pool.

Dynamite is at hand, housed in an iron shed along the seaside wall of the cavern. A sense of reckless excitement mounts as the wires come festooning down from the catwalks and all but the final terminals on the plunger are wired. But that, too, is about to transpire.

Shift perspective a step backward. One hour before the first bomb explodes Gustav Gebbler gets out of bed and lights a cigarette. The cigarettes are a new habit and he smokes them with almost sensuous pleasure. The easel and canvas are also new, as if a new identity is being acquired. His shoebox full of Gaelic verse is in the closet. Spending the war on a pinnacle in the middle of nowhere has been bad enough, but now the war is lost—everyone knows the war is lost.

Some three months ago he decided maybe Schaub was right. Krantz the nerveless incompetent is really Krantz the traitor. It isn't just the length of time they have been at it. He expected that. Archaeological digs take years, and this site is larger, the sought after object exponentially smaller, than most. Besides, the prize means nothing in the short run, nothing to an immediate war effort.

No, the thing about Krantz is the consistency of his incompetence. There is method to it. Always the slowest, the riskiest way, always the crucial piece of machinery that breaks, disappears or gets short-ordered. Certain broad areas of the cliff have been ignored while others are pointedly honeycombed. Krantz seems to know where he is going...and maybe where he shouldn't.

Could it be that the young Josef Krantz made a deduction on that first reconnaissance years ago? Does he, in fact, *know* where the reservoir is? Heydrich thought so then. Heydrich is dead. Blown up. But Himmler never trusted Krantz either. If the Führer hadn't personally picked him...

So, three months ago, Gebbler made up his mind: keep a file on Krantz's every order and decision.

He cannot judge the excavation technicalities for Berlin, but given the least tangible evidence of treason he will bring charges. No one from the base will back Krantz. The architect had always been on trial here, and with the men demoralized and afraid of the Russians, they need a scapegoat.

Against the shadows of the room in the hour before the attack, Gebbler's white face catches some of the floodlight reflecting through the window. He can see his expression in the mirror wreathed in cigarette smoke and is surprised at how haggard he looks. He tries to exhale through his nostrils but coughs. It was stupid to start smoking. Untidy. He has always been neat. Quiet and neat. The calico cat he found last week crawls into the mirror and he strokes it. Such purring. But a few seconds later he knows it isn't the cat.

Plane engines!

And then the first concussion rocks him, launching the cat to the corner. Seconds later the raucous horns begin bleating, and he is on his feet, looking for his boots.

By the time he reaches the telephone, ground batteries are pounding. Successive checks take another several minutes. The gun captains tell him they are under attack by American bombers, a fact he confirms in the overcast morning light on his way down in the cage. Every post is functioning. Thank God something is going right.

And then he reaches the cavern and sees the charges being set.

In his office safe he has a standing order from the Führer that in the event the base is about to be overrun, he is to collapse the cavern in order to bury all traces of the excavation. Let the enemy believe they have discovered a damaged U-boat base or something other than what it is. Because what a blasphemy it would be if *Slavs* somehow found and utilized the genetic matter of the ultra-race. What a betrayal of Aryan superiority! The legacy must never fall into foreign hands, even if it means that the Grail remains dormant for another era, or gets destroyed. The order struck Gebbler as an example of the Führer's megalomania, the same tyranny that cost the Wehrmacht hundreds of thousands of lives in futile Russian stands.

And here is Krantz rushing to carry it out.

"What in hell are you doing?" he shouts at no one and everyone in a voice not much lower in decibels than the first bomb blast.

The sense of command within the cavern shatters at once. A score of men look like a score of boys caught in indiscretions.

"The Russians are in our laps, in case you haven't noticed," Krantz bellows back. "In case you haven't noticed, we're being bombed. You don't think I'm going to leave this site open for the Russians against the Führer's orders?"

"In case you haven't noticed," Gebbler counters lividly, "it's the Americans who are bombing us. Check with the gun captains, if you won't take my word for it. In fact it sounds like they've finished bombing us, in case you haven't noticed!"

"Gustav"—Krantz lowers his voice—"it's only a matter of time before we're overrun. I've given the order to set charges, and I'm ordering you to keep your opinions to yourself."

"Don't pull rank on me, Josef. I'm Security, not a part of your pecking order! You've turned this mission into a farce. You've blocked every expeditious move. You've bungled one approach after another. Berlin will—"

His lips continue to move, but his voice drowns in a sudden rush from the inner wall of the cavern as the natural parapet of stone protecting the reservoir, long weakened, begins sheering off layer by layer. Choking in dust, a half-blind column of men rushes into the lock.

"One good jab with a drill and that cavern will collapse like a *soufflé*," is the way someone describes it the next morning.

In a matter of weeks, perhaps days, the Russians will stand on the Hel peninsula and pound their chests.

"There's no point in challenging me now," Krantz tells Gebbler face to face at the end of the pier later that afternoon. "By the time everything's shored up, the war will be over."

"Don't imagine for a second that your treason will escape its consequences," Gebbler replies.

"File your report, Gustav."

"Some day, Krantz, some day when you least expect it, a man will appear. Maybe behind you. Maybe when you're asleep. Those of us who keep faith will see to it that a man appears."

Krantz grasps the rail above the pilings, Baltic surges collecting in his forearms. "I did what needed to be done," he says ambiguously.

"You *are* a traitor," Gebbler assures him. "I see that now. I believe you even know where the damned thing is. Where to look, anyhow. Right? You *know* where the Grail is!"

Slate gray waves rush at Krantz, roaring accusations from Atlantis, Hyperborea, Thule, which Gebbler translates into a less certain, less powerful language. Krantz could pick the little man up and throw him in the sea, but what then? Take the slow victory, Josef, he counsels himself. Go back to Berlin. Gather up the pieces.

"You can be sure of this," Gebbler imparts ominously, "the dream isn't finished yet. Too many of us know. I'm taking this to Himmler, and he will convince Hitler. This site will stay open!"

12
AUSCHWITZ

Like thirty pieces of silver, they gleam in the autumn sun—the Jews of the Sonderkommando. White hands, white faces. No outdoor work for them. Moreover, their food is adequate. But inside they are white, too—bloodlessly white—because that is where their holocaust is taking place.

Zolkower thought he had seen it all at Treblinka. Bones made into razor handles, pillows stuffed with hair, flesh made into soap. The saponifying of the bodies was the worst. An indelible formula—eight ounces to a pound of caustic soda, ten quarts of water, twelve pounds of human fat—will boil and cool in his memory forever. But being a Sonderkommando at Auschwitz is worse still.

Thirty of them wait behind the knolls built over the gas chambers. They are just able to see the mushroom-shaped vents in the manicured lawns, hidden by flowerbeds so that those approaching from the other side see only the façades of the buildings housing "showers." SS Sergeant Moll struts in front of the thirty, issuing orders.

"At the conclusion of today's assignment you will place your boots and gas masks on the lorry! Then you will return to your barracks for reassignment!"

Reassignment. They are to be shot. Zolkower has heard the rumor: *Himmler has ordered the crematoria dismantled.* Things must be prettied up before the Russians arrive. The greatest *Vernichtungslager* of them all is going out of business.

From the railroad siding beyond the knolls they hear the train jolting to a stop. In a few moments the doors will be rolled back and the moaning will be heard. The stench of urine and defecations will waft out of the freight cars along with the dying and the surviving—terrified souls who have been packed together for three days too tightly to fall down. And the dead—a few—still in the arms of their loved ones. And when the terrible cargo is fully discharged stunned into the sunlight, the screaming will begin. The guards will try to temper it, but mothers being separated from the children hiding under their skirts and tearful farewells between husbands and wives cannot be quieted.

A few years ago the arriving Jews would have been given *Waldsee* postcards (*"Doing fine, anxiously awaiting your arrival"*) to be sent back to their relatives by the Germans. But these internees have had neither food nor water for three days. A camp doctor channels them right or left with God-like prerogative as they file away from the snake-like train. The able-bodied go to camp. The others are to take a shower.

In his mind's eye, Zolkower follows the approach of these last toward the knolls. He knows they are on the way because there is suddenly music in the air. A string quartet of pretty young girls—inmates—in white blouses and navy blue skirts is playing in the courtyard before the showers. Zolkower closes his eyes whenever they play, but he cannot shut his ears. This morning's selection vastly amuses the guards: "The Merry Widow." By the time the Sonderkommandos are led around to the now sealed doors, the young girls are somberly packing their instruments away in the empty courtyard.

Inside, the whole dreary line is herded into chambers—half capacity today—and the awful suspicion begins. This is the cruelest time. Eyes roll heavenward, a woman keens, others cling to absurd hopes and denials as they merely pray softly or try to comfort each other with trembling assurances. The smell of fear is thick and rank.

They are told to undress. Some are even issued towels. Three or four of Sergeant Moll's SS watch through thick glass portholes on the knoll above them, making crude jokes, "Oy! Where are the drains in these showers?"

Then the tireless sergeant gives the signal: "All right, give 'em something to chew on!"

Blue crystals of Zyklon B go rattling into the vents, which are immediately sealed. Moments later the uncanny, entombed chorus of the damned begins. A thousand souls expiring…

It lasts three to fifteen minutes. When the huge mass of humanity piled at the doors no longer writhes, the pumps are started, the tomb opened.

Enter the Sonderkommando.

Zolkower wields a hose to wash away blood and feces. Then it is the hook and noose to pull down the blue, well-clawed and clammy pyramid. He looks but doesn't see. How can you see, touch, smell, after you have heard…? He has been numb since that first time. The horror, the unbelievable cruelty. So you have to go dead inside, have to flood your reeling brain and heaving gorge with something else.

For Zolkower it is is that first monster, the man with the amputated finger. It is not Zolkower who tugs rings off still warm fingers and yanks gold from broken teeth. Not he who shears skulls and breaks jaws. The child-killer from Niski Kosciol—he is the one who rapes the dead. That one.

As he loads bodies on the rail wagon for the short run to the crematoria this final day, Zolkower notices the lorry. It is there for the boots and masks the Sonderkommandos will no longer need. And where are they taking them? Back to Farben's? The giant chemical trust has built a synthetic coal-oil and rubber plant at Auschwitz to derive the benefit of slave labor. Zolkower long ago surmised the manufacturer of the boots and masks. Another circle of irony. Jews making boots for Jews to bury Jews in. And when they are too starved and tired to make boots or bury Jews, they themselves become the buried.

The pile of wet gristly things on the lorry is almost as ghastly as the showers, but for the man who survived by crawling through the hole in an outhouse, it is a ray of hope.

If I can hide on the lorry, if I can escape to the marshes…

Sergeant Moll is eating pistachios, which he somehow acquires on a regular basis from Bulgaria. Zolkower waits for the sergeant to call one of the Sonderkommandos to pick up the pistachio shells from the curried lawn atop the knoll, and as the hand with the ragged, red fingernails points here, there, Zolkower swings onto the back of the lorry. And there, amid the smell and moisture of his fellow Jews still clinging to the boots that cover him, he conjures up the face again.

Child-killer, I'm coming for you. I'm coming for you, child-killer. May you live, so that I can kill you.

13

Somewhat sparser, white rather than silver, Mika Lott's hair now arcs back out of his temples once more and sprouts above his lip. He is actually thinner than he was in Buchenwald, but increasingly stronger.

Willi Oberstein brings him a pair or two of reading glasses once a week—the legacy of genocide—and out of each several of these he finds one which is an improvement over the last. The remainder go into a drawer until they begin to remind him of the obscenities he has escaped: mountains of shoes, a pile of clothes over thirty meters high, the glittering bramble of eyeglasses next to the one of rings and watches. So he cannot bring himself to discard them. Instead they fill a drawer until the Frau of the house discreetly removes them.

In the farmhouse between Bamberg and Bayreuth, Mika is once again a quiet spinner of webs, casting out subtle lines, waiting for tremors. Fieldwork and memory feed his files. The memory is his, the field work Oberstein's and the others. They can't risk losing him again, Willi insists, so sad-eyed Mika sits in the center of his web, analyzing and interpreting the often bizarre odds and ends that trickle in. It is almost logical, he fears, the way the insanity pervades Germany's hierarchy.

An aide to General Dornberger, for instance, has talked freely about how Hitler held up V2 rocket tests for two months at Peenemunde. The reason given was that they might disturb etheric forces from the cosmos layered above the earth, forces from the mystic well which the Führer taps into during his trances.

Then there is the business of skywriting. Place: Montségur, France, the mountain of the Grail. Time: March 16th, 1944, the seven hundredth anniversary of the Cathari massacre in defense of the

Grail (it is the "greening of the laurel" every seven hundred years that represents the return of knowledge, symbolized by the Grail, Mika has read). And on this anniversary a Fieseler Stork plane carrying Alfred Rosenberg flies overhead, tracing Cathar emblems in the sky.

Hitler, in explaining the meaning of the National Socialist movement, tells his gauleiters that creation is unfinished and will yield a new, infinitely superior species soon. Humanity ascends one level every seven hundred years, he says, and the end results will be the sons of God.

"That so?" chortles the Frau, a gentile they call Hedda but whose given name is Hadu, when Mika explains this to her. "'Protect them from the son of perdition,'" she quotes, "'the evil one'—John, chapter seventeen. That's what the real Son of God said! To hell with Hitler's sons of Gods."

But despite the flow of information, Mika hears nothing about Josef Krantz and the Spear of Longinus.

Find Krantz and you know where the search for Hyperborean cells has gone, he believes. Where was it that Krantz and the Thulist led them all those years ago? The village in the Polish Corridor—it is one of the obscure names he cannot remember. But he recalls gathering information from a Professor Tromblein at the Institute of Technology in Berlin. The professor was forwarding mail. He is probably dead now.

And then one morning—no thanks to the maps Oberstein has brought him—he awakens and remembers. *Niski Kosciol.*

Progress. Word is sent to Cracow asking for help from the Jewish Resistance—asking if anyone can reach Niski Kosciol. There are other fish to fry, however, and the name of the Polish village drifts to the back of Mika's thoughts. He directs that Wolfram von Sievers, Occult Bureau chief, be keyed on in the hope that a cross-connection to the Grail turns up. As for the Spear, they know only that after the first RAF raid on Nuremberg all the treasures in St. Katherine's were moved to the vault of Kohn's Bank on Königstrasse, and that after Stalingrad they were moved again.

Rumors, hysteria, chaos—the winding down of the war has its upside to someone who can read the confusion, and Mika pounces on every exposure of the Reich's underpinnings for revelations.

In October, 1944, RAF night runs and US Flying Fortress day bombings turn the ancient fortress city of Nuremberg into a burning shambles. Of unappreciated importance to the Allies, who aim at such targets as the panzer engine MAN plants and the Siemens-Schuckert electrical factory by the railyards, is the demolishment of a centuries old house in the Oberen Schmied Gasse. The doors of an exterior building there are blown away, revealing a much more sophisticated façade. Neighbors describe a secret, sliding wall on the other side twisted by the bombing into a steel knot. By late in the day a rumor is circulating that a gaping tunnel with damaged ductwork leads down to an air-conditioned bunker with massive iron doors.

Mika insists on traveling the few kilometers to Nuremberg to see it for himself. But by then the damage has been camouflaged.

"You took a risk for nothing," Oberstein complains.

"On the contrary. They hid it, didn't they? And you see where it is in relation to the Fortress."

"So?"

"There is, indeed, a tunnel, Willi. There always were tunnels—a medieval warren leading three hundred meters underground beneath the Fortress. That's where the Spear was hidden in 1796 to keep it away from Napoleon. That's where it is today. They've added an air-conditioned bunker and moved the treasures there."

And on the heels of that, there is news from Cracow that one of the Temple Guardsmen sent to Niski Kosciol was shot on the spot and the other returned shaken. The week after that, a cell in Cracow sends word that they have a new recruit, an escapee from Auschwitz named Zolkower, originally from Niski Kosciol.

"I have to talk to him," says Mika.

Willi sighs.

It takes another week. In the interim, the first reports on Wolfram von Sievers, Occult Bureau chief, come in, and once again Mika feels his stomach tighten as new pieces of an old puzzle fall together.

While in Buchenwald he heard about the work of Sievers and Dr. Eugen Haagen in a certain Block 46. From inmates involved in the collecting and shipping, he learned that special Jewish types at Auschwitz had their heads severed according to Sievers' specific anatomical instructions, after which each head was sealed in a hermetic container and forwarded to Buchenwald. Testicles, spleen, bone marrow, blood and skin were also collected and processed. Inexplicably, "processing" included the powdering or dissolving of these items, and subsequent dilution, and finally, the injection of such solutions into Jewish inmates. The meaning of this has eluded Mika until now. Especially since more sinister things were being injected in others, including the gamut of human diseases.

But now come reports that ashes from the gas ovens are being scattered all across the Reich at the behest of Himmler *and Sievers*. Why Sievers? Why *all* across the Reich? There are simpler, quicker ways of hiding ashes. The Baltic, for instance, or a lake. And Sievers would have no interest in such a cover-up unless it had something to do with his function.

His experiments.

That is when Mika realizes the truth and the connection with Himmler. Himmler, the young man who once lived above an apothecary shop. Himmler, the graduate in farm chemistry. Himmler, the lab assistant in a fertilizer plant. Himmler, the poultry farmer whose Munich-Trudering land was overrun with rats. Himmler who, in 1929, became interested in something called the homeopathic potentiation method of pest control. A method almost identical with the Sievers-Haagen experiments at Buchenwald.

First you take the powdered essence of the designated pest, then you potentiate it, then you spread it on the wind. Or inject it. Something tangible is thus conveyed—fear, death—driving the living pests from the area. It is crazy, of course. Even though there are documented cases of success. Rabbits in Silesia on the estates of a Count Keyserlingk, for example. The Royal Homeopathic Hospital in London. Himmler himself set up a branch of the Ahnenerbe to try it on rats near Auschwitz. And now they are trying it on human beings, these Godless, ghoulish Nazis.

And into this comes Zolkower, skinnier, more electric-eyed than ever.

"Tell me about Niski Kosciol," Mika asks after the escapee has been served a glass of wine and his boots—rubber boots made by Farben on the outskirts of Auschwitz—sit drying by the fire. "Is there something important to the Nazis there?"

Zolkower shrugs. "It's the coast."

"Of course, but is there anything else—anything specific that might draw them to that area?"

"Like what?"

"Old ruins."

Zolkower sips his wine, coughs. "Whatever was is rotted. Can't even find my father's grave anymore."

"What about stories...legends?"

"Plenty of those."

"Teutonic history?"

Zolkower's brows gather, oddly soft and gray because they are just growing back.

"Knights," Mika probes.

"There were knights once," replies Zolkower.

"Have you ever heard mention of the Holy Grail?"

Zolkower frowns. "The Nazis steal that, too?"

For some fifty minutes Mika questions him. The answers are laconic. It may be that Auschwitz has stunned Zolkower, or it may be a natural rural reserve, but the two of them seem unable to communicate. Even after Mika tells him that he himself was at Buchenwald, the onyx-eyed farmer from Niski Kosciol seems indifferent. Until he mentions Josef Krantz.

"Krantz will die," Zolkower croaks immediately.

"You know him?"

Breathless and pale, the words are wrenched out of wild-eyed Zolkower syllable by syllable in a heap that only another victim of the holocaust can measure as what happened on that horrific afternoon in the village of Niski Kosciol is described. When it is finally over, Mika ponders the imponderable. He hadn't thought it likely Josef Krantz could commit atrocities.

"I knew him when he was vacillating," he tells Zolkower. "I thought I knew him. But he mustn't die. I absolutely need to question him"

Something passes through Zolkower's face akin to shock then, congealing his expression into scar tissue. "Is this what I came all the way from Cracow to hear?" he gets out in a tight, shaking voice. "Let me tell you, let me tell you, I'll go back to Auschwitz today... today, if it means I can kill Josef Krantz!"

14

"Defend Nuremberg to the last drop of blood!"

So speaks the Führer as the US 7th Army encircles the citadel of National Socialism in Berlin, and the blood begins to cascade on April 16th, 1945.

Four days of merciless fighting fulfills Hitler's command, and the mauled but victorious 7th runs up its flag on the Adolf Hitler Platz amid smoldering Gothic ruins. Within that army is a special task force, commanded by a Captain Walter Thompson, whose purpose is to trace the Germanic treasures once housed in St. Katherine's. Rumors have reached Churchill that the *Werewolf* Nazi underground is already planning a resurgence, central to which is the Spear.

The Allies are taking no chances.

Oberbürgermeister Willi Liebel, the inner circle Nazi leader in charge of the treasures, quickly becomes the object of an intense manhunt. Meanwhile, a burial detail made up of German civilians and American soldiers enters the Palmenhof Gestapo headquarters and there, in a cellar stacked high with looted luxuries, discovers a putrefying corpse half collapsed into its own cavities. One of the discoverers wears a gas mask and drags the remains upstairs. Outside on the Jacobplatz, the body is hosed and the face wiped clean of dried blood with cotton wool. Willi Liebel's bulky features appear with a bullet hole through the temple.

The next day an SS Colonel and garrison commander under persistent questioning reveals that Liebel committed suicide. He also maintains that the Imperial treasures have been sunk to the bottom of Lake Zell. But his version of things, including the whereabouts of certain folders concerning the transfer of the Imperial regalia, contradicts Liebel's secretary, Dreykorn.

Ten days later, a group of GIs prodding the ruins of the Oberen Schmied Gasse for caches of loot discover a yawning chasm where one corner of the building has been blown away. Descending by flashlight some three hundred meters through a wide tunnel, they come to massive steel doors with a barrel dial locking mechanism. HQ is notified, and the ranking Nuremberg authorities, Dr. Konrad Freis and Heinz Schmeissner, are interrogated. Freis breaks down, producing the key to the dual locking device, and Schmeissner, who knows the five-digit code, follows suit.

Secretly they believe the Spear is no longer in the vault. When American forces reached Gemunden, and all appeared lost, Himmler ordered a hasty deception. A plumber by the name of Brau made special copper containers in which the six central holy relics (the so-called Reichsheiligtümer) were placed, wrapped in glass wool. They were then spirited away to a rock cavern beneath the cellar of a nearby school in the Panier Platz. But the Maurice Lance, as the Spear is sometimes known, was mistakenly displaced by the Maurice Sword, a piece of lesser importance in the collection, by the uninformed aides of the frantic Willi Liebel. It was the suicidal Liebel, in a frantic state, who delegated this assignment and thus served fate in adding one more irony to the incredible history of the Spear.

When the vault is opened and the generator light floods over a vast array of priceless treasures, Captain Thompson's eye falls on an intricately carved altar upon which rests an ancient leather case. The United States of America takes possession of the Spear of Longinus on April 30th, 1945.

Only minutes later, beneath the surface of another city, in another bunker, the man with the metamorphosed soul, known as the Führer, puts a Walther 7.65-calibre pistol to his right temple and pulls the trigger.

Legions of dead rush forward to bear witness.

THE RESERVOIR

1
POSTWAR BERLIN

Krantz gets a haircut. He earlier made up his mind to go see his dentist on the Fasanenstrasse or else get a haircut, and, since his dentist is Jewish and long gone, he comes to a barber who is Dutch and German and an atheist. The barber says it is funny but since everything collapsed, business is booming. He cut seven heads this morning and was paid with cigarettes mostly. Also chocolate, firewood from the denuded Tiergarten and dietary advice from a man who recently had rectal surgery.

Krantz offers him occupation money and the barber shrugs. It isn't as negotiable as cigarettes, especially in the Russian sector, but what the hell, he will cut hair for free, he confides. Haircuts are the secret commiseration of Germany. A tiny bit of normalcy in a disordered world. And isn't it a shame that Himmler didn't get all the Jews?

Freshly shorn, Krantz wanders Berlin. Occupied by four powers, the city is a mansion turned boarding house. One sees its pyres, its pulverized stone, and retreats into memory. His old office at the Institute of Technology is now his living quarters. The last apartment he lived in is rubble. And his father's house, rubble.

The city is landscaped with slopes of brick and mortar swept up against wounded buildings. Dust and death and machine oil waft out of pockets as the wind traces new configurations down old streets. And this wind, carrying these unwelcome refugees, is the only thing that moves freely. The city is dammed with checkpoints, severing its arteries. The Berlin express comes only as close as Wannsee some twenty-four kilometers away. And within this stagnancy, little eddies of people drift, gathering scraps, fighting for the splintered wood of a park bench, reading hand-printed notices on street posts in search of missing relatives.

Despite the stultifying occupation, Krantz feels a certain boundlessness. If he has given up membership in the Fatherland, he has taken out world citizenship. The barber's comment about Jews is incomprehensible. He knows the barber's experience. Everyone's experience is the same. How could anyone live through all that they have lived through together and not learn? Events of such magnitude have to make a difference. They *have* to. And the hard-core dispossessed—the diseased, the satanic, the twisted—they have to be cut off from power.

Is it only because he is damned that he understands this?

Niski Kosciol can never be forgiven him. But he achieved his ends at the reservoir, and the only thing that bothers him is that men like Gebbler know the reservoir is still there. It was left intact within the rubble of an apparently destroyed submarine base, as Gebbler vowed, devoid of any trace of archaeological excavation. The advancing Russians forced a cloture over the ongoing issue before Krantz could manipulate Berlin into ordering its total burial.

He thought he understood Hitler well enough to believe permission was possible. Hitler liked total annihilations. The Führer's legacy, had it been carried out, would have been a "twilight of the gods" Armageddon: flooding Berlin's population in the subways; the Wehrmacht dying to the last man; Poland's reservoir reinterred in a holocaust of dynamite. Hadn't Hitler compared himself and his followers to barbarians, saying the present world was nearly finished, that their only task was to sack it?

But permission was never granted Krantz. He couldn't even get through to the Führer. Power was fragmenting and a resurgent underground of *Werewolves* was already forming to protect and rekindle Nazi cults in the wake of the occupation. The road to the Hel peninsula lies open still. To anyone.

That is why he is considering going back.

So he isn't really surprised to find the zombies waiting for him the day he picks his way up to the fourth floor of the damaged Institute building, as he does about once a week. They are there in his office, Bruckner and Wolff, looking dumpy and misshapen in civilian clothes. When he turns to retreat, Lugert appears at the staircase end of the corridor, grinning his saurian grin, and as Krantz pirouettes helplessly toward the blind end of the building, they merely lumber after him like a trio of golems.

A blaze of light marks the bomb damage where the facade was sheared off in the only direction open to him. It is unsafe, but so are the zombies. Scrambling under a rope cordon, Krantz grasps a steel rod spiraling out of broken concrete and drops down a level. Dust rains off the slabs as heavy feet break into a run above him. No longer lumbering golems, his three pursuers fan out with SS precision. Krantz weaves over the rubbled floor of a classroom wing, but Bruckner manages to outflank him close to an exterior wall. Lugert and Wolff herd him toward another blind end.

"This could be easier," Wolff calls.

"You know…this wing is ready to collapse," Krantz puffs hoarsely.

"We'll all die then," grins Lugert.

"Maybe just the heaviest of us."

"Lots of true Germans left," says Wolff. "But you've got us all wrong. We want you to live."

Krantz glances from one to the other. Escape is hopeless. But if they wanted to kill him, they wouldn't have let this happen.

"All we want is for you to finish what you started," Lugert calls softly.

"I couldn't do it with professional miners and a full base, how do you think I'd do it with a Russian occupation?"

No one is moving now.

"Either it's readily accessible, or you know just how to go about it," Wolff says. "You wouldn't have wanted to bury the cavern if it wasn't accessible."

"That's Gebbler's paranoia talking."

"As for the Russians, Poland is independent, haven't you heard? And we can get by the Poles."

In desperation Krantz zigzags half a dozen steps in the difficult area between Lugert and Bruckner, and amazingly, he gets through before either can negotiate the footing. But he is gasping now. The impaired lung that took a bullet in Poland seems to be doing all the work. And already Bruckner is moving parallel and abreast along the exterior wall. Twisting, Krantz hurls a concrete chunk straight at his exposed temple.

It is almost comical to Lugert and Wolff. They are three of the Fatherland's finest SS, and here is a mediocre specimen of sedentary citizenry challenging them with a rock. But a nearly bloodless wound flashes white as Bruckner staggers and falls against the precarious brick of a window frame. Then the casing grates. In an instant their comrade reels through and is pinned momentarily from the thigh down by a rain of bricks. Above the dull thudding of the bricks they all hear the sharp crack—Bruckner's head on the side of the building, or maybe his spine—and now he simply slides into silence.

Krantz is too riveted to avoid Lugert's rush. The SS man has him by the hair, his stark olive eyes staring down. "You lucky fucker," he says, as if the act of killing one of their own should be beyond Krantz's capacity.

Wolff crunches through stone chips for a look over the edge. When he straightens, his rugged face is calm. Shaping his left fist in his right palm, he picks his way back and delivers a pile driver punch that wrenches Krantz forward, vomiting down his shirt.

"You come with us to the reservoir now, Krantz. You find the damned thing to make it easier on your miserable skin. Then we won't have to pare you down with razor blades like a carrot."

2
VIENNA

Like a tarnished pendant, Vienna hugs the right bank of the Danube. An array of architectural jewels—St. Stephen's, the Imperial Palace where the Hapsburgs once lived, others—lie lusterless in post-war debris. The Ringstrasse is a dreary boulevard of tombstones, no longer gay, but gray and martial. Like Berlin, Vienna is another mansion turned boarding house, sharing the same foreign occupants.

On this particular morning a sudden cold downpour sends the pedestrians on Morzinplatz scurrying for cover. One of them is a scrawny man with darting onyx eyes. Saul Zolkower.

Created of spring steel, he bears few outward marks from the concentration camps, but inwardly he has begun to suffer fugues, lapses, deep depressions. There are moments when he must close his eyes to let the confusion pass. It started when he came to Austria were Mika Lott sent him. There really wasn't any place to go except the underground. And now that the war is over and the Temple Guard has surfaced, *where is Josef Krantz?* The thing that sustained him through all those horrors at Auschwitz has been set aside somehow, and so, as if his reason to survive has also been set aside, he has these spells.

The one that is coming over him at this moment is because of the rain and the steaming humidity inside the damaged office where he has taken refuge from the shower. The office is a temporary center for registering school children. And it is as damp as a shower...a shower...a shower.

And full of anxious people.

Waiting.

Zolkower shuts his eyes tightly. *I am here. The showers have stopped. The world is in order.*

One of the people waiting is a woman who is talking loudly to the clerk. "You told me to bring his birth certificate, well, there it is," she says. "Now, I want to register my child. You wouldn't accept him last year, and now he'll be a form behind."

The shrill voice is motherhood and it brings a silence while she speaks, and another silence afterward.

Zolkower's darkness extends all the way back to Niski Kosciol six years ago, but a note of pathos in the motherhood forges a link, and he listens with his eyelids closed to the woman and the silence and a rustling among the clerks until one of them says consolingly but firmly: "Madam, we cannot register your child."

"Why not? You tell me, why not?"

"We have told you, Madam. You know why."

"Listen to me, I want him registered. You can't refuse him. He's ready. I've taught him all his sounds and he can count to ten. How many do you have who can count to ten and know all their sounds and…you think he's Jewish is that it?"

"Your child is dead, Madam," says the clerk softly. "He died in the bombing. You know that."

Zolkower opens his eyes.

She is fat and wrinkled and overdressed for the weather. Her lips glisten because she licks them compulsively with a gray stub of a tongue. "No," she says pensively. "No," turning away. "You have no right to say that. Hans is alive and he knows all his sounds and he can count…count to…."

Zolkower trembles and returns to the rain. How could he have forgotten the children? How could he languish while the Child Killer roams free? He has it in the back of his mind that the Temple Guard will eventually lead him to Krantz. But they haven't yet.

He returns to the apartment on Ballhausplatz. Gabriel, the arthritic spindle of a man who once hosted Mika during the *Anschluss* of Austria, has given Zolkower the sofa and shares his bird-like meals.

"I've found a Nazi named Krantz," Zolkower baits Gabriel as they play cards. "I think he's on the run, maybe trying to make contact with ODESSA. Know anything about him?"

"That's the one Lott's been looking for," declares Gabriel. "This could be important. Where did you see him?"

Zolkower's answers are vague, but Gabriel promptly contacts Willi Oberstein, who has just arrived in Salzberg.

Willi is tracing one report that a four engine Heinkel 277 V-1 carrying SS elite from the Black Order left the region bound for the Orient, and another report that the Innsbruck-Salzberg road was blocked at the end of the war to allow a convoy secret passage from Hitler's Berghof to the Schleigeiss glacier, where a lead chest was buried. The presumption is that such a chest—if the report is true— may contain a badly damaged chalice from Montségur. But Willi doubts it. Even though an Austrian Lieutenant named Gottleich and two other mountaineers searching the area were murdered and mutilated.

When Willi hears that Zolkower claims to have sighted a Nazi named Krantz in Vienna he doubts that, too. Krantz was seen in Stettin, Poland, just yesterday in the company of two former SS men trying to rent a car. He confides the basis of his doubts to Gabriel, and it is another two hours before he realizes his mistake: that Gabriel will tell Zolkower about Krantz in Stettin, and that Zolkower may have pulled off a ruse.

Willi risks a call to Mika over the much monitored lines to Berlin. Mika's sigh of exasperation at the news is scarcely distinguishable from the background hiss of the patched call.

Post-war events, so illogical to the Allies, are crystal clear to Mika. The Russians found over a thousand dead Tibetans in Berlin, dressed in German uniforms and lying in ritual suicide rows. Professor Karl Haushofer was also found dead, having committed hara-kiri after killing his wife. A poem written by Haushofer's son, Albrecht, a former Nazi who renounced the Party when he saw that Germany was under demonic control, has come to light. In it he laments that his father unleashed the Beast of the Apocalypse when he initiated Hitler into the Thule.

Albrecht was beheaded in Moabit prison by the Gestapo because he aided Rudolf Hess in contacting white magic adepts in England, and because of what he knew. Allied Intelligence analysts categorically dismiss these unfathomable reports as meaningless, but for Mika, such enigmas are more often neat endings.

It is Zolkower he is slow to understand. Send him to Vienna, he thought. A simple farmer who knows the seasons, the Auschwitz refugee will remember how to live; and eventually he will see past the monsters. His agrarian instincts will bring him to plow the past under, to sow new life. It was a very flawed assessment. They should have seen it after that first interview in the farmhouse. For Zolkower, life cannot resume until he kills Josef Krantz.

Mika intends to cross the border as soon as the Temple Guard definitely locates their quarry, only now he may lose control to Zolkower if he waits. Moreover, he is certain—as Zolkower must be—that Krantz is headed for the general area of Niski Kosciol. Better to hang onto his fellow refugee, he decides, and leaves for Vienna in the hope of keeping Zolkower there.

But at Ballhausplatz early the next morning he is too late. Gabriel has already relayed Willi's story, and sometime during the night "that ungrateful scarecrow Zolkower" stole the Temple Guard cash box from behind the radiator along with certain forged papers, passports and Gabriel's .32 calibre pistol.

"Aspern," Mika decides—the airport splattered over the southeast landscape. Zolkower is going to take a plane.

Air travel—like everything else—is unpredictable these days, and Mika rushes out of the apartment, hoping it is not too late. But it takes him nearly half an hour to locate a taxi, and then the aging Renault crawls along the battered Schwarzenbergstrasse like a blue-black dung beetle, up and down craters, skirting mountains of rubble. If only Zolkower has to wait long enough for a flight, he prays.

At Aspern, the taxi driver gazes at his passenger in a way that tells Mika he looks ill. And he is ill—feverish, in fact. Every nerve and instinct inside him is jangling. Krantz is the key, he is certain now, and keeping him alive in order to be sure the Reich can no longer summon its occult power is as important to Mika as killing him is to revenge-crazed Zolkower.

A Doppler effect of car horns marks Mika's reckless passage across the street to the terminal, there to endure sniping marble echoes and jostling crowds as he glances down the departure board. *Flight twenty-seven to Danzig.* That will put him near Niski Kosciol.

Boarding area twelve. Scheduled departure 10:20 a.m. In his pocket is a watch, a fine watch with a silver case and leather strap to replace the one of Katya's they took away at Buchenwald—the only thing of value he has acquired since the war—a watch that he never winds because from the time of her murder he never wound the one it replaced, and he has had this one inscribed the same as that silent silver original: *Love Forever Katya.* So now he must look around for a clock—this watchmaker, this guardian of time. He walks, runs, walks, following the signs to the boarding areas, and there above the fifth one is a clock. 10:24 it says. Four minutes late.

His great sad eyes wide with fear and hope, Mika scurries through the concourse. Boarding area ten…eleven…twelve—the big AUA carrier is still there! But the passengers are already filing through the restricted area. And there is Zolkower. Behind glass. They stare at each other like captured insects in separate bottles. Zolkower's rotten teeth flash.

Mika rushes forward, but flight guards restrain him. They have seen these Jewish refugees before. Confused, panic-stricken at the thought of something going wrong, maybe thinking they have glimpsed a relative.

Slowly the tower is wheeled away. The AUA's props begin to hum.

"An eye for an eye," Zolkower is thinking as the plane lifts off.

"Vengeance is thine, O God—not Zolkower's," Mika prays, studying the departure board for the next flight to Danzig.

3

His shirt still smells like vomit, even though Krantz washed it the first night after the zombies took him across the border to Poland. They gave Stettin as their destination at the border, and, out of fear of being traced, they now spend two days in a bombed-out market until Lugert shows up grinning at the wheel of another car. After that it is an evasive three hundred kilometer trip and a series of acquisitions by theft. These include a shovel in Drawsko, food and maps in Neustettin, a pickax and more food in Lebork, battery lights in Leba. Lugert whistles, grins, bathes naked in the Baltic, cleans his pistol. Wolff drives.

Nearly five kilometers from the Pomeranian coast, they leave the car in a forest of yews. On foot they make their way around a Kaszubian fishing village festooned with eel traps and from there past an abandoned resort to the sea. Then they follow the shore, forced now and then to enter the icy surf whose hissing seems to be part of the act of drowning the sun.

"Should've stolen those field glasses in Leba," Lugert says when they stand at last on the western flank of the moraine. Dropping his pickax, he skirts the approach for a better view of the summit.

When he returns, they pass to the catwalk and the pier in twilight, their footsteps diminished by the slap and run of waves against the granite face of the cliff. At the spot where the lock once stood they turn on their lights.

Before the Case White team abandoned the site, they dismantled the outer face of the lock and employed every piece of heavy equipment they could get their hands on to backfill and bulldoze a scree slide of stones and boulders over its poured foundations. They expected the Russians to at least discover that, if not the cavern itself—left to look like a U-boat base under construction. But the scree is undisturbed.

"Stupid Russians," says Wolff.

"Maybe the Kaszubs forgot to tell them we had something going here." Lugert scuffs his boot over loose gravel. "Maybe they mistook the pier for a tourist marina."

"Superstitious Kaszubs probably didn't tell them anything!"

Wolff pokes around the top of the scree slope with his shovel, while Lugert sets his light on the catwalk to illuminate the operation.

Krantz perches on the catwalk rail to watch and wait. If the cavern is as they left it, then the dynamite charges that he and Gebbler argued over are still inside, still set at crucial stress points. He had entered one last time with Gebbler just before the sealing off and took pains to notice. It didn't matter, he told himself then. With the bombing and all their excavation, the cavern was almost certainly too shaky to last. But the damned thing still hasn't collapsed. That possibility has haunted his dreams since the retreat to Berlin.

He has a vague idea of what Lugert and Wolff expect. They must think that some minor excavating will instantly produce the Grail. And the fact that they haven't just tortured him for the information means that they think his structural skills may be necessary to avoid disaster.

As the two SS clear rubble shielding the lock, a slash of paint is revealed across the face of a dozen uneven stones. This was left deliberately by Gebbler, so that a future expedition would know whether or not someone breached the site and then resealed it. The paint is uniform across the uneven stones. It is certain now. All is as they left it. The dynamite is untouched. Inwardly Krantz exults. He has only to enter by himself and finish wiring the charges to the plunger.

"Let me go in alone," he says when they have cleared as much of the slope as the receding tide permits.

Wolff straightens. "Like hell."

Krantz steps down from the rail. "Why should I give you what you want without at least a chance to save my own skin? You have to let me go in alone, and when I get you what you're after, you have to be at the end of the pier when I bring it out. If you're any closer than that when I'm coming out, I swear I'll dump the thing right here. But if you're at the end of the pier—the very end—then I'll set it down and take my head start. You move before I get another fifty meters, I'll come back and heave it in the Baltic."

He sees in their faces that they are as unsure of what the Grail might look like as he is. Nor do they know that he has never seen it either. For all any of them know, it is exactly what the legends say: a chalice, a cup, holding the stuff of divinity—construed by less sophisticated ages as the holy blood of God incarnate. They cannot take a chance that Krantz is bluffing, that he hasn't a clue, that the Grail is not something as easily breached and corruptible of its genetic content as Onan spilling his seed on the ground.

Wolff meets his eyes with raw scorn. "Do we have to take an oath on our SS daggers for you?"

"They tell me an SS oath isn't worth a damn anymore."

"Your choice could be between death and horrible death," suggests Lugert.

"You can't get the Grail without me," Krantz says. "It won't do you any good to know where it is. Get some asshole in there who doesn't know how that cavern's been fractured and you can forget about the chalice until after the next ice age."

Lugert gestures Wolff aside for a whispered conference and presently starts down the catwalk leading to the beach. Wolff confronts Krantz.

"We agree," he says.

As long as they stay on the end of the pier, he can fly like a bat out of hell through the lock opening, playing out wire and carrying a plunger, Krantz believes. And if he has placed his charges right he will make it to the beach and maybe get some of the pier, too, before they can reach the wire. Unless they start shooting.

Well, every plan has a flaw.

"You'll have to leave your guns halfway to the end of the pier," he adds, only slightly disturbed that Wolff makes no objection.

"Lugert will be back in a few hours," the Goliath says. "You go in then."

And that is the first time Krantz realizes that Lugert is gone. But what can they possibly do that he hasn't anticipated?

And then, just at dawn, Lugert is back. And he has someone with him at gunpoint. Someone who is supposed to be dead. A female someone. Lutka.

"I should have known," she says, contempt flowing out of her.

She is back from the dead, and Krantz is drowning in the meaning of her presence. The Gestapo lied—*We've killed your girlfriend*—and now like a play of Wagner's, she has been brought back to life in order to finish the drama.

"All these years..." he manages thickly, "you were there in Niski Kosciol, and I never went back."

"I wouldn't think you could. But then, who knew anything about you?" Her scorn is even more malevolent than Wolff's.

Lugert grins, rolls the gun barrel in a little circle. "We're very happy for you, but you'll have to carry out your reunion on the pier while we finish digging through the lock."

Slowly they walk to the end of the pier.

"What is this?" she demands acidly.

Krantz shrugs helplessly. "You're a hostage. Lutka, I'm sorry—"

"Yes, yes, you're a very sorry fellow. Whose hostage am I?"

"Theirs. We're both hostages. They want me to find something. But I can't."

"Same bungling Josef. The only thing you ever did efficiently was murder half the children in Niski Kosciol."

"By all that's holy, Lutka, I swear, there was nothing I could have done to stop that. It was written on a piece of paper. An order. I—"

She glares without softening. "So, after you don't find this thing, what then?"

"I haven't the faintest idea. I'm not sure it makes any difference what I do."

Her lime eyes in the sunrise all but saw him in half.

"Maybe...if I'm dead, they'll let you go," he says.

"Forget about being a hero. It doesn't suit you."

He once thought he would go to hell just to avoid facing her. Maybe this is it. Hell. Everything has caught up with him. How could one pacifist architect, one cowardly lover of all that is good and serene have come to this crossroads? And if he throws himself on the zombies' mercy and confesses his intention to collapse the dome, will they let her go? Christ! Such a betrayal. He *has* to bury that evil. Because if what lies within the sub-cavern is really a rejuvenation of Hyperborean roots, the fate of Niski Kosciol's children will become his lesser sin.

"You know," she says, "I didn't think I could hate anyone as much as I hate you." The twitter is completely gone from her marinated voice, and her expression is tight as a drum. "I hoped for a long time to be able to tell you what I'm going to tell you now, Josef. When I left Berlin the last time, I was pregnant." She pauses to soak up his horror. "I had a girl, Josef. Your daughter. A child when you arrived with your Einsatzgruppe. That's right…you ordered her rounded up with the others…and you took her to that farm. Zosia…I named her Zosia. *Your* Zosia, Josef. And that's all I'm going to tell you."

She turns her back on him too rapidly to see him wrestling down wave after wave of revulsion, mimed by the sea's relentless thud. But waves always win.

There isn't the slightest flicker of personal survival left in him now. He will gladly die in the commission of this last act. Except… that he needs desperately to know the answer to the hellish possibility she has raised. Zosia…she said her name was Zosia. Did he order his own daughter buried alive?

Lutka feels him edge a step closer, and the pathos of what she has done begins to rack her. But this moment has been predetermined since that ghastly night of the Einsatzgruppe. There is no free will about it. At the first pitiful syllable out of him, she whirls and spits in his face.

When the zombies come for him, Wolff has to hand him one of the lights and prod him into the lock, and even Lugert's grin flags.

"The Grail, Krantz!" he shouts after him. "Everything turns happy when you bring out the Grail!"

On the brink of entering, Krantz remembers the conditions he imposed on his captors and slogs back over the broken lock foundations still a meter deep beneath the tide to watch the two SS and Lutka move to the end of the pier. Neither zombie leaves his gun at the halfway point, but it doesn't matter now. He won't be coming out.

Hot middle-earth odors radiating from the inner wall of the cavern push down on him like a hand as he enters. His light sweeps slowly from one end to the other. The deep, beckoning phosphorescence of the pool and its grim spire that once impaled the SS sentry Lichter are not nearly as forbidding as the honeycombed façade that separates the sub-cavern. Is it more pockmarked and fractured than before, or has he simply forgotten?

Thank God the charges appear to be intact. Working his way around the perimeter, he checks and places the ones farthest from the interior wall as possible. The wire ends are beginning to corrode but the insulation has protected the long runs, which are still flexible. But the dome has to be shaken at each support, and the final pack of dynamite should go at the foot of the deepest interior point, he reasons. Tingling in every nerve, he wades around the flooded perimeter near the drop into the pool. And as he runs the wire to a crevice at the base of that inner wall, he hears a single shot.

At the end of the pier, Wilhelm Lugert has been struck dead by a single shot. But before his massive body can even splash into the slate gray swells, Wolff sweeps Lutka in front of himself with one arm like a shield. Krantz, the miserable traitor, has come up with a weapon from the cavern, he believes at first. Firing twice indiscriminately at the lock, Wolff drags his captive forward. But now another shot splinters the piling to his left, and this time he sees the source. There is a sniper very close on the west flank of the moraine.

All the way back to the lock, the woman struggles like a rag doll in the SS soldier's crushing embrace. Why has the sniper stopped shooting, Wolff wonders. And then he hears the catwalk over the Baltic thrum faintly with his adversary's pursuing steps. Good. All the cards will be in his favor when they reach the cavern. Inside, he will have darkness and a shield. His attacker will be silhouetted against the entrance.

But when he enters the cavern, facing down death suddenly becomes secondary, because there in the illumination of his own light is Josef Krantz frantically splicing wires together.

Goliath Wolff, sworn to the ultimate cause of a mission he knows must not fail, immediately gets off a wild shot meant to distract the traitor from his efforts. But Krantz, only glancing at the fine rain of debris from the precarious crevices in the dome, continues to work. Still clutching Lutka like a bag of groceries, Wolff slogs dangerously near the drop-off into the pool where he pauses to fire more accurately.

This time he sends Krantz scrambling to douse the light. But now, in the sudden darkness, the SS titan steps into an erosion on the flooded edge. For a moment he strains to shift all his leverage onto his left leg, and if the woman in his grasp could have shifted with him, he would have borne both their weight and regained his balance. But flailing weakly, she throws her weight in the other direction. Wolff's iron grip on the collar of her jacket loosens, and then she tears free.

Lutka Krantz nee Gerlak slices into the cold water.

Instantly the chill revives her, and reflexively she spreads her arms. There is more air in her clothes than her lungs as she goes under. She feels her jacket balloon. Despite the shock and the constriction in her chest, something wordless flashes through her brain. She has done this before. There was a baby in her womb that first time, and it was not far from here. And all because of the same man—Josef Krantz. Was she no less a child-killer that day? At least by intent. Even if it all ended well. *Only where is the bottom this time?* There was one that winter's day on the ice pond a decade ago.

Clawing fiercely, she begins to rise, but Wolff—perhaps for expediency's sake, perhaps only to simplify the drama ensuing in the cavern—stiff-arms her just below the surface. She struggles fiercely as the roar in her ears crescendos, demanding, hoping... too soon yielding to the fatal reflex of a swallow. And that is all it takes. One breath without air. One mistake. One. The burning in her lungs and the blaze in her mind fade gently into extinction.

Three living souls in a cavern under a moraine on the Baltic have become two, but only for a moment. Because seconds later the sniper fires from the entrance.

Wolff crouches, bringing the Luger around with two hands. He has to aim directly at the patch of light in order to silhouette his own pistol sight. Where is the bastard? And suddenly light bursts all around him. *The traitor Krantz has spotlighted him!* He is vividly illuminated for the sniper. Notching the Luger left, he squeezes the trigger.

The concussion merges with the sniper's return shot, which he never hears anyway. Because by the time the sound reaches him, the bullet has already ripped bloodlessly under the base of Wolff's skull, severing his spine. Like a dollop of mud, the SS warrior slides into the water with a faint splash, arms drifting out as if to recapture the frail female bundle floating close by.

Convinced that the other shooter cannot be his enemy, Krantz slowly straightens and steps in front of the light. Whoever is firing from the mouth of the cavern, the two of them have acted in concert to eliminate a mutual threat—a double threat, it occurs to him, because the second body he sees floating in the lake must be Lugert's. So the stranger wading toward him, dark and intent and thin as a rail, wishes him no harm. He probably came to rescue Lutka, and she is already safe out on the pier.

"Watch the drop-off!" Krantz shouts. "On your right...stay to your left!"

At twenty meters some of the darkness of a beard resolves itself in fresh gouts of crimson on the stranger's chest and shoulder. His ally has been hit. Krantz starts forward to help.

But at ten meters, the pistol in the stranger's slack hand comes up.

"I have reserved this pleasure for myself, Josef Krantz," says Saul Zolkower in a voice not unlike the hiss of a snake in that vast hellacious cavern.

And Krantz, horrified, pleads for the necessary moments needed to complete the single most important deed of his life.

"Please...listen, please. I'm going to die. I want to die. But for the sake of all that's holy, help me destroy this place!" Dropping to his hands and knees, he begins to crawl over the rock floor, gathering the wire ends together like a bouquet. "See, the wires just have to be hooked to the detonator."

Zolkower's onyx eyes cloud and he shivers once just before he pulls the trigger.

When the reverberations of the gunshot die away, he seems to see the wound in his chest for the first time. *For the sake of all that's holy, this place is destroyed*, he says—believes he says—though in fact it is only Krantz's plea echoing in his thoughts before he sways and collapses.

Like the White Rabbit, ever tardy in a world beyond reality, Mika Lott comes. From Danzig he hires a car to take him to the village of Niski Kosciol, and in that hamlet, finding no sign of Saul Zolkower, he inquires about for an archaeological site; and when that also fails, he makes small talk with a group of children in front of Rudnicki's until the local center of German war-time occupation, the base at the moraine, casually comes out. The directions are rather vague, but one child in particular is insistent about the way to the coast. Mika is struck by her blue eyes and blond hair. And startled by her name.

Zosia Krantz.

It is twilight when Mika leans over the catwalk rail on the pier to observe a much-battered body in the backwash of the cliff. At the foot of the lock sits a dry cell light, a pickax and a shovel. He picks up the light. Inside the cavern, another light flickers orange on the point of extinction. Mika surveys the vast chamber with a sense of having finished a journey. This is it. There is no doubt in his mind whatever. None at all.

Several meters in front of him a Goliath of dead flesh sits chest deep in water, seeming about to drift loose in the rising tide. Close by another floats face down. Carefully he skirts them, drawn by a more accessible pair of bodies beyond the water. Mika thinks immediately of the little girl named Zosia when he sees Krantz, and their relationship is obvious. No doubt in his mind about that either. None whatsoever.

This is the reservoir. The carnage screams default. Whatever was under way here is incomplete. And Mika knows what is under way here—that the Grail is nearby. The thing that possessed Hitler invests this moraine. "Will" reeks in this place so thick as to be palpable, a force that vibrates the very atoms of the stones. No wonder it looks as if it is about to collapse.

From the maze of wires and planted charges, it is clear that Josef Krantz was going to bring the dome down. The exact "why" is scarcely important. Maybe he met the real Krantz on the morning following *Kristallnacht* after all. The man in the ruins of that synagogue wasn't capable of serving a demonic Reich. At any rate, Zolkower's version of Josef Krantz has paid the price. And Mika's Krantz has come close to collecting his demand from the Thule, from Satan, from an ancient enemy of Mika's last seen wearing the uniform of a Prussian soldier and riding a pale horse in the Pale of Settlement. It is ironic that the final physical act should be left to the child of that long-ago day, the mere behind-the-scenes strategist. He can defeat the Prussian himself now. Then the horse will ride away with an empty saddle.

Slowly Mika sets to work carrying the detonator and drawing

out wire through the ruins of the lock along the catwalk as far as it will go up the beach. He is old beyond his years, and the effort of all this chasing has set his blood pounding. A long time ago he was a watchmaker, wasn't he? A married, about-to-be father, peaceful watchmaker mending time. How did it come to this? Wheels within wheels. Circles of destiny like gears in a watchcase. He is still a mender of time. That is why he has been brought to this point. Only—God preserve him—time could stop for him at any moment now.

And then he sees the body in the Baltic Sea again, rising and falling in the swells. *Leave it,* an inner voice admonishes. *You've got the detonator out here, and the wires, just complete the thing before something happens or someone else comes along.* But the body twists and rolls like a leftover spring from an escapement, and you cannot mend time without putting all the pieces back in the case that holds wheels within wheels.

Because what if the corpse signifies in some way what went on here to others? No, *this* final solution must be without human traces.

Wheezing a little, Mika makes his way over the rocks and begins to drag the cadaver to the cavern. He has him in a bear hug, a monstrous man, shot through the chest and made heavier by his water-soaked clothes. Just before he gets him to the lock, Mika sees the flopping hand with the untanned circle on its ring finger. Lots of untanned ring fingers these days where SS death's-head bands have recently been removed. He stumbles in the lock and they fall together in the shallows with unnerving animation. No more! The corpse feels alive; and anyway, this is far enough for entombment.

Pushing Lugert away, Mika sways to his feet and sloshes back to the Baltic end of the lock. The air is suddenly pressing down on him like a shroud. What is happening? He has to get out of here.

Waves of nausea synchronize themselves to the crash of the sea as he struggles to the beach. Consciousness draining, he sees only the wires leading to the detonator on the sand. And now what? Does it matter which wire is hooked where? He kneels shaking over the device and fumbles to secure the contacts. "Kein ayin horoh," he prays huskily, yielding one last fear to the Prussian Nemesis of his life-long nightmare. But when he drives down the plunger, and the sand lifts several centimeters off the beach, and the mighty moraine shudders and collapses into the cavern, and a cloud of boiling black dust climbs skyward, and the endless slate waves of the sea pause and for several seconds reverse themselves, Mika Lott knows that he has blunted the will of a predator civilization in remission, and that there is a God in heaven.

There is no doubt in his mind whatsoever. None at all.

And slipping the silver watch from his pocket with the inscription *Love Forever Katya*, gently he begins to wind it.

AFTERMATH

It is 1945. Among the many political and military leaders who visit the treasure bunker beneath the Oberen Schmied Gasse in Nuremberg after the war in Europe ends, only George S. Patton realizes the significance of the Spear of Longinus. Like Hitler, Patton has a deep and life-long love of history and a phenomenal memory for detail. He also believes in reincarnation, has researched the Holy Grail, and once made a special side trip to the castle of the Landulf of Capua (Hitler's antecedent) at Kalot Enbolot in the middle of the Sicilian campaign. Patton examines the Spear at length, sending his aides out looking for local experts to answer his many questions about the talisman. Then, while still grasping it, he utters a remarkable warning that America is tottering on the brink of an even more evil era than the one just ended.

On August 6, 1945, while still in possession of the Spear of Longinus, the United States of America detonates its own explosion at a place called Hiroshima. Only instead of sealing a reservoir of forces, it unleashes one.

Still later come the Nuremberg Trials where Cartesian judges wallow through the irrational evidence of an irrational world. Most of it is simply not understood. How can it be? The pertinent testimony is reduced to evidence of a quite mindless sadism and an overwhelming mountain of eccentricities. It is impossible for the judges to fathom the intricate and ancient evil at the core of the Reich, with its Faustian overtones, or to connect it to the independent acts of millions of followers who themselves merely clutched the magic hem of the Führer's cloak. They are faced with a truth so staggering that it cannot be grasped.

When the death sentences are passed and Wolfram von Sievers waits with the condemned in their cells, he has a visitor. Friedrich

Heilscher, yet another occult figure in the Reich's hierarchy and the creator of satanic oaths taken by the SS in the "Ceremony of the Stifling Air," incants a Black Mass as von Sievers kneels at his feet. The event is fully witnessed by death row guards, who dismiss it as a peculiar prayer to God.

ABOUT THE AUTHOR

From his first introduction by the *Chicago Tribune* as "…a John Barth or a John Irving, with a touch of William Gaddis and maybe a dash of Kurt Vonnegut, Jr.," Thomas Sullivan has been eclectic. His over ninety publishing credits across the spectrum of fiction categories include short stories and novels translated into more than a dozen languages. The novels include *Born Burning* (optioned for a major Hollywood film), *The Phases of Harry Moon* (a Pulitzer Prize nominee), *The Martyring* (a World Fantasy Award finalist for Best Novel) and *Dust of Eden* (a Borders national selection). Numerous short story honors are as diverse as inclusion in *Best of Omni #2* to a Hemingway Literary Days Festival cash award to a Catholic Press Association award.

His personal history is also broadly based. A former All-American athlete in two sports, he has lived in a dozen countries and been a gambler, a "Rube Goldberg" innovator, a coach, a teacher and a city commissioner. Currently he writes full-time in Minnesota and speaks internationally in venues as diverse as the House of Literature in Oslo, Norway and American schools and universities. His inspirational monthly newsletter (Sullygram) is available free on request.

Website: www.thomassullivanauthor.com
Contact him at: mn333mn@earthlink.net

Curious about other Crossroad Press books?
Stop by our site:
http://store.crossroadpress.com
We offer quality writing
in digital, audio, and print formats.

Enter the code FIRSTBOOK
to get 20% off your first order from our store!
Stop by today!

Printed in Great Britain
by Amazon